Water Dressed in Brown

Dan O'Hare

Dan\OHARE

Cover Design by Caroline O'Hare

Edited by Jaime Coyne, Megan Leslie

Design by Dan O'Hare

First edition

ISBN 979-8-9994425-0-5

for Sharyn, Caroline, and Olive

thank you

Contents

1

The Prelude

Whether Laura likes it or not, Trey matters.

They met as children in 1982. It was a time when all manmade light was tungsten, save for the buzzing fluorescents of the office or school. A time before screens dominated our lives, when privacy and loneliness were both manual and physical. Together from second grade all the way through high school, Laura and Trey learned math, science, English and all the other languages they would come to need—secret, unspoken, or otherwise.

Laura Byrne's family had moved from Chicago, Illinois to Ocean Pines, Maryland. The sprawling neighborhood, only 14 years old then, was yet a mostly unrealized idea. It was an empty, quiet place. On one hand it felt a little wild and unbuilt, and on the other it felt abandoned. While there were the sporadic seasonal vacation houses tucked in the thick woods, by Labor Day they were vacant. Their black windows and the thick dressing of dead leaves made it easier for Laura to imagine Baba Yaga as her neighbor, rather than the sunburned, crab-feasting family that would one day reappear.

Not long after the moving truck had left, the Byrne's were welcomed to the neighborhood by Trey's mother, Dolores Buckingham, carrying an enormous pot of paella. The dish had become Dolores' trademark since she chose Trey's father over returning to her native Denia, Spain. Along with the gift of food,

Dolores brought her son, who carried a bouquet of autumn asters, zinnias, freesias, and blue thistles, all hand-picked and arranged by Dolores, all grown in her garden.

Dolores was thrilled another family had finally moved into the neighborhood, and offered to help make the transition easier. Since both of Laura's parents worked in the nearby town of Berlin, an arrangement was made that Laura would go to the Buckinghams' house every day after school until her mother could pick her up.

Laura and Trey were not fast friends. He could barely read while she was already voraciously consuming chapter books. He refused to play house or school with her, because he said boys didn't do that. She was unimpressed by his loud attempts to skateboard, his fort building skills, or his clichéd expedition to China via a hole in the woods.

There were some "Trey activities" that she enjoyed, like exploring the woods, looking for salamanders under rotten logs, or checking the canal for blue crabs. Laura had a quick, curious mind. She was alternately described as either precocious or smart, though the latter was usually intended to be an insult. While it's true that with each book she read her tongue sharpened, through the years that sharpness rounded into wit and charm. If, perhaps, only to those who also read books.

Laura's favorite thing about those early autumn afternoons at the Buckinghams' was riding her bike. They rode bikes together almost every day, around the cul-de-sac, up to the bend in the road and then back again. She had never experienced this kind of freedom and maturity before, riding without an adult, on an empty road, in an abandoned world.

But it often led to racing, and Laura was faster than Trey. When she sped away from him, he would snap. He would throw his bike to the ground in disgust. He would accuse her of cheating. Sometimes he would cry. On one occasion, he tried to rage-climb the impossibly large red oak in his front yard. Knowing what we know today, well... at the time Laura assumed that he was a typical eight year old boy.

As the early fall morphed into late autumn, Laura experienced true darkness for the first time in her life. The combination of a heavy canopy of needles and leaves, the vacant houses, and a lack of streetlights created the feeling of an abyss, not unlike being in a cave.

The night didn't stop them from exploring. These first two children of Ocean Pines were alone together, in a wild, forsaken, and dark world. They were the first adolescents nurtured in this womb, thrust together by nothing more than chance and scarcity.

That winter, on one chilly and damp afternoon, Laura pushed the always unlocked front door open and crept inside the house to see if Dolores was more interesting than Trey. The home was black except for the kitchen, with its warm golden glow bulging a little into the hallway. She heard Dolores before she saw her, singing along in French to a Françoise Hardy cassette tape playing on her Marantz stereo.

Laura shut the door quietly behind her and crept up the seven stairs and slid along the wall of the hallway, careful to stay in the shadows, while looking through the kitchen entryway. On the right she could see a single empty chair and a curved edge of the round kitchen table. To the left was the stove with a four quart pot releasing wisps of meandering steam. Straight ahead the sink hid a portion of a yellow colander overflowing with the red, orange, and green of the peppers and carrots. Sudden and occasional flashes of color glided in and out of the doorframe, as Dolores—alternating between humming and singing—stirred, chopped, and mixed, in what was more of a dance than a task.

Dolores was dressed in one of her bright, vibrant, and flowing outfits. She was a shock of color in an otherwise brown and gray world. Her long, wavy hair was recently dyed with a tiny hint of red, a subtle and almost secret rebellion against the winter.

Dolores knew she was being watched. She waited a dozen moments or so before she spoke to little Laura, who had stopped right at the edge of the shadow, standing with her hands behind her back and her back to the wall.

"Nena," Dolores gently asked while stirring the onions to keep them from burning. "Do you need something?"

Laura stepped into the light.

"Can I watch you?"

Dolores looked at her and smiled. Unlike most Americans, she only smiled when she really meant it.

"No," she said, opening the refrigerator and pulling out a bag of green beans. "You can help. Sit."

She patted the table to show Laura where she wanted her and then produced a shiny metal bowl from the cabinet next to the stove.

"Here, let me show you," she said, sitting next to Laura and demonstrating how to snap off the end of the green beans. "You see, like this. Don't snap off too much, just the very end, and we throw this part away."

Laura snapped a green bean in half.

"That's a little too much," Dolores said kindly.

Laura rolled her eyes with far too much sarcasm for an eight year old. Dolores picked up the pieces and pinched the ends off.

"It's still going to taste the same."

Laura tried with another green bean and soon got the hang of it. Dolores went back to cooking and humming along to the music. Laura asked her what Françoise Hardy was singing about.

"Love," Dolores answered.

"She sounds sad."

Dolores stirred the onions and didn't respond.

***

Afternoons for the rest of that school year were spent with Dolores. The kitchen glowed with warmth and music. Whether she was cooking, gardening, or reading her bordering-on-pornographic romance novels, she had her trusty Marantz piping jazz or classical music into the air. Even when she was in places without music, like a hospital or courtroom, she would softly hum to herself.

By the time school let out for summer, Laura was skilled at cleaning beans, shelling peas, peeling carrots, chopping peppers and onions, and mincing garlic, and was not half bad at rolling out dough or kneading bread. She helped prepare soups and stews, casseroles, tortilla de patatas, albóndigas, empanadas, and paellas. While she always ate dinner with her family at home, she often got to taste the results of her cooking, and in the process, expanded her palate far beyond what most American children in small towns were exposed to.

In the summer, Ocean Pines was no longer a lonely place. Once empty driveways filled with cars, the cul-de-sac buzzed with bikes or balls, and the canals were patrolled by little hunters armed with crab nets and chicken necks. Both kids joined the Ocean Pines Swim Team and attended the Ocean Pines Day Camp at White Horse Park. Since these places were only a few blocks – albeit long blocks – away, their parents allowed them to ride their bikes. The swim team, camp, and cul-de-sacs were full of children from Baltimore, Pennsylvania, New Jersey, and Washington DC. Laura got to know them for a week and then literally never saw them again the rest of her life.

When school started up again, Laura slid back into the routine of cooking with Dolores, but was a little friendlier with Trey, a little closer, a little more familiar.

Through riding bikes, meeting new kids that would soon be gone, and swimming together, Trey became a fixture. In a resort town, so many people come into your world in fits and spurts, all of them awash in an unusual energy. It's passion, some might call lust, that slips into the soul in these short bursts of experiences outside of one's regular routine. But these summer friends were in Laura's life for days at best, sometimes only hours. Since neither Trey nor Laura had either siblings or other neighbors, they became the only constant of their peer group.

As the years progressed and the adolescent need arose to pretend they were sweet on someone, out of convenience she chose Trey. He was easy and safe.

But in those early days, it was Dolores who she really loved. Dolores was her teacher, grandmother, aunt, and best friend all rolled into one. She was her other mother. For those first three years in Ocean Pines, it was probably Dolores who was her best friend.

***

But when Laura was eleven years old everything changed. In one night her childhood fractured. Her mom, Joyce, became suspicious that Laura's father was cheating on her. She hired a private investigator who eventually exposed that he was indeed having an affair. Laura's father was disgraced and ostracized, not only because he had an extramarital affair, but because it was with a man. Joyce, like anyone who watched the nightly news in the US in the mid 1980s, was terrified of AIDS and was convinced that every gay man had it. Partly because of that fear, and partly because of her deep sense of betrayal, she destroyed Laura's father so thoroughly in the divorce that he had no option but to move out of town and temporarily out of Laura's life.

Laura blamed her father for cheating on her mom and her mother for destroying her father, and, unless you count Dolores, she was left without a family member to trust or love. For the first time in her life she was really, truly angry. As providence would have it, this time coincided with school-sponsored team sports. She soon discovered that it was not only perfectly acceptable, but almost encouraged for her to take her rage out on the athletic field. Starting in sixth grade she played field hockey, basketball, and lacrosse; was usually the fastest on her team, and was always the toughest. In fact, when she was still only in sixth grade, she gained a bit of a reputation for her ferocity, even if it was usually qualified with a "for a girl."

While athletics ended her regular afternoons at the Buckingham household, since Trey also played sports it became very common for Dolores or Joyce to pick the kids up from practice together, and from time to time Laura would share a meal with Trey and Dolores at their home. Sometimes, out of the blue, Laura would walk over with dessert and sit and visit with Dolores for hours. Perhaps because of her ease in the Buckingham kitchen, or because Dolores taught her the first real skill, or because she had that foreign mystique that gave her advice a hint of secret well-traveled knowledge, Laura cherished her counsel.

It was at a school dance in autumn of seventh grade when Trey and Laura first kissed. It was nothing more than a peck on the lips, but Laura regretted it immediately, and Trey was a little hurt by that. He didn't understand that Laura was spiraling. She felt her parents had destroyed her traditional family and was worried that this innocuous kiss would be such a momentous event that it would somehow turn her last uncomplicated "family" member, Dolores, into someone she couldn't be around. That didn't happen. Trey got over himself, and Laura and Trey eventually became better friends for it. Not too long afterwards they even pretended that they were okay joking about it.

Unbeknownst to Laura, her mother was really struggling. But after a year had passed and multiple HIV tests came back negative, and with the help of psychotherapy, Joyce had finally gained some perspective on the matter. She had not forgiven her ex-husband, but she was no longer afraid that his infidelity was literally going to kill her. Her sessions with her therapist became less about her and her husband, and more about her and her daughter. Eventually the "my child hates me" transformed to "my child is mad at me for taking away her father." So when Laura was almost thirteen her mom allowed her to go to Chicago for Christmas to visit her father, and just like that, Laura's father was back in her life. He was wracked with guilt, embarrassed, and in general a bit of a mess, but she didn't care. He was her favorite pen pal, and he had no problem letting her call collect anytime from anywhere.

As he rebuilt his own life, he would gently nudge her to mend her relationship with her mother. It was a long and often challenging road for all of them. But after some difficult years of screaming, slammed doors, and tears, Laura emerged as a confident and intelligent sixteen year old who had a healthy friendship with both of her successful parents.

The summer between sophomore and junior year of high school, Laura went to Chicago and lived with her father, working as a barista in the coffee shop on the first floor of her father's Lakeview apartment building. She met her father's boyfriend, Todd, a vivacious free-spirited bon vivant. Together, Todd and her father introduced her to an array of remarkable characters, artists, connoisseurs, and people passionate about life. They took her shopping for a completely new wardrobe; they took her to underground theaters, arthouse films, piano bars, fabulous restaurants, and parties. She was exposed to innovative art and vibrant culture, she tried pesto and sushi, and through work she developed serious thoughts on what made for a good cappuccino—a drink yet unknown to most Americans.

With less than two weeks remaining in her summer, on Todd's advice, she had cut her hair short for the first time in her life. He was right beside her the whole way, and even held her hand for the first and most terrifying snip. Then Todd took a week off work and took her to Hollywood Beach every day.

"Lift your chin, sweetie," Todd instructed that first morning as a cool breeze came off Lake Michigan. "No one wants to kiss someone with a pale neck."

"Who said I want to kiss anyone!" Laura snapped trying out a little extra attitude in a safe environment.

"You, every time you talk about your *friend* Trey."

"I do not want to kiss Trey Buckingham!"

"Uh-huh. Well, whether you do or do not, a good tan is all part of the new you. I'm not sending you home without a summer-with-a-gay-best-friend full makeover. I would be ostracized if I did."

"By whom?"

"The community, dear. The community."

Todd winked.

"If you follow my instructions you will be worshiped."

Laura scrunched up her face.

"I'm not sure I want to be worshiped."

"Even so," Todd said, raising an eyebrow. "It will be fun to try."

That's when Todd explained to her the virtue of smiling with one's eyes.

"Lips are the way people lie. Never trust a smile that isn't in the eyes."

***

There's one more very important part of the prelude that has gone unmentioned. There's no other way to say it... Dolores married an asshole. He owned two bars in nearby Ocean City, Maryland. He was a drunk who sold enough cocaine to use it habitually without ever paying for it, and he terrorized his family.

The occasional criticism of Dolores shortly after Trey was born, evolved through the years into regular beratement. A too stern rebuke of Trey's innocuous childhood behavior morphed into obsessive terror. If Trey did anything imperfect his father would either scream at him from the jump, or worse, be very silent until Trey was within his grasp. He was like a lion stalking a lamb, and nearly as ferocious when he had his prey. For years Trey's father beat his child irregularly, often without reason or warning, and when Dolores protested he grabbed, pinched, pushed, and slapped her. As Trey grew it got worse, with the violence peaking at age 11 or 12. After that Trey became more deft at avoiding his father's wrath. Still, unpredictability is the trademark of abusers, and as careful as Trey and Dolores were, they were never truly safe when he was around.

Dolores hid her bruises with those long, flowing colorful outfits that led to her reputation for being fashionable. Trey didn't need to hide his bruises. Most boys, especially rough and tumble boys like Trey, had the odd bruise.

The only saving grace was that, outside of the weekends, this man was almost never home at the same time as Trey. His father spent less and less time at home. He never took a day off, or at least never claimed to, though this was due to him being an alcoholic who preferred to drink at his own bar. He also had multiple affairs with waitresses and patrons alike, which is time consuming. In fact, for as much as Laura was at the Buckingham household, by the time she was a junior in high school she had only seen Trey's father a handful of times, always in passing.

It was that same summer, when Laura was in Chicago, that Dolores, who was a staunch Catholic, had finally started to consider a divorce. Her mistake was using a local priest as her confessor. Instead of offering any helpful advice he reminded her that divorce was a sin, suggested that she pray for her husband's soul, and smugly told her that God had a plan.

That same summer Trey grew almost four inches taller. He spent his mornings working at the Berlin Ice Plant loading trucks with hundreds of 20 and 40 pound bags of ice, and his evenings at Waterman's Crab House in West Ocean City steaming crabs by the bushel or bussing tables. All this work led to his forearms practically doubling in size, his biceps bulging against his shirts, and his shoulders... well, they could only be described as broad. In one three-month period it seemed he had transformed from a gangling adolescent to a grown man. He had been a good athlete before, but this growth spurt changed everything.

When she came back to school, Laura was looking forward to seeing Trey's reaction to her. She had it planned—a practiced head-turn with smiling eyes. She heard him coming down the hall from the locker room, joking with one of his teammates as they headed out to preseason soccer practice. She stepped outside into the afternoon sun, and bent down to retie her shoe. She stood up slowly, turned her head to face him, but the smile in her eyes was replaced by surprise. Instead of seeing her old friend, she locked eyes with a man.

Even though she knew that she herself had changed so much in her brief time away, she didn't assume others could have done the same. After all, she left—he stayed where he was. Sometimes, especially when you are young, when you leave somewhere you expect the world to freeze as it is, while it waits for your return. And yet, it only took one look to know that here before her was undeniable evidence that her "friend who was a boy" had suddenly become a man.

Up to this point, Laura and Trey had never really dated each other, nor anyone else. While they went to the Homecoming Dance together freshman and sophomore year, it was more out of convenience. She was sweet on Trey, in an innocent way. These kids were still in many ways, children. But childhood ends sometime, and this "sometime" for both of them happened to be the exact same summer.

Suddenly Laura caught herself looking at her friend in a way she had never done before. She liked how his shoulders looked, she liked his jaw, his back, his calves. He had let his hair get a little long, and she liked it that way, but right when school started he cut it short and she liked that too. She liked that she could see the outline of his traps beneath his shirt. She stole glances in literature class, where he sat directly in front of her; and more than once she lost track of the conversation as those glances became stares. She liked watching him play soccer, she liked watching him walk towards her, and she loved watching him walk away. She found more and more excuses to visit him at home, hoping for a glimpse of him coming out of the shower, or just walking around with his shirt off, as he always did.

She thought about him when she was waking up, in that moment between a dream and veritas where the mind can make anything seem real. She thought about him while she was in the shower, and she wished he was in there with her. She felt lust for her friend, her first real deep lust, and when she closed her eyes she fantasized about him kissing her, holding her with those muscular arms, touching her in places no one had ever touched before. Sometimes when she would think about him she would shake her head to try to snap out of it. She would remind herself that this was her best friend, and it would be a mistake. Other times she would let herself go, and get lost in the fantasy. Especially in the shower.

Of course, it wasn't like Trey and Laura were alone in this world. Other girls noticed too. So did some guys. Even teachers noticed the change in Trey, as would anyone when someone suddenly transformed from awkward teen to stone cold fox. No wait, that's not entirely fair. He didn't look like a fox. He was too big, too thick, to be a fox. He was more like a wolf.

In fact, the only person that didn't seem to notice Trey's change was his own father. Many bullies are certain that they are always going to be stronger than those they terrorize, and Trey's dad was no different. And so it happened that one autumn evening, only minutes after Trey had returned home from soccer practice, Trey's father came home surprisingly early and unsurprisingly drunk and immediately started yelling at Dolores in the kitchen.

His rage built so quickly and was so intense that he didn't notice Trey had left his bedroom and was standing with fists and jaw clenched in the hall. In fact, Trey stood frozen in almost in the exact same spot from which Laura had first watched Dolores cook. His father snarled at Dolores, saying unrepeatable things.

She resisted. That's when the worthless piece of shit that was Trey's father grabbed Dolores by the hair and raised his right hand to strike her.

With one dexterous move, Trey leapt into the room, caught his father's raised hand, squeezed it tight, and pulled it, quickly jerking it down towards the floor. With that single motion, Trey tore his father's rotator cuff and bicep, and popped his shoulder out of its socket in the process. He damn near ripped his father's arm clean off. His father, too drunk to feel the true pain of the tear but still stunned into a confused moment of inaction, focused his full rage on Trey. His nostrils flared, his eyelids vibrated with hatred. He released Dolores' hair and grabbed a flower vase off the kitchen table and flung it at Trey's head. Autumn asters, zinnias, freesias, and blue thistles floated in the air while the vase crunched into Trey's cheek and eye, though not shattering until it hit the floor at the base of the refrigerator.

But then, with one massive swing that contained all the kinetic energy which had been building for sixteen years, Trey's fist shattered his father's jaw, knocking out four teeth and removing consciousness from the body. His father crumpled on the ground completely motionless. Trey thought he had killed his father. And he wasn't sad.

This is where our story begins. The father is with Dolores at the hospital, the son is sitting at the kitchen table, holding a bag of frozen peas to his eye and drinking one of his father's beers. And that's when Laura, holding half a pan of cherry cheesecake, knocked on the door.

2

Rain on Autumn Leaves

"Go away," Trey said with a quavering voice. He took the bag of peas away from his eye for a second and looked at the door, but the act of looking caused the pain to return, so the peas went back to his eye as Laura pushed the door open.

"I brought dessert..." her words and smile faded as she took in the scene. She was standing frozen at the doorway holding the remainder of her mother's signature graham cracker cherry cheesecake. She was wearing her favorite orange sweater, the one Trey once said made her eyes brighter, and jeans that might have been a little too tight. She had come over hoping to catch Trey coming out of the shower, as he usually ate dinner before he showered, and the Buckinghams almost always ate later than she and her mom. Laura had hoped to sit with Dolores and talk about Chicago, about Spain, about music, about anything Dolores wanted to talk about until Trey came out of the shower, still a little wet, glistening like a dream, grinning like a fool.

But instead of seeing Trey all glistening, golden, and goofy, he was strangely pale and looked, for lack of a better word, fragile. Even though his sleeveless shirt exposed his thick biceps which he was likely unconsciously flexing because a girl was present, and even though he was still breathing hard from the anxiety of what he had done and what unknown fate awaited him, he looked shrunken. Laura had no idea about the violence or the abuse. She didn't know that Trey and

Dolores lived with a monster, and she didn't even know that Mr. Buckingham was a drunk. She knew Trey looked so different than when she last saw him that afternoon, just before soccer.

To Laura, the whole scene was wrong. The floor was wet and littered with broken flowers and glass. Her friend was still. He never sat still. It was quiet. Whatever had happened here made no logical sense to Laura, but her body processed the need before her mind could understand, and she unfroze and walked inside and straight toward Trey. She wanted to touch him, to inspect him, to make sure he was okay. But he looked away.

"What the heck happened here?" She asked herself softly as she carefully walked through the debris and slid the dessert into the fridge.

Laura turned off the oven and removed the casserole that was about to be ruined. She opened the cabinet beneath the sink and pulled out the trash can. She stole the occasional glance, but each time she did Trey felt her eyes and they caused him a confused pain that bordered on rage. She picked up the flowers and large shards of glass one by one and began throwing them away. Trey wanted to tell her to stop. He wanted to tell her to leave. Neither sentiment came out. As she picked up and threw away the flowers he could smell them. He could smell everything, the burnt edges of the casserole, the dirt on his knees, the blood on the floor. He could smell the peas as they were starting to thaw against his cheek. They were losing their frozen lifelessness, and regaining their peaness. Or was that smell the first moments of decay? Trey moved the bag away from his face and tried to speak, but no words came out.

All Trey could do was try to not cry. The harder he tried to hold back the tears, the more his face hurt. He stood up, dropped the peas on the kitchen table, walked out the front door, and slammed it behind him.

Left alone in the kitchen, Laura was so confused. She thought about following Trey outside but instead, for reasons she didn't understand, she finished cleaning up. She sopped up the water and what was clearly blood with a paper towel. She used a broom and dustpan to get all the tiny bits of glass. She noticed a spattering of blood on one of the chairs and cleaned it with some kitchen cleaner. She took the trash bag out of the can, put a new liner in, and dumped the old bag in the outdoor can in the garage. Then she went back inside, washed her hands, and looked around. The kitchen looked the way it had always looked, the way it was supposed to look. But somehow it looked different. It looked wrong. It wasn't just the missing vase and flowers. Something about that kitchen was broken.

She went out into the Ocean Pines night to look for her friend. There was no moon, and though many deciduous leaves had recently fallen, the sky and the pine trees conspired to make it even darker than it usually was in autumn. Clouds hid the stars. Only the kitchen light of the Buckingham house was illuminated, and from the driveway the kitchen window wasn't visible. Laura tried to let her eyes adjust, but there was no light to adjust to and the darkness was so complete that her mind rejected it and placed a false silver sheen over the shadows. Trey could have stayed hidden anywhere in that night.

It was chilly and damp. The wind smelled like rain. Laura walked to the street side of the home. Trey's bedroom had a small bay window that protruded out from the house's foundation. Laura stood next to it, perfectly still, looking into the abyss and listening.

Laura let out a long exhale, and then stayed silent. That's when she could hear Trey's heavy and uneven breath coming from under his bay window's overhang. It was too dark for her to see him, but she could sense him, almost like she could feel an invisible aura, right next to her, beneath her, cowering.

"Can I come in?" She asked gently, like a mother to a hiding child.

He held out his hand towards her voice, and with his fingers brushed her thigh, just above the knee. She reached down with her left hand and caressed his fingers, and followed the contours of his hand and wrist, down to his bare arm and finally to his shoulder. She then crawled under the overhang and behind him, into an even deeper darkness, in the process wrapping both of her arms around him, and pulling him into her. She felt his back muscles tense against her chest, she curled her legs around him so they outlined his own, and she pulled him towards her so she could nestle her chin on his shoulder, and her throat against the nape of his neck. She could smell his dried sweat, the clover and dirt that was stained on the skin of his knees, and the early decay of autumn leaves. They were out of the wind, but he still shivered and his arms had goosebumps. She rubbed her hands slowly over the length of his arms, back and forth, until she could feel his muscles start to relax, and then she folded his arms in towards himself and enveloped him in a hug. She had wrapped herself around him like a sweater, and he felt a warmth that he had never known before. She held him so tight that he melted and after one long and last breath of resistance, his tears finally fell freely. The more he wept the closer she pulled him towards her. Laura didn't speak, and she didn't understand. But that night she was so strong that she squeezed a lifetime of secret rage out of a child.

Trey was not healed of course, for as powerful as a loving touch can be there is no magic that great. It was more as if he had taken his first breath of the person he was soon to become. He was made new.

Laura had never felt so much in her life. The outline of each one of Trey's back muscles against her breast and stomach. Where her jeans had ridden up exposing her ankles and lower shin, the hairs of his legs against the tiny stubble of her own. His shoulder under her chin relaxing with each exhale, his forearm tendons shifting as his hands unclenched their fists. The wet of his tears dripping onto her arms. Beneath her, the soft earth that only exists in places hidden from the exposure of the sun.

It wasn't until Trey almost spoke – when the tears had subsided and the silence began to be uncomfortable— that a stiff wind gathered up some leaves and swirled them around the base of that huge red oak. Moments later, large drops of rain fell one at a time, striking the dry leaves and stilling the wind. There was no great storm that raged, no cathartic cleansing of the world that is the occasional gift from the sky. It was only the occasional fallen water on dead leaves that provided sound so Trey didn't need to. And while this child finally felt safe again, Laura buried her desire to kiss his neck or to taste his tears. For the first time she understood the selflessness of strength.

3

Jessica's Music

When the police arrived, Trey climbed out from under the overhang. The rain had stalled and almost stopped. Trey still hadn't said a word to Laura, and while she wasn't certain why the police were there, their presence plus the kitchen blood frightened her. Trey reached down to help Laura up, and then walked right up to the police officer and held out his hand to meet the shake. The officer asked what had happened. Trey told them both everything. The violence, the torture. Not only that night, but how it had been his whole life. Laura was stunned into silence. It was as if she was hearing him tell a story about a family she didn't even know, not one that had basically been her surrogate family for the last eight years.

The police officer was kind. His attention was mostly focused on Trey, but he stole a few glances at Laura, noticing her jeans had dirt on them, and there were a few leaves clinging to her orange sweater.

"Did you witness any of this?" he asked Laura.

She shook her head. She couldn't yet use words, there was too much new and contradictory information crowding her mind.

"It's probably best if you leave then," he said matter-of-factly.

Even though she lived a ten minute walk away, she had driven to Trey's that night because of the chance of rain. And so she looked on from her car as the officer continued to question Trey in the driveway. As always, she had parked along the drainage ditch across the street, and as she watched the scene unfold she noticed for the first time that Mr. Buckingham's car was parked in the driveway. Trey was speaking calmly while the officer took notes. Five minutes later, the police officer opened the back door of their cruiser and Trey stepped in. She noted that his hands weren't cuffed, but nonetheless, she was pretty sure that he was being arrested. She had no idea what to do, so she slunk down further in her seat and waited until the taillights of the police cruiser disappeared around the corner.

Without thinking she went back inside the house. She spooned some casserole into a bowl and sat at the kitchen table, having no idea what to do next. Laura had already eaten dinner, but unconsciously she felt like Dolores had made the casserole to be eaten, and the least she could do was eat some. Food cooked and uneaten felt like a sin.

She picked at it. It was pork, onions, peppers, fennel, and garlic. Laura knew this recipe. It was one of the first meals she made with Dolores. She couldn't find an appetite. But she smelled it and smiled sadly.

It was as if she had entered a different universe than the one she had lived in that very morning. This emotional state reminded her of the night when her mother came home late and suddenly started screaming and hitting her father. Except that was somehow very different from this night. After all, that night with her parents was a sudden, loud, and violent experience, almost like an explosion. Trey's house was still, vacant, and uncharacteristically unfamiliar. It was never silent, never empty. But that night, there was no music.

Laura wondered in the moment *how* she should think about what she had just learned. But there were too many thoughts. Her brain flooded.

If this were to happen today, people would pull out their phones, click links, check socials, and get their tiny dopamine hits to calm their mind to the typical state of low-grade anxiety in which much of society exists. But it didn't happen now, it happened then, at a time when one was really alone with their thoughts, cut off from the greater world.

In Laura's time and place, when brains were overloaded, people sometimes spoke out loud to calm or slow their mind. And in this case, that's exactly what

Laura did. First, she started mumbling while she picked at the food. That morning all that mattered to her was a calculus test. So she said "calculus" out loud. She sort of spit it out, like the word equivalent of something between an unripe berry and a watermelon seed. She remembered that morning when she had said to her friend Candace that she was "all stressed out" over the test. She sneered the word "stressed" in the empty kitchen, and then heaved a great sigh. School seemed so petty now. And then she managed to say the first and most terrifying fully formed thought.

"What if Trey is going to jail?"

The words hung in the empty house. She looked around and her eyes slid out of focus as if she could see the space between things, as if she could see the actual silence hanging in the air of the kitchen. It was thick and unhealthy. She needed to leave.

She went quickly out the door, speeding up as she walked until she was almost running by the time she got to her car. She got in, cranked the radio, and started driving without a destination in mind. The station was playing another Top 40 song. She popped in a mixtape that her friend and former teammate Jessica made for her before Jessica went off to start college at NYU. T-Rex and The Velvet Underground guided her through the inky black autumn night. She drove out of Ocean Pines, out of the cocoon and darkness of the protective trees and into a real wind and rain of a growing storm, and onto the route 90 bridge to Ocean City.

Ocean City, Maryland is a resort town on a long sliver of a barrier island—really a thin peninsula, but everyone calls it an island—just south of the Delaware State line. It was and is lined with hotels, condos, restaurants, and t-shirt shops. Truly, it can only be considered a "city" in the summer, when it swells with hundreds of thousands of tourists. The rest of the year it has a population of around 7,000 residents. Nowadays the tourism board in Ocean City has done well to build up the "shoulder seasons" of spring and fall, but in the early '90s, Ocean City was an absolute ghost town after Labor Day. Most bars and restaurants shuttered for the winter. In fact, Trey's father closed one of his bars. The other, called Buck's

Tavern, was one of the few establishments that stayed open, supplying locals with a year round watering hole and cocaine distribution center. Still, because the tourists were gone, many aspects that make a city an actual city disappeared. So much so, after Labor Day weekend the town made all the stoplights on Coastal Highway flashing yellow lights.

Going to school in nearby Berlin, Maryland and living in Ocean Pines, Laura hadn't yet found an excuse to go to Ocean City that autumn. Even though it was fifteen minutes away from her home, it was fifteen minutes in the wrong direction. So this night happened to be the first time that year in which she had seen the flashing yellow lights. To a kid who grew up in the area, it was akin to seeing the first Christmas lights in your neighborhood pop on. Those flashing yellow lights represented everything there was to love about living year-round in a coastal summer resort town. Even though it was a chilly night, she rolled down her window and smelled that unique Ocean City autumn wind which was a mixture of rain, sea, and the cold.

To those poor souls that have never stood in the presence of the ocean, you might believe that the wind smells of salt. That is because you have heard it described that way so many times. But the sea does not actually smell like salt; it smells like birth, death, promise, and memory. Like life, it's rich, dirty, and complex.

She drove south first, all the way to the Inlet, and paused to look out at the chaotic waves in the place where the ocean meets the bay. Then she turned around and drove north the full length of Coastal Highway letting the blinking yellow lights reassure her. The "city" was taking a breath, relaxing, meditating.

The cassette tape finished and flipped over to start again. David Bowie was singing about the end of the world. Laura missed Jessica. Her friend was two years older, and after graduation she moved up to New York City to attend NYU's Tisch School of the Arts and pursue acting. Jessica was the youngest child of an airline executive, her nearest sibling was seven years older. She would be the first to admit that her parents had checked out by the time she was in high school, and so, for the most part she was left to her own devices. Albeit well-funded and supported endeavors. Her mom was a social drunk who smoked really long thin cigarettes. Her father would probably be considered an alcoholic today, but was just considered successful.

Jessica's family had moved from Philadelphia when she was in eighth grade to nearby Salisbury, Maryland for a year, then to Ocean Pines for a year, before settling in a bayfront neighborhood in north Ocean City called "Little Salisbury."

Laura decided to drive past Jessica's home, the way you do when you long to see someone you know isn't there, but seeing where they once were is in some ways the next best thing. She went looking for a ghost.

To her delight and surprise, the light in Jessica's room was on. So she knocked on the door. Through the window she could hear a stereo blasting with a female singer she didn't recognize. She knocked again and rang the bell. But it was impossible to hear anything over the music, the volume was so loud it was rattling windows. So Laura waited with her finger hovering over the doorbell until the song ended, and then rang the bell three times in succession. From inside she heard a squeal and cascading footsteps down the front stair.

Jessica whipped the door open, her once blonde hair now streaked with purple.

"Oh my god, bitch, why didn't you call me back?"

Laura's eyes widened. She hadn't seen Jessica since Laura had left for Chicago, and again, while Laura had changed, somehow Jessica had changed more. It wasn't just her purple hair. It was her energy. Everything about her now seemed to vibrate at a different frequency.

"Did you just..." Laura tried to ask.

"Bitch, give me a hug! Oh my God, I love your haircut!"

Jessica pulled Laura in for an all-time great hug. Distance had indeed made both hearts grow fonder. But this distance was not only physical. For the first time they were old friends with new stories to tell.

Laura needed that kind of hug more than Jessica knew. Laura needed that kind of hug more than Laura even knew. Jessica felt it, and didn't let go, and waited the twenty seconds or so for Laura to release. Which she finally did, as she confusedly asked:

"Did you just call me a bitch... twice?"

Jessica laughed.

"Why didn't you call me back? I've been waiting like two hours."

Laura was so confused.

"I don't know what you are talking about."

"I left a message with your mom like two hours ago. She said you were bringing Trey over some dessert," Jessica bopped her head up and down. "I bet you were."

Laura laughed for the first time in hours.

"I don't know what you mean."

"I bet you don't, bitch."

"Okay, stop. What's up with the 'bitch' all the time? What's that about?"

Jessica smiled an almost condescending smile.

"It's just something my roommates and I say. They call me bitch all the time. I love it."

"I don't think your roommates like you very much."

Jessica sighed.

"I have so much to tell you," she was suddenly far more serious, dragging Laura by the hand into the den. "We need to talk."

Laura hated that phrase. She had heard it too many times in her youth. Laura's mom would always say it to her before delivering bad news. And Laura's mom delivered more than her fair share of bad news. But Laura sat dutifully, sliding onto one side of a tan leather couch in front of a cold tube television.

Jessica took a deep breath. "Okay, here goes." She paused and looked Laura in the eyes, then looked away, gathered herself and looked back at her again. "I'm a lesbian."

Laura let out an uncontrollable chortle. Jessica's eyes widened and mouth opened as if to say, *How dare you?*

"No you are not," Laura dug herself deeper. "What about Teddy Pearson?"

Jessica was incredulous.

"What about him?"

"Didn't you guys... you know... like date?"

"Because we had to. You know Teddy is gay, right?"

"What?!? But he was, like... so good at sports."

Jessica smiled a full on condescending smile. But in her defense, this is a moment condescending smiles were made for.

"Oh sweetheart, you've got so much to learn."

Laura was struggling to keep up.

"But you said you two had sex after prom."

"We did..." Jessica started to explain but realized this was going to take a while. "Wait, look, that's not what this is about. I'm trying to tell you that... I'm different, and I need you to be okay with it."

Laura shrugged.

"Of course I'm okay with it, you know that right? I love you."

"Yeah," Jessica nodded and put her hand to her heart, genuinely touched. "I know what you are saying and you are awesome, but also like... I need you to hear me when I say that, things are going to be different for me now. Like... I've always been told I had to be a certain way, but some things for people like me, like... some things are hard, and they're just not... it's just, they are different, you know?"

Laura nodded trying to understand. "And it's different for Teddy, too?"

"Oh yeah," Jessica said looking up and smiling. "It's really different for him. He'll figure it out eventually."

"Oh," Laura was trying to process. "So wait... You mean you don't know he's gay?"

"I know. Believe me, I know."

Laura's mind was racing. For the second time that night she was trying to find puzzle pieces from a shared past and make sense of what a friend was telling her. "When did you know?"

"About me or Teddy?"

"Why are we talking about Teddy?" Laura said even more confused.

"You brought him up."

"Because you slept with him! I mean you, when did you know about you."

"I don't know exactly," Jessica said with a shrug. " I think I knew for a long time, but I didn't want to admit it to myself, you know? It wasn't until I was up in New York. The city, it just lets you be who you want to be, you know? Because it like... doesn't care but in a good way, you know? Not like here where there's all these close-minded, like... well, you know, rules and... I don't want to get into it. Does this make sense?"

"Yeah, I guess so. I don't. Wait..." A thought flashed in Laura's mind. She buried a smile. She knew it was delicate and she wasn't entirely sure where to begin. Jessica saw her friend struggling and sat on the edge of the recliner, watching patiently.

"I don't know if I should ask questions, is that okay?"

Jessica nodded. Laura composed herself with a breath and looked her friend right in the eye.

"Okay. And... well, like I've known you a long time, and you know I love you right?"

"Of course," Jessica smiled, nodding.

"Good. Because, like, we played sports together, and well... we like, showered together."

"We didn't shower together," Jessica corrected her, as she shifted a little in her seat and felt her cheeks get warm.

"Well, we showered next to each other. I mean, you've seen me naked a lot."

"Uh huh," Jessica sat back in the chair clearly dreading the sudden direction of the conversation.

"And, well, I don't know how to say this without sounding, you know... It's just that, I mean, I know I'm really hot..."

Jessica picked up a pillow and chucked it at Laura's head.

"You bitch!" Jessica said laughing.

Laura blocked the pillow and finally allowed herself to smile.

"See when you say it that way it sounds like it's a bad thing."

"It can be both!" Jessica yelled as she stood up and walked towards the kitchen. "I need something to drink."

"Wait," Laura stood to follow her friend. "I want to know who else is gay and doesn't know it yet."

4

Soft Lights, Small City

Jessica pulled out gin and vermouth from her parents liquor cabinet and started to mix martinis. Laura opened the refrigerator and noticed it was mostly empty other than condiments, sodas, a few apples, and a pizza box, from which she stole a slice of cheese pizza. Jessica pulled out two martini glasses but Laura grabbed a soda and poured it in her martini glass.

"So your parents aren't home?"

"I never know with them," Jessica said with a faux exasperated wave of a hand while she used the other to plop two olives in her martini. "They are always coming and going, I can't keep track."

They clinked glasses and drank, both drinks tickling the backs of their throat. There was a moment of silent reflection before Laura spoke.

"Are your roommates all lesbians too?"

"Bitch, is that all we are going to talk about?"

"But..."

"Let's go upstairs, grab your drink."

They walked up to Jessica's room. It looked much as it did before she left for college. The wall was full of posters: The Cure, Siouxsie and the Banshees, Duran Duran, The Smiths, and David Bowie. Jessica plugged in the white Christmas lights that she had strung around her room in February of her ninth grade year, and turned off the overhead light. There was a large window facing east, from which you could see Coastal Highway on a clear day, but tonight was a splatter painting of drops of rain, and a hint of the distant blinking yellow stoplights. The rest of the room was scattered clothes, a stereo, and a cassette collection of around 100 tapes, including dozens of Jessica's own mixes.

"So, I just finished this for you." She popped a tape out of the stereo and put it in Laura's hand. "You are going to flip out when you listen to it."

"Aw, I love your mixes," Laura said smiling. "Thank you."

Jessica shook her head.

"It's not a mix. It's a full album. It's this singer I saw in a little club in the East Village. Her name is Ani DiFranco. She's going to blow you away."

Laura nodded and took the tape.

"Awesome, thank you."

"No," Jessica didn't let go of the tape. She shook her head and looked Laura dead in the eyes. "I need you to hear me when I'm saying this. This matters. Ani's going to blow your fucking mind. You don't have any idea what you are about to hear."

Laura nodded seriously.

"All of your music blows my mind. I was just listening to one of your mixes on the way here."

"Which one?"

"Dudes in Tight Pants."

"That was a good one," Jessica looked up into her memory for the track listings.

"Great for rainy nights," Laura confirmed while looking at the tape in her hand.

"It is. But that tape, that belongs to another time. It's like the past, like soon to be two generations of music ago. Music is changing. You might not know it yet, because everything takes two years to get down here from actual civilization, but I'm telling you the scene is like... evolving. And that doesn't even sound right, because even calling it a 'scene' kinda cheapens it and it shouldn't be cheapened. It's becoming so fucking raw and authentic and... just... it's becoming real."

Laura was nodding along. She was used to her friend going on about music. Laura was spinning the tape slowly between her fingers. She was listening, but not entirely present. The calm of the moment let her mind wander back to Trey.

"Like have you even heard Nirvana yet?"

"I don't think so."

"You would fucking know it if you heard them. Your brain is going to melt the first time you hear *Smells Like Teen Spirit*. I didn't bring it down with me. That's the Seattle sound, it's like the new thing, like everyone is talking about it. But that's not what tonight is about."

Jessica went to her stereo and fast forwarded a tape, pausing it occasionally to check her progress. Laura heard a preview of a single guitar and a sonorous and soulful voice.

"Ani isn't a part of that Seattle thing, she's like... so New York City it hurts. Honestly, it's my music... it's the perfect music for me right now in my life. It's literally the soundtrack for my life. Wait, just listen to this song."

Jessica was still rewinding and fast-forwarding to get to the right place.

"She kinda reminds me of Joni Mitchell," Laura offered from the snippets she heard.

"Eh, no. Not really. You know I love me some Joni, but they are so different," Jessica thought about what she had said for a moment before adding, "That said, maybe in some ways she's kinda like a Joni for our generation, but I don't think so. I would say she's more like Woody Guthrie for our generation."

"Who's that?"

Jessica sighed, still focused on the stereo.

"I'll make you a mix, though he's not important right now."

Laura nodded and Jessica still scanned.

"What's the name of the album?" Laura asked.

"No idea," Jessica shrugged. "I bought it from someone in a bar, it just says Ani DiFranco on it."

"What song are you looking for?"

"I don't know the song title, but this is it."

The song that Jessica played for Laura is the second to last song on the eponymous debut album from Ani. It's called *Out of Habit*. And yes, it contains the lyrics *and the coffee is just water dressed in brown.*

It's a song about a girl eating in a late night diner. But it's about much more than that too. For these two teenage girls in this moment, it wasn't just a song, or a poem. It was an experience, more like a painting that burned its image into their memory. A moment that was raw, personal, secretive, and yet shared.

From the first words Laura knew she was hearing something special. But then she heard the line that stayed with her forever.

my cunt is built like a wound that won't heal

Laura actually put her hand to her own mouth when she heard the lyric. She laughed nervously, thinking for a second she misheard the words. At the same time she felt like she had done something illicit. She got goosebumps. She didn't know what to do with her hands. She didn't know where to look. So she looked up at her friend.

Jessica was watching her and grinning.

"Right?" Jessica said loudly and triumphantly over the music.

The song stopped and Laura tried to process it. This might have been the most perfect song she had ever heard.

"Play it again."

Jessica cackled and hit rewind.

Partway through the second playing Laura thought how she wanted to someday play this song for Trey. She felt a pang in her stomach and lost track of the song. She sighed and looked at the rain.

Jessica, who had been singing along, this time with her eyes closed, opened them to see her friend looking out the window. Laura's damp eyes reflected the Christmas lights like tiny stars. Jessica tried to read Laura's face.

Laura could feel Jessica looking at her, but kept her eyes fixed on the storm. She cleared her throat.

"Play it again."

The wind picked up and rain pelted the window, causing long streams to run down the glass. In the distance, the lights of Ocean City blinked yellow.

5

School

Laura was home one minute after her 11PM weeknight curfew. When she got home, her mother was surprisingly already asleep, but had left a note for her that both Jessica and Candace had called. Laura went up to bed, ignoring her homework. She fell asleep immediately. The stress of the day, from the calculus test on, had taken its toll.

That night she dreamt of her little coffee shop in Chicago, and her father, sitting in the corner, reading a book, sipping a cappuccino. She came out of the dream in a comfortable ease that only lasted a few moments before the memories stormed their way into her brain. After a quick shower she flew down the stairs hoping to stop at English's Family Restaurant for coffee and a scrapple sandwich, when she smelled the unmistakable scent of cooking bacon and brewing coffee coming from the kitchen.

Joyce was never one to cook breakfast. Getting herself and a child out of the door in the morning had been a challenge since she had become a single parent. Breakfast at home was at best microwaved oatmeal or cold cereal. When Laura was younger they would go to English's roughly once a week for a hot breakfast, where Joyce would get the "Fast Fare" which was eggs and ham cubes scrambled together with buttered white toast while Laura would go for the scrapple sandwich. It was at English's that Laura first tasted coffee when she was twelve, and she still drank it like her mother did: four creams and three sugars.

"Bacon? Coffee?" she said, stunned and smiling as she looked at her mother who was still dressed in her nightgown. "Did you quit?"

Her mother was always dressed by this time in the morning. Joyce laughed as she poured herself a cup of cream, sugar, and coffee.

"I didn't tell you last night?"

Laura hopped up and sat on the counter of the kitchen island, took her mother's coffee right out of her hand, drank it, and shook her head.

Joyce was unfazed, as she was used to her daughter stealing her food, and got out another cup for herself as she explained. "HR told me that because I haven't taken a vacation day in nine years I'm going to forfeit them. I have two months' worth of vacation days and eight months to take them before I start losing them, so, my two-day vacation starts today."

"Two whole days?"

"I have a big project on Friday I need to present. But being out of the office will give me quality time to work on it."

Laura drank the coffee and her eyes narrowed as she focused on her mother.

"I'm not sure what is sadder. That you have not taken a single vacation day in nine years, or that in nine years you have only accrued eight weeks of vacation, or that when you finally take two days off after nine years you are going to spend them working anyway."

Joyce rolled her eyes. As she spoke she made herself a plate of toast and bacon, and was putting butter on the toast.

"You are not going to make me feel bad about my time off. I have made myself toast, bacon, and coffee, I'm going to finish my book this morning, and I'm going to the Salisbury Mall to get a new coat, and maybe even some new clothes."

"You going to the Centre or the old mall?"

"The Centre," Joyce said, putting the butter away. Laura took the opportunity to steal her mother's plate and make herself a bacon, toast, and butter sandwich.

"Ik 'an go 'ith ou," Laura said with her mouth full.

Joyce sighed and got the butter out of the fridge again.

"Not a chance."

Laura shrugged, slugged down the coffee, hopped off the counter, gave her mother a greasy kiss on the cheek, popped the other half of the bacon sandwich in her mouth, grabbed her backpack and gym bag and glided out the door.

The morning sun was clean, and the world glistened in the way it only knows how after a good rain. The grass was a brilliant green. The Black-eyed Susans, bent low from the storm and season, were radiant. They looked brighter than they had in weeks. The chill from the night before was gone and the heat of the morning was hinting at a few days of an Indian Summer. Laura drove to school with Ani DiFranco cranked up and her driver's side window down.

As she pulled into the parking lot she saw Trey's car wasn't there. He always parked as far away from school as allowed. Laura drove past his empty space and parked in her usual spot next to Candace, who had just closed her own car door, waved, and waited for Laura to get out of her car. Laura closed her eyes for a second and breathed deep. She could still taste the butter and bacon on her tongue.

As she pushed her car door open Candace stepped forward into the space, far closer than anyone should. She spoke in a hushed tone, even though there was no one around that could hear her.

"Did you guys have it out last night?"

Laura stood up into Candace's space, and gently moved her out of the way of the car door as she closed it.

"What are you talking about?"

"Your mom said you were over at Trey's. And you never called me back. I figured you two maybe had it out or something. Finally." The last 'finally' was said with a little all-too-knowing smirk.

"No. What would there be to 'have out' or whatever you mean by that?"

"Hello? Because of Homecoming."

"I don't... what?"

"Do you not know? Katherine Bounds asked Trey to Homecoming yesterday after soccer practice and he said yes."

Laura's face flushed. She had no idea she could be jealous, but suddenly at this moment she was. It wasn't a conscious thought, after all, she had nothing to be jealous about. She wasn't dating Trey. She knew Homecoming was a couple of weeks away, but she figured Trey would ask her like he did last year, for them to go as the usual "just friends" as they had done in the previous two years.

"*She* asked *him*?"

Candace nodded. Katherine was a senior, and widely considered the prettiest girl in the school. Last year, when she was a junior, she had dated senior star athlete and prom king Chuckie Burbage, but the rumor was that he broke up with her right before he went off to college. Katherine was smart, like Ivy League early admissions smart, and kind too. She didn't play school sports but she rode horses competitively and her family was crazy wealthy. Laura liked her the way everyone seemed to like her, from afar. But they weren't friends or anything.

"Huh," was all she could manage to say.

"Trey didn't mention this last night?" Candace was building a drama in her mind.

"I wasn't there that long, just for a minute. I went to see Jessica."

"Oh," Candace was always a little intimidated by Jessica's relationship with Laura. "She's on midterm break? How's she?"

"She's a le..." Laura was in a daze and almost said something she would regret. "She's great. She's all over the place, as usual."

Candace looked worried for her friend.

"Are you okay?"

Laura forced a smile and nodded that she was. But she was lying. She felt off. She was a little dizzy and a little nauseous as she walked with Candace into school.

First period on Wednesday was English Literature. Trey always sat in front of Laura, but the seat remained empty. They were discussing *To Kill a Mockingbird* which Laura had read the summer between her seventh and eighth grade year at the suggestion of her father. It was one of his favorite books. She enjoyed it then, or at least enjoyed talking to him about it then, but she had not bothered to reread it for class, and was struggling to keep up with the conversation. She started to get a headache, and she thought she was maybe dehydrated, so after English Lit she went to the water-fountain and drank as much as she could.

Her next class was Study Hall. She tried to work on her Western Civ homework that she hadn't done the night before, but her headache got worse and her stomach started to hurt. Every time she heard the door open she turned her head and looked, and each time that it wasn't Trey she felt worse. Finally, the bell rang, her homework wasn't done, and when she stood she felt for a second like she was going to pass out.

Laura went back to the water fountain again. After two more sips of water she felt okay. Then it hit her. She held onto the water fountain with both hands as a wave of the worst menstrual cramps she had ever had gripped her insides and twisted. She breathed through the pain. Candace came up behind her and put her hand on her back.

"You don't look so good."

"I don't..." Laura said between breaths, "feel so good."

Candace walked with her to the bathroom and went to her locker for some Midol. Then she went to tell the school nurse, Mrs. Pruitt, who – as a rule – was generally unsympathetic to most illnesses. However, as a former teenaged sufferer of painful menstrual cramps herself, she made an exception for that ailment. In fact, Mrs. Pruitt was known to say, perhaps in jest, that two of her five children hurt less when they were born than her worst teenage cramps.

Candace got a hastily written hall pass from Mrs. Pruitt for Laura, and made it to Western Civ as the teacher was closing the door.

Laura, left alone in the bathroom stall, wept. It started as simple tears of pain, but through the waves of agony she started thinking about how Trey was suddenly gone, and the more she thought about Trey, the more she let her mind invent horrible futures.

What if he was in jail right now? What if his dad had died and he went to jail forever for murder? Did that happen to sixteen year old kids who were just defending their mother? And what if he didn't go to jail, would he still live with his dad? Wouldn't his father want to kill him? Didn't his dad have a gun?

At that thought another wicked spasm on her left side wiped out her thoughts. She breathed through the cramp. More tears came. The tears helped with the pain.

She thought about Dolores. She had never seen Dolores cry. She had seen her own mother cry dozens of times, but she never remembered Dolores crying once. *Would she see Dolores cry now? Had Dolores changed just because Laura learned a secret about her? How had Dolores hidden this secret from her for all these years? How would she ever be able to laugh or joke with Dolores again? Would Dolores even let her back into her life?*

The Buckingham house was crashing down. Her fantasy lover, her ideal mother both stolen by this monster she didn't even know.

She started rocking back and forth to try to mitigate the pain. She was making a noise that was a mix between a moan and a sob, which was why she didn't hear the bathroom door open, or the footsteps that walked right over to her stall door. As her eyes were closed, she didn't see the shoes, but when she heard the knock on the door it ripped her back into reality.

"Hey," the voice was familiar but Laura couldn't place it right away. "Do you need help?"

"I'm okay," Laura squeaked through a shallow breath.

"Well, you clearly aren't okay. Can I go get someone for you?"

Laura recognized the voice. Of course it was Katherine. The realization was followed instantaneously by a spasm that went through her midsection, apparently twisting her organs into poorly tied knots. She let out an uncontrollable sound that must have been something to hear from the other side of the bathroom stall door.

"Oh jeeze. Cramps, huh? It sounds like you got them pretty bad."

"Actually, I could be dying. It feels like I might be dying."

The voice on the other side of the door sounded concerned.

"Are you serious?"

Laura flushed the toilet for no reason other than habit and then stood up and opened the door. She had one hand on the sidewall to steady herself.

"Partly. I don't think I'm actually going to die, but I can't imagine it feels much worse than this."

Katherine smiled.

"I've got some Midol in my locker. If you want some, I could go grab them."

"I just took some. They haven't kicked in yet."

Katherine nodded and looked at her. Laura couldn't shake the sensation that she was being sized up somehow. She was cognizant of the stark dichotomy of this beautiful, tall, perfectly postured senior and her own tear-streaked face, her hands clutching at the walls, and her back hunched like Quasimodo.

"Come on, I'll help you to Mrs. Pruitt's," Katherine said encouragingly, offering her arm.

Laura thought *She's really leaning into this princess thing* and shook her head not sure what she should do next. Just then another spasm, which Laura assumed was her spleen imploding, made her knees buckle. Katherine reached out and caught Laura's arm and helped to keep her from hitting the floor. She put her arm around Laura and held her up until the worst of the sudden pain passed. And she kept her arm around her and slowly moved her towards the door.

"It will be better for you to get to Mrs. Pruitt's room. She turns off the lights, and gives you a warm washcloth. It's really the best thing, until the drugs kick in."

Laura nodded, exhausted from the pain. She managed to whisper a "thank you" which made Katherine smile.

"You know, I haven't said this to you yet," Katherine continued as they walked down the hall. "But I really like your haircut. I know you might have done it because of sports and all, but it really frames your face so much better than your long hair did. It's a good look for you."

Laura just nodded and pretended there was another small spasm. She was surprised Katherine thought about her at all, but she wasn't in the place to have a real heart to heart about her own face. They got to Mrs. Pruitt's door. With poise and ease Katherine pushed the door open and nodded to Mrs. Pruitt, who immediately stood up and walked over to the girls. Katherine slid her hand cautiously across Laura's back until she held her shoulder.

"You know," she said as sweetly and gently as anyone had ever spoken to Laura. "You're really beautiful."

Mrs. Pruitt, who was likely in her mid-sixties, but to the students, seemed as old as possible, replaced the future prom queen's hand with her own and Katherine exited.

Mrs. Pruitt was best described as the toughest five-foot-one and ninety-three pound broad you would ever want to meet. There might be tougher five-foot-one and ninety-three pound broads, but you don't want to meet them. She was at least a grandmother, possibly already a great-grandmother, and was as no-nonsense as they came, especially to "sick" children. She led Laura back into the "sick room" which was really a bed in a large windowless closet. She took her temperature and asked her a couple of questions, but knew right away what Laura was dealing with. She asked her when she took the pills and wrote it down in her notebook. She asked if this was the worst her cramps had ever been, and Laura confirmed that they were. She felt Laura's abdomen, which was tender, but not where her appendix was, so that was a relief. And then she asked a question Laura didn't see coming.

"Have you had any unusual stress the last couple of days?"

Laura looked at her and her eyes leaked water.

"It's okay," Mrs. Pruitt handed her a tissue box. "Do you want to talk about it?"

Laura shook her head. Mrs. Pruitt nodded and stood up, and walked over to the light switch, flicking it off. With one hand on the doorknob, she turned her head and spoke softly before pulling it closed.

"Okay then. Close your eyes. It will be better soon."

The drugs kicked in and Laura fell into a dreamless sleep, was woken at lunch, and was given the option of going home or going back to class. The pain was still there, but it was as if the steak knives in her sides had been replaced by butter knives. She planned on going home, but on the way to her car she saw Coach Hartman, her field hockey and lacrosse coach, who told her to suck it up, so she stayed in school for the last couple of classes and even went to field hockey practice. Trey never showed.

Laura was starving. As soon as she walked in the door she could smell her mother had been cooking. Stuffed cabbage, mashed potatoes, and cucumber salad. She trudged into the kitchen, exhausted and sore. She felt as if she had been beaten up by a gang of short people wielding sacks of lemons. Joyce was spooning the cabbages into a serving bowl and didn't break her concentration, even when Laura grabbed a pinch of mashed potatoes right out of the pot.

"Get," she tried shooing her daughter away. "Go wash up."

Laura washed her hands and started setting the table.

"How was the Day of Mom?"

"Hmm," was her mother's only response.

"That good, huh? So you worked all day?"

"Let's eat," Joyce said, putting the cabbages on the table.

Joyce paused and closed her eyes, as if to pray. She knew it was time to tell Laura her secret.

6

Joyce and Bubby

Unbeknownst to Laura, that previous spring Joyce had received a job offer from a competitor. It was substantially more money, but would have required that she move to Baltimore, which was about a three-hour drive away from Ocean Pines.

Joyce weighed her options: long-term financial security versus allowing her daughter to finish the last two years of high school with all of her friends. She considered how tough it was on Laura the last time they moved. It seemed wrong for Joyce to take the Baltimore job, but at the same time, it was a huge opportunity. So instead of accepting it outright, she told her own company about the offer, which caused a mild panic in her firm. Losing Joyce would likely mean losing clients they couldn't afford to lose. However, as they were a smaller company, they couldn't match the substantial offer from the Baltimore firm, though they did manage to give her a promotion, a modest raise, profit sharing, and some other perks.

One of those perks was a travel budget. For years she had chosen to not go to out-of-town conferences or work with out-of-town clients because she was a single parent. But that summer, while Laura was with her father in Chicago, her company sent Joyce to New Orleans, Las Vegas, and Charlotte. And it was in Las Vegas, at a craps table in the newly built Mirage Casino that she met Bubby Davis. Yes, Joyce met the Sheriff of Worcester County two thousand miles away from where they lived less than a ten minute drive from one another. Bubby, who

Joyce never voted for, was a young widower. His wife had tragically died from a rare form of cancer a year before he was elected Sheriff.

Bubby and Joyce were not natural bedfellows, but kismet being as intoxicating as their seven-and-sevens, one thing led to another and a Las Vegas tryst occurred. Bubby was conservative, religious, and a fan of sports, hunting, and fishing. Joyce was a reader, listened to NPR, and didn't understand the rules to any major team sport, including the ones her daughter played. Bubby, who had only been with two women in his life, was instantly ready to marry Joyce. While she enjoyed the attention, Joyce was not remotely interested in marriage. In fact, while she had fun with him, she wasn't even really sure she liked Bubby.

When they returned to the Eastern Shore he sent flowers to her office. A few days later Joyce and Bubby got coffee at English's. The next week, they had lunch at Rayne's Reef, an old fashioned soda fountain largely unchanged since it was built in 1901 in downtown Berlin.

The following day Bubby went into Ocean City to get crab cakes from Weitzel's. Long since gone, Weitzel's was a high quality, casual, almost fast food seafood restaurant. To go to 50th street in Ocean City in the mid-day summer traffic, just to get the best crab cake sandwiches, was a truly sacrificial act. And he didn't even light up the gumball or use his siren.

Their first real date was dinner at Thompson's Sea Girt House, one of the two nicest fine dining bayfront restaurants in the area. They shared a bottle of white wine. They were seated as the sun was setting over the marsh, and as the windows blackened the dining room glowed with soft candlelight. Bubby told funny stories, and he had plenty of them. Joyce spent that night at Bubby's. They didn't see each other again for a week, as Joyce was in Charlotte. When she got back, they went to the other fancy bayside restaurant, The Hobbit, for happy hour drinks. After drinks they ate dinner out on the deck. Her mood was different this time. She wanted a "real" conversation and she could see Bubby struggling to meet her. Joyce wanted to talk about books that he hadn't read and movies he hadn't seen. There was an awkward lull. And then she did the unthinkable.

"Tell me about your wife," she said while looking out at the bay. It was a kindness not to meet his eyes at that moment.

He never expected the question, and it hit him hard in the gut. His eyes pooled before he could catch himself. He sighed and put his fork down.

"Well," he started, not knowing where he was going. "I guess... I guess you would have liked her."

Joyce was confused but smiled to hide it. "Why's that?"

"Well, unlike me... she could read."

He grinned as she laughed. With the cool breeze coming off the bay, they drank their coffees and shared a dessert and an honest conversation. They talked about her ex-husband and his late wife and all the challenges in their young lives. Again Joyce stayed over. The following day, Laura came home from Chicago.

Joyce was unable to explain to herself or Bubby why she couldn't be honest with Laura about her new relationship. It could be that she was using Laura as an excuse to not jump into the deep end of the pool with someone that honestly had much stronger feelings for her than she had for him. She liked him. He loved her.

But also, she liked her freedom more than she was willing to admit. She liked being able to stay up and read a book and not have anyone disturb her. Laura and Joyce had a rhythm to their lives and she wasn't ready to add another band member.

But then again, young Bubby Davis had that "aw shucks" crooked grin mixed with a very real pain behind his sparkling blue eyes. And he had enough charm to be elected sheriff five times.

So, while Joyce wasn't ready to dive headfirst into the Bubby pool, some "late nights at the office" were not really spent at the office, and some long lunches might have really been just a Your Store sub at Bubby's kitchen table.

Now back to this day in question. Joyce did finish her book, go shopping at the Centre at Salisbury, nearly finish her Friday presentation, and cook dinner;

and yet, she still found the time to meet Bubby for lunch in Salisbury at Curley's Garage, a kitschy restaurant with walls full of automobile memorabilia.

And it was at lunch over iced teas and taco salads that he told her all about what happened at the Buckingham household the night before, about Trey and Dolores and the alleged abuse they had suffered for years, and what was about to happen that evening to Mr. Buckingham's bar. The Ocean Pines police had brought in the Worcester County Sheriff's department, the Maryland State police, and the Worcester County State's Attorney, as it became much bigger than a simple domestic violence issue. As if domestic violence is ever simple.

So, as Joyce and Laura sat down to eat stuffed cabbage and mashed potatoes, the talk was small, but the weight on both of their minds was heavy. They talked about the weather, Laura's upcoming field hockey game, the film *The Fisher King* which was still playing at Sun and Surf Theaters and how Joyce loved it and wanted Laura to see it with her. It wasn't until Laura was clearly done eating that Joyce said the phrase which Laura hated.

"We need to talk."

Laura sighed. She wondered how much her mother knew.

"Sweetheart, this is going to be hard for you to hear, but I want you to know that I'm going to be here for you no matter what happens next. I know how much you care for Trey..."

"Mom," Laura sheepishly protested.

"Wait, just let me talk. First off, I think he's going to be okay. I don't know how to say this... I'm just going to... Mr. Buckingham is a drug dealer and his bar was raided earlier today by the police."

Laura's mouth hung open. She was stunned into silence.

"Last night at the hospital the police were called. Dolores told them everything. She told the police that he tried to kill her, and also she suspected that he was on the cocaine. This was an open secret in Ocean City for years, that he sold cocaine. Dolores didn't know much about it, but she gave them enough for a warrant. He's going to jail for a long time. Even if he gets out on bail, he should be prevented from going near Trey and Dolores. I hope so, at least."

Laura shook her head to snap out of it.

"Mom, how do you know all of this?"

Joyce looked up at the ceiling.

"Well, that's a whole other thing I guess we should talk about."

Two hours later Laura was lying on Jessica's floor looking up at the ceiling and the glowing sticker stars, listening to "Kid Fears" by the Indigo Girls on repeat. Laura said she didn't want to talk about it and Jessica didn't press. It wasn't the first time they had listened to "Kid Fears" on repeat, and it wouldn't be the last. Jessica was comfy in her bean bag chair, reading *Get Shorty* with the help of a clip-on book light, and singing along with the Michael Stipe parts.

7

Going Home

The following morning was gloriously warm, the second day of the Indian Summer. Laura shined to match the sky when she saw Trey's car parked in his usual spot, ridiculously far from school.

Again Candace was waiting for her. Again, to gossip about Trey, but this time about his father, and the police, and drugs. In the days before the internet or social media, for Candace to already have this knowledge was pretty impressive, and she knew it.

"I know," Laura cut her off before Candace got to some of the more wild and lurid rumors. "Mom filled me in last night."

Candace looked at her with shocked suspicion.

"Is that why you didn't call me back?"

Laura got her bags out of the back. She shook her head and sighed a little. "No, I went to Jessica's. I didn't really want to talk to anyone."

Candace heard *I didn't want to talk to you* even if that's not what Laura meant. She never explained to Candace that Jessica would allow her to just be, and not talk. Laura had no intention of relegating Candace into a second-class friend. They had been friends since eight grade and Laura felt like she could tell her anything. Even if she was a huge gossip, she would keep Laura's confidence. Probably. But at this moment Laura didn't know how to tell Candace all of this.

"I just need... I don't know, like a moment."

She looked at Candace to see if her friend understood. It seemed like she did. But Candace was uncomfortable with silence.

"Wait, how the fuck did Joyce know?"

Laura smirked. Everyone in the county knew Bubby Davis, but no one knew he was dating Joyce Byrne. This was a gift Laura could give Candace. She linked her arm under Candace's and they started walking towards school.

"Alright," she said with a smile. "You're never going to believe this."

While Trey's car was in the parking lot, Trey was not in the first two classes. But at mid-morning break, she finally saw him, standing by the door that led to the gym, talking to his soccer coach and the Athletic Director. The soccer team had a game that day, and the discussion was most likely whether or not he was allowed to play, because he had missed practice and school the day before. He stole a glance at Laura. Laura smiled. Trey didn't. He looked back at the AD and pleaded his case. He looked smaller than Laura remembered. Paler.

They didn't share any more morning classes, so Laura didn't see Trey again until lunch. She took her time getting to the lunchroom. As bad as she wanted to see him, she wasn't sure she was ready to talk. But as soon as she walked down the steps into the lunchroom, he spotted her and stood up. He walked right over to her, and for a second it seemed like he was going to hug her, but then he awkwardly stopped.

"Um," she said, looking around for Katherine and realizing she was outside at the senior class picnic tables. "Can I hug you?"

Trey fell into her the way few high school students would ever dare. The lunchroom, always so loud, dropped one octave as many of their peers' jaws slacked. Even the teacher's table, known for their constant chatter, was stunned into silence by such an honest and raw hug.

Once he finally released her, he spoke almost nervously.

"I have to go out to my car. Do you want to go with me?"

Laura nodded and they walked out into the afternoon sun.

Trey drove a 1980 Ford LTD 4-door that was baby blue where it wasn't rusted, that had bench seats and an occasionally broken tape player. It was huge, and it always smelled like a mixture of Drakkar Noir and his lacrosse pads, which were kept in the trunk but still permeated into the car when the windows were up—an admittedly rare occurrence. He usually had three to four large packs of cinnamon gum jutting out of his otherwise unused ashtray and always had a box of mini chocolate donuts on the floor in the passenger side. He kept them on the floor to keep them out of the direct sunlight, though in the summer they were always melty and in the winter they were often frozen.

They didn't speak on the walk to the car. Katherine waved at both of them as they passed. A practiced, confident wave that somehow intimidated Laura. Laura smiled and offered an awkward half-wave reply.

When they got to the car, Trey opened the passenger side door and leaned in, moving a sweatshirt out of the way while looking for something. He picked up the box of mini chocolate donuts, ate one and offered the box to Laura. She popped one in her mouth whole, then set the box on the passenger side seat. Trey put it back on the floor in the shade. He stood up, having found what he was looking for.

"Last night I wrote you a letter," he said as he handed it to her.

She went to open it.

"You aren't going to read it in front of me, are you?"

Laura shrugged in confusion.

"Where am I supposed to read it?"

"I don't know," he said, looking around for a solution.

"Can we just talk?"

He shook his head.

"You should read the letter first."

Laura rolled her eyes.

"Well, turn around then."

He nodded and complied. She opened the letter.

Laura,

I don't know how to say this so I am writing you a letter. I don't want to talk about what happened last night. But I want to thank you for being there. I don't know what else to say about that.

We've known each other a long time, and I swear you knew everything there is to know about me except for this one thing. In a way, I guess that wasn't very fair to you. So many times I wanted to tell you, but I was scared. I've spent my whole life being scared, I don't want to be scared anymore.

You are my best friend. I can't imagine my life without you in it all the time. I don't want that to ever change. I'm sorry I lied to you for so long. I swear I did it to protect you, even if I don't think that was the right thing to do anymore. I don't know what's going to happen, but whatever happens, I hope you are a part of my life.

Also, I wanted you to hear from me, Katherine Bounds asked me to homecoming and I said yes. We aren't dating or anything, I think she just wanted someone to go with and I guess I wasn't thinking. I didn't know if you wanted to go with me as just friends as usual. After last night though now I feel bad. I'm sorry. I don't know how to say this, but... I love you.

Trey

Laura sighed. Her stomach felt like it was doing flips. She turned her head slowly to look at Trey out of the corner of her eye. He was facing away from her, looking out towards the soccer field. His right leg was quivering. He let out a long, nervous exhale. Laura smiled. She wanted to hug him again. She wanted to kiss him. She wanted to jump into his arms.

But she also saw a figure walking towards them from the back of the school. It was a fast walk, not a jog, but a very quick and determined step. It was Candace, and she was looking right at them.

Laura knew she only had a couple of seconds before Candace was in earshot of anything she was going to say to Trey. She wanted to tell him that she loved him too, but she was also not remotely ready to tell him that. And she had nowhere to hide the letter. She folded it in half, turned away from Candace, slipped into her bra, and cleared her throat.

Trey turned to look at her. She offered a half-smile and then motioned to Candace. Trey glanced at Candace and then back at Laura trying his best to read anything in her body language. But she was looking at Candace.

"What's up, Candace?" Laura said with more frustration than she planned.

"Trey, the police are here. They are at the front of the school," Candace was almost breathless, not from the walk but from the excitement. "They are looking for you."

The two girls looked at Trey expectantly. Trey opened his passenger seat door and pulled out the donuts, popping one into his mouth and offering them to Laura and Candace. Laura took another, but Candace just gave the floor donuts a suspicious side-eye.

"Maybe," Candace said, thinking out loud, "you should save those for the cops?"

Trey snorted a laugh and tossed the box back on the floor, grabbed a stick of gum, and walked slowly back towards the school, and straight to the main office. Five minutes later, one police officer was carrying Trey's backpack and gym bag, and placing it in the trunk of the cruiser, the other was opening the back door for Trey. There was a whole contingent of schoolmates who swear that he was handcuffed at this point, but Candace said he wasn't, and it's probably best to take her word on it.

8

The Game

That afternoon was one of the biggest soccer games of the year. Interstate rival Cape Henlopen from Delaware was undefeated and featured two senior all-star strikers, who at that time were #1 and #4 in the state of Delaware in goals. It can't be overstated how big this game was. The stands were full of cheering parents and students from both sides. Even alumni who had moved away would mark the Cape game on the calendar, just in case they could find a way to get back to the Shore. It was a big deal.

Trey was the anchor of the team's defense, and not having him in the lineup was noticeable from the beginning. He was the best player on that team, for even though Dylan Hayes would go on to play college ball at University of Maryland, he was only a freshman keeper that year and hadn't really hit his growth spurt yet. Dylan was getting shelled, as the two Cape strikers were finding opportunities almost every time Cape had possession of the ball. Despite some acrobatic saves, Dylan had already let in 2 goals by halftime. Without Trey, the game seemed hopeless.

Laura and Candace had come to watch the game with the rest of the field hockey team. At halftime the mood was somber, as the home crowd had little to cheer about. Candace nudged Laura to let her know that Katherine was in the stands, sitting with her mother and a few senior girls. Laura regretted looking, but Katherine didn't seem to notice her. Laura thought she overheard snippets of their conversation mentioning Trey, but couldn't say for sure.

Just as the final seconds of halftime ticked down, a police car turned into the service road behind the field and pulled up as close as possible to the bench. The police officer got out and opened the back door, and Trey jumped out, already dressed in his uniform, and even wearing his shin guards and cleats. At first the crowd was a mixture of cheers and whispers. Trey ran right out onto the field taking his spot moments before the start of the second half.

That's when one of the eight grade boys, either Chris Tawney or Paul Green yelled, "You're fucked now, Cape!"

In the crowd, most of the mothers smiled and the fathers laughed. The furious AD made a beeline to the group of eighth grade boys to figure out who to threaten. The field hockey team let out a smattering of woos, and the Cape fans pretended to be offended.

Laura was watching Trey who was looking at the ground to center himself. When he heard the boy curse he looked up and smiled. That smile was so honest. From that point forward Laura didn't watch the game, she watched Trey. He was big again, strong, brimming, and confident. It sounds like a cliché, but everyone there will tell you it's true... that when the sun hit him right, he shone golden.

Trey was an immediate gamechanger. Less than a minute into the second half he scored on a penalty kick. With Trey directing the defense, Cape's two star strikers were stymied. Trey played with a focus he had never shown before, he glided over the field, always one literal step ahead of the two seniors. It was, without a doubt, the best he had ever played.

Though with less than ten minutes left in the game and still down one, his coach had no choice but to send Trey up on offense. When he became an attacking midfielder, the game really got exciting. Both keepers pulled off some magic saves to keep Cape in the lead.

With less than a minute remaining in the game, Trey found Tyrone Stewart on the right wing, who had come all the way up from fullback and Tyrone buried it in the back of the net. All tied up, the game went to overtime.

Only a minute into overtime Blair Cathell got tackled from behind in what was a pretty violent play, in fact ending his season. Tensions were high both in the stands and on the field, and it looked for a second like Tyrone was going to get in a fight with the Cape defender. But the refs and players separated them. Tyrone helped Blair off the field. A yellow card was issued to the Cape defender. Cape set the wall too close to the ball. Both coaches were barking at the refs and a warning was given to both benches. One of the refs backed up the wall.

The entire time, Trey stood absolutely still. He was standing over top of the ball and looking intently at the goal, ignoring everything else. It was as if all the distractions and chaos that swirled around him couldn't actually touch him. The ball was on the left side of the field, a little more than 25 yards out. Trey closed his eyes and breathed. When he opened them again the world had gone silent. He took one more deep breath, and then struck the ball perfectly. It curved around the wall and into the top right corner of the goal, past the diving goalie. As soon as the ball hit the net the team and spectators went berserk, except for Trey, who fell to his knees and covered his face in his hands. To this day no one knows if he was actually crying, but it sure looked like it.

Laura and Candace were cheering, laughing, and hugging. The entire field hockey team was screaming so loud you could hear their cheers echoing off the school. Parents were embracing one another, shaking hands, awkwardly high fiving. Trey's teammates mobbed him, smacking him on the back, hugging, screaming, and laughing.

Like a good captain he pushed them away, got them to chant "Rah, rah Vikings" and then lined up and shook the opponents' hands. Trey was in the back of the line, the last player before the coach. He knew his place. Even before the hands were all shaken, the fans had begun to meander onto the field. Laura didn't, of course, she knew the rules, but the parents, siblings, and others didn't seem to obey them.

Neither did Katherine Bounds. She walked right up to Trey who had just finished talking to the Cape head coach at midfield. She grabbed his shoulders first, until he was looking at her. He smiled. Then with both hands, she grabbed his face and kissed him deeply.

Everyone saw their first kiss. No one knew it was their first kiss, or would even assume that it was. After all, you didn't do that kind of thing in high school. Maybe in movies, but not in real life. But in October of 1991 in Berlin, Maryland it actually happened and it was just like a movie.

It seemed everyone was looking at Trey and Katherine. Except for Candace. She was looking at Laura. She was the only one that saw her friend desperately trying not to react to what was obvious physical pain. Candace would actually never even know what it was like to have her heart broken. This was the closest she would ever get to it.

Laura felt betrayed by life. She turned her back to the field and walked quickly towards her car, Candace walking beside her, offering her apologies for something that was in no way her fault. Laura thought for a minute that she might throw up.

She went home. Her mom wasn't there. There was a note on the fridge saying she had to go into the office. So Laura took a quick shower and threw on her comfiest jeans and an old Cubs sweatshirt of her father's. Then she got in the car to go see Jessica. But instead, she drove to the Buckingham house to talk to Dolores.

9

Garlic Soup

Laura knew that Dolores was home before she even knocked on the door. She could smell the garlic from the driveway.

She thought perhaps Dolores was making pernil, as that pork recipe calls for so much garlic you can usually smell it from the street, but there wasn't a greasy meaty smell that usually accompanies the roasting pernil. This was cleaner. Fresher.

Laura knocked on the door. A minute later Dolores, with an unusual hint of fear in her eyes, opened it. She immediately put her hands together in front of her lips, as if she was a little child praying, but with her eyes wide open and darting back and forth between Laura's eyes and mouth. In that moment, looking at this girl who in many ways was her daughter, Dolores' heart was a morass of emotions: concern, fear, and shame—and yet, deep pride, respect, and love. Dolores knew that at a time like this, with crime and violence hanging heavily over her home, only a truly brave and kind person would have the strength to knock on her door. Overcome with emotion, Dolores tilted her head softly to the right side, unable to speak.

Laura lifted her hand in a stilted half-wave greeting. She studied Dolores' face. These eyes that she knew so well, and yet it was as if she was seeing them for the first time. The autumn air swirled in the doorway, and Laura could smell a mixture of garlic and toast. She could hear Billie Holiday singing the first words of *No Good Man* coming from the Marantz in the kitchen.

Laura, weary from emotion and pain, finally spoke.

"Can I come in? Can we talk?"

"Always, Mija," she said as she spread her arms wide. Laura fell into them. Dolores instinctively rubbed Laura's back and cooed a few *it's okay's*, though it was unclear to whom she was saying it, Laura or herself.

She held Laura just inside the threshold, and slowly rocked back and forth. Somehow, through the magic of a home she had worked so hard to create, Dolores shed the skin of a victim and became a mother again.

"Come and eat. Healing soup is ready."

Dolores' own mother's recipe for "healing soup" was something she made whenever someone in the house was sick. Laura knew it well, and could even make it herself. It was a simple garlic and almond soup, made with vegetable broth, white wine vinegar, salt, pepper, paprika, and drizzled extra virgin olive oil on top. Dolores always served the soup with buttered sourdough toast and, of course, green grapes. Dolores was not strict on many things, but in her house garlic soup could never be served without green grapes.

There was a silence between them as they walked into the kitchen and prepared the meal. Dolores got two bowls out of the cupboard, while Laura pulled two spoons from the silverware drawer, and placed them under folded napkins across the round table from one another. Then Laura opened the fridge and pulled out the bowl of already washed green grapes, placing them at the center of the table, next to the basket with the sourdough toast.

Dolores set Laura's bowl on the table, then moved her place-setting over ninety degrees to be closer to Laura. Neither woman smiled or even made a sound, other than that which was made by the ceramic and silver resting on the table. Sounds that were largely covered by the strained voice of Billie Holiday. Laura sat first, but didn't pick up her spoon. Dolores' silence and collected expression belied the storm raging in her mind.

"You didn't go to the game today," Laura almost blurted out. Her voice came out of her unexpectedly, both interrupting Billie Holiday as she was beginning *God Bless The Child* and causing a little twinge of pain in Dolores.

"I couldn't, not yet," she said as she looked at her soup.

"We won. Trey won it for us. He was..." Laura was at a loss for words. She kept seeing him kiss Katherine in her mind, and she couldn't think of the right word.

Dolores looked up and nodded. "He made it? That's good. He needed that. It was very nice of the police to take him. I was worried he had missed it."

"He got there right as the second half started. He had two goals and an assist, and we won three to two so..." Laura trailed off, again, thinking of the kiss.

"I feel bad. This was his first game I have ever missed."

Laura waited for Dolores to continue but she didn't. They both tasted the soup. It was hot, maybe a little too hot still. Laura scraped some butter onto a piece of sourdough toast.

The longer they went without saying anything, the easier it got. Perhaps this is a phenomenon that can only happen with family, whether blood relations or not. Laura had gone over to the Buckingham household almost unconsciously, but also, in the back of her mind, expectantly. She felt there would be some sort of big confrontation, or confession, maybe an apology, or even a long explanation. But instead, all she got was garlic soup, sourdough toast, Billie Holiday, and a hug.

So Laura talked a little more about the game. Dolores relaxed. She asked about school. She asked about Homecoming. She wanted to know "who this Katherine girl was" and if Trey was really dating her. Laura told her about the kiss. Dolores cursed in Spanish. Laura wasn't sure if she was upset that Trey had kissed Katherine instead of Laura, or if she was upset that this happened in the one game in Trey's career that she missed.

Likely it was both. After all, Dolores loved her romance novels.

Time moved quickly as they chatted, but once it got to be nine PM and Trey still wasn't home, Dolores became a little agitated. She wanted to see her son. She wanted to know about the game, and the kiss, and most importantly that he was safe. This wasn't a regular day for her, she needed her son, but his curfew was eleven PM, and she knew he was likely to not show up until then.

So perhaps that is why Dolores, out of the blue, changed the conversation to something much more substantial than soccer games and dramatic kisses. She had switched out the Billie Holiday cassette for Françoise Hardy's *Comment te dire adieu* album. They were still sitting at the kitchen table, the bowls in the dishwasher, the soup wrapped up and in the fridge, the sourdough and butter gone, and only three grapes left untouched between them. Dolores had made coffee and put out some butter cookies, which Laura snapped on the plate before each bite.

"I don't know," Dolores began slowly as if searching for the right words, "what is going to happen."

"With what?" Laura asked, not aware yet that the timbre of the room had changed.

"My husband."

The word hung in the kitchen while Laura remembered the blood she cleaned up off the chair she was currently sitting on. She wondered why it had taken her so long to realize that it was the same chair.

Dolores stood up and walked to the tantalus where she pulled out a bottle of tawny port, offering some to Laura who shook her head. She poured herself a glass, speaking to the bottle and the glass.

"He was so beautiful once. So wild and full of life."

She picked up the glass and looked up at Laura with broken and wistful eyes.

"You know, he used to write me poetry, almost every day. After college he wanted to move to New York City and live in Greenwich Village. He almost dropped out of college in fact, but his father stopped him. His father was a real bastard."

She stopped talking, lost in a memory. Laura waited.

"I don't think he ever loved his son, just the idea of having a son... that is all he loved. He gave him the land in Ocean City, and just enough money to make sure he couldn't say no."

Dolores shook her head and sighed.

"When Trey's father proposed, he promised me he would never be anything like his own father. And yet, every day we lived here, a little piece of the man I loved chipped away. And what was underneath..."

Dolores drained her port and poured herself another glass and sat back down at the table.

"It wasn't like," she continued, "he became a demon overnight. It was just tiny moments. Incrementally. Little things. And the little things got bigger. Then, when his father died..." she cut off again shaking her head.

Dolores' left hand was on the table. Laura wanted to hold it, or to put her hand on Dolores' hand, but she didn't know if that would have been okay. So she put her hand right next to Dolores' hand, which caused Dolores to smile through damp eyes and reach out and grasp Laura's hand and squeeze twice.

"Do you want more coffee?" Dolores asked.

"Sure."

Dolores stood up and brought the pot over to the table, only filling Laura's cup halfway, knowing her propensity for adding lots of milk and sugar. She replaced the pot in the coffee maker and sat back down. She was tired, and Laura could see it.

Laura stirred the sugar into her coffee. Her mind was so full of thoughts none of them could gain precedence over one another. But she felt the need to speak. She wanted to express how she was there for Dolores, how she wanted to help her. She wanted to offer Dolores her home if she needed it. She wanted Dolores to know she would fight for her. She wanted to say how angry she was, how much she hated Mr. Buckingham and how she hoped that they would get divorced and he would disappear forever. She wanted to thank Dolores for being her second mother, in many ways, her best mother, for teaching her to cook, for introducing her to so much music that helped fill her life with meaning. Instead she said:

"I think I'm in love with Trey."

A huge grin washed over Dolores' face. Suddenly she wasn't tired.

10

Timing

Laura couldn't believe what had come out of her mouth. Consciously, of course, she immediately regretted telling Trey's mom that she was in love with him, but oddly beyond that conscious fear, she felt good. She felt almost as if something inside of her that had been dirty was finally clean.

Dolores put her hands together in front of her lips again. This was no futile attempt to hide an expression, it was just a reflex. Other than her hands to her lips, neither of the women moved. They froze with eyes locked, one pair in terror, the other in unabashed joy.

Dolores broke first. After giving Laura about twenty seconds to take back what she had said, Dolores moved her hands down from her lips.

"Does Trey know that?"

Laura shook her head.

"Mija," she said admonishingly. "Why not?"

Laura shrugged. Dolores' smile widened, melting across all of her features.

"Maybe you should tell him."

"I almost did. I think that's why I was coming over here the other night, when I found him, when I found..." It was all too cluttered and fresh for Laura to explain. "The timing has been really bad."

"Oh my dear, it's never good."

"Well," Laura said with a kind smile. "There's not good, and then there's us. Our timing has been terrible."

At that very moment the front door opened and Trey and Katherine walked into the house.

***

Sometimes, especially with young love, the timing is just dogshit.

From Laura's perspective, Katherine seemed to have suddenly arrived on the scene. It was as if she came out of the ether only to get in the way of the inevitable romance that should have been Laura and Trey's destiny. But that's not the case at all.

To understand Katherine and Trey we must first go back in time, to the previous school year when Katherine was truly in love with her former boyfriend, Chuckie Burbage. Chuckie was the first person outside of her family that had ever told her that they loved her, her first real boyfriend, the first person she was ever "with" in every sense, and someone she had dated for eighteen months, which in high school years is a very, very long time. There was even discussion about marriage when she had a pregnancy scare just before Valentine's Day. She was so sure he was "the one" and they would be together forever that she couldn't envision her future without him in it. And then over the summer he callously, cruelly, and unceremoniously, dumped her less than an hour after they had sex. It was the night before he left for college. She was shattered.

Chuckie did come to regret his decision. After "having some fun" with other freshmen in college he realized his massive mistake, and a few weeks into September came home to try to win her back. Katherine told him to get lost.

Even as a teen Katherine was a pretty tough cookie. She had self-respect, and had no time for those that didn't recognize that about her. The oldest sibling in her family, with 4 younger brothers, she had a drive that most young people didn't seem to have. She had no problem sacrificing the present pleasure to ensure future success. But there was another reason why she rejected Chuckie with his guilt gifts of flowers, chocolates, and a diamond chip bracelet. She had come to really like Trey Buckingham. She didn't love him or anything, but she certainly fancied him. She found him worth her time.

She hadn't noticed Trey until the lacrosse season in Trey's sophomore year when Katherine was a junior and Chuckie was teammates with Trey. Chuckie, who was not one to dole out compliments, mentioned how impressed he was with Trey's toughness. Katherine correctly recognized toughness was not physical quality, but a mental one. And it was perhaps the quality she most admired in others.

Katherine's parents were wealthy, but she didn't have everything handed to her. Sure when she turned sixteen she got a 1967 Ford Mustang convertible as a gift from her parents, but that same month they made her pay stable fees for her horse. Because of that, she kept a job waiting tables at Waterman's Seafood House in the summer, coincidentally working with Trey.

This is how the two of them got to know each other. As one does working in restaurants, they chatted in the downtime, and flirted when it got busy. Katherine was impressed that Trey chose to make his own way and not work at one of his father's businesses. Like everyone else, she didn't know why, but it seemed like an honorable decision from the outside. And she liked Trey's easy sense of humor. He could talk to girls without being nervous and trying to show off, and she was attracted to that confidence. Of course, we know he had Laura to thank for being comfortable around girls, having a girl for a best friend makes flirting natural.

When Chuckie broke up with Katherine she didn't tell anyone other than her parents. They were as disappointed as Katherine was heartbroken, and when she was home they treated her as if she was delicate and about to break at any minute. She hated being treated as if she was sick. So she picked up as many shifts as she could at the restaurant, and when she wasn't working she was riding or taking care of her horse, a gorgeous gray Andalusian named Dulcinea.

At the "end of the summer party" for Waterman's Katherine noticed Trey wasn't there, and wished that he was. Not long afterwards he showed up, making eye contact with her as soon as he walked through the door. He smiled and nodded, and then helped one of the cooks tap a keg.

A few minutes later, they found themselves in the corner of the room.

"You alright?" he asked.

"Yeah," she lied.

Trey swallowed a little laugh. Trey was not what you would call book-smart, but he was pretty good at reading people. He knew she was lying. But he didn't press.

"So," he said before taking a sip from his red cup. "Looking forward to school starting?"

Katherine shook her head a little.

"Really?" he was genuinely surprised. "I thought you were like... smart. I figured you were one of those people that liked being graded."

Katherine closed her eyes.

"Chuckie broke up with me."

She opened her eyes and looked at him. He was looking around the room, and she wondered for a moment if he even heard her. Then he sighed and shook his head.

"Well," he said, still looking around the room. "Chuckie is a fucking idiot."

Katherine smiled. They chatted a little more, and he asked her about Dulcinea. But nothing changed between the two of them. He went on treating her exactly the same way he had, with flirty kindness. When school started back up, Katherine noticed that no one at school had found out that she and Chuckie had broken up, which meant he clearly hadn't told anyone. She was concerned he would be as flirty at school as he was in the restaurant. But when she saw Trey, she waved, and he waved back and smiled. But he didn't come over to joke around. He didn't try to sit with her at lunch. He expected nothing.

So naturally Katherine started to flirt with him. As school is very different from a restaurant, flirting is not something one does lightly. But she was sly about it. Katherine remembered a day that summer when she was reading a magazine and he looked over her shoulder and pointed out the model, saying she was cute. The model was Niki Taylor, who did not look entirely dissimilar to Katherine herself. So, Katherine started to cut pictures of Niki Taylor out of magazines and put them in Trey's locker. At first, Trey was confused, then he was embarrassed. Once he finally caught Katherine doing it, he embraced it. But he didn't push. He never overstepped. He didn't get greedy. He didn't put pictures of Patrick Swayze in her locker or anything, but he did do one thing that she found so endearing. He asked her to stop.

Not in a *leave-me-alone-you-are-bugging-me* kinda way, but in one of the best ways possible. It was at lunch, and he saw her walking towards his locker with a glossy magazine photo, and he intercepted her.

"You know," he said with a smile. "My locker is filling up. It's starting to look a little serial killer-y."

"You said you thought she was pretty," Katherine teased.

"She is pretty. But it's not like she's as pretty as you."

Well done Trey, well done.

So yes, Katherine fancied Trey. She wasn't in love, but she liked him, in every sense of the word, even in the "like, like" sense of the word(s).

So she asked him to Homecoming, and he said yes. It wasn't a big deal. She needed someone to go to the dance with, and Trey was friendly and handsome. If nothing else, it would be a good photo for the yearbook. Then, suddenly and unexpectedly something happened with his father and the police. Trey was arrested. The school was buzzing with rumors. Everyone already liked Trey, but now he was mysterious, and maybe, dangerous. When he returned in dramatic fashion to win the game for the school Katherine was swept up in the romance of it all. Just like in all the movies these kids saw growing up, the hero got a kiss from the prettiest girl in school.

All of a sudden, life was no longer mundane. Katherine felt like she was living in a movie.

Trey hadn't told Katherine he loved Laura. He did tell Katherine that Laura was his best friend. Was Katherine jealous of Laura, when she watched the two of them out of the corner of her eye walking to his car parked a million miles from school? Yes, she was. Did she want him more because there was another girl in his life? Of course. That's how all this works.

After the dramatic kiss, Trey was mobbed by his teammates. They were separated. Katherine and Trey locked eyes, but they couldn't talk over the chaos. Trey was still very sweaty, dirty, and a little bloody. He yelled for Katherine to wait for him. He ran back to the locker room, showered and got dressed back into his school clothes. Katherine was leaning on his car, waiting. They drove separately to Boomers, a burger joint in Berlin just off of route 113, got cheeseburgers, fries, and chocolate shakes to go. He followed her to her home, which was not far from Boomers, where she dropped off her car, got into his, and they went to the stables so she could show him Dulcinea.

At the stables, they ate on the hood of his car. They talked about the game. She teased him about having floor donuts. The last of the sun was being swallowed by thin clouds in the western sky, and they both silently watched it sink.

"Do you..." she began, but paused. She wanted to ask about the police and his father but she didn't know how.

"Do I what?"

"No, it's okay."

"What?" Trey pressed. He could see there was something she really wanted to ask, but he had no idea what it was. He was still high on the win, and the kiss.

"If you want to talk about your dad..." Katherine stopped when she saw Trey's face change. She immediately regretted bringing it up.

Trey shook his head, unable to answer. He suddenly felt like he couldn't breathe. He slid off the hood of the car and took a few steps away, towards the pasture where Dulcinea had discovered some wildflowers.

"I'm sorry," she said, walking after him and reaching out for his arm.

He tried to turn away but there was nowhere to turn. He blinked twice and tears fell. He couldn't stop them.

"I'm an idiot. I'm so sorry," she said, sliding her hand over his cheek and catching a tear with her thumb.

He tried to put his head down. Trey was exhausted. She gently lifted his chin with her hand, leaned in, and kissed his cheek. She could taste the salt of his tears. She kissed his other cheek. He closed his eyes. She kissed his eyelid.

He breathed deeply and slowly. She kissed his lips. It was a lingering, gentle, salty kiss.

She whispered, "I'm sorry," one more time.

He smiled and shook his head. She kissed him again, hard this time, and grabbed his ass and squeezed. He opened his eyes and she was grinning.

They heard a truck coming down the long driveway, the owner of the stables was coming to lock up for the night. So they left and drove into Ocean Pines, both chewing cinnamon gum while talking about Homecoming, and if they should go to dinner beforehand with another couple or two. Trey thought of Laura, but didn't say her name.

They went to the boat ramp. It was quiet and empty. He parked and she asked if they could go for a walk. They walked along an old logging road into the woods, and they kissed again, he slid his hand up to her left breast. She kissed his jaw, and then his neck, and then she bit him a little and giggled when he winced.

For a second, both of them thought they were going to take things further, but both of them seemed to pull back at the same time. Just a nervous misunderstanding.

As they walked back to the car, Katherine asked Trey about his mother. He talked about her lovingly. Katherine asked if she could meet her. So instead of driving her back to her mansion, he took her to his humble home.

His first pang of guilt hit when his headlights turned to face the cul-de-sac and he saw Laura's car parked in the usual spot along the drainage ditch across the street. Since he didn't want to blindside Katherine, he told her that Laura was there, and that she was often there, as Laura and Dolores were very close.

Katherine thought about what that meant. For a high school boy, having a girl as a good friend, who was "just a friend," was rare enough. But when that girl was so close that she hung out with your mom when you weren't even there… that was strange.

By the time the front door opened, Katherine was intimidated.

So here they all were, looking at each other, everyone wondering what was going through the minds of someone else.

Katherine was nervous. Trey was guilty. Laura felt betrayed. Dolores was overjoyed. Not only was this love drama on display in her home and before her very eyes, but it was the perfect distraction for her and her son from her horrible husband and their legal and financial troubles.

Laura bailed as soon as she reasonably could, about two minutes after Katherine and Trey showed up. She hugged Dolores goodbye, high-fived Trey and said "good game" and just waved to Katherine. She had rarely felt so awkward in her entire life.

Katherine stayed at the Buckingham house for about an hour, and had a lovely conversation with Dolores, mostly about Spain. Katherine had long been fascinated with Spanish culture, as her horse was an Andalusian, which meant the breed was originally from the Andalusia region of Spain. Katherine was only ten years old when she got Dulcinea, and her young mind was convinced that since Andalusians were originally from Spain, she would need to speak Spanish in order for her horse to understand. So she learned Spanish in order to communicate to the creature that was dearest to her heart.

When she learned that Dolores was from Spain, she grew two degrees fonder of Trey. Dolores, for her part, was impressed that Katherine tried speaking in Spanish as much as possible. Between the two languages they had a nice conversation, but as much as Dolores found Katherine to be pleasant, she didn't warm to her. Perhaps it was because Katherine refused the garlic soup. In Katherine's defense, she was full after the large dinner, and she didn't want to eat a bowl of garlic before kissing her new boyfriend. But the refusal didn't help with Dolores.

While Katherine and Dolores spoke, Trey took the opportunity to change. He put on jeans and a black t-shirt. While he was changing he thought about calling Laura, just to make sure she was okay, but something inside of him told him that that would be wrong, so he didn't.

After the hour long visit, Trey drove Katherine home. They made out in her driveway. She was a good kisser; gentle and considerate, but passionate. He needed some work. It was a few minutes before 11 PM when he watched her walk inside, giving him a last demure wave before turning off the outdoor light.

Instead of going home, Trey drove directly to Laura's house, and knocked on the door.

11

Law and Order

Joyce was not crazy about a teenage boy knocking on her door on a school night after her daughter's curfew. She would normally have told him to go home and see her at school tomorrow, but as she was well aware of everything that was going on, she made an exception. She was concerned for Trey, and good mothers do not make it a habit of turning away children that they are concerned about. So she let Trey in, went upstairs and interrupted Laura's phone call with Candace to tell her that Trey was waiting in the living room, and then got her book and went into her bedroom to read.

Laura was wearing boxers and the same comfy Cubs sweatshirt. She stood at the entrance to the living room, watching Trey, unsure of what to do. Trey was pacing back and forth. Laura felt cold, as if he had let in too much of the autumn air. She entered the room and gave him a wide berth, plopped herself cross-legged on the couch, and pulled a crochet blanket over her lap.

"It's a little late, isn't it?" she teased. They both knew she wanted to see him as much as he wanted to see her.

"Can we talk?" he asked earnestly. "Like really talk?"

"Always."

"Okay," he began, not sure of where to start. He was still standing and moving, almost pacing around the room. "Okay. Alright. Shit. I'm not even sure where to start."

"Do you want to talk about Katherine?"

"Not really."

"Do you want to talk about your dad?"

"Not really."

"Do you want to talk about why the police took you from school today?"

He sighed and slowly nodded.

"Yeah, that's fair."

Laura waited patiently for Trey to collect his thoughts. He stopped pacing and looked at her for a moment, though his eyes couldn't stay still. He looked at the window as if to find his thoughts there. It was so dark outside he could only see the reflection of the living room.

"Okay, after, you know, the other night, they just took my statement. They had to come pick me up I guess, because my dad was hurt, and they wanted to be sure they got both sides of the story. But mom told them everything, how he's been terrorizing us, how he was attacking her at the time, and how what I did probably saved her life. At least, that was her words."

Trey started pacing a little again, not quickly though. Like his thoughts, his feet couldn't stay still. His hands were gesturing more than usual.

"Originally I wasn't going to be charged with hitting my father because they said it was self-defense, and honestly, from the beginning my dad had said he wasn't pressing charges. But then, when my mom was questioned about the drugs... I swear she doesn't know much about what my dad does, but she's had her suspicions for a while. And I guess she gave them enough for them to confirm what they had been waiting for, and they got... um, like a warrant for the bar. Because of the raid, my dad got a lawyer from like Baltimore, and everything changed. The lawyer said the cops should have arrested me and charged me with assault, and he was trying to make my dad out like the victim. Which is... fucking lawyers."

Trey took a deep breath and continued.

"That's why they came to pick me up today, to get another statement for the police. Like the Ocean Pines Police never even went inside the house, the night... you know. My mom let the detectives in today, she fed them and everything, of course she did, right? But they didn't find anything at home."

Laura wondered for a moment if Dolores had given the police the same garlic soup. She didn't think she would do that. Healing soup was for family.

"I don't think they ever really have any intention of arresting or charging me or anything. But then I had to give another statement to a judge for the restraining order."

"Wait," Laura interrupted. "He isn't going to stay in jail?"

"He's not even really in jail now, he's just in custody. He's actually still in the hospital. He had to get surgery on his jaw, so I guess he's just like handcuffed to a hospital bed at this point. I think he gets out in a couple days. He's already posted bail."

"And then what? He just comes back home? He can't be near you and Dolores."

"I don't know exactly. He is allowed to come back to the house to get things, but I think he needs to inform us and I think he's supposed to be supervised or something. I am kinda confused by the whole thing, and I really just wanted to go as fast as possible today to get to the game, you know?"

"But isn't that an important thing to know?"

Trey shrugged.

"I think they explained it but I wasn't really paying attention."

Laura laughed, sighed, and shook her head all at the same time.

"What?" Trey grinned, relaxing a little.

"I'm very familiar with you not paying attention to things," Laura said coyly.

Trey nodded in agreement at first, but then thought about what she had just said and was confused.

"I don't, wait..." He paused. "Laura, I swear to God I have so many things in my head right now... I really don't know what you mean. Do you mean, like, us?"

"No," Laura flushed, a little embarrassed. "What are you talking about? There is no us, right?"

Trey sighed heavily. He sat down on the couch, but as far from Laura as he could. He had his back to the armrest, so he was facing her. She turned her head to look at him, but not her body, so she could easily look away.

"What do you mean?" he said seriously, his voice dropping in timbre. "When you say, there is no us, it hurts me."

She looked at him, confused.

"Hurts you?"

"Okay," he looked at the black window again and saw his distorted reflection. He looked like a monster. "Not hurt I guess. Maybe I mean scared. Maybe it's just that I don't know the difference between the two."

"I don't want to hurt or scare you."

"I know," he started not sure of where he was going with what he was saying. "It's just that, I don't know, like in these last couple of days, it's like... Am I living a nightmare? Or a dream? Or both? Maybe that's all dreaming is. Unreal. And... I guess, I'm really worried that when I finally wake up, things will be different. And there are some things I don't want to be different."

"Like what?" Laura asked, dropping any hint of teasing from her voice.

"Like the other night, under the window. You know, after I hit him, I wasn't scared. I was angry. I was angry he made me do that. But I wasn't just angry at him, I was just angry. And then when you came into the house... I don't know... I didn't want you to see me angry. So I hid. I guess that's what you do when you are scared, but I didn't want you to have to... to see... to know that part of me... It's like..."

He let out a big sigh again, and Laura felt that Trey might be on the verge of crying. He wasn't, but he had so much energy swelling inside of him that he was shaking.

"It's like... something inside of me snapped... when I hit my dad... and it felt like, maybe that was it... like I was broken for good. I couldn't calm down, I couldn't think, I felt like I couldn't even breathe. And then... under the window, just listening to the rain, and I could feel your breath on my neck, and it was just like... I don't know, it was like you taught me how to breathe again."

He took a moment to breathe consciously.

"It's like... whatever was broken, you picked up and held together for me. And I guess I can figure out how it all fits back together... but I wouldn't have even known where to look if it wasn't for you. I don't know, this all sounds crazy, but... I don't know why, but somehow I think that was the best night of my life."

Laura nodded in silence. And then she smiled.

"You mean, up until that point."

Trey shrugged.

"Okay, like, so far."

"Including tonight?" Laura asked, honestly surprised.

"Yeah, I mean... don't get me wrong, today was pretty cool. Anytime you beat Cape is a good day."

"Come on."

"What?"

Laura took a second to gather her thoughts. She was besotted. He was everything, fragile and strong, broken and powerful. And beautiful. She lusted for him, loved him, and wanted to help him. She knew she could jump on him and kiss him right now, and he would kiss her back. She could tear off his clothes and have sex with him right now, and she wouldn't regret a moment of it. Though she did wonder if he had already done that once tonight. And more importantly she knew, at this moment he needed a friend more than a lover.

"I..." Laura started to say that she loved Trey, but changed her mind as soon as the "I" came out of her mouth. "I want... to be sure that you and I are good. You know. That we're always going to be friends. So go ahead. Talk about Katherine."

Trey said nothing for a moment.

"What about her?" he finally asked.

"Come on," Laura was surprised to find that she enjoyed this little game. "You guys kissed before, there's no way that was a first kiss."

"I swear, we had never kissed before," Trey's leg was shaking a little.

"What?" Laura's eyes widened. "That was a pretty epic first kiss. Jesus. It's going to be hard to top that."

Laura softly laughed a little.

"I know you don't know her," Trey said, searching Laura's face. "But she's a good person. I think you would really like her if you got to know her."

"I'm sure I will."

Neither of them said anything for at least thirty seconds. Both of their teenaged brains were racing, a chaotic morass of fear, sex, and humor. Finally Laura won by speaking first.

"Did you touch her boobs?"

Had Trey been drinking something at that moment he would have spit it out. He laughed and shook his head while sighing.

"I mean..." he paused. "Seriously?"

"Come on," Laura prodded with a huge, honest grin. "She has a great rack, you're telling me you don't want to touch them? She's hot, I don't blame you at all."

Trey was positive he was about to walk into some sort of trap. But he couldn't stop himself from going forward. He smiled sheepishly.

"Eh... just like, a little bit."

Laura suddenly felt hot on her cheeks, and was worried she was blushing. But she continued.

"Like under the bra or over?"

Trey's eyes got big. Blood started to rush to his penis and he started to sweat.

"Oh my god."

"Look, buddy," Laura said, still with her teasing voice. "We should be able to talk about this right? Come on, we're friends."

The way she said *friends* almost had a hit of contempt for the word in the voice. Almost. It just didn't sound entirely right when she said it.

Trey looked down, scared to meet Laura's eyes. He was trying to will his penis to not become erect, but largely failing at his task.

"We should probably talk about something else," he said to the floor.

Laura felt bad. She didn't realize she had excited Trey, and thought his attempt to change the subject was more due to emotional reasons than physical ones. So, she did the absolute worst thing she could have done, she slid next to him and put her hand on his shoulder.

"Hey, I'm sorry, I shouldn't have been teasing you," Laura said to the side of Trey's face. With her other hand she reached up and gently touched his chin.

"Hey, look at me, I'm serious."

Trey looked at her. His heart, and everything about him, was swollen with love. Laura spoke slowly and sweetly.

"You are my best friend."

Trey wanted to kiss Laura so bad, but he could still taste Katherine's kiss on his lips. He wanted to hug her, but he was afraid she would feel his erect penis. So he did the only thing he could.

"I love you," he said as sincerely as he had ever said anything in his entire life.

Laura felt as if she had just been kissed. And she would have kissed him like no one had ever been kissed before, had any circumstances been different. But they weren't. She couldn't change the fact that, only a few hours prior, he had a very public and very emotional kiss with the prettiest girl in school. Plus, apparently, he touched her boobs some. Katherine could have his lips, Laura had his heart. She smiled at the thought, and let his three small words wash over her and remind her that she is beautiful, and she is seen. Her eyes burrowed deep inside his, and she very slowly leaned in close to him, her hand still on one shoulder, and the other on his chin, and she whispered her response.

"Good."

Laura slid her left hand behind the small of Trey's back, and leaned her head on his shoulder. Her right hand slid slowly down his neck, down his chest to his ribs, hugging him with her head on his shoulder. His right arm was trapped, and he felt uncomfortable, but Laura sensed it, leaned back, took his arm and wrapped it around her and then went back to holding him. And there they stayed, in a silent and perfect embrace.

About fifteen minutes into their hug, Joyce appeared at the living room door, relieved to find them both dressed, and told Trey it was probably time for him to go home.

He left. Laura called Candace back and they talked until they fell asleep together on the phone around two am.

Trey went home, went right to bed, fell asleep immediately, and dreamt of Laura and Katherine and lots of sex.

12

The Three Dates

There were ten days between the legendary on-field kiss and Homecoming. For Katherine and Trey, Homecoming would technically be their fourth date, not counting the cheeseburgers at the barn. Their first actual date was at The Sun and Surf theater the Friday after the kiss. They got ice cream after the movie. They made out a little in the car while parked in her driveway.

They didn't talk during the movie, and the conversation over ice cream was casual. It was an easy date, almost too easy. To Katherine, it seemed they were already more comfortable together than she had ever been with Chuckie. Since Katherine and Trey were friends first, and since they had flirted for so long before ever kissing, she felt like they had been together much longer than they technically had.

Physical things were still exciting. Holding hands in the theater was electric. He kissed her ear when she was saying "good night" and a shiver went through her body. She still hadn't danced with him yet, and she hadn't seen him naked... well, she hadn't seen him without pants on. Everyone had seen Trey without a shirt on. While physically, things were new, mentally Katherine jumped almost directly from the kiss to *he's my boyfriend now*. There was no in-between.

Which is why their second date was Sunday dinner at the Bounds' household. Sunday dinner was more important than church to the Bounds family, as they never skipped it. Every Sunday at three PM the family and occasional guests would gather to feast on some type of roast meat, potatoes, vegetables, and a fancy dessert. It was a big deal for anyone in Worcester County to be invited to share their table, much less a boy that had been on one date with their daughter.

Dinner was a challenge for Trey. He tried to keep up with the conversation but he felt like it was a tennis game played with seven players and three balls. Mostly he stayed quiet, smiled when people laughed, nodded at everything, and only spoke in response to a direct question.

Eventually he figured out how it worked. Katherine's mother didn't actually participate in the conversation, but she tossed out the topics, and then Katherine and her father would debate, while Katherine's four little brothers would chime in with their two cents which went largely ignored.

For instance while cutting her youngest son's roast beef she said, "Rose Tingle just got back from touring East Berlin. You know she taught English there in the '60s. She said it's a very stark difference between East and West."

"Reunification is going to cripple their economy," her husband said, picking up the thread. "I don't know how any country can withstand that kind of financial strain. It'd be like us opening up the Mexico border and saying, Come on in!"

"But Dad," Katherine protested. "They're Germans. How can they turn their back on their own people?"

"Are they?" he responded with a slight eyebrow raise. "Or are they communists?"

"Just because someone is a communist doesn't mean they aren't still German."

"Well," he took a small sip of wine to give his words more gravitas. "I think that's exactly what it means. Communists, after all, talk about internationalism. I don't think we can ever trust in the national loyalty of a communist, do you?"

"I've never met a communist, so I can't say. But I know they didn't look very communist when they danced to rock music on the Wall as it came crumbling down!"

"We'll see," her father smiled. "But mark my words, Germany will be one of the poorest nations in Europe before the end of the decade."

"Germans made the best tanks," James, the second son said, probably referring to World War II.

"No they didn't, they made the best subs," Andrew, the oldest son corrected him.

"I like subs," said Stephen, who was the youngest.

"Andrew," Katherine's mother said, looking at her oldest boy. "You have sour cream on your cheek. Trey, what do you think?"

Suddenly everyone stopped talking and eating and looked right at Trey.

"Um... well... If we're talking about Berlin and who has the best subs, I think Your Store is better than Boomers," he said with a slight smile.

Everyone laughed and Katherine's mom lobbed a new topic to the table. Trey exhaled and took a bite of beef. Honestly, the family had been halfway through the conversation before he even realized they were talking about Germany and not Berlin, Maryland.

After dinner all the kids did the dishes together. Then Trey went outside with Katherine's brothers and played basketball until it got dark. Katherine's mom stood next to her daughter in the parlor, looking out the window at the boys playing and smiled. She nudged Katherine with her elbow, and then walked away. Katherine knew she approved.

Katherine's father, on the other hand, wasn't as easily won over. He knew Trey's father, but he didn't like him. Trey's dad didn't hunt or fish. He didn't serve on any boards, and he wasn't in the Rotary, Optimists, or Lion's club. He wasn't involved with politics or known to give to charity.

To him, Trey was just some dumb teenage boy who came from a lousy family. Her father had endured Chuckie because he had come from a great local family. Chuckie's and Katherine's fathers served on three different boards together and they were in most of the same clubs. Trey didn't have the same leeway Chuckie had.

But at dinner he saw the relaxed smile in his daughter's eyes. He caught her looking at this new boy in a way he had never seen her look at the old one. So before the evening ended he was on the phone with his good friend, the States

Attorney for Worcester County, to find out everything there was to know about the Buckingham household.

It was late when Katherine walked Trey to the car to say goodnight. He tried to shake her hand goodnight as he was convinced someone in the house was watching them. She laughed and gave him a lingering kiss on the lips.

Their third date started off as a bit of a disaster. It was Thursday of Homecoming week, two days before the dance, and Katherine suggested that they go for a drive together and just talk.

It was a cold, rainy evening, and Trey was still dressed in his soccer shorts from practice. He convinced Katherine to ride with him to his house so he could change. Trey suggested that he drive his car, which was his first mistake.

Trey's car didn't have the most reliable fuel gauge, so he usually just added gas when he felt it was the right time, but with all the events of the previous week or so, he lost track. They were on route 90 about a mile from the off ramp when they ran out of gas. Trey got out and pushed in the rain, Katherine steered, and thirty minutes later they made it to the 7-Eleven. Trey was shaking with both hunger and cold and his clothes were soaked through.

After putting seven dollars of gas in his car they drove to his house so he could shower and change. Dolores wasn't home, but Trey expected her anytime so, after raiding the fridge, they left and drove to the boat ramp behind White Horse Park.

At this point it was dark and the rain had really started to come down. They couldn't even see the marsh which was no more than twenty feet in front of them. Trey turned off the headlights but had the car running so they could listen to the Grateful Dead *American Beauty* album for the eighteenth time.

"Please turn your car off," Katherine begged.

Trey thought she didn't want to hear the music. He didn't realize she was calculating his mileage versus seven dollars of gas and the distance to her home.

"So, you wanted to talk?" he said, expecting a serious heart to heart.

Katherine slid over to Trey and kissed him. She put both hands on his face and climbed into his lap, her knees digging into the bench seat. He was so shocked by the suddenness that he forgot to breathe. She flicked her tongue against his lips and swirled her hips, pushing into his stomach. He pulled back in order to take a breath. She watched him, reading his thoughts as he realized they weren't going to "talk." She smiled. She knew he was innocent.

She pulled off her sweater and was reaching behind her to unclasp her bra when he slid his hand along her back and kissed her. His hand was freezing and she twitched. His elbow bumped the steering wheel and the horn honked, scaring them and causing them to giggle.

Katherine took the opportunity that the laughter provided to remove her bra. He dove right in. He was far too eager and violent for her taste, so she put her hand on his chest and pushed him back against his seat.

"There's no rush," she whispered.

She pulled off his t-shirt and he nodded. She slid her hand down his chest to his stomach and slid a finger under his belt buckle. His heart was racing. She kissed him again, and very slowly unbuckled his belt and unzipped his jeans.

"Seriously?" she said, looking down at him.

"What?" Trey's eyes went wide with fear.

"You're going commando?"

He smiled, and shrugged. She slid her hand into his pants. He wiggled and jerked to take them off as quickly as possible, in the process hitting her left breast with his forearm. She put her hand on his chest again.

"Relax," she said, louder than she had spoken before. "There's no rush. I'm not going to disappear, and I'm not going to change my mind."

She kissed him again, on the lips, on the chest, and lower. When it was his turn to return the favor he gave it his best shot. While he lacked experience, he certainly had exuberance.

13

Homecoming

At first Laura planned to go solo to the Homecoming dance, then agreed to tag along as a third wheel with Candace and her new boyfriend Tyrone. But at the last minute Jessica convinced Laura to let her come down from NYC and go as her "date" in order to--as she put it--shake things up in Berlin, Maryland. Jessica had it in her head that they were making a big statement by two girls going together to Homecoming.

In truth, two girls going to a dance together as a date would have been a big deal if it wasn't for the three important facts. The first being everyone at school knew and liked Jessica. The second being Jessica hadn't come out as a lesbian to anyone other than her parents and Laura. And the third "fact," was actually more of a rumor.

Three days before homecoming, Mrs. Warhol, the French teacher, mentioned in the teacher's lounge that she heard Trey and Laura were secretly dating. Since all the teachers adored Katherine and had a rather neutral opinion of Laura, this spread around the school pretty quick.

It should be noted that Katherine took Spanish, as did Trey and Laura, but Candace took French.

It had been seven days since Trey and Katherine shared that epic kiss, so pretty much everyone at school knew they were dating. And everyone in all of Worcester

County knew about Trey's father. The Cape game, the police, the kiss—it was a pretty big story for a week. But just as it died down the rumor about Laura and Trey took hold.

While it's true that in some ways Trey and Laura were closer than they had ever been, not much had actually changed about how they acted around one another. Yet suddenly people noticed that these two "supposedly" platonic friends always sat together, shared food, whispered secrets, and made each other laugh. Even if there were doubts that anyone would cheat on someone like Katherine with someone like Laura, the mere implication of the Trey/Laura secret relationship meant that no one thought Laura was a lesbian. Which meant no one, at least at the time, thought Laura and Jessica were going to Homecoming as anything more than just friends.

Jessica's father got a limo for Jessica and her friends. Joyce dropped Laura off at Jessica's house, and Jessica presented Laura with a wrist corsage, which Laura found funny, until Jessica called her a bitch.

As the limo pulled up Jessica grabbed a bottle of Peach Schnapps from her parents' liquor cabinet, and a pack of her mother's cigarettes. Jessica's mom saw her do this, and stopped the girls in the foyer.

"Listen," she said in her most motherly tone. "I know you girls are going to smoke, but don't smoke the cigarettes past half way. Otherwise they are really bad for you. Also, be sure to drink plenty of soda or something at dinner, you don't want to get dehydrated."

She gestured to the Schnapps.

"Be sure the limo has ice, because that's not chilled and you don't want to drink that warm, it's not good for your stomach," she said before hugging both Laura and Jessica. "Have such a good time girls, and don't do anything I wouldn't do!"

"Honestly," Jessica said as they climbed into the limo which was thankfully stocked with plenty of ice. "What do you think she wouldn't do?"

Laura smiled. "Best not think about it."

"Yeah," Jessica said looking through the tinted window at her waving mother. "I think I should get a therapist."

Both girls giggled, even if Jessica wasn't entirely joking.

They picked up Candace and Tyrone, before taking the limo to the Phillips Crab House on 21st street in Ocean City. The massive two story brick building always felt like a castle—in contrast to the old, wooden, single-story restaurants that were typical at the beach. Tyrone worked as a busboy there, and it was a popular pre-dance choice. Tyrone, to the protestation of Jessica, even paid for all three girls, which created his reputation at work for being a "ladies man."

The foursome got to the high school gym about a half hour after the dance had begun. There was a good crowd already, with a few dozen dancers and pockets of punch drinking gawkers on the sidelines. Culture Club's *Karma Chameleon* was playing and all four of them immediately ran onto the dance floor.

Once Laura got on the dance floor, she didn't leave. Fueled by crabcakes, cola, peach schnapps, big drums, kicking bass, synthesizers, and the raw uncomplicated abandon of dance, Laura let the outside world fade into the shadows beyond the gymnasium. Jessica, Candace, and Tyrone were never far from her side, and one by one, seniors came up to greet Jessica, and generally stayed nearby to dance, so Laura felt like there was always so much positive energy crowding around her.

Jessica was the perfect date: focused on Laura, happy, a little drunk, and totally lost in the music. She even slow-danced with Laura, so nothing ever broke their dance floor flow. Indeed, unbeknownst to Laura, Jessica was going through some complicated emotions. After all, here she was, back in the world she had left behind, the same gym, the same music, many of the same people living the same exact lives. There was an ease to life that Jessica had not felt in a while, and that both relaxed and bothered her.

During Alphaville's *Forever Young* Jessica put her head on Laura's shoulder and actually teared up a little. Of course, in the light of day, Jessica knew she wanted her life in the city. But that night, in the dark of a small-town gym, surrounded by so much positivity, for a fleeting moment, she missed being in high school.

Laura didn't even realize that she hadn't yet seen Trey, until he walked into the gym with Katherine when there was under an hour remaining. A-ha's *Take on Me* was playing and during the musical interlude in-between the sing-along parts,

Laura happened to look towards the door right as Katherine and Trey stepped through. They were holding hands. Trey was wearing jeans and a white t-shirt with a leather jacket, which Laura was sure he didn't own. Katherine was wearing acid wash jeans, mid-calf leather slouch boots, and a burgundy boat neck sweater. She looked a little dressier than him, but neither of them looked like they were dressed for Homecoming. Everyone else at the dance was in dresses or coats and ties.

As soon as they entered the gym, a few senior girls and most of the boys' soccer team started to migrate over to them with questions and concerns, the result being that they were surrounded by people who didn't want to dance. Laura tried to wave from the dance floor, but she was pretty sure Trey didn't see her. She went back to dancing with her crew.

It wasn't long before Candace leaned into Laura and whispered very loudly: "They're here. Do you see what they are wearing?"

Laura, in one of her cooler moments in her life, smiled and didn't even look in Trey's direction and kept dancing.

***

Katherine had started the day of the Homecoming dance in Hartford County competing in a horse show. She came in second. She was frustrated that she didn't win, but only mildly annoyed because the show meant she was missing Trey's soccer game. By this point she already knew she was the Homecoming Queen, and was excited for her date with Trey. She had decided that tonight was going to be the night that she and Trey would have sex. She bought six condoms, just in case.

On their third date they finally saw each other naked and traded turns at oral sex. There's no good word that sounds less clinical than oral sex or cunnilingus, but Jessica's mom used to refer to any act of oral sex as a "tropical kiss," which--unfortunately for Jessica--was a phrase her mom used often.

Trey, for what it is worth, was not a natural at the tropical kiss, so Katherine had low expectations for their first time making love. She was correct in assuming he was a virgin. But he also looked really good without his clothes on.

Trey was clueless to Katherine's intentions. His whirlwind October meant he was struggling to keep up, and he had no expectations. Though he was hopeful to get another blowjob soon. Sorry, tropical kiss. Beyond that, he had no plans.

When Trey arrived to pick up Katherine for homecoming he was wearing a new, off the rack suit that his mom had helped him pick out the Saturday before from one of the anchor stores at the Centre of Salisbury. Dolores had great taste and was skilled with the sewing machine, so she hemmed the pants, and even took the jacket in a little to give it an almost fitted look. He looked as good as you could in an off the rack suit from Salisbury, Maryland. Katherine was wearing a tight white suede dress with a little matching suede jacket that likely cost more than Trey's car, which admittingly was a low bar to cross.

They went to Reflections restaurant, perhaps the most expensive, white tablecloth, oceanside restaurant in Ocean City. Trey had made reservations, and they were the only teenagers in the restaurant, something Katherine relished. She was starving from the already long day, and she ordered the surf and turf with a baked potato, and finished the entire thing. Trey had the same. They drank cola, and chatted about their respective competitions. They split a chocolate cake for dessert. Everything was great, right up until Trey asked for the check.

The waitress, assuming she was delivering positive news, leaned in and told them both that their bill had already been taken care of by the man sitting at the end of the bar. Trey looked up, and at the end of the bar saw his father. He was drunk and doing his best to stare daggers at the couple while smiling. It was unsettling. Trey looked back at the waitress.

"I'm sorry," he said, shaking a little with rage. "But I don't want him to pay for me. Can you please bring me the check."

The waitress was confused and superficially apologetic.

"I'm so sorry, it's already been closed out," she said, not imagining this was a big deal.

But it was a big deal. A more mature Trey would likely have just left the restaurant. In fact, had he done nothing, had he walked away, he was going to have sex. But see, he didn't know that.

Instead he chose to walk Katherine out of the restaurant by way of the bar. When he was about ten feet away from his sadistically grinning father he said, "I don't want your dirty fucking money."

His dad grabbed a full carafe of red wine off the bar and flung it at Trey. The carafe bounced harmlessly off him onto the ground, but the wine sprayed Trey, Katherine, and five other diners, ruining Katherine's suede outfit, Trey's suit, and... well, the mood. Absolute chaos ensued, Trey's father was detained and then arrested again. Katherine and Trey, after giving statements to the police, went back to Katherine's house so she could change. While there, Trey put on a pair of jeans he had in his car, and he borrowed a t-shirt and a leather coat from Katherine's father.

Katherine certainly could have put on another dress, but she didn't want to make Trey more uncomfortable than he already was, so she dressed to match his outfit. She asked him if he wanted to go home to change, but he didn't have another suit, and they were barely going to make the dance as it was.

Katherine's parents were obviously concerned. Trey was the definition of contrite, profusely apologizing. He offered to pay for Katherine's dress, which her parents were never going to allow. It was unlikely that he could afford it anyway. He blamed himself. Katherine's mother, in her kind gracious way, tried to calm him down.

"Oh sweetheart, don't worry about it. It happens," she said as if it was the same as someone spilling a glass of water while reaching for the dinner rolls.

But her father knew that this wasn't something that just happens. This was a problem. And as soon as the kids left for Homecoming, in fact before they were all the way down the driveway, he was again on the phone with the State Attorney, working on a plan to get Trey's father out of the picture.

There would be no bail for Trey's father this time. It turns out, without even realizing it, he had threatened the only daughter of the wrong, very well-connected rich man in a small town in the early nineties. And there were repercussions for that. As unjust as that society was, and it was very unjust, occasionally one can glean the rare positive from it. Stopped clocks being right twice a day and all.

14

After Party

Not long after they arrived Katherine was named Homecoming Queen, Trey was named Junior Prince, and Candace was named Junior Princess. Then, the court each had to dance with their counterpart to Diana Ross and Lionel Richie's *Endless Love*, which meant that Candace and Trey danced together.

Before Candace even put her hands on Trey's shoulder, she gestured to his outfit.

"Alright, spill. There's got to be a story here, right?" she asked with a knowing grin.

Trey sighed. He had already told the entire story to the Ocean City police, most of it to Katherine's parents, and snippets to three of his teammates. He was tired of talking about it. But he knew if he told Candace it would get around school faster than if he took out a radio ad on 93.5 "The Beach." He figured at least he wouldn't have to tell the story again. He gave her a thorough statement that was less embellished than the one he gave the police. It took the entire duet to explain.

After that, the DJ went straight into Bon Jovi's *Livin' on a Prayer* which got the whole student body on the dance floor singing their hearts out. It was the final song of the night, and after it ended the lights came on and the dance started to break up. Katherine and Trey never even had a chance to dance a slow song together. The evening was off the rails, and they both felt it.

As they walked to the parking lot Jessica suggested they go to a spot called "The Point" in Ocean Pines, which was not far from where she used to live. "The Point" that she referred to then is not the neighborhood currently called "The Point" in Ocean Pines, but is actually where townhouses called Marina Village now reside. Long before the townhouses and Pines Point Marina were a twinkle in a developer's eyes, that waterfront could be accessed by entering Yacht Club Drive, turning right immediately onto an old logging dirt road and driving past a no trespassing sign, winding through a woods and a marsh, and emerging by a decrepit bulkhead. It offered a stunning view of Assawoman Bay and the distant twinkling lights of Ocean City. The few teenagers in Ocean Pines all knew about "The Point" and there were cigarette butts, beer cans, and condoms littering the otherwise serene and natural peninsula.

However, the limo driver refused to take them there, saying he would get in trouble if he drove on either a dirt road or past a no trespassing sign. Tyrone, came up with the plan for Trey to follow them to the Yacht Club, then everyone would pile into Trey's car and they would all go together to the point.

Katherine didn't love the plan, but she had given up on the idea that they were going to have sex, so she decided to go with the flow and let the night take them where it would. After the limo parked in the empty Yacht Club parking lot, Jessica grabbed the peach schnapps and a couple cassettes, Tyrone grabbed his Strawberry/Kiwi Mad Dog 20/20, and everyone jumped into Trey's Ford LTD. Even though there was plenty of space for six people in that car, Candace sat on Tyrone's lap, and the rest of them had a seat to themselves, Katherine riding shotgun, and Laura sitting directly behind her.

The conversations in the car were divergent, but mostly had to do with kids who had been to "The Point" explaining to those who hadn't that it was worth it, while those that hadn't been there recounted urban legends that bordered on slasher movie motifs. Granted, if you had never been there before, and you had seen pretty much any 1980s horror film, you could assume that you were about to be murdered as you drove down the tunnel of twisted trees on a potholed and abandoned logging road.

But once they arrived at the bayside, with lights of Ocean City reflecting off the bay, the moon lurking behind slender clouds overhead, and the gentle lapping of the waves along the bulkhead, those who had never been to The Point understood why the journey was worth it. They had entered a secret place, a place just for teens, and it was magnificent in its beauty.

Candace was the first out of the car and took in the view. She had never been to The Point before.

"Okay," she said just loud enough for the people in the car to hear. "If we're gonna be murdered by an escaped mental patient, this view is worth it."

Tyrone got out of the car next and shouted "woo-hoo" and opened up his Mad Dog, offering it to everyone as they exited the car. Only Trey accepted, taking a very small sip.

Jessica took a swig of lukewarm Schnapps and then walked to the water's edge. It was a clear night, and a gentle breeze was coming off the east, bringing the smell of brine with it.

Laura got out and joined Jessica by the waterside.

Katherine and Trey stayed in the car longer than everyone else. Katherine was looking at Ocean City. Trey was looking at her.

"I'm sorry about tonight," he said, watching her face for a sign through the shadows thrown into the car by people walking by.

She smiled with the smallest hint of longing escaping her almost perfect poise, but was otherwise motionless as she looked across the bay to Ocean City.

"It's okay," she said, and then finally turned to face him. "I like spending time with you. I was just hoping for a dance."

She leaned over and kissed him gently on the lips, and opened the door.

At this point everyone broke up into small groups. Katherine sat alone on the hood of the car. Candace and Tyrone walked off together and started making out in the dark. Trey walked up to Jessica and asked her what music she brought, and she started listing the songs, half of which he had never heard of. Laura walked away a little, saw Katherine sitting alone on the hood of the car, and then walked over to her.

"Candace told me what happened tonight," she spoke cautiously, with a mix of emotions: genuine sympathy for Katherine, jealousy, and a little sadness for Trey. "I'm so sorry. I can't imagine how scary it must have been."

Katherine nodded.

"Thanks. Honestly it happened so fast, I was more confused than scared," just realizing how scary it must have been for her parents to hear her retell the story.

"He's a good guy," Laura spoke unconsciously. Katherine was a little surprised by the statement.

"I know."

Trey and Jessica had walked back to the car and were fiddling with the tape player. Laura turned away from Katherine and looked out at the water. Candace's laughter echoed, originating from somewhere shrouded in darkness. Jessica had found the song Trey wanted. He cranked the volume. It was *Lady in Red* by Chris De Burgh. He walked over to Katherine and held out his hand.

"Would you like to dance?"

Katherine fell in love with Trey at that moment. She slid into his arms gracefully, and put her head on his shoulder.

Laura felt a tightening and twisting in her stomach. She looked away from the dancers, but stood still, her feet frozen. Jessica came over to her, and placed her hand on Laura's elbow, guiding her away from the car. They walked towards the water.

"*Lady in Red*?" Laura whispered with an accusation in her voice. "Really? Why do you even have this on a mixtape?"

"A good song is a good song."

Laura looked out at the water. Between the notes she could hear Trey and Katherine's feet scraping along the rough ground. When Katherine giggled it felt like something stabbed Laura in the side. She wondered what the hell she was doing there, and started to calculate how long it would take for her to walk home. She was pretty sure she could hear them kissing, and it was killing her. Jessica reached out and held her hand, and whispered to her: *It's okay. Just breathe.*

But as the song started to fade out, Jessica grimaced. She looked at Laura, who felt her looking and turned and mouthed: *What?*

Jessica leaned over and whispered right into Laura's ear: *The next song is Eternal Flame.*

Laura rolled her eyes. She whispered back *Who the fuck were you making this mix for?*

Jessica laughed, and turned to look at the couple as *Eternal Flame* by The Bangles started. She saw pure joy in Katherine's face.

Don't look at them, Jessica whispered. *I think they are going to fuck.*

Seriously, Laura hissed. *Where is Ani DiFranco when I need her?*

Jessica's eyes got wide.

"Literally next," Jessica spoke louder as the song was swelling. "though it's *Both Hands* which is kind of a love song."

Laura looked out at the water, learning to hate The Bangles forever.

When Ani started, the dancing stopped. Everyone listened, with all but Jessica and Laura unsure of what it was that they were listening to.

"What the hell is this?" Tyrone said walking up to the car with Candace.

"It's weird," Katherine said unconsciously.

Trey was silent and listening. Something about the cadence of the guitar and her voice reminded him of Jacques Brel. It was hard to hear the lyrics on a tape that was copied from a tape and on his crappy car speakers, but he liked the words he was able to make out.

"Who is this?" he asked Jessica.

"Ani DiFranco," Laura answered.

"You know her?" he asked Laura.

Laura nodded in a way to say: *oh yeah, I've known about Ani for ages.*

"You ever play this for my mom?" he asked Laura. "I think she would love it."

Katherine regretted saying it was weird.

"No, but I bet she would."

At this moment six teens began a rapid-fire conversation.

Jessica – "Your mom legit has the best taste in music."

Trey – "Yeah, but she hates everything I really like."

Jessica – "Oh, really? Like what?"

Trey – "I don't know. Led Zeppelin. Grateful Dead."

Jessica – "Huh. What's your desert island album?"

Trey – "My what?"

Jessica – "Desert island album. If you had one album that you could bring with you to a desert island, what would it be?"

Trey – "Guns N Roses, *Appetite for Destruction*."

Laura – "Really? Not *Wish You Were Here*?"

(Trey shook his head, sticking to his Guns.)

Katherine – "That surprises me."

Trey – "Why?"

Katherine – "I've only heard you listen to Grateful Dead."

Trey – "The tape was just stuck in the tape player. I got it out though."

Tyrone – "How did you get it out?"

Trey – "A comb."

(Tyrone nodded, as if that was the most reasonable tool for the job.)

Candace – "Can it be a greatest hits tape?"

Jessica – "Nope."

Candace – "Prince, *Purple Rain*."

(Jessica nodded with respect.)

Katherine – "Can it be a soundtrack?"

(Jessica thought for a second and shrugged.)

Jessica – "Yeah, I think that's fair."

Katherine – "*The Breakfast Club Soundtrack*."

(Everyone thought about it for a second.)

Katherine – "No wait. I gotta change my answer. *Footloose Soundtrack. Almost Paradise, Let's Hear it for the Boy, Holding Out for a Hero*... come on."

Jessica – "What about you Tyrone?"

Tyrone – "*Eagles Greatest Hits.*"

Katherine – "It can't be a greatest hits album."

Candace – "Don't you listen?"

Tyrone – "That Beatles album. You know, the blue one."

Katherine – "That's a greatest hits album."

Tyrone – "Shit. Um, oh, I like The Police album. It's uh, *Every Breath You Take.*"

Jessica – "Dude, that's a greatest hits album."

Tyrone – "Seriously?"

Jessica – "Yeah."

Candace – "Do you only like bands with 'the' before their name?"

Tyrone – "Yup."

Candance – "What about Prince?"

Tyrone – "Nope."

Trey – "What about Michael Jackson?"

Tyrone – "Nope."

Laura – "What about The Jackson Five?"

Tyrone – "Sure."

Candace – "You're so weird."

Jessica – "What about The The?"

Tyrone – "The what?"

Jessica – "The The."

Tyrone – "That sounds weird."

Candace – "You sound weird!"

Tyrone – "Oh. *The Big Chill Soundtrack.*"

Jessica – "Oh right on."

Candace – "Really?"

Tyrone – "Yeah. It's great. It's all hits."

(Jessica laughed and then nodded to Laura.)

Jessica – "You gonna go or what?"

Laura – "Can I pick one of your mixes?"

Jessica – "As flattered as I am... no."

Laura – "Fuck. This is tough."

Trey – "Everyone else answered in like a second."

Tyrone – "I came up with four options."

Candace – "Only one of them counted."

Laura – "See the problem is, if you were only going to listen to the same thing over and over again forever, you might eventually learn to hate it. As much as you love it now, it might start to drive you crazy."

Katherine – "But how often are you really going to listen to it?"

Laura – "If I'm alone on a desert island I think I would want to listen to it constantly."

Tyrone – "Is there an album that would tell you things you need to survive on a desert island? Because that would be helpful."

Trey – "That brings up a good point, are you choosing to go to this desert island or did you get shipwrecked?"

Candace – "Yeah, and is anyone with you or are you alone?"

Jessica – "Umm, let's say you are choosing to go and you are alone."

Tyrone – "Who would choose to go alone? I can't imagine that."

Katherine – "I could see it."

Laura – "Can I bring books too?"

Jessica – "You can bring one book."

Laura – "Bitch."

(Jessica stuck her tongue out at Laura.)

Tyrone – "You should bring the Bible."

Candace – (laughing) "Why?"

Tyrone – "Because it's super long. You can use the paper to start fires or something."

Jessica – "So you are suggesting bringing one book just to burn it?"

Katherine – "And he's suggesting burning the Bible."

Tyrone – "Well, no, not like that. Wait, are we allowed other paper?"

Candace – "Why do you need paper?"

Tyrone – "To start fires."

Candace – "Why are you so obsessed with starting a fire?"

Tyrone – "I'm not going to a desert island and not having a fire!"

Trey – "I'm with Tyrone on this one. Like, what's the point?"

Tyrone – "Right?"

Candace – "You are going to bring the Bible too, to burn it?"

Trey – "Hell no. I don't need paper to start a fire anyway."

Candace – "Prove it."

Tyrone – "Yeah! Let's start a fire."

Jessica – "No."

Candace – "Aw, come on. A fire would be nice."

Jessica – "Cops will come."

(Jessica walked over to Candace and stood close to her and pointed to a house far in the distance.)

Jessica – "Whoever lives in that house always calls the cops when we start a fire. We can be here all night if we don't start a fire, or fifteen minutes with a fire."

Tyrone – "Bogus."

Trey – "Laura still hasn't answered."

Laura – "Pass."

Tyrone – "You can't pass!"

Jessica – "Yeah, sorry babe, no passing."

Laura – "You didn't answer."

Jessica – "I'm letting you have first choice."

Laura – "It's too hard. If I had a million books, then I would pick some jazz for sure. Like Billie Holiday or something. It would be pretty wonderful reading a book, listening to jazz, sitting by a fire with a gentle breeze."

Tyrone – "So you *do* want a fire."

Laura – "But only one book, that sucks. I would die. I wouldn't choose to go."

Jessica – "You have to go."

Laura – "Says who?"

Jessica – "Okay, because I don't want you to die, you can have as many books as you want."

Laura – "Cool, then some jazz."

Jessica – "Which one?"

Laura – "Probably Billie Holiday. What's the one with *God Bless the Child* on it?"

Jessica – "I don't know jazz that well."

Trey – "I think it's "*Lady Sings the Blues*."

(Everyone looked at Trey.)

Trey – "It's one of my mom's favorite albums."

Tyrone – "What about you Jessica?"

Jessica – "I don't know? Something I have never heard before."

Katherine – "Are you insane?"

Jessica – "Why?"

Katherine – "You are choosing something you don't even know to be the only thing you can listen to for the rest of your life?"

Jessica – "Yeah."

Katherine – "But what if you hate it?"

(Jessica shrugged.)

Jessica – "Eh, I like to try new things."

Katherine – "But it will only be new to you once."

Jessica – "Yeah, so I will get to try new things one more time than I would if I picked something I had already heard."

Katherine – "But then you are stuck with it."

Jessica – "You are stuck with a lot of things in life. Might as well take a joyous moment when you can."

Katherine – "I can't... I don't even know where to begin..."

Jessica – "What?"

Katherine – "You are going to regret it."

Jessica – "Perhaps. It's very likely though that I will regret any choice I make. No matter what, someday I am going to long for another album. But if I chose something I have never heard, I'll always have the memory of discovery, on my own desert island."

Katherine – "But what if the album is terrible?"

Jessica – "Then it will be a funny memory."

(Katherine shook her head and threw up her hands, refusing to accept anything Jessica was saying. Tyrone pulled Candace back into the darkness. Trey walked with Katherine and reached out to hold her hand. Laura stayed still, and kept looking at Jessica, narrowing her eyes and scrunching up her nose. Jessica walked up to Laura.)

Jessica – "What?"

Laura – "I think that was a cop out."

(Jessica smiled.)

Jessica – "Yeah, but it was a good cop out."

Laura – "Bitch."

Jessica – "There you go."

(Jessica leaned her shoulder into Laura. Laura put her arm around her friend and they laughed about nothing in particular. The wind picked up, and Laura and Jessica got into Trey's car and listened to the mixes. Laura sat in the driver's seat.)

It was two in the morning when Trey turned his engine off in Katherine's driveway. She was looking at her house, and without turning to face him she smiled.

"That's not like you," she said.

He looked confused. She turned to face him.

"Cocky," she explained.

"What?"

She studied him. He was beautiful, especially in these shadows. The white t-shirt, the leather jacket, his hollow cheeks, his styled hair all mussed with one wild strand falling into his eye, his gentle lips, his sad eyes that had seen too much, and his jaw which he was clenching in anticipation made him look like he was from another time. Like an actor from a black and white movie.

He opened his door and got out of the car. She watched him, confused for a second. He opened her car door and held out his hand for her. She stood up, and they stood by the car for a moment.

"I'm sorry again..."

"Stop saying that," she cut him off.

"Okay," he nodded. "Thank you."

He took off his jacket and put it over her shoulders like a cloak. She almost swooned. The t-shirt was too tight on his arms and her gaze drifted along the curve of his shoulders. He held her hand and they walked to the door. She slid her fingers in-between his, interlocking them.

"Thank your father for me, for the jacket."

They stood facing each other, not moving. The world was still and silent. Trey could feel his heart beating. When he spoke, the words came from deep inside his chest.

"Thank you for saving me."

Katherine kissed him wildly. When she stopped she could barely stand. She was in love. She went inside and watched him until the taillights disappeared into the night.

15

Halloween

Jessica's first NYC Halloween was spent exactly how everyone's first Halloween in NYC should be spent, at the Greenwich Village Halloween Parade. If one had come from a small town in Maryland and gone to the Greenwich Village parade in the early nineties, he/she/they would have seen the largest collection of beautiful and scantily clad women they had ever seen in their life. Even if few of those ladies would still be women in the morning. It was quite the experience.

But alas, this is not her tale to tell. Laura is still stuck in a sleepy town; so sleepy in fact that it actually outlawed Halloween. Well, not Halloween per se, but Trick or Treating. The Ocean Pines Board of Directors said it was because there were no streetlights and they were worried children would get hit by cars. The few kids who lived there year round denounced this explanation and rather were convinced the ban was actually due to the grumpy diabetic retirees not wanting to buy candy. Either way, Halloween wasn't celebrated in Ocean Pines. Since it was celebrated in Berlin, that's where Ocean Pines kids went.

In the late '80s, long before Budget Travel's national contest crowned Berlin, Maryland "the coolest small town in America," it was nearly dead. The downtown had more vacant buildings than occupied ones. Other than Farlow's Pharmacy, Rayne's Reef Diner, the Style Guide, a barber shop, a junk store, and a small grocery there was nothing that remained of a once thriving economy. Then, completely out of the blue, a few lawyers, accountants, and business owners got together and renovated the historic Atlantic Hotel, the first step in resuscitating Berlin. Even so, in October of 1991 it was still almost a decade away from charming the location scouts of the Hollywood romcom *Runaway Bride*, and seeing the return of retail stores, bougie eateries, and antique shops that it is known for today.

Sleepy as it was, the old Victorian and Edwardian mansions of Main Street were not vacant like the storefronts, but rather were inhabited by lawyers, doctors, dentists, and small town old money types. Berlin, with its sidewalks, streetlights, old sycamore-lined streets, and wealthy inhabitants was a perfect place for kids to trick-or-treat, and because of that, not only children from Ocean Pines, but from all the rural areas nearby descended on Berlin for Halloween. Even those who lived on quiet streets right outside of town, like Katherine, would drive downtown and walk Main Street for the excitement of it all.

Trey and Laura had spent their youth being driven to Berlin for Halloween, and even though they had stopped trick-or-treating in seventh grade, they still went to Berlin this year. Trey was helping Katherine, who was taking her youngest brother door to door, and doing her best to keep an eye on her other brothers, as they were right on the cusp of being more concerned about tricks than candy.

Laura and Candace were volunteering at the haunted house that Candace's little sisters did for the 4H club. Laura was dressed as a vampire, wearing a tight black dress, white face makeup, black eyeshadow, ruby red lipstick, fake plastic fangs, and her hair slicked back and held in place with all the mousse. She had come up with the idea over the phone with her father's boyfriend, Todd. Since neither of them had any idea what a sexy vampire should look like, they drew inspiration from the Robert Palmer "Addicted to Love" video, and then added plastic fangs.

Laura was good with kids, so her job was greeting the little ones and convincing them that the haunted house wasn't actually that scary. In-between groups walking up to the haunted house she would eat a piece of candy corn, one color section at a time, tip to base. She didn't like candy corn, but there was nothing else there.

The rest of the teenage volunteers, mostly girls from the field hockey team, were hidden throughout the haunted house, waiting to scare the kids. Candace, who was dressed up as a ghost bride, and Tyrone, who was dressed as a zombie soccer player – as he had forgotten to turn in his uniform after soccer season, and had no other costume – took the opportunity to hide behind a hay bale and make out, doing terrible things to their respective makeup.

Laura was trying to decide if she could taste the difference in the colors of the candy corn when a handsome teenage boy in jeans, work boots, and a flannel shirt and a child dressed head to toe as Spiderman came up the brick walkway. The teen smiled when he saw her.

"Welcome... to the haunted house!" Laura said, making her voice a little deeper than usual, and adding a touch of a generic eastern European accent. She smiled at Spiderman.

"Is this your house?" Spiderman asked.

"No," Laura crouched down as best she could to meet him at his level. It wasn't the easiest thing to do in her tight skirt. "I'm just helping out a friend. It's her house."

"Timmy," the teen said to his brother. "I think you're gonna want to go through this yourself. It's just fake ghosts, not like the real ghost we have in our house."

"AL – LEX!" Timmy protested.

"Timmy," Laura was still crouched down. "Alex seems like a bit of a meanie, but he is right, it's all just pretend. I can walk through with you if you want."

"Nah, Timmy wants to be brave. Just like the real Spiderman, don'tcha Timmy."

Timmy nodded, though anyone could see real fear in his eyes.

"Okay," Laura stood up. "But Timmy, just so you know, I already think you're pretty brave. I mean, you're braver than Alex, that's for sure, he didn't even dress up for Halloween!"

"Hey, I'm dressed up as a farmer."

"Did you wear that outfit anytime in the last two weeks?" Laura said without even looking at him.

Alex looked down and thought about it. "Yeah."

"Then it isn't a costume," Laura said to Timmy, and gave him a little wink.

"Plus," Timmy added as he walked up to the front door. "We live on a farm, so we are farmers."

"Timmy, I like you already," Laura called after him.

"What about his older brother?"

Laura's eyes got wide. She could flirt with the best of them, but this guy was a complete stranger and he was coming on way too strong. She looked at him to be sure that she had never seen him at school, or didn't know him from camp or anything.

"Excuse me? Do I know you?" she said. She thought that would be enough to get him to back off. It was not.

"You have very impressive balance," he said, undeterred. He took a few steps closer to her, getting far too close for her comfort, and looking at her dead in the eyes. With his right hand he reached into the bowl and helped himself to a candy corn. "Am I being too... corny?"

She took a step backwards and opened her mouth to say something, but couldn't come up with the right words. He just smiled and waited.

"Who are you?" she finally asked.

"I'm Alex, but you know that already. Alex the meanie who wasn't brave enough to dress up for Halloween. Who are you?"

"I'm Laura."

"Laura. That's a good name."

"Oh," Laura rolled her eyes. "I'm so glad you approve. So how come I've never seen you at school? You get held back or something, still in middle school? You get kicked out? You go to juvie?"

"Do people go to juvie?"

"You tell me, you would know."

He snickered a little.

"Okay. Well, we live in Snow Hill," he explained. Snow Hill is a town about fifteen miles south of Berlin.

"So why don't you trick or treat in Snow Hill?" Laura said, picking up another piece of candy corn.

"Because there's prettier girls in Berlin."

She rolled her eyes again.

"Actually, it's a long story. If you want to give me your number I could call you and tell you all about it."

At that moment Timmy ran out of the haunted house.

"I did it, I did it!"

Laura high fived him. "I knew you could!" she held him the candy corn bowl for him. "And you have the best timing!"

"Way to go Timmy," Alex said. "You want to go through again?"

Both of them looked at Alex.

"But, it was scary!"

"I bet you a dollar you can't go through again," Alex said, pulling a dollar out of his pocket to show Timmy he was serious.

Timmy gritted his teeth and struggled with the decision, but eventually went back inside.

"So," Alex smiled triumphantly. "I think you were about to give me your number?"

"I don't... know..." Laura said, unsure how she was supposed to respond. She thought Alex was cute, and he was bold as hell, but he was a total stranger. No boy had ever asked her for her number before. It was exciting and random. "I mean, I don't even have a pen."

"Oh no worries," Alex said and pulled a small notebook and a mechanical pencil out of his back pocket.

"Okay, well that's a red flag. So I guess you do this often?"

Alex smiled confidently. He handed her the notebook and flipped through the pages so she could see it. It was full of pencil sketches. Mostly comic book characters with skin tight outfits and exaggerated features. Some of them were shooting what looked like lasers from their hands or eyes.

"Woah," Laura said, seriously surprised. "You did these?"

"Yeah, it's a hobby... for now. But as you see, no phone numbers in there."

Laura looked up from the book and opened her mouth to speak, but thought better of it. Instead she took the pencil and wrote her phone number on a blank page.

"Well," she said. "Now you have one."

Timmy appeared again and announced it was time to go. Alex promised to call Laura the following day. Laura watched them walk away. She saw Alex hand his brother the dollar and heard him tell Timmy that he was proud of him.

Moments later Katherine and Trey showed up with two of Katherine's brothers. The brothers were both dressed as Ghostbusters. They ran right into the haunted house. Katherine and Trey were both dressed as sexy pirates. Katherine walked up close to Laura, inspecting her.

"I love this costume. You look like, really good," Katherine said. "You kinda look like one of those models from the *Addicted to Love* video."

Laura blushed but it couldn't be seen under her makeup.

"I don't know... really?" she managed to say.

"Hmmm," Katherine murmured as she looked at Laura's backside. She almost told Laura that she had a great body, but changed her mind.

"You guys look really good too," Laura said out of duty. They did look good, but she wouldn't normally tell Trey he looked good. The last thing he needed was that kind of confidence boost.

"Arrrrrrr," he said..

Then no one said anything. A full minute went by, and they awkwardly looked at each other. Laura and Trey ate a candy corn. Katherine refused with a gentle head shake. They all looked around not sure what to do. Katherine wanted to whisper to Trey that he was hot, but she thought that would be rude. She looked at him and smiled. He returned her smile with a dumb grin.

Laura noticed something was different about Trey, but she couldn't put her finger on what it was. He was more confident than usual, and just, kinda dumber.

Laura didn't usually think Trey was dumb. Well, technically she did, she called him dumb all the time, almost always to his face. But she didn't *mean* dumb like he couldn't do math or read a good book. She meant dumb like he would make a sandwich out of sliced bread, two hot dogs, American cheese, crushed potato chips, hot sauce, and maple syrup. Or how he once bit into an onion like an apple, winced in disgust and possibly even a little bit of pain, choked a little, coughed, and then after catching his breath took another bite. Or how he would inexplicably park as far as he possibly could from school, even during a torrential downpour. So she didn't mean dumb, she meant goofy, or weird.

But on Halloween Trey wasn't acting goofy or weird. He was... for lack of a better word... *dumb*. As if he wasn't capable of thoughts beyond the most basic. Laura suspected something had changed.

When Katherine's brothers emerged, they waved their goodbyes and Laura was left alone. And she felt really alone. She didn't like how it seemed Trey had nothing to say. Maybe he just had nothing to say to her.

Not long afterwards it was time to wrap up the haunted house. Candace and Tyrone emerged from behind the haybale and with their makeup smeared and exchanged. Upon seeing them Laura let out a small "Agh!" as that moment was the scariest of her night.

She went home. The house seemed quiet and empty. She called Jessica, but got the machine, as Jessica was still in the Village at the parade.

***

When Alex called the next day, Laura agreed to a date. He offered to pick her up from her home, but she wanted to meet him at the movies. She reasoned that she didn't want her mom to meet Alex, not because she was embarrassed by either of them, but because somehow it would be less real if they didn't meet. It's not something that made sense. Laura was lonely and in love. Of course she was in love with Trey not Alex, but Trey was off somewhere being dumb with Katherine. So Alex would have to do.

She wore acid wash jeans and a pink and white checkered sweater. She thought about wearing her orange sweater that Trey liked so much, but felt it would be dishonest somehow.

They went to the Sun and Surf theaters and saw *Frankie and Johnny*, a romantic film starring Al Pacino and Michelle Pfeiffer. Laura spent the first half of the movie thinking about Trey, until Alex started holding her hand, and then, just like that, she stopped thinking about Trey. It was almost magic.

Alex walked her to her car, chatting unimportant thoughts about the film. When they got to Laura's car, Alex reached out and held her hand again.

"Listen, why don't you leave your car here, I'll drive you to Dumser's for some ice cream and then I'll drive you back to your car."

"Or I'll just follow you to Dumser's since it's on my way home anyway."

Alex studied her face which was half in shadow, half in a soft yellow glow of the streetlight. Without opening her car door for her, he smiled, nodded, and walked to his car.

Dumser's Dairyland was one of the few Ocean City establishments open year round for ice cream. They served the typical burgers and fries too, but everyone went there for the homemade ice cream. Alex and Laura ordered a single mint chocolate hot fudge "super sundae" to share – which honestly was enough for four people – and cherry cokes which were made the old fashioned way, by putting cherry syrup into the coke.

Laura noticed that Alex was a little more reserved at Dumser's than he had been earlier that evening. It was almost as if he was anticipating being rejected. This embarrassed Laura, and she started to think that she was a bad person for leading him on and yet being closed off to him. Or maybe just not being entirely present.

Technically this was Laura's first real one-on-one date. She had kissed a few boys here and there, but they were never real kisses, and in some ways they were never real boys. Not like Trey. And now that she was sitting across from Alex, on her first real date, she realized, not like Alex either.

"So," she said, sipping her cherry coke. "How's Timmy?"

"Timmy's a good kid," Alex said. Then he smiled at a memory. "He thinks you're pretty, but don't read too much into that. Timmy's grown up on a farm, and he's not too bright."

"Oh well..." Laura smiled. "But didn't you grow up on a farm too?"

"Yeah, but I'm really smart."

"And modest."

Alex shook his head and bit his lower lip. It looked as if he wanted to say something but wasn't sure if he should. Finally he shrugged.

"You know what? Modesty is overrated. I am smart. I'm too smart for the farm, too smart for my school, and way too smart for this town. I'm not going to stay here a minute longer than I have to."

"Where are you going to go?"

Alex shook his head ever so slightly, wondering if he had messed up. Laura's face was placid.

"Anywhere but here. A city. Somewhere where people don't just say, 'I don't get it' when they hear a poem or look at a painting. Europe maybe? I don't know."

"You want to do art?" Laura asked, not sure how to say it.

"Yeah," Alex smiled. "I want to do art... somehow. But, enough about me, what about you? You're smart. What are you going to do? Doctor? Lawyer?"

"I'm not that smart."

"Bullshit."

"I'm not. I mean, I get mostly As, but I have to really work at it."

The waitress brought over the sundae and set it between them. Laura thanked her, Alex kept his eyes on Laura, but didn't speak again until after the waitress left. They picked up their spoons and started picking at the sundae.

"That's not what I mean by smart. The smartest kids I know don't necessarily get the best grades in school. But they like, have a spark, you know. Something... some passion. And it's not just art. Like, they play music, or they're into science fiction, or do theater, they play dungeons and dragons, or, I don't know... whatever... they just... they just care about something out there..." he gestured with his hand that wasn't holding the spoon.

"And you think I have that, after knowing me for like seven minutes?"

"I know you have it. I knew after knowing you for seven seconds. I can see it."

Laura shook her head.

"How?"

"How what?"

"How can you see it?"

"I don't know, I just can." He saw Laura was doubting him. "I'm not joking, and I'm not full of shit. Some people have a spark and some people don't. You do."

Laura smiled and shrugged at the same time. She didn't entirely believe him, but she wasn't immune to compliments.

"I mean, I guess I'm good at sports. I'm good with kids. My guidance counselor told me I would be a good teacher or coach. Oh wait, I think he said teacher and coach."

"Okay, *guidance counselor*, as if there is a more useless profession. Whatever, look, you're going to stay in this town forever?"

"No," Laura said firmly. "I spent the summer in Chicago with my father and it was awesome. It was the best summer of my life. I know what you mean about the spark, the people there... they were more alive."

"Exactly!"

"And we went to galleries, art films. They had book stores everywhere. I loved it. But I don't know how to do any of that stuff."

"Well you learn."

"No," Laura shook her head. "It's not that, I don't have that in me. I'm not going to be an artist because I can't draw."

"But that's not..."

"No," she cut him off. "It's not just that. My brain doesn't work that way, you know?"

"So, then what do you want to do?"

"I don't know," Laura said, digging a big spoonful of ice cream and cookie with her spoon. "Isn't that what college is for? Doesn't someone there tell you?"

Alex smiled and put his spoon down. He was looking at her trying to figure out if she was serious or not.

"Like... a college guidance counselor?"

Laura shrugged. Her mouth was too full of sundae to respond.

"So," he continued. "You're going to go to whatever college they tell you to go to and then you're going to get a job wherever they tell you to get a job and then you're going to move to wherever they tell you to live. Is that it?"

He stood up to go pay the check. Laura was a mixture of annoyed, embarrassed, and a little angry. She put down the spoon and sighed. This wasn't how she imagined dates normally went. A minute later Alex slid back into the booth.

"Well," he said without giving her a chance to talk. "I don't think you are going to do any of that. I think you are going to wake up one day and realize that you only have this one life to live and then you're gonna go live it however the hell you want to."

"So, don't take this the wrong way," Laura said with a hint of annoyance in her voice. "But I can't really tell if you are trying to be nice or trying to be a jerk."

Alex shrugged.

"Well, neither. I'm just trying to be honest," he said and then spoke quickly as Laura sighed and shook her head. "No wait, listen. Every other guy you meet is either going to try to be nice to you or be a jerk to you to get in your pants. I'm not like other guys."

"Is this your sales pitch?"

"Yeah, how am I doing?"

She smiled.

"It needs work."

"Dammit, I thought it was going well."

"I'm still stuck on who "they" are that you kept talking about. Is it like a club or something. Some sinister cabal."

"See," he said, pointing at her. "Right there. One, you picked up on the fact I was implying there is a conspiracy to control our lives to keep us all mindless drones. And two, you just said *sinister cabal*. You don't belong here anymore than I do."

Laura smiled. "Maybe that's just what they want you to think."

Alex grinned, impressed. They stood up and walked out of Dumser's. He walked her to her car and opened her door for her. The night was cold, and the wind coming off the ocean made them both shiver. She went to get into her car, but he reached out and held her arm stopping her. She looked at him, with a surprised look.

Alex kissed her. It was relatively quick. It wasn't a big open mouth kiss, but his lips were a little parted. She honestly wasn't expecting it at all, and her lips were not closed. His breath tasted minty and sweet.

When he pulled back from the kiss he was sporting hopeful eyes and a guilty smile. At first she was stunned into a moment of inaction. Then, a little awkwardly she slid her hand up his chest to his face, and then gave him a soft and playful slap. He never stopped grinning. Laura thought about pushing him away, but instead grabbed his neck, leaned in, and kissed him deeply. The second kiss is the one Laura counts as her first real kiss.

That night Laura dreamt that Trey died, and she woke up crying.

16

Alex and that Four Letter Word

Laura and Alex went on two more dates in Ocean City. They went to La Hacienda for Mexican food with Candace and Tyrone. On the next date they went bowling. Laura still hadn't introduced Alex to Joyce, nor had she introduced Alex to Trey.

Trey and Laura had, almost overnight, grown distant. She went over to the Buckingham house once to have dinner with Dolores, but Trey was out with Katherine. Laura thought about telling Dolores about Alex, but in the end she didn't. And throughout dinner, Dolores never even mentioned Katherine.

Just as Laura realized how much she loved Trey, he faded from her life. Yes, she saw him in the classes they shared, but as he now ate lunch with Katherine and the seniors she barely even saw him at school.

When Alex invited Laura to his home, for their fourth date, she didn't know what to expect. She assumed, other than seeing Timmy again, she was going to meet his parents. She was nervous about that. She had never met a boyfriend's parents before, and she knew nothing about them.

It was late in the afternoon on a mild autumn Saturday, one of those gloriously golden Delmarva days. As Laura drove south past Berlin, the fields stretched away from the highway as far as she could see in both directions. Every third or fourth field had its own rangale of deer picking through the corn stover, and the occasional lazy turkey vulture glided overhead.

She had her driver's side window half down letting in the clean autumn air. Laura sang along with Ani DiFranco, by now familiar with every word of that album. She got lost, but didn't mind. It was a beautiful drive. After turning around a few times she finally found Alex's address.

The Cook homestead was set back at least two hundred yards from the road. In fact, one could barely see the 1850's farmhouse from the start of the drive, but the huge red barn or the silver grain silo was likely visible from space. Behind the barn was an abandoned grey and white chicken house that was falling down. There was a huge white oak in front of the house, a beech tree with a tire swing and a few small pines out back. Otherwise there were no trees until the distant horizon.

Laura parked between Alex's truck and a brand new green and yellow row crop tractor. The screen door opened and Alex emerged.

After a quick greeting she learned that they were alone, as his parents had taken Timmy to a friend's birthday party at a nearby farm.

"Do you want to come inside and see my room?" Alex asked abruptly.

Up until this point Alex and Laura had done nothing more than making out in a car. Going into a bedroom with him was a leap that Laura wasn't ready to make.

"Um...no," she said flatly. "Was this... like was this the plan all along?"

Alex scrunched up his mouth so much that his right eye was almost closed, and he scratched his head.

"Um, I mean," he was at a loss. "I don't... I thought... ah shit, never mind, it was dumb."

Laura sighed and smiled ever so slightly. She felt bad for Alex. And it's not like she didn't want to see the inside of his house, or even his bedroom, it just seemed so sudden.

"I'm sorry," Alex said. "I just... I thought you would get here sooner. We only have so much time before my parents get back."

"I got lost," Laura explained. "But, don't you want me to meet your parents?"

"It's not that, they're just... They are really uptight, you know? Especially my dad. Um... actually... well... he's just an asshole."

He shook his head.

"I'm sorry. You want to go for a walk?"

"I guess."

They started to walk towards the abandoned chicken house.

"Alright," Alex began. "Look, my parents are weird. You're not a farm girl so, they aren't going to like you."

"Wow."

"But so what? I like you, and you are super sexy. And yes, okay, I wanted to see you naked, in my bedroom, or wherever. I even changed the sheets. But I get it, I fucked up."

Laura nodded. She wasn't really upset, but she did enjoy playing with Alex.

"How much time do we have?"

Alex didn't have a watch. He shrugged.

"About an hour. If you are wondering, I don't need anywhere near that long."

Laura blushed and laughed. Alex was grinning. She kept walking towards the chicken house.

"So you want me to be gone before they get home?"

"I don't know," Alex sighed. "They don't like anything different. They don't even like me. They don't like change, you know?"

"This changed," Laura said, pointing to the dilapidated chicken house.

"Yeah," Alex admitted. "Well, we stopped chickens before I was born. We only do grain now."

Laura looked around. "How big is your farm?"

"Six hundred acres." He pointed as he showed her. "We go all the way over to the road there, and then all the way to the Onley farm over there. Becca Onley is the first girl I kissed, if you were wondering."

Laura laughed. "I wasn't."

"Who was the first boy you kissed?"

Laura was looking out at the empty fields and towards the setting sun.

"Trey Buckingham."

They watched the sunset while leaning on the hood of Laura's car. Alex was standing behind Laura and had put his arms around her and left them that way, as they faced the final moments of sunlight in silence.

They left before his parents got home and went to a party at The Rickety House, an old, abandoned farmhouse that was basically The Point for Snow Hill kids. There were about fifty high schoolers there, and someone brought a keg and someone else brought a boom box that played nothing but Bruce Springsteen. Laura walked away from the crowd and into the field. The soil had been disked and she walked parallel to the rows, but she stumbled occasionally on large hardened clumps of earth. But she wasn't looking at the ground, she was looking up.

The sky was clear and they were far away from any unnatural light. Growing up in Ocean Pines, Laura always had trees in between her and the sky. In Ocean City, even in the hibernating winter, the city was full of streetlights and blinking yellow stoplights. But now, far from the trees and the pollution of electricity, Laura had never seen so many stars in her life.

It was a crisp night. Alex gave Laura his coat and they laid down on the ground and looked up at the sky. Laura saw her first shooting star. She gasped and pointed to the sky. But Alex didn't see it. He was looking at her.

He kissed her and she pulled him close. He tasted of cheap beer, but she liked his warmth. He climbed on top of her and kissed her neck. She inhaled with base carnal pleasure but kept her eyes open, looking at the most magnificent night sky she had ever seen.

He kept kissing her lower and lower. He pulled up her sweater and she didn't protest. He kissed her stomach, and then he pulled her sweater higher, and kissed her side along her ribs. She pulled her bra up revealing herself to him. He gently kissed her. She responded with a shudder.

He slid his hand down her stomach and into her jeans. For a moment Laura froze. Then she could feel the top of her jeans cutting into her waist, and felt like the button was going to break.

"Wait," she said, removing his hand. She unbuttoned her jeans and then put his hand back where it was.

He kissed her and then whispered in her ear, "I have a condom."

"Good for you," she said. "But you aren't going to need it tonight."

She sighed as he pushed his finger inside her. She reached out and unbuckled his pants, pulled down his boxers and grabbed him.

"Unless," she whispered in his ear, pausing to exhale. "Unless Becky Onley is here."

He laughed and she did too. They kissed and played some more in the field. They didn't have sex that night, but Laura thought for the first time that maybe she would like to make love with Alex.

Sex was confusing and complicated for Laura. She never spoke of sex with her mother. The health class she had freshman year of high school included one week of Sex Education. It was taught by a coach that spent more of the class yelling at the students to "stop laughing" than actually passing on important information. She had only seen a penis because Jessica showed her a Penthouse magazine that she had stolen from one of her parents.

Laura's concept of love was derived largely from teen movies made in the 1980s. Films that were obsessed with the concept of virginity. Men couldn't be virgins, and girls had to be. Beyond the incongruous virginity equation was the idea that one true love existed for everyone. And if you found that one true love, you needed to fight for it.

Up until meeting Alex, Laura felt the whole universe had conspired for her to love Trey. But then things got messy. Trey disappeared right about the same time Alex showed up. Alex kissed her and made her feel good. He made her feel special.

She thought she might love him too. Maybe not in the same way as Trey. Trey was comfortable, Alex was exciting. Could Laura love two people at once? Was that even allowed? According to the Hollywood of the 1980s that marketed films to teens… nope. But then again, there weren't any movies about a man falling in love with another man, and her father and Todd certainly seemed to be in love.

Cracks started to form in the cultural windshield that was her worldview. Just tiny, almost imperceptible slivers that signaled something was wrong.

A week later Laura and Alex had sex for the first time. It was in Alex's pickup truck. They were all alone, parked in front of the Rickety House on a cold and windless night. Through most of the physical act, Alex wasn't thinking of Laura. Her skin, which only moments before had been hidden from him, glimmered in the moonlight that was shining through the foggy windshield. Alex stole glances but mostly looked away, trying to stave off the energy which was building inside. He was trying to last as long as he could. He even slid her shirt back over her breasts at one point to hide them from his peripheral vision. Finally, Alex closed his eyes in a desperate attempt to try to hide from the lust Laura inspired. Alex was actually thinking about baseball, even though he didn't even really like baseball. He had heard that it worked. It didn't.

Laura wasn't thinking of Alex either. She was at first, when Alex was pushing against her, stabbing her crotch with his condom covered hard-on. She even giggled a little. The first few times he wasn't even that close to finding his mark. She reached down to help guide him, and at that very moment a tiny little voice deep inside thought *this is a funny thing that I can't wait to tell Trey*. And the next moment she was no longer a virgin.

The following day she was upset about what she had done. But she wasn't sure if she was upset that she had had sex with Alex when her universe-ordained true love was clearly Trey, or if she was upset because she was thinking about Trey when her boyfriend penetrated her for the first time. Had she perverted the hallowed act of bestowing the most precious gift a woman had to give, or was she cheating on her one true love for lust?

But if on one shoulder was the Hollywood devil of a love made from golden cheese, on the other shoulder was the angel of Ani DiFranco. *My cunt was built like a wound that won't heal* echoed in Laura's mind balancing the doubt and mitigating some of the suffering.

Still, like many teenagers, she struggled. She suffered because she cared and she analyzed. An awful combination for a human being, especially one going through adolescence, is to be both thoughtful to the point of philosophic, and also empathetic.

Through Thanksgiving she suffered. She ate a quiet meal with her mother, and they went to the movies together in the evening. They saw *The Addams Family*, and she laughed, forgetting her troubles. Afterwards they went to Dumser's Dairyland and split a mint chocolate cookie sundae and Laura thought of Alex and got sad again.

She wanted to tell her mom everything. She wanted her mom to be her friend and her confidante. She wanted to confess to someone, and her mom was there, right in front of her. But she was scared. She didn't know how her mother would react to something this big. She thought there was a very good chance she would be okay with it, but there was just enough doubt to keep Laura quiet.

So the next day, Laura got up early, stole her mother's coffee, and got in her car and drove. There's something special about the day after a holiday, like that Friday after Thanksgiving. It was an extra day, not a weekend, not a school day, a rare unscheduled day without commitments. She decided to let the horizon guide her. To get lost on the back roads of Delmarva.

Before she even left Ocean Pines, she first drove past the Buckingham home, both Dolores' and Trey's car were in the driveway, but she didn't stop. She drove into Berlin. She turned onto Main Street and rolled slowly through the sleepy downtown passing no pedestrians and only a few cars. She drove past her school, which was barren and dark.

It was one of those autumn days with that deep blue sky and the occasional fluffy and round white clouds. The air was crisp and clean. She was wearing jeans and a green sweater, but she drove with the driver-side window halfway down, as she liked being cold.

She continued south on back roads towards Snow Hill. The fields that she sped past all had the memory of corn or soybean from the recent season, and the occasional solitary deer wandered through looking for remnants. Groups of turkey vultures circled in the morning sun, looking for the previous night's roadkill that had limped into the fields before breathing their last. She crossed route 113 time and again, avoiding the highway as best as she could, while driving in a roughly parallel path south. Eventually she drove past Alex's farm, but even though she saw his truck in the driveway, she didn't stop.

She drove down the lonely and familiar road, which was gravel and didn't even have a street sign, and pulled up to The Rickety House. While this was her third time at the former home, it was the first time she had seen it during the day.

The farmhouse had been abandoned for more than thirty years. The broken or warped wood siding had lost all traces of paint and was a sun-bleached gray. Leafless gum and maple trees had taken root inside the house and had pushed their way through what were once windows, like tiny arms growing from a wide body. Moss grew on clumps on the north side. Vines crawled through the siding and along the tree limbs. Birds flitted in and out. The house was now a home for the wild. A paragon of entropy.

Laura rolled down all of her windows and turned off the engine. The cool autumn air cleansed her car and chilled her skin. She heard a crow caw. Branches scraped against one another in the breeze. A leaf bounced against the ground as it repeatedly seemed to try to jump in the air, like a desperate attempt to return to its former home in the sky and undo abscission. A squirrel skittered through tall drying grass, gathering something unseen. Laura listened to the squirrel move, she listened to the birds flap their wings, and the dancing leaf. Autumn sounds are cleaner than summer sounds. They are more severe. Lonelier.

Her coffee was empty, so she sat motionless and listened. She closed her eyes, and the sounds of the season bathed her mind. Far away she thought she heard a howl. Just as the wind paused, she was certain she heard a single peal of a child's laughter.

There was no epiphany, no clarity, no decision, no goal achieved, no answer to an unknown question. It was just a lengthy drive alone, sometimes with Jessica's music, sometimes with the music of the abandoned world. It was a beautiful day spent in the wilds of Delmarva, and the secret and forgotten places.

After an unknown time at the Rickety House, she got back in her car and drove away from that place, never to return.

17

Giving Thanks

After the drive Laura went home and called her father's apartment, but only Todd was home. Which turned out to be perfect. She needed to talk to someone who wouldn't judge her, or at least, not in any actionable or predictable way. She told Todd about Alex on the condition that he promised not to tell her dad. He agreed on the condition that she always promised to use protection.

That night she went over to Jessica's house, but Jessica's parents were there and Jessica and her mom were already drunk by the time Laura arrived. It was uncomfortable. Laura made her excuses and left early.

The following day was Saturday, and she went shopping with her mom. Saturday night Laura and Joyce went to dinner at the Cactus Café in Selbyville with Bubby Davis. One would think this would have been a more momentous occasion, but it really wasn't. Laura wanted her mom to be happy, and she was so preoccupied with her own life that she just enjoyed the chips and salsa and shrimp fajitas. Also, she liked how polite Bubby was towards both of them. He knew how to talk to teenagers, and wasn't awkward like most adults were. That night she called Candace and had a nice chat about their holiday, but still hadn't told Candace that she and Alex had had sex. She wasn't ready for that.

Then there was Sunday...

Sunday morning Laura went to church with Dolores. Sunday afternoon Jessica came over to her house. Sunday night she slept with Trey.

18

Sunday Morning

Laura was surprised to find Dolores knocking at her door early on Sunday morning. Laura had woken up only minutes before, she hadn't yet showered or had breakfast.

Dolores asked Laura if she would accompany her to church. Laura was confused. While she grew up Catholic, and even went to a Catholic school for Kindergarten and first grade, she hadn't really kept up with it. In fact, neither she nor her mother even went to Easter Mass the year before, and she had never been to mass with Dolores before. But she was not in the habit of letting Dolores down, so she threw some water on her face, slipped into a dress, and was in Dolores' car in three minutes.

Through small talk and silence they drove into Ocean City on route 50, and went to St Mary's Star of the Sea on South Baltimore Street. Laura had never been to this particular church before. Whenever she had gone to mass she went to St. Luke's on 100th Street or Holy Savior on 17th Street. Both of those other churches were bigger, and as Laura correctly guessed, newer. In fact, St. Mary's Star of the Sea was built in 1877, long before Ocean City became a tourist destination. Laura liked the modesty of the smaller and older building. It was more intimate, and felt somehow more honest.

Mass was crowded, but not like it would be at Christmas or Easter, or on any Sunday in the summer. Laura had already found out that Trey wouldn't be there, but she was surprised not to see anyone else that she knew. It reminded her of a ghost story she had heard at camp when she was younger, about a woman hearing church bells and thinking she was late for church. After rushing there the woman noticed she didn't recognize the people sitting in her usual pew. She scanned the other parishioners until she finally found someone she recognized... someone who had recently died. That's when the woman in the story realized she was at a mass for the dead. Laura couldn't remember how the story ended, but she touched Dolores' arm, checking to make sure she was real. Laura smiled at her own thoughts. Dolores smiled back.

The mass went quickly for Laura. Like most kids that grew up Catholic, mass was memorized. Other than the homily, the service was just going through the motions. That day the ritual gave her mind a chance to relax. She sat, stood, kneeled, spoke, and sang on cue. She found comfort in unison with all of these unknown neighbors. Her eyes focused on the circular stained glass window behind the altar, depicting an image of Jesus on the cross. He suddenly reminded Laura of Trey. Neither of them ever seemed to be wearing a shirt.

Laura giggled at the thought, but later apologized to Jesus while in line to receive communion.

Afterwards they drove uptown to General's Kitchen for creamed chipped beef over biscuits and scrambled eggs. Once they ordered and Laura had used all the cream for her coffee, Dolores told her why she had woken her up that morning.

"Mija, I have something to tell you. Things are going to have to change very quickly for our family. Our financial situation is very complicated." Laura gave Dolores her full attention. Dolores went on to explain how a coked up accountant gave her husband the idea of putting everything into Dolores' name, which meant she owned not only the house but both bars and the land they sat on. The physical building of the downtown bar, which shuttered in the winter, was in pretty bad shape and would need serious renovations to be able to open the following summer. And the bank account was nearly empty. Dolores had a modest offer from a real estate developer to purchase the land, and she agreed in order to have a lifeline.

The bar that remained opened in the winter, Buck's Tavern, had been closed since it was raided by police. Out of necessity, Dolores would reopen the bar immediately and run it herself.

Laura listened intently. She asked questions, and then there was a bit of silence, a pause in the conversation. Laura asked the waitress for a little more coffee and much more cream.

"You know," Laura said as the waitress poured the coffee, "you could put some of your recipes on the menu. Like your albóndigas, you could put that on the menu."

Dolores smiled.

"People here," she said looking around at the restaurant but meaning all of Ocean City, "want deep fried cheese and light beer. I don't think I can afford to try to change that."

"Maybe not right away," Laura said, shrugging.

"Mija," Dolores leaned in conspiratorially, "I am not going to be able to be there for Trey anymore, like I have been his whole life. I need you to promise me that you will help me, that you will look after him."

"Trey's not a child anymore."

"But he is always my child," Dolores said with a pained smile. "And he is going through so much. I worry about him."

"He has Katherine," Laura dutifully pointed out.

Dolores leaned back in her seat, in a moment debating the outcome of two opposite scenarios. She shook her head, more at her own idea than at what Laura said, but Laura interpreted a different meaning.

"Did something happen?" Laura pressed.

Dolores shrugged with a sincere desire not to betray her son's confidence.

"Katrine is a nice girl. But for my life, I do not understand what my Trey sees in her. She does not hold a candle up to you."

Laura blushed. "I think you're biased."

Dolores nodded. "I am. And I always will be."

Dolores picked up the check, and went to the cashier to pay. Laura looked forward, towards Coastal Highway, and the blinking yellow lights, but not at anything in particular.

"Are you ready?" Dolores asked.

"Can we go by Buck's? I have never actually been there."

Dolores nodded and smiled.

Even though it was a clear and sunny day, the restaurant was dark, with black wooden booths when you first walked inside, to your left, and a few tables pushed up against north facing windows to the right. Beyond the booths there were about a dozen round tables that could seat six people comfortably, and that area opened to a large bar that had huge western windows which overlooked the bay.

The air was heavy in there, and smelled of stale beer, mildew, and bleach. The chairs had been flipped over onto the tables, and Dolores moved through the dining room to the kitchen, turning on lights as she went.

Laura followed her into the kitchen. The fluorescent lights buzzed and one flickered, but they did their job, bathing the kitchen in pale, brilliant light. Silver pots and pans were stacked above the line, lustrous and shiny. The dishwasher area was full of flatware in racks, and the heavy iron stoves were black and clean. Laura walked through the kitchen, looking in the reach-ins, at the salamander broiler whose base was littered with blackened former cheese, the walk-in freezer which was full of boxes of chicken fingers and mozzarella sticks, and the walk-in cooler, which was empty. She had never been in a kitchen so big, in a place with so much possibility.

"Can I work here?" she asked, dreamily. She looked at Dolores with hopeful eyes. "I want to help you."

"Mija," Dolores said with all her love.

19

Sunday Afternoon

Laura got home around noon, and was trying to decide how she was going to spend the rest of her day when she heard a knock on her door. Jessica didn't wait for her to get there before she opened it and stepped inside. As soon as Laura rounded the corner to the door she was hit with a surprise.

"Hey bitch, this is for you," Jessica said, shoving a bulging black trash bag into Laura's arms.

"Oh, you brought me your trash. How kind."

"It's my Christmas lights. I'm bequeathing them to you. Come on, let's go upstairs. Hang on," she pushed the front door open and yelled outside. "Dad! Ten minutes!"

Her father was waiting to drive her back to Wilmington, Delaware, in order for her to catch the train back to Manhattan. He left his Mercedes running and looked in vain for football on the radio.

Once upstairs Laura pulled three rat's nests made of white Christmas lights and green cords out of the trash bag. She started untangling them and spreading them out while she talked.

"So, I realized when I get back to the city I'm going to buy Christmas lights there. And I don't want to take these on the train, and besides, I'm not really here to enjoy them anyway. They really do provide the best lighting, you know? Plus,

I don't know... I didn't really like how we left it on Friday night. I might have gotten a little drunk, and my family was being assholes as usual, but it wasn't just that, was it? There's something else going on with you, I think. Right? So anyway, I invented this excuse to come over here. What do you think?"

"About the excuse?" Laura asked.

"I don't know," Jessica said, busy with a complicated knot. "About anything I guess. What's going on with you?"

"I'm okay."

"Don't." Jessica was ever so slightly shaking her head and looking at Laura with penetrating eyes. "Don't give me that bull shit, I'm not just someone you know."

Laura stayed quiet, but Jessica didn't give in. She kept looking at her until Laura finally spoke.

"I have been dealing with some stuff."

"Lay it on me, sister, that's what I'm here for."

Laura wasn't sure how to begin.

"Do you," she said after a big sigh, "believe in soulmates?"

"Ew. Wait... you can't be talking about Alex, can you?" She looked at Laura with penetrating eyes. "Oh... you guys fucked?"

"Um..." Laura sighed. "That's a complicated question."

"Which question, the fucking or the talking about Alex. Both seem pretty straightforward to me. Oh, is he into kinky things? S&M? Golden showers? Did he pee on you? Don't let a guy pee on you."

"No!"

"Babe, can I be really honest with you for a second? I don't like Alex. I had met him for like two minutes and he told me he's going to be this great artist. Okay, dude, that's cool, but then he kept talking about how he couldn't wait to get out of this town and do something great. Look, I know a lot of artists, and the ones that spend all their time talking about themselves and what they are going to do, they kinda suck. The ones that are about the journey, not the destination, they are the interesting ones. So yeah, he thinks he's special because he's gonna leave this town. Like no shit dude. Stop talking. Everyone with half a brain leaves here, you know? I left, you're gonna leave..."

"What about Trey?"

"Well..." Jessica stopped talking and looked at Laura with a sudden understanding of what Laura was going through. "Oh shit, babe. You fucked Alex and you love Trey. Damn. That's no joke, I'm sorry."

"So do you believe in soulmates?"

"No," Jessica said flatly but without a hint of condescension.

"You mean," Laura was confused and a little surprised, "you don't think there's just one person out there for you? Like you could have true love between multiple people?"

"Ehhh..." Jessica was trying hard now not to take over the conversation, but she knew it wasn't going to work. "I mean to say, I don't even believe in the soul."

"What? What, do you think we're just animals?"

"Well, yeah," Jessica said smiling. "But that doesn't have anything to do with my idea about whether or not there is a soul. Look, if you think about it, it's more likely that a dog has a soul than a person. Like people change, so much all the time, but like, dogs don't change much, you know? You're so different than you were last spring, and you are going to be such a different person a year from now, much less five years, or ten years."

"I mean, I changed my hair, but that didn't change me."

"Laura, this has nothing to do with your hair. Or, for that matter, who you are fucking or what music you're listening to. I'm not talking about that stuff, I'm talking about what makes you human. That's changing, and it will keep changing. You don't notice because for you it's slow, it's like, incremental. But it's obvious to me because I only see you from time to time, and all those small, I don't know, increments... add up to be something bigger... more obvious."

"So wait," Laura was processing the idea, "are you saying that I could change so much or you could change so much that we wouldn't be friends anymore?"

Jessica nodded.

"Is that already starting to happen?" Laura was visibly upset.

"No, come on... no," Jessica said reassuringly. "Why would I be giving someone I didn't like my Christmas lights? Honestly, babe, I love the change. It's like you are just starting to wake up. Look, other than the fact you're a smart-ass, you've always been, like, really nice, like to the point of almost being a pushover. But, and I swear I mean this in the best possible way, you are not as nice anymore. Like, you are starting to carve out a little slice of the world for yourself."

"You don't think I'm nice?"

"Of course you are, you're just not a pushover, you know? I think because everyone has said for years how scary you were when you played sports, that maybe you were like, overcompensating in regular life. I think we're getting off the rails a little bit, but to go back..." Jessica's voice lowered a notch. "Look, I like how you have changed, but if you don't like how I change, you don't have any obligation to be my friend."

"That's so fucked up," Laura felt like Jessica was breaking up with her. "How can you say you are not going to be there for me no matter what?"

"Because I don't know that it's true."

Laura shook her head, getting angry. "That's so selfish."

"Alright," Jessica shrugged, going back to untangling the strands of lights, "fine, I'm selfish. I think I'm just being honest, but you can look at it anyway you want. Okay, so now you know the answer, I don't believe in soulmates. Where were you going with that?"

"What does it matter now?" Laura asked.

"I don't know, why did you ask me about it in the first place?"

"Because I thought you would say yes!"

Jessica put down the lights, looked at Laura, and smiled. Laura tried to be mad but her friend's adoring condescension made her crack. She took a long slow breath and a big exhale.

"Go ahead," Jessica said grinning. "You know you want to."

"Bitch."

"See how it makes things better?"

Laura forced a frown. "I can't believe you are going to ditch me someday!"

"Can't know that," Jessica shook her head. "You might be stuck with me for life, you never know. But I am dead serious about this, you don't owe me anything."

"You can say that..." Laura was picking up a strand of lights and focused on them. "You can say that because you have siblings. You have a sister and a brother, who will always be your sister or your brother no matter what they say or do. Not everyone has that."

Jessica looked at her and thought about how cavalier she had been. Laura was her best friend, and had been her best friend for years. Laura was closer to her than any of her siblings, or her roommates, or anyone else in the world. But she hadn't considered what it was like to be Laura.

Without thinking any further about it, Jessica held up her right hand and spit on it.

"Ew," Laura said, looking up, shocked.

"Spit on your hand," Jessica said.

"No."

"Spit!"

"That's gross."

"Spit on your hand," Jessica demanded, "Or I am going to hold you down and lick your face."

"Why?"

Jessica smiled.

"Because that's what sisters do."

Laura sighed as she looked at Jessica through misty eyes. She spit on her left hand.

"It was supposed to be your right hand," Jessica corrected her.

"I'm not spitting on another hand."

Jessica reached out and interlocked her fingers with Laura's.

"Now we're sisters. Okay? Everyone else in my life I can get rid of, but not you."

"Well," Laura corrected her. "Not me and your real sister."

Jessica shook her head.

"You are my real sister."

20

Sunday Night

Laura had many good qualities, but skill at interior decoration wasn't one of them. After about an hour and a half she managed to get all of the Christmas lights untangled and strung up along her wall and around the single window in her room. To secure the lights in place she employed a mixture of thumbtacks, scotch tape, and a spare shoestring in a slapdash and haphazard way. In the end, the lights gave a soft and romantic glow to her room.

Joyce knocked gently on her door as Laura was switching cassettes. She had been listening to *Out of Time* by REM, but she wasn't crazy about the second side of the album, so she was putting on *I Do Not Want What I Haven't Got* when her mom pushed the door open.

Joyce was wearing a cocktail dress and makeup, clearly going out for the evening. Laura's eyes got big upon seeing her.

"Hubba hubba!" Laura teased.

"I'm going out tonight."

"Wait, really? That's not how you usually look on a Sunday night when you are staying at home, curled up with a good book?"

Joyce rolled her eyes.

"Okay. Look, Bubby is taking me to a cocktail party in Easton. It's a work thing for him, and we might be pretty late."

"Easton? That's like half way to Baltimore."

"Basically," Joyce agreed. "It doesn't start until nine, I don't expect we will be home until after one AM. I expect you to be asleep, as you have school tomorrow."

"Honestly Mom, I'm so exhausted after this weekend. I expect I will be asleep in about an hour."

Her mother nodded sarcastically knowing what she was saying was completely unlikely. She looked around the room at the Christmas lights.

"Interesting decorating choice."

"You like them? Jessica gave them to me."

"Just," her mother was trying to not be critical. "Do your best not to burn the house down."

"Yeah," Laura said, confidently hopping on her bed, "I can't make any promises."

Joyce paused, and then sat on the edge of the bed.

"Who is this?" Joyce nodded to the stereo.

Laura raised an eyebrow. Her mother never asked her about her music. Laura had gotten to the point that she believed that her mother couldn't actually hear music if it wasn't classical.

"It's Sinead O'Connor. She's Irish."

Her mother smiled.

"With a name like Sinead O'Connor I could have guessed. Is she your favorite these days?"

Laura tilted her head and narrowed her eyes, trying to read her mom's intention.

"I don't really have a favorite. I mean, I like Ani DiFranco, I've been listening to her more than anyone else lately. Why?"

"Just curious."

Joyce fiddled with the neckline of her dress.

"You know," she started slowly. "If you ever have anything you want to talk about, you can talk to me, right? About anything."

"Same goes to you mom," Laura volleyed the conversation back.

"I'm serious."

Laura shrugged.

"You know what mom? So am I."

"I mean, if you are worried about anything, I just..." she exhaled as she trailed off. "Look, I know that things haven't always been the easiest, but, you know, I only want the best for you."

"I know."

"And I think we're at a place where, maybe we can tell each other things." Joyce was struggling to get to her point. "It's just that, I don't want you to think that you are going to get in trouble for telling me something, I would rather know than not know."

Laura looked out the window not sure what she should say.

"I don't mean to push," Joyce broke the silence.

But she did mean to push. Bubby had gotten in her head, telling her one horror story after another about drugs, alcohol, and other terrors destroying the youth of the era. To his credit, he had said the parents who let kids drink at home were keeping their kids safer than the ones who forced the kids to hide it and drive to the Rickety House or The Point.

Of course Laura was reading something else from this conversation entirely. She had no idea how her mom seemed to know that Laura was no longer a virgin, but it was pretty obvious that she did. It didn't help that Sinead kept singing the lyrics *feel so different* over and over during this whole conversation.

"Please, think about it. I promise, you won't be in trouble. I only want you to be safe."

Joyce leaned down and kissed her on the forehead. "Goodnight, sweetheart."

Laura did her best to recover. "Don't do anything I wouldn't do!"

Joyce stood at the doorway and looked at Laura as if she was trying to figure something out.

"Open or closed?" Joyce said.

"Open, please," Laura turned the volume up on her stereo as "I Am Stretched On Your Grave" began. She laid on the bed and stared at the ceiling and wondered why Alex hadn't called her in two days.

About an hour later Laura was spooning a comically large scoop of ice cream into a bowl when she was startled by a knock at the front door. She peeked around the corner and through the sidelight saw the familiar frame of Trey Buckingham standing there, his shoulders hunched perhaps more from the cold than his mood.

Laura opened the door. He was wearing a white t-shirt, black Levi's, and untied light brown work boots. She was barefoot, wearing boxer shorts and the Iowa Hawkeyes sweatshirt that her grandparents had sent her four years prior. It was getting threadbare, but it was her favorite comfy sweatshirt. Even so, Trey had never seen it.

For as many times as Laura was at Trey's home, it was very rare for Trey to go to Laura's house. Since she was always over there, she planned what outfits he saw her in. There were occasions he had been to her home, but it was rare and other than the one time earlier in the story, it wasn't like him to surprise her.

He looked right into her eyes. He was sad. Not that he had been crying sad, but he was damaged. He had no flirt left in him. Luckily, something in Laura's teenage brain snapped, and she had enough flirt for the both of them. She peeked around his shoulder at his car.

"Anyone with you?"

He shook his head. She opened the door wider to let him in.

"Want to eat ice cream and listen to sad music?"

A smile crawled across his lips.

Trey kicked off his boots and placed them at the door. Laura watched him. Her mind was a flurry. She hadn't talked to him in days, and he had absolutely no reason to be there. What's more, her mother was out for the evening, with no chance of coming back anytime soon. They were alone, truly alone, for the first time since they listened to rain falling on the leaves beneath the bay window, before Katherine, before Alex, before the police arrived and took him away.

Trey stood still. He didn't know where to go. Laura kept looking at him, torturing him with her quizzical and wicked grin. He sheepishly laughed.

"What?" he pleaded.

She let him off the hook and turned to the kitchen.

"Come on, the ice cream is melting," she said over her right shoulder.

They walked into the kitchen. There was a small bowl on the counter with three huge scoops of cherry chocolate chip ice cream overflowing from the bowl.

"So..." Laura walked around the kitchen island to the cabinet and indicated the bowl on the island. "This is mine. Would you like your own bowl?"

She reached into the cabinet and picked up a bowl, but Trey had walked up to hers and taken a spoonful already.

"I'm fine," he said as he slid the bowl closer to himself.

Laura closed her eyes in what could have been a very long blink, or maybe it was her way of taking a break. Giving her mind a moment to make a decision that she wasn't sure she was ready to make. She put the second bowl away.

"Come on," she walked out of the kitchen and upstairs towards her room. "And bring *my* ice cream."

Trey grabbed the bowl. He never even considered grabbing a second spoon, but in his defense, teenage boys don't really think about things like that.

By the time Trey got to Laura's room, the Christmas lights were the only illumination in the entire house. Laura was digging through a stack of cassettes, until she found the right mixtape.

The creation of the mixtape, an artifact unique to that generation, was a true craft. It's not like throwing a playlist together with the endless possibility of options and unrestricted runtimes. Since each side of the tape had limited space, every decision was precious and strategic. That's not even considering the suffering Laura and countless others of her generation felt when they had waited forty-five minutes to record a song off the radio and the DJ decided to say something stupid over the last few lines of the song, ruining the mood.

And mood was everything with the mixtape. Some were happy, some were sad, some were good for working out, some were made for dancing, but the best, the truly special mixtapes took you on a personal journey of the mixer. If you ever listened to a mixtape that someone made for themselves only, then you knew something about that person. You saw into their soul.

Laura found the tape. It had no name, only a line of teardrops drawn in blue pen on the little sticker where one could label the cassette. This was her tape. She never played it for Jessica, or Candace, or Alex. She popped it in, rewound it to the beginning, and hit play.

Trey sat on the floor, his back against her bed, looking out the window, holding her ice cream. The lonely and sonorous notes of *Something I Can Never Have* by Nine Inch Nails filled the room. It's a brooding song that starts with the line *I can still recall the taste of your tears*, and from there only gets darker. Laura hopped on the bed and laid on her stomach, her face behind Trey's left ear. She leaned close.

"My ice cream," she whispered as she slid her fingers down his arm to his hand. She grabbed the bowl and placed it on her bed.

She shifted her position so that she was laying on her left side, and pulled a pillow beneath her left arm to prop herself up a little while she ate. Trey half turned and pulled his knees up towards his chest with his elbows on his knees. He kept stealing glances at Laura, then looking away before she met his gaze. Shadows dominated the room. But as Trent Reznor sang *I just want something I can never have* she caught him looking. He smiled and recovered.

"Is this song about that bowl of ice cream?"

She simpered and fed him a spoonful of cherry and chocolate. He looked into her eyes as she watched his mouth. Once he closed his lips around the spoon, their eyes met, and in the soft glow of the Christmas lights everything else disappeared. Up until that moment, it was the most intimate moment of either of their lives.

The next song on the mix was *Alone* by Heart. It was impossible to have listened to the radio in the 1980s and not heard that song one thousand times, and there's a reason for it. It's a damn good song. When Laura put it on the mixtape, she was thinking of Trey. After all, it's about them. Whether they were capable of admitting it or not, they were deeply in love. So maybe every love song was now about them. In the end, maybe that's all love is, finding the person that gives music meaning.

Laura had put the spoon in the bowl. She adjusted the pillow. She sighed. Trey kept looking at her. She smiled nervously. At first she was avoiding his face, but then she gave in and looked him dead in the eyes, challenging him. He didn't avert his gaze. She made a silly face at him that was basically asking him *what are you going to do?*

Trey could have kissed her then. Laura could have kissed Trey then. It would have made sense. After all, Ann Wilson was cooing: *You don't know how long I have wanted to touch your lips and hold you tight. You don't know how long I have waited, and I was going to tell you tonight.* All either of them needed to do was lean a little bit towards the other, and that tension, that terrible tension that had been building up for eight years would finally be broken. Just a little lean. Laura readjusted her elbow. It was almost a lean, but it wasn't.

Laura had the tiniest pang of guilt for Alex and Katherine. She couldn't be the one to break the tension. If Trey did, she was sure she would melt into him. But a lifetime of always seeking to do what was right could not be undone by a little taste of cherry chocolate chip ice cream.

Trey didn't move. He looked at her, waiting for something.

So she gave him another spoonful. They let the moment pass. They were friends again, the moment of perfect lust had faded into the next song. Which happened to be *Stockton Gala Days* by 10,000 Maniacs. Trey knew it from the first chord.

"Oh man, this is a great mix," his eyes still twinkling in the reflection of the Christmas lights. "Did you make this for me?"

Laura frowned with her lips and smiled with her eyes.

"I made this for me."

He closed his eyes and sang along. *How I learned to please, to doubt myself in need, you'll never, you'll never know.* Laura sang with him. The ice cream started to melt.

"You like all the music I like," he said, looking back out the window.

"I like all the music I like. You just happen to sometimes have good taste."

"Sometimes?" He looked back at her.

She nodded. "Yeah, that's what I said. Sometimes. Sometimes your taste leaves something to be desired."

Trey snatched the ice cream bowl back and took an enormous overflowing spoonful and jammed it into his mouth.

"Hey!" Laura swung the pillow under her arm at his head, but he ducked it with chipmunk cheeks full of ice cream. She sprang from the bed and tackled him onto the floor. He swallowed the ice cream in one gulp, nearly choking in the process.

"Stop, wait..." he pleaded as he felt a brain freeze coming on. He rolled on his back while she straddled his waist. "Brain freeze!"

"Ha!" She leaned in towards his pained face. "Karma's a bitch."

She stayed motionless on top of him, not sure what to do next. She knew she shouldn't be there, but she also knew she didn't want to move yet. Her brain raced to come up with some reason to stay straddled on his waist, but she couldn't. She was about to get off when he grabbed her right wrist with his left hand.

"Wait," he pleaded. "Don't move."

She stopped and looked at him questioningly.

"It makes my head feel better."

She smacked him in the arm and climbed off him.

"Which head?" she teased as she climbed back on the bed.

The saxophone of the next song made Trey smile as much as Laura's comment.

"*Careless Whisper*?"

"It's a great song."

"Yeah, but, is it?" The song was so popular by then that it had already become a bit of a cliché.

"Yes, it is."

He sincerely listened to the words he knew so well, as if he would hear something he hadn't heard before.

"But," he pressed, "it doesn't fit with the rest of the tape."

"Well..." Laura began while gathering her thoughts. "One, you haven't heard the rest of the tape, and two, it's not for you, it's for me."

"Well yeah," he was unconsciously bobbing his head to the chorus. "But you are sharing it with me."

"I guess that means I like you."

He picked up the pillow and handed it to her. Then he sat on the floor again, with his back to her. She propped herself up on the pillow again, but a little bit closer to him this time. He looked out the window, into the darkness. She could see the chaotically hung lights reflecting in his left eye. She saw his jaw muscle by his ear flex. Trey swallowed.

"Katherine broke up with me."

He sighed and kept looking out the window. She sat up, and almost spoke, but then thought better of it. Then she stood up and walked to the light switch as she felt the need to suddenly see him better. But she stopped before she got to the switch, not entirely sure she was ready for the extra light. She turned around and faced Trey. He was looking at her, but he hadn't moved. He wasn't sad. It was something else. He looked small. And then she realized what it was. He was scared.

Now what Laura probably didn't put together is that Trey was always scared of disappointing everyone. That's the child of an abusive alcoholic. They are scared to deliver bad news, and look to appease people. Trey was no different. He could sense that Laura was upset.

What Trey didn't know is that Laura was upset because she was close to cheating on her boyfriend with someone who she loved, but, in her mind, would have also been cheating on his girlfriend, so there would have been a balance to the whole thing. It wasn't like she plotted all of this, or balanced the cosmic justice of the whole thing beforehand, but she had sensed it as a shared danger. Now the realization that the danger never actually existed for Trey bothered her.

Meanwhile, *I should have known better than to cheat a friend* and saxophone, saxophone, saxophone...

Laura didn't turn the light on, but instead she sat next to Trey, with her back to the bed and facing the window. She patted his right knee with her left hand three times, and he looked at her with a crooked grin.

"Why did she break up with you?" she asked. "Was it because you were bad in bed?"

"Holy shit."

"Seriously though. Did you guys do it?"

Trey nodded. He wanted to ask about her and Alex, but he didn't want to hear the answer. The saxophone had finally ended and the *Careless Whisper* faded out. T'Pau's *China in Your Hand* was the next song.

"Well," he nodded to the stereo. "I didn't see T'Pau coming."

"Maybe you need to start expecting the unexpected," she looked at her feet for a second, needing to take a break from his eyes. "Alex and I had sex."

Trey nodded and took a deep breath.

"Were you listening to T'Pau at the time?"

Laura punched him in the arm.

"So," he said looking back out the window. "I guess... uh... we're even then?"

"Huh?"

"Never mind, that was dumb."

"Oh," she suddenly got what he was getting at. "Hmm. Is everything in your life a competition?"

"Yes."

"That's healthy."

He kept looking out the window. They listened to the song. More saxophone. Trey cleared his throat.

"You know what makes you unbelievable?"

She craned her neck to see his face better, to see if he was being sincere. He turned his head and looked directly into her eyes. Each eye held two individual lights.

"That's random," she said, meeting his gaze and searching back and forth between his eyes, trying to find a crack. "What makes me unbelievable?"

He paused to think one last time before speaking.

"You don't care what other people think."

She laughed.

"Of course I care what other people think."

He leaned back ever so slightly.

"Then you are far braver than I will ever be."

Laura smiled.

"Well, yeah."

Trey fidgeted. He felt like he should be doing something. He thought maybe it was time to leave, but he didn't want to go. Laura noticed he was uncomfortable.

"So," she started. "Why did you come here tonight? Other than to steal my ice cream."

Trey shook his head.

"I don't know entirely."

"Well, why *partially* did you come here?"

Trey thought for a moment.

"Because I wanted to see you. I feel like something wasn't finished from before, I guess, and I feel like we are never alone with each other, and, I don't know. I feel like we needed to be. To like, talk, or just, I don't know, be together without everyone around us all the time."

She waited.

"Or maybe I was just lonely."

T'Pau gave way to a solitary piano and Bob Seger singing *We've Got Tonite.* Trey laughed.

"What?" Laura smiled widely.

Trey shook his head and sang *I know your plans, don't include me, still here we are, both of us lonely...*

"You know," he spoke so low it was almost a whisper. "I'm never going to hear this song and not think of this moment."

Laura slid her hand under his and their fingers interlocked. He looked at her to make sure she was okay. She leaned her head on his shoulder. They stayed that way until the song ended.

The tape had flipped over to side two. *Please, Please, Please, Let Me Get What I Want* by The Smiths set the B side tone.

"I love The Smiths."

Laura lifted her head off his shoulder.

"I know."

He turned his head to look down into her eyes.

"Seriously, did you make this tape for me?"

Laura smiled.

"I told you, I made this tape for me."

He nodded, not entirely believing her. He then looked away and arched his back, stretching.

"Are you uncomfortable?" she asked.

He shrugged.

"Yes. But I don't want to move. I like sitting next to you. It's just... my back hurts."

He hadn't let go of her hand. She slid her fingers free.

"Get on the bed, I'll rub your back."

He looked at her trying to tell if she was joking or not.

"I'm not going to offer twice."

He dove against the bed with such speed and violence that the frame slammed against the wall. He sheepishly apologized. She climbed on top of him, sitting on his lower back, and with her right thumb and forefinger started massaging his upper neck. He closed his eyes. When she got to the base of his neck she used both hands and with her thumbs pushed deeply into his muscles. He released a hollow moan, so she pushed harder.

"Is this too much?"

He kept his eyes closed. "Is it okay if I fall asleep?"

She dug her nail into his skin right beneath his shoulder blade.

"Um, no. After I'm done I expect you to give me a backrub."

The Smiths had ended and *Don't Give Up* by Peter Gabriel was playing. Laura moved further back, until she was sitting on Trey's ass. She slid her hands under his shirt and made small circles with her thumbs just to the right and left of his spine. She had never touched Trey like this before. In fact, she had never touched anyone like this before.

Her bare knees rubbed against his exposed ribs. His back was so muscular that she had to push harder and harder to get the muscles to move. She leaned low and could smell his skin, and for a fleeting moment wanted to kiss his back.

Laura was worn out, both from the massage and the excitement. When the song ended and *All I Want Is You* by U2 started, she collapsed beside him, and he turned to face her. They were so close their noses were almost touching.

"All I want is you..." she paused unnecessarily long. "To give me a backrub."

Trey's heart was racing as he climbed on top of Laura, and he did his best to mimic exactly the same thing she did. He was a little too rough, and his fingers moved too quickly. When he went under the shirt like she had done, Laura was worried he was going to break her in half, so she asked him to just softly scratch her back.

Love Will Tear Us Apart by Joy Division had started by this point, and Laura had closed her eyes. Later, she couldn't be sure she remembered Trey lying next to her, but he did, continuing to softly trace figure eights on her back through *Drive* by The Cars. She didn't see the pain in his face, or hear his voice catch when he sang *Who's gonna hold you down when you shake, who's gonna come around when you break.*

Sometime during Billy Joel's *And So It Goes* he fell asleep with his hand on her spine.

Joyce stood stock still at the open door to Laura's room. She had seen Trey's car in the driveway, and his boots by the door, so she was relieved that both Laura's bedroom door was already open, and that Trey was fully clothed and above the covers. It was almost two in the morning on a school night and she had no idea what to do. Her mind replayed the conversation she had earlier that evening with Laura.

Joyce walked downstairs and opened the front door and then slammed it. She heard muffled voices and a scrambling of movement in Laura's bedroom. Joyce walked into the kitchen to make some tea and pretended she didn't hear footsteps on the stairs or see Trey's tail lights disappear into the Ocean Pines night.

21

Christmas Break

The following week Trey and Katherine ended up getting back together. Like many teenage relationships, it was a convoluted route.

Katherine broke up with Trey the Friday after Thanksgiving, roughly the same time Laura was alone at The Rickety House. Katherine's father convinced her that if she wasn't going to marry Trey, then this was all a dangerous waste of time. It wasn't an easy conversation between the two of them, but Katherine's father exerted a strong influence over his daughter.

Saturday she woke up early and went to the stables. She took Dulcinea into the woods, following an old logging road until she found a stream that she didn't know existed. She dismounted and crouched close to the water, surprised to find it was crystal clear. Dulcinea ate some grass growing near the stream, in the shade provided by a large loblolly pine. Katherine walked around a bit and then lounged beneath an old maple tree that had lost all of its leaves. She was comfortable in the dappled light, the shards of sunlight warming her left leg and right shoulder. She fell asleep under the maple.

When she came home that afternoon her father called her into his library and had her sit down in one of the high back leather chairs by the fireplace.

"Congratulations," he said with a knowing smile.

Katherine shook her head not understanding. He held up an opened envelope. Katherine recognized the Brown University logo.

"You've been accepted early admission," he handed it to her. "And you will have a spot on the equestrian team. You can even bring Dulcinea, I've already worked it out with the university."

Katherine pulled the letter out of the envelope. She felt cold. As she unfolded it and read, she didn't speak.

He waited. He was truly proud, both of his daughter and his alma mater. He inexplicably expected to be thanked. But Katherine just kept looking at the letter.

"Where's mom?" she finally asked.

Her dad shrugged.

"In the kitchen maybe?"

Katherine stood up and walked out without saying anything.

At Sunday dinner the following day, try as she might, Katherine's mother could not get Katherine to debate her father. No matter what topic was broached, no matter what salvo her father attempted, Katherine did not engage. She picked at her food, sipped her water, and started washing the dishes long before anyone else had finished eating.

That evening, while Katherine was sitting on her bed reading the Emily Dickinson poem *Hope is the Thing with Feathers* and listening to "Hymn to Her" by the Pretenders, her mother came into her room and sat on the edge of the bed. She sat there quietly for a moment letting the room settle. Katherine didn't look up from the book.

"You know," her mother said. "He only wants what's best for you."

Katherine flipped a page.

"It's not his life."

"But you're his only daughter."

Katherine slammed her book down on the bed.

"It was my letter to open! Not his. Mine."

She sighed and picked up her book.

"And not for nothing mom, but I wanted you there with me when I opened it."

Her mom smiled and patted Katherine on the foot.

"Oh dear. You know, Brown is his thing. It always has been." She stood up then and walked to the door. "But thank you."

As Katherine sat in her bed, she was not only angry, she was lonely. She blamed her father. Trey was kind. Considerate. And not for nothing, he was sexy. He made her feel good. So that's when she resolved to get him back.

At that very moment, Trey was walking up to Laura's bedroom with a comically large bowl of cherry chocolate chip ice cream.

Both Trey and Laura were nervous that Monday morning. Laura couldn't even look Joyce in the eye at breakfast. On the drive to school Laura thought about how close she came to cheating on Alex, and how she was a terrible person. By the time she got to school, she had reasoned that it was mostly Trey's fault.

When she pulled into her parking spot, Candace was again waiting for her. She didn't wave. She had a serious look on her face. The moment Laura opened the door Candace stepped towards her and said, "We need to talk."

"Candace, you know I hate that phrase."

"Yeah, but that doesn't mean it's not true."

Laura looked at her friend. She was never this serious.

"What's wrong? Are you okay?"

Candace shook her head.

"No, I'm angry. But it's not about me." She lifted her hand and beckoned to Tyrone, who was standing on the sidewalk by the school, with his hands in his pockets and looking at the ground. He walked over and nodded hello to Laura.

"Tell her. Tell her what you just told me," Candace demanded.

"Um... okay, uh, you know my older brother Lamont? He's a senior at Goucher."

Laura shook her head indicating that she didn't know him.

"Well, he was home for Thanksgiving and... well, he smokes weed and when he's home he buys his weed from this guy named Greg who goes to UMES. They went to school together, like high school not college."

"Ty!" Candace broke in. "Get to the point!"

"Right, sorry. So, Greg lives with this girl named Kim, who goes to UMES too, but they're not together because Greg is dating a girl named Brandi who is in Pittsburgh or Philly or something. Anyway, my brother says this girl Kim is kinda hot and so he was wondering if she was available, but Greg says she's robbing the cradle with this high school kid named Alex from Snow Hill."

Laura could feel a pain twist in her stomach. She thought for a second she was going to get sick. But she recovered.

"There's got to be more than one high school guy in Snow Hill named Alex," Laura tried.

"That's what I said too, but..." Candace said, prompting her boyfriend to finish.

"Yeah, except Lamont was there buying weed last night, and he was like hanging out. He saw Alex. He described him to me. It's your Alex. He even showed Lamont his notebook, with like comic characters, you know, that he shows everyone. It's your Alex for sure."

"I'm so sorry," Candace said, putting her hand on Laura's shoulder. "Tell me what you want me to do."

Laura's eyes went wide and darted back and forth. She started walking towards school. Her head was shaking ever so slightly. Thoughts flew so fast she couldn't grasp any. Candace and Tyrone walked with her.

"He's not my Alex anymore," Laura said as they opened the doors to the school.

Laura avoided Trey all day. After first period she went to Mrs. Pruitt's office and said she didn't feel well. Mrs. Pruitt used her palm to take her temperature.

"You don't feel warm," Mrs. Pruitt said. "Do you have a test or a quiz now?"

"Study Hall."

Mrs. Pruitt sighed and opened the door to her sick room. She left the lights off. "One hour, and then go back to class."

Laura looked at Mrs. Pruitt with damp eyes. She wanted to hug her. Mrs. Pruitt nodded, and closed the door behind her, leaving her in darkness. She stayed there until after morning break. She was in a daze through her other classes and ate lunch alone in her car.

Trey looked for Laura at lunch. Instead he found Katherine, who was taping a picture of Niki Taylor to his locker.

"What are you doing?" he asked with a hint of annoyance in his voice.

"Apologizing," Katherine said sheepishly.

Laura skipped basketball practice and drove to the Cook farm. Alex was tossing a football with Timmy when she drove down the driveway. He was surprised.

"Laura!" Timmy exclaimed and ran right up to her but stopped just short of hugging her. "Watch what I can do!"

He kicked the ball which bounced about seven feet in front of him and then he chased it while explaining that wasn't what he was trying to do. Alex was studying Laura's body language and that plus her showing up out of the blue confirmed to him that something was wrong.

"That's great Timmy," Alex said calmly. "Hey buddy, can you go inside? I have to talk to Laura."

Timmy waved goodbye three times and then went inside.

"So, what's up?" Alex asked.

"Who the fuck is Kim?"

Alex's eyes got wide with surprise. Laura knew at that minute. She didn't even wait for him to respond. She turned to go back to her car. "Fuck you!"

"No wait," Alex said, chasing after her. "Wait, listen, I don't..."

But Alex stopped. He had nothing to say. He was wrong and he knew it. He silently shook his head.

"What the fuck could you say to me right now?"

Alex shrugged.

"You're right. I am sorry. But you know what, you would have left me eventually for Trey anyway, so whatever."

And Alex turned and walked back to his house. Laura was purple with rage. She got in her car, slammed the door and screamed.

After basketball practice Trey looked for Laura, in the parking lot, but she wasn't there. Instead, he saw Katherine leaning against the hood of his car with a bag of cheeseburgers and fries and a sly smile on her lips.

***

Laura spent the next week licking her wounds. She didn't speak to anyone on Monday night and stayed home from school on Tuesday. Tuesday night Candace called her and told her Trey and Katherine looked like they were back together. Laura tasted bile and got off the phone.

Wednesday she went back to school, and when she saw Trey and Katherine laughing, it felt like they were laughing at her.

In December, everything seemed to be rushed. Dolores had reopened Buck's and hired Laura as a hostess and waitress. Between work and basketball she never had a free moment.

Basketball allowed Laura to lean into her anger. This was the time period when she would make a sound that was akin to a growl when she got a rebound. It scared the hell out of the other team, and even some of her own teammates. While Candace was the better basketball player, people talked about Laura. Some said it was performative, others said it was frightening. All agreed it wasn't "ladylike."

About a week before Christmas Trey was kicked off the basketball team. He got into a fight at a game down at Chincoteague, which honestly was nothing new, there were fights there all the time. One of the opposing team's players called his mother a whore in Spanish, and since Trey was fluent in Spanish, they decided to settle their dispute with fisticuffs. In the melee, Trey accidently broke the nose of the referee, and therefore was kicked off the team.

Trey took advantage of the newfound free evenings to work with his mother at Buck's Tavern.

Laura and Trey hadn't been speaking much since they fell asleep in Laura's bed. They waited too long, and then it was awkward, and then Katherine was there. Working together eased them back into familiarity.

Jessica came home for the holidays and finally remembered to bring some grunge music with her. Nirvana for Laura and Pearl Jam for Trey. Joyce bought Laura a CD player for Christmas, and presented her with her first CD, Enya's *Shepherd Moons*.

The week after Christmas, Katherine's family went skiing, and Trey was not invited. Katherine's father was starting to like Trey less and less, especially after he got kicked off the basketball team. He was concerned about Trey continuing the cycle of violence, and he never really liked Trey that much anyway. He couldn't stop his daughter from dating him, but he certainly wasn't going to invite him on the ski trip. In fact, Trey hadn't been asked back to Sunday Dinner.

Joyce took one of the mornings of Christmas break to talk to Laura about birth control. It was an awkward conversation, and it was pretty raw for Laura, as she had recently broken up with the only person she had ever had sex with. Laura told her mom that she would make every boy wear a condom if her mom promised to never talk to her about this again. Her mom sensed that wasn't true, but backed off for the time being. At least there was no yelling, just a lot of "eeew! Mom!" and stuff like that.

Two days before the new year, Laura came home from shopping with Candace to find her mother in the kitchen cooking.

"Smells good!" Laura said as she lifted the lid of the pot.

"I'm making chicken and dumplings for dinner tonight. It's Bubby's favorite."

"Oh la la," Laura said sarcastically.

Chicken and dumplings on the Eastern Shore were made with "slippery" dumplings, which are basically large flat noodles, about the width of a lasagna noodle. It's a hearty, stick-to-your-bones type of cuisine.

"I invited Trey to dinner," her mother said nonchalantly.

Laura's eyes got wide.

"Why?"

"He called for you earlier. I said you were out, but that he should come to dinner. They should be here soon."

Laura disappeared from the kitchen, emerging a minute later with her orange sweater and favorite pair of jeans. Joyce noticed out of the corner of her eye and smiled.

Trey and Bubby arrived at the exact same time. Neither knew the other was coming.

"You know I heard about the fight down at Chincoteague," Bubby said as Joyce was transferring the contents of the pot into a serving dish. "Damn shame if you ask me. Chincoteague has been pulling the same shit since I was in school, probably even before. Just bad luck that Ben stuck his nose in there I guess."

Bubby laughed as if everyone knew who Ben was. He was the ref who got his nose broken.

"How'd the fight start anyway?"

"I'd rather not say."

"One of their players called Dolores a whore," Laura said as if she was commenting on the weather. Joyce gasped at the language. Bubby's eyes got wide and then he slapped Trey on the back.

"Good for you son. Good for you."

It was not lost on Trey that this was the first time a man had called him son and meant it as a complement.

After dinner, Bubby and Joyce went for a "drive." Trey and Laura did the dishes together in the kitchen.

"Sheriff Davis seems nice," Trey remarked as they finished the dishes.

"Do you think it's weird that they ate dinner here and now they are driving to his house to have sex?"

Trey burst out laughing.

"I don't think you should be thinking about that," he said through the chuckles.

"But I mean, come on. They are... right?"

"Probably."

Laura sighed. She stood there looking at Trey, waiting for something that wasn't going to happen. She was standing on a precipice and she knew it. It had been a good night. She liked having him as a friend, it was better than not having him in her life.

"My mom got me a cd player for Christmas. She gave me Enya's *Shepherd Moons*. I think because I was listening to Sinead O'Conner once, she thinks I'm into Irish music or something."

"You like U2," he said.

"I do."

"I love U2."

"Say that again," she said smiling.

"What? I love U2."

She smiled. He wasn't understanding what he was saying to her. She blushed a little.

"Come on," she said walking out of the kitchen and upstairs. "Let's go listen to Enya."

Laura turned off all the lights in the house other than the Christmas lights. The soft glow was a perfect companion to Enya. Trey was standing up, not sure if he should sit on the floor or the bed. Laura laid on the bed and cleared her throat.

"I made you dinner, you give me a backrub."

Trey smiled and climbed on top of her. Laura liked being touched again, as it had been a month since a boy had touched her. But Trey was as bad at the massage as he was the time before. After about a minute she told him to stop and lay down. She climbed on top of him.

"See, you need to go slow," she said as she pressed into his shoulders with her thumb. "The slower the better. Sometimes."

"That feels nice," Trey said, closing his eyes.

"No no no, I was just showing you. Get up!"

They switched places again. Trey started, slower this time.

"Honestly," he began earnestly. "I think the problem is this sweater. It's hard for me to get a real grip."

Laura turned to face him, and narrowed her eyes. After pausing for a moment she sat up and pulled her sweater off. She was only wearing her bra underneath. It was pink, and she had put it on when she put on the sweater. Then she laid back down. Trey swallowed hard and then continued the massage on her bare skin.

"Honestly," he said with a smile in his voice. "I think the problem is these bra straps."

"Nice try."

After a half hour Trey collapsed on the bed exhausted. He had done a much better job this time, but she was too tired to return the favor. She turned on her side and faced him, her nose only a few inches from his own. She reached behind him with her right hand and softly rubbed his neck muscles in slow counter clockwise circles. He closed his eyes. She leaned even closer so that their noses were touching, and she could feel his rhythmic breath on her lips. With her right pointer finger she delicately caressed his earlobe, using all of her willpower to fight the urge to kiss him while he slept.

22

Alive

When school started a few days later, Trey seemed distant. Laura mistook his distance for something she had done.

That January Trey experienced what we could call today either clinical depression or major depressive disorder. He couldn't sleep at night. He started missing days of school, and days he did show up he fell asleep in class. He lost his appetite, and when he did eat, he ate trash. He became antisocial, stopped doing his homework entirely, and watched too much television. He even drove his car into a ditch, probably accidentally, but luckily, other than some whiplash, wasn't really hurt.

It seemed to come on suddenly, and no one knew what was happening to/in Trey, not even Trey himself. There was a combination of lots of things at work here. First, Trey's childhood was littered with abuse. Second, he likely was genetically predisposed to depression as his father was bipolar at best, and probably schizophrenic, though both went undiagnosed. Third, the crazy hormonal changes natural in teens mixed with lack of sunlight and vitamin D might have contributed to seasonal affective disorder. Fourth, his diet got much worse, now that his mom wasn't around to cook for him, and when he ate at the bar it was usually fried cheese. Fifth, he was super confused and conflicted about his emotions towards Laura and Katherine. And finally, his lack of exercise after being kicked off the basketball team probably threw off his serotonin, dopamine, and cortisol levels. Combined with the fact that Buck's place was so quiet in January that by the end of the month he was only working one shift a week, put him in the absolute toilet, moodwise.

Laura, however, was convinced that Trey was acting weird towards her because of something she had done. While other people noticed the change, no one thought it was depression, or even had an understanding of what depression was. "Down in the dumps" was as close as anyone would get to understanding. Though at lunch one day Candace pulled Laura aside and asked her if something had happened to Trey.

"I don't know," she responded. "I think he's being a huge weirdo about nothing."

"About what?" Candace pressed.

Laura sighed.

"We fell asleep together like twice and..."

"You what?!"

"Shhh." Laura tried to quiet her. Luckily the din of the lunchroom prevented anyone from hearing. "Look, I might have just touched his ear, by mistake, while he was sleeping."

"Where?"

"Right here," Laura showed Candace on her ear.

"No," she said laughing. "Where were you when he fell asleep?"

"In... uh... my bed."

Candace raised her eyebrows and smiled. She didn't say anything hoping for more details.

"It's not a thing, he's just being weird."

"Uh huh."

Katherine broke up with him twice in January, but both times they got back together the following week. Both breakups seemed like they didn't even phase Trey, which frustrated Katherine even more. In Katherine's defense, she had no experience with depression at all. It just didn't run in her family. Depression was so alien to her that even with a college course or two about psychology she likely wouldn't have recognized it in Trey. She thought he was starting to fall out of love with her, and so she vacillated between breaking up with him and doubling down on her efforts to please him, which created more tension and stress in his life.

Dolores didn't notice because Trey seemed fine at work. When he had tasks to do he handled them. He also knew how to fit in at a restaurant, laughing when everyone else laughed, or pretending to be busy when he didn't feel like laughing. So his depression went mostly unnoticed by those around him, or, if not entirely unnoticed, then misdiagnosed.

But Trey was in a very, very dark place. Crashing his car might well have been the precursor to something far more tragic if not for Pearl Jam and their debut album, *Ten*.

It was on one Thursday afternoon in late January. Trey was looking at a pile of homework that needed to be completed if he had any chance to play lacrosse that spring. He couldn't find the strength to pick up a single piece of paper. Instead, he finally popped in the tape Jessica had given him at Christmas, closed his eyes and listened. The third song, "Alive," might have saved Trey's life.

Whatever one thinks "Alive" is about, they are correct. But for Trey, that song was written about him. He listened to the full album over and over again, but every time he got to "Alive" he played it at least twice. Had it been a compact disk he could have put it on repeat, but it was a tape. Sometimes he could manage himself to get up and rewind the tape, sometimes he couldn't. But he always played it at least twice.

The second time he heard the song he sang along to the chorus. He didn't understand all the different versus, but he didn't need to. It was the third verse that held him down, that tethered him to this plane of existence and gave him the space to explore the thoughts of destruction while in the safety of an ocean of sound. That's the verse that has the lines:

You're still alive, she said
Oh, and do I deserve to be

Is that the question
And if so... if so... who answers?

Trey sang it loud. He sang it through tears. He sang it instead of doing his homework, instead of watching television, instead of driving his car into another ditch. Trey sang it until his throat was raw and his body was exhausted. And then he finally slept.

One song did not fix Trey, and lots of other factors contributed to him "turning it around." One of them was his lacrosse goalie, Scott, who asked him to shoot on him a couple days a week.

Another was Katherine, who drove him home after school while his car was being repaired after the "accident." She made a detour on the way and took him to the stables and taught him to ride a horse. He was not good at riding, but learning any new skill really helps combat depression, and the connection with those magnificent creatures calmed much of Trey's misplaced rage.

Once he got his car back from the shop he started lifting weights, jumping rope, and running again, and by Valentine's Day he had finally made up most of his missed assignments and gotten his grades back to acceptable levels. The days were getting longer. Dolores, sick of eating like crap as well, started doing family dinners at Buck's that were much healthier than the food they had on the menu.

Trey wasn't healed. In fact, he would go on to deal with depression occasionally for most of his life. But in his darkest moment, one song helped drag him back into the light. Or maybe, it just walked beside him through the darkness.

23

The Winter

This was the season Laura learned to love the ocean.

While everyone in her life was busy with their own stories, Laura was left alone. Trey was with Katherine or his depression, Candace was with Tyrone, Joyce was with Bubby, and Dolores was at Buck's. So Laura spent many nights after basketball wandering in solitude. There are hundreds of backroads in Delmarva to explore, but since the winter sun set so early, those dark roads and the fields that flanked them look awfully similar at night. But Ocean City—with its yellow blinking lights, its closed hotels, and its dark condo windows facing the lonely ocean—was peculiar and forsaken, and somehow mysterious.

The story of the winter at the seaside is in some ways unlike any other story told. For when you travel inland, far from the relentless tides and infinite horizons of the ocean, winter is a time of slumber, hibernation, and lifelessness. There is almost a sterility to the winter air in these landlocked locations, especially in the northern reaches, where snow and ice blanket the landscape and the wind becomes heartless and cruel.

That sterility never exists by the ocean. No matter how cold the air, no matter how violent the wind, one can always smell life. That is the gift of the sea.

It is said that we are drawn to the sea because it holds the memory of our beginnings. Akin to staring into a fire, one can stare at the ocean endlessly, for it is like looking back into the past. Not only at your own life's history but all the countless lives that ever needed to thrive in order for you to exist. But Laura didn't believe that.

She found memory in things like the frozen pond, or the slumbering field where the once soft and fertile earth has turned to a massive lifeless brick. Memories were in the visions of the hibernating animals who dreamt of vernal sunshine, gathering streams, and golden shoots of days gone by. Memories were for candlelit nights gathered around a hearth sharing tales of fiction and family.

But she found no memory in the sea. The sea never stopped living long enough to remember. For Laura, a child of the Eastern Shore, the sea created the day. She never paused, she never hid, she never slumbered. She just continued to breathe.

Laura would often find herself on a dark winter beach, walking with the resonating crash of the waves meeting their termination. The frigid night wind off the ocean would be so unkind to her face and fingers, but the sound, that music that is unique to the sea, always bathed her in reassurance that there was something more that existed—somewhere else for her—and if she kept walking, perhaps she would find it.

After a particular frigid late-January walk Laura went into Buck's to warm up and see Dolores. She found her surrogate mother working by herself on the kitchen line. Her scheduled cook had pulled a "no show." Laura did what she had always done, threw on an apron and asked how she could help. She worked the fryers while Dolores manned the grill and flattop, and together they got out the three dozen or so meals without too much stress. It was, after all, just a weeknight in January, but both of them were figuring it out as they went along.

Once a rhythm was established, Laura realized she was having fun. Working the fryers was easy, hot, and loud. There was something so satisfying about dropping a basket of frozen food into the impossibly hot grease and hearing the explosion of sound from the diametrical forces.

When all the tickets were done, Dolores made some coffee and they sat at the bar.

"Would it be crazy," Laura asked after they both had sipped their coffee twice in silence, "if I worked in the kitchen a couple of nights a week?"

Dolores smiled and looked at Laura, thinking before she spoke.

"You are a pretty girl with a warm personality. You will make so much more money in tips from old men," and then Dolores raised one eyebrow. "And even young men."

Laura rolled her eyes.

"But I like cooking."

"I like cooking too! But line cooks... how do I say this... it's less cooking than it is organized insanity. Line cooks are a different species."

Laura laughed.

"You mean to say they aren't human?"

Dolores didn't answer, as she pondered the question. Laura continued.

"How about I just try it, like one day a week. That's all, just working the fryers or something. I just want to try it."

Dolores sighed. She knew that Laura would be worth much more to the restaurant if she was working in the front of the house, but at the same time, she couldn't say no to Laura. Especially because it wasn't fair that she was a pretty girl, and who was to say that she always would be. It wouldn't be fair for Dolores to deny her this, so she capitulated.

This is why on Friday, February 14th, 1992, at ten PM Laura walked out of the kitchen at Buck's smelling of onion rings, French fries, and sweat. Her hair, which had spent the shift under a hat, was partially matted to her head, and she could feel the grease on her forearms and neck. She had a cup of coffee in one hand and a plate of mozzarella sticks in the other, and was backing through the door on her way to the staff booth to eat her post shift meal. When she spun one hundred and eighty degrees to face forward again she locked eyes with Trey and Katherine, dressed semi-formally as if they had been to a dance. They had, in fact, been at a party at the home of a friend of Katherine's parents earlier that evening. They had decided to go to Buck's because Katherine wanted to get away from her parents but didn't want to go to Trey's house, because she wasn't in the mood to have sex, and she knew he would expect that, being Valentine's Day and all.

Laura sighed, knowing she must have looked and smelled terrible. Still, she walked up to them and held out her plate.

"Mozzarella stick?" she offered.

Trey took one. Katherine politely shook her head, and took a small step backwards.

"I need to sit down before I collapse," Laura said, smiling at them and walking away to the staff booth.

She sat in the booth, her back to the wall, her legs on the bench and crossed at the ankles. She took one bite of the mozzarella sticks but then realized she didn't want them. She drank her coffee and looked around the restaurant at all the couples squeezing in a last drink or two before heading home to do whatever they planned to do on this official day of romance.

She thought about Trey, and how it had been more than a month since they had spoken. They never joked around anymore, they never flirted, they never even spoke. She missed her friend. She was lonely.

She made a point not to look at Trey and Katherine. She did see Trey sneak into the service bar and make a gin and tonic for Katherine. Neither of them acknowledged Laura again that night. Laura finished her coffee and went home.

Laura saw a note from her mother on the refrigerator that read, *Staying at Bubby's tonight. I love you.*

She went upstairs, undressed, and showered for the better part of a half hour before she was sure all the grease was off her. By the time she got out of the shower it was almost midnight. She brushed her hair, and looked at her pajamas, but didn't put them on. Instead, she put on a pair of jeans and her orange sweater. She looked in the mirror. No rational thought came to her mind. She looked at herself, smiled, nodded, and walked down the stairs and out the door.

She stood by her car, frozen in a minute of indecision. The full moon reflected in her windshield. She studied the image and watched as a cloud slowly sailed past. She reached out to try to touch it, but her shadow made it disappear. She sighed a small laugh at herself and looked down at the dappled moonlight in the driveway, and on the hard winter soil surrounding it. She looked at her mother's garden and thought how sad it was that the dead or slumbering plants covered in fallen leaves couldn't feel this cold light. Reflections were pale and without heat. Without life.

She missed her friend, and she wanted him back. *Just as a friend*, she told herself. She needed him. But going over there at midnight was not the solution. That would have been selfish. Because what if something else happened? The last two times they were together and alone, something almost happened. If she went over there at that moment, she was going over there to make Trey a cheater. And she hated cheaters.

It wasn't right. She told herself it wasn't fair to Katherine as she walked back towards the house. But she knew, had she gone to Trey's house that night it wouldn't have been fair to anyone.

She got undressed and slept naked and alone.

24

Breakfast

The following morning Laura woke up at dawn, waited about fifteen minutes, and then called Trey and woke him up. She asked him if she could buy him breakfast. She said she would drive and made a joke that didn't land about wanting to get to the restaurant alive.

The talk couldn't have been smaller on the ride to English's. Trey was a little tired but played it up more than he was, as teenagers are sometimes so fond of doing. Laura mentioned the weather. It was a cold, gray morning with an occasional misty rain. Laura asked about Katherine, Trey responded generically with a "she's good."

It was quiet in the non-smoking section of the restaurant, which relieved Laura. Trey ordered the scrapple and eggs. Laura just got coffee. Trey raised his eyebrow at that, he had never known Laura not to eat. She couldn't explain it, but she had lost her appetite.

It was between the first coffees and the food that Laura started to really talk.

"Are you avoiding me?"

Trey looked confused. "What do you mean?"

Laura was frustrated but did her best not to show it.

"I mean we haven't spoken since Christmas."

The words hung between them. Trey hadn't realized that they hadn't spoken since Christmas, but then again, he hadn't done much since Christmas.

"I didn't..." Trey sighed. "I didn't even realize..."

Trey stopped talking when he saw Laura's face. It wasn't a hard emotion to read. Trey was very, very good at noticing other people's feelings. It's a trait you pick up when you are trying not to get hit by someone you live with who is twice your size. But even someone who was bad at reading feelings would be able to pick this one out of a lineup. It was anger.

Laura would have left at that moment if they didn't drive together. She would have thrown ten dollars on the table and stormed out. She really wanted to, but she didn't want Dolores to have to wake up and come get Trey, or have Katherine find out what happened. So she just seethed.

"Look," Trey tried to defuse the bomb. "I don't know what's going on with me, but... I just don't know."

"Did you really not notice we haven't spoken in almost two months?"

"No, I mean, I knew, like, that we hadn't spoken in a while and all, I just didn't realize how... like... how long it had like been, I guess. You know?"

Laura stayed silent. The waitress brought over Trey's food. He kept looking at Laura, but Laura thanked the waitress and asked for more coffee. The innocent bystander released a little of the pressure that had been building in her.

Laura looked at the coffee cup while she poured the milk and sugar. She could feel Trey looking at her. He hadn't picked up his fork. He hadn't moved.

"Eat your food."

Trey didn't move. He kept looking at Laura. She stirred her coffee very slowly, not looking at Trey. Finally, while still looking at her coffee, she spoke.

"Was it the ear thing?"

Trey tilted his head a little to the left, like a confused dog.

"What ear thing?"

Laura hadn't thought through this scenario. She had convinced herself the only reason Trey had to act weird around her was because she caressed his ear. She shook her head.

"Never mind."

Her eyes went up from her coffee to meet his. He was confused. Not confident, not teasing, just confused, and a little lost.

"I have no idea what you are talking about."

"Eat your eggs."

Trey picked up his fork and slowly put a bite of scrapple into his mouth while stealing glances at Laura. It was almost as if a small part of him thought he was about to be poisoned. He chewed slowly and carefully. Laura shook her head.

"Why are you acting so weird?" she pressed.

Trey swallowed. "I guess because I'm afraid of you?"

Laura tried and failed to prevent a smile from cracking her frown.

"I mean for the last two months. Not just right now."

Trey sighed. "I don't know."

"But you admit you are acting weird towards me, right?"

Trey shrugged. "I mean, I guess. But it's not just you."

"Then what is it?"

Trey shook his head. He couldn't answer even if he wanted to. But he didn't want to. He was getting frustrated. Laura waited for him to answer, but he stayed silent. The air was heavy between them. Laura broke first.

"So it's nothing I did?" she asked.

"No! I swear. I don't know what it is, I just don't feel right... I guess. I don't know."

Laura picked up his fork and took a bite of his scrapple. He shrugged with his palms up in mock protest.

"What? You weren't eating it."

Trey snatched his fork back. "I was worried it was poisoned."

Laura sipped her coffee and looked closely at Trey. She could tell there was something physically wrong with him. He looked off. Sallow, and almost shrunken. He had only started to hit the weights that week and the small amount of work he had put in wasn't showing yet. And he hadn't slept well the night before. Things were tense that week with Katherine, but he didn't want to tell Laura.

"So," Laura sipped her coffee for a dramatic pause. "You aren't actually avoiding me?"

"Not at all."

Laura nodded and put her coffee cup down.

"Then you are okay with me calling you? Just to talk?"

"Anytime."

Laura had both hands on her coffee cup and looked at it in her hands. She didn't want to meet his eyes.

"Because I wanted to talk to you last night," she said, taking a deep breath. "But it was late and I thought it would have been wrong... I mean, it was like midnight by the time I got all the grease off me. The fryer station is pretty gross."

Trey nodded, taking her word for it.

"Yeah, even at midnight," he took a bite and offered his fork to Laura. She shook her head no, and then stole a quarter of his toast. "Honestly, midnight is a good time to talk, I'm up anyway, and my mom is never home until like 2 AM. And Katherine likes to be home by 11. She likes her sleep."

He looked at her. She opened up a strawberry jam packet and dipped the toast straight in it since she didn't have a knife.

"Call me tonight?" he asked.

"Okay."

And that's how it came to be that almost every night Laura would call Trey, sometimes at midnight, sometimes earlier, and they would talk about absolutely nothing for hours, often falling asleep together on the phone.

This annoyed Joyce to no end, so after a week she got Laura her own dedicated phone line, which was a pretty big deal. It even had call-waiting for when Candace or Jessica wanted to talk to her too.

Somehow it got around school that Laura and Trey fell asleep together every night on the phone. The Trey/Laura secret relationship rumor was rekindled. It became so prevalent that on St Patrick's Day, Tuesday March 17th, Katherine heard the rumor from two different people that belonged to two vastly different social groups.

That day happened to be the first lacrosse game of the season for both Trey and Laura. Laura had three goals and four assists. Trey scored eight goals, breaking the school's single game record. It was in the paper, and he even got coverage on the local nightly news. Laura's game wasn't mentioned.

After the game, Trey and Katherine went to Boomers for cheeseburgers with a few of his teammates and their girlfriends. Katherine was quiet until they were in the parking lot after dinner. She asked him to sit in her car with her so they could talk. Trey was still smiling from the game.

"Trey, I'm only going to ask you this once," she said. He nodded along. "Are you and Laura Byrne having an affair."

Trey laughed. It was ill-timed, but he thought her use of the term *affair* for a high school relationship was funny.

"No," he said while trying to stifle his laugh.

"Do you spend every single night talking on the phone with her? Do you fall asleep together on the phone?"

Trey shrugged.

"Yeah, sometimes. She's my best friend, we talk, that's it."

Katherine shook her head.

"That's not it. It never is."

"What?"

"Trey Buckingham, if you want to be with me, you have to stop talking with her. Do you understand?"

Trey nodded. He was sad. He really did love Katherine. There was a long pause while he thought.

"Yeah, I do." He opened the car door. "Goodbye Katherine."

25

Lacrosse Season

Trey was worked up. He hated having to choose between his girlfriend and his best friend. Even more so, he despised being accused of something he didn't do. His father did that. By the time he got into his car he felt real rage. He cranked Pearl Jam as loud as his stereo allowed. He didn't even get out of the parking lot before he started punching his steering wheel. He hit it so hard and often that he knocked it back to how it was before the accident.

But then something sort of magical happened. After a couple of songs, the rage morphed into another feeling. Pride. He was proud of himself for standing up for his friend, and not for nothing, himself. At that moment he knew for certain he had done the right thing in breaking up with Katherine. He was energized. And, not for nothing, about ninety minutes prior he had completed the best individual lacrosse game anyone that had ever gone to his school had ever played.

So he took his energized self over to Laura's house. Laura answered the door with wet hair and in red and black checkered flannel pajamas, and let Trey inside. The house still smelled of corned beef and cabbage, but dinner was long since eaten and the leftovers stored away. Joyce was reading on the couch in the living room. She looked up.

"Oh Trey," she smiled, genuinely pleased to see him. "How did the game go?"

Trey was looking at Laura not Joyce.

"We won," he said, offering no other details. Laura grabbed his shirt and pulled him out of the room and up to her bedroom.

"That's nice," Joyce said, looking back at her book.

A moment later she realized what had just happened. Her daughter had taken a boy upstairs. Wordlessly pulling him by his clothes. She put her book down and looked around the room in a confused state. *Did I see what I thought I saw?* She stood up to go upstairs to check on them, and then stopped. Bubby's wisdom rattled around in her brain. *It's better they were in her house than off drinking and driving.* She sat down again. She read one more page before she stood up a second time. *Maybe I'll just ask her to keep her door open? But then they will leave. And probably go do drugs.* She sat back down again, and reread the same page. She put her book down and stared straight ahead. *Maybe I'll go upstairs, and they can come down here?* She stood up again. But then she would need to come down to disturb them if she wanted to be sure they weren't doing anything inappropriate, and her stairs creaked, so they would hear her coming anyway. She put down the book, made a cup of tea, and then stared out the window into the darkness of the Ocean Pines night, and the abyss of the struggle of being a single parent to a teenage girl.

Laura had shut the door but not locked it. She put on *Shepherd Moons.* She plugged in the Christmas lights. She didn't know why Trey was there, but she could see he was invigorated. Or better yet, enthused. Prior to the word being co-opted by coaches, teachers, and political pundits, the actual original meaning of the word "enthusiasm" was inspiration or possession by a god. That was how Trey looked. Part man, part god. For the first time in a while he was not coming to Laura in a broken, sad, or depressed state. He was bigger, inflated, and so very alive.

He told her about the talk in the car, and the ultimatum. He told her how Katherine called it an "affair" and how he stood up for Laura, how he said goodbye all cool and collected, and how he slammed the door while Katherine stared at him with her mouth agape. Laura's heart swelled. She wanted to kiss him. She almost did in fact, but he then said one thing that tripped her up.

"I'm not going to let anyone or anything come between me and my best friend."

They were best friends. For the last month they had spoken every night on the phone, falling asleep together, dreaming together. What would happen if she kissed him now?

So she hugged him. He hugged her back. They held the hug for a long time. She broke the hug. He asked about her game. She showed him a bruise on her thigh. She had to pull down her pajama bottoms so he could see. She was wearing teal underwear. He asked if she had any other bruises to show him. She laughed a wicked laugh.

She wanted to take off her clothes and have him take off his. But instead she grabbed his hands and placed them on her shoulders, and laid down on the bed, asking for a massage without uttering a word. He complied. In her mind, she repeated the same mantra over and over. *We're best friends, we're just friends, we're best friends, we're just friends, we're best friends...*

He slid his hands under her pajama top, along her spine, halfway to her neck. She wasn't wearing a bra. While still laying on her stomach, she pulled her top up so it exposed most of her back. He focused on one shoulder blade at a time, and then both together, with pressure in the middle of her back, and getting more gentle as his hand descended to her side. His powerful hands squeezed the tension out of every secret muscle in her back, while his fingertips occasionally brushed her ribs, stomach, and the sides of her breasts. His hands shook a little with excitement. She shivered, and more than once breathed dramatically. Eventually the budding ecstasy melted into a more relaxed comfort. Enya sang them one sonorous love song after another, soothing them into a different state, that of peace, and calm.

Exhaustion finally hit Trey. It had been too much for one day. He collapsed on the bed. She asked him if he wanted a massage. He said sure. She didn't move but rubbed his neck with her thumb and forefinger softly for about seven seconds and then patted him on the shoulder. He laughed quietly and fell asleep. She gently scratched his shoulder with her fingertips, back and forth softly and slowly, like a boat rocking on Enya's peaceful Irish sea.

Joyce knocked on the door, offering to make them some tea. Laura chuckled and opened it, wanting to reassure her mother that they were both fully clothed.

Her mother gave her a knowing look.

"We're just friends," Laura whispered.

Joyce looked past her at Trey who was asleep in the bed.

"He had a long day," Laura tried to explain. Joyce gave her a questioning look.

"What?" Laura said. "Where's my tea?"

26

Fools

For a week after that night, Laura and Trey spent every evening together, at one of their houses, in one of their beds, with their hands all over each other, but somehow still never crossing the line of their lips touching. It was a strange time in an unusual relationship. The tension that was so present when they first shared a bed became relaxed, and they became more and more comfortable touching one another. Backrubs were expected, and if not offered, demanded.

Katherine had inadvertently brought them together in a way that neither Trey nor Laura anticipated. Because of her, these lifelong friends became friends who fought for one another, who sacrificed something in their life for the other, who slept together, who touched one another, and who spent every waking moment together. This bond became very strong. And yet, technically they had not crossed the line into lovers.

Trey didn't even give it a second thought. He liked the relationship. If Laura wanted to take it further, he would go with her, and if she wanted to keep it the same, he was happy. He needed Laura in his life, and was willing to have her in whatever way she chose.

Laura, on the other hand, was probably giving it too much thought. Each night she thought that would be the night they would kiss, and yet each night she found a reason not to.

It was Wednesday April 1st when things got really, really confusing. The date was mostly inconsequential, Gen X wasn't really into April Fool's Day or pranks the way Boomers or Millennials were. What was far more important than the date was the weather. It was a dark gray morning, with low fast moving clouds and occasional wind gusts promising quite the storm. A nor'easter was settling in, and to Delmarva that meant at least one solid day of rain, if not three. Though it hadn't started raining yet.

***

When Trey woke up on April 1st, he was neither aware of the day nor date. He hadn't slept well. He had a nightmare about his father killing his mother and woke up in a sweat. Before his shower he checked on his mom, who was sleeping soundly and unmurdered.

When he got to school he opened his locker and a glossy page from a magazine fell out. He picked it up and looked at it. It was Niki Taylor, in a black and white polkadot bikini standing in the water at a beach, with a caption bubble drawn in orange highlighter that read *We should talk*. Trey looked around. He knew it was from Katherine, but she wasn't there. He didn't see her before the bell rang. In fact, he didn't see her until lunch.

***

For Katherine's part of this tale, we actually have to go back to the evening of March 31st. Katherine had rode Dulcinea that afternoon, ate dinner with her parents, took a long bath, and then spent the evening reading a book. For seniors at this time of year, schoolwork was unnecessary, and she was uncharacteristically listless and unfocused.

She missed Trey terribly. While she was certain that she had made a mistake trying to get between him and Laura, she still blamed Laura. She was convinced Laura was duplicitous, plotted against her, and was by now having sex with Trey.

It was about nine PM when the phone rang. Chuckie Burbage had heard that she had broken up with Trey, and said he was calling "just to talk." Chuckie probably didn't care at all why she broke up with Trey, but he wanted to sound like he did, so he asked her, and she explained that it was because he was spending so much time with Laura. Which is when Chuckie started to laugh that forced, laughing-too-hard fake laugh that frat boys do.

"What?" Katherine asked, annoyed. "Why is that funny?"

"I'm sorry," Chuckie pretended like he was trying to catch his breath or reel-in his fake laughter. "You are talking about Laura Byrne, right?"

"Yeah."

"She's a carpet muncher."

Katherine thought she heard something else. She asked Chuckie to repeat it.

"She's a dyke. You seriously don't know that?"

"She is not."

"Uhhhh, yeah she is. Like how do you not see it? Wait, was she fucking Trey?"

Katherine paused.

"I mean... I guess, no. Trey said they didn't do anything, that they were just really good friends."

"Yeah, cause she's a total lesbo."

Katherine was silent. Her mind raced.

"That's funny," Chuckie went on trying to fake laugh again.

"Wait. How do you know?"

"Okay, so last year Teddy used to fuck Jessica occasionally, like, I guess it was like a casual thing and all... but he was up in New York this January, and he looked her up and they like... hung out at this bar, right? Teddy said it was all like, full of hot girls, I mean wall to wall... like he thought he'd died and gone to heaven, you know? And then Jessica tells him, she's a lesbo, and so is everyone in that bar. Can you believe that? A whole bar full of dykes? So needless to say that night turned out pretty crappy for him, you know?"

"Okay," Katherine said, surprised about Jessica but still confused. "What does that have to do with Laura?"

"Are you kidding me? *They went to Homecoming together*. You didn't know that? They are always around each other. Plus Laura cut her hair short, and she's like way too good at sports for a regular girl, if you know what I mean. And did you know her dad is a fag? I heard he has AIDS, but Teddy said that's bullshit, so, whatever, I guess not, but, you know, you should probably be careful I guess."

Katherine shook her head, like she was trying to get water out of her ear. She realized at that moment how much she hated talking to Chuckie Burbage. He went on for a while, she offered a few "uh huh's" for his trouble, and then told him she had to get to a ton of homework.

Katherine hung up the phone and stood perfectly still, allowing her mind every ounce of her energy. What did this mean, that Trey had a lesbian best friend? She didn't like that Laura was a lesbian, but that definitely changed things, right? And was Trey somehow better than she thought before, standing up for his friend, who by all rights should be an outcast? Did he actually choose friendship over sex? You know who else would do that? Jesus, that's who.

She walked up to her room slowly, like she was in a trance. She sat on her bed and thought for a second what it must have been like to be Trey, being told by his girlfriend that his platonic lesbian friend had to be cut out of his life. What kind of monster was she?

It was perhaps an hour later that she started pacing around her room, formulating a plan to get Trey back. She saw the magazine, thought about Niki Taylor, and smiled.

The next day at lunch she met Trey in her car. The wind was wild, but the rain hadn't fallen yet. Trey was leery of getting in the car, not because he feared Katherine, but he was nervous of confrontation in tight spaces. He had been cornered too many times. He was put a little at ease by Katherine's smile. It looked like a real smile.

"Hey," he said, sliding into the passenger seat. "You wanted to..."

"I'm sorry."

Trey nodded. He wasn't used to people saying that to him, and he didn't know how to respond. He waited for the next thing. Katherine was hoping he would either say he was sorry too or at least accept her apology, but he just looked at the swirling clouds.

"Okay, well, look." She thought to give it some context. "I don't like how I behaved with you, asking you to choose between your friend and me. I thought you... I thought the two of you... oh it's just so silly now. I just didn't know... I didn't know the facts."

Trey looked at her, trying to figure out what fact or facts she was referring to. But he still didn't speak. He still thought this could be a trap.

"Alright, so, look, I know about it, okay. And I totally understand why you aren't saying anything, and I promise I won't say anything either. But I think you should know, I think you are pretty brave."

Trey nodded in agreement, having no idea what she was referring to.

"And I think you should know that I'm very sorry about how things worked out between us. I misjudged you. And I hope that we can at least be friends, if not something more, and either way that's totally up to you. Oh Trey, you must think I'm such a monster!"

"No," he finally spoke, putting his hand on her shoulder. Trey knew monsters. "You're not a monster."

"Thank you. I just didn't know everything beforehand, and now that I do... God, I was so blind before. I just really do love you and I thought I was losing you and I was so stupid that I ended up actually losing you when I should have known that... I guess that wasn't even a possibility? I was dumb."

"Okay, uh... what the fuck are you talking about?"

"Laura, obviously."

"What about her?"

"That she's a dyke."

"Wha..." Trey was stunned into partial silence.

"I'm sorry, I'm sure she wants it to be a secret, though, I don't know if it was that smart to go to Homecoming with Jessica if she's trying to hide it. I mean, if Chuckie Burbage knows, probably everyone knows anyway."

"Chuckie?"

"Yeah."

"Is this like an April Fool's joke?"

"No, it's really not. Are you okay?"

Trey was not okay. Trey was confused. How could he not know this about his best friend?

"How?" he said unconsciously out loud.

"Oh, he heard from Teddy Pearson."

Trey shook his head with the hope the motion would get more synapses to fire.

"Teddy told him about Jessica, and that's why they went to Homecoming together. I should have figured it out, like when Laura cut her hair short, and how she is so good at sports, and you know her dad is gay, right? Plus that music she listens to? And let's be honest, you guys are like really close and both pretty good looking..."

Trey smiled in agreement.

"And nothing has happened between you guys, so, you know, it kinda makes sense."

"Yeah," Trey went back to looking at the clouds.

"I swear I won't say anything," Katherine said honestly.

"Okay."

"Do you think that, maybe, you could find a way to forgive me?"

Trey nodded, still looking at the clouds.

"I think so," he said slowly, not even sure what she had just said.

The wind suddenly whistled against the windows. That's when the rain started. It was a fine mist. The droplets covered the car, hiding them.

"I miss you," she said kindly and honestly.

"I miss you too," he said still in a daze.

She reached out and brushed a lock of his hair behind his ear. He closed his eyes. Not because he liked how her hand felt, even though he did, but because he was trying to focus. The mist started tapping the windows harder as the gusts picked up strength. Katherine looked towards the school.

"We should probably get inside before it gets too bad," she suggested.

Trey shook his head.

"You want to stay here?" she suggested suggestively.

It should say something about the state of shock Trey was in, that a teenage boy missed a clear sign like that. He just kept staring at the windshield, running different scenarios through his mind.

Trey knew Jessica was a lesbian, she came out to him at Christmas, and he wasn't that surprised. Trey liked Jessica, she had great taste in music and she was fun to be around. Trey, unlike many of the teenage boys of that era in rural America, wasn't homophobic. Trey knew Laura's dad was gay, and knew it long before anyone else in their class knew. He didn't know Mr. Byrne well, but he seemed nice, and unlike Trey's straight father, Mr. Byrne was always kind to his child. Laura also raved about how wonderful Todd was, so his experience with gay people, while limited, was one hundred percent positive.

Trey didn't think Laura was a lesbian. He had no indication that she was. Well... almost no indication. She did really freak out when he kissed her at that middle school dance. Trey knew that didn't make her a lesbian, but it seemed an overreaction for just a little kiss. The second is that she only dated Alex for a minute. Though she claimed they had sex, it was only after he admitted to having sex with Katherine that she told him about her doing the same. So he thought it could have been a lie. The third reason, which was perhaps most important, was that they had just slept in the same bed for the last few weeks and never even so much as kissed.

So, while Trey didn't think that Laura was a lesbian, his mind did wander enough to wonder if that explained why they hadn't done anything. After all, it was pretty clear that they both had very strong feelings for one another.

Suddenly Trey realized he was wildly, madly, passionately in love with Laura. He didn't want Katherine, he wanted Laura. His best friend.

But he smiled as he thought, *Am I really in love with a lesbian?*

It was a fleeting thought. After all, he would have known. They talked every night about everything. He knew everything there was to know about her. If she was a lesbian, she would have told him.

Trey nodded. He looked at Katherine, who had been trying to make sense of his face as he swept through divergent thoughts. Katherine leaned forward and kissed him. He unconsciously kissed her back.

It was a short kiss, but a sensuous one. Trey had forgotten himself. He couldn't speak, he only shook his head ever so slightly. Just another reason for him to not trust tight spaces in the future.

"We should get back to class," Katherine said.

They left the car and ran through the rain, and into two very different worlds.

***

On April 1st Laura woke in an agitated and elated state. From the moment her eyes opened, in fact, perhaps from the moment *before* her eyes opened, she wanted to see Trey. She even thought about driving over to his house and sneaking through his bedroom window. She giggled, imagining waking him up, naked, in his bed.

She breathed an exaggerated sigh to try to shake away the fantasy, but it lingered. She got out of bed and showered. She took a long, hot shower, first scrubbing and then touching herself, letting the steam fill her lungs and the water heat and caress her skin. The shower didn't fix it. She was in a mood. Before she even left for school, she was sure that was the day she would push things with Trey. She wanted him. All of him.

Perhaps it was the weather. Laura loved rainy days. There was something about how the wind smelled when it rained near the ocean that was life affirming in a way sunny days could never be.

The promised rain fell during lunch, and it was announced that all after school sports were cancelled that day in order to save the fields from ruin. Trey wasn't at lunch. In fact, it just so happened that Laura and Trey only had one class together that day, which was in the afternoon, and they hadn't seen each other at all prior to that class. Laura brightened up the moment she saw him. He looked a little extra goofy today, and for some reason she liked that. It seemed like Trey was smiling through the whole class, and he kept stealing glances at Laura, but looking at her in a strange way. Laura giggled and rolled her eyes. She was so sure that this would be the night.

After school she went over to his house, but he wasn't home. The wind had picked up and the rain was falling in sheets. She waited a few minutes and then drove home. Her mother was there, home early from work and getting dressed for a night out with Bubby. She asked Laura if it would be okay if, because of the storm, she stayed over at Bubby's that night. Laura laughed and repeated "because of the storm" while doing air quotes.

Laura was still in her skirt and button down shirt she wore to school when, at around six PM, Trey knocked on the door. She didn't hear him knock the first two times, but he just stood in the rain. He was nervous. He was wearing a black t-shirt, jeans, and flip flops, and by the time Laura got to the door he was shivering. Neither spoke as he stepped inside and kicked off his flip flops. Wordlessly, with a massive smile, she grabbed his hand and pulled him up the stairs and into her bedroom. She touched his shoulder as he walked through her bedroom door, and it felt like he had swam there.

"Eagth," she emoted as she touched his shirt. "Why?"

"You didn't hear me knocking."

"What is it with you and the rain?" She smiled, looking at him. "Take off your shirt."

He started to, and then stopped. He mouthed to her, *Is your mom here?*

"Mom?!?" Laura said as loud as she could without yelling, and then paused to pretend to listen for an answer. "I guess not."

Trey peeled off his shirt, and a fine mist spurted into the air when he pulled it over his head. He had been working out, and it showed. In fact, he had just come from the gym, so he looked a little extra. Oh, and he was wet. Glistening. She stared at his torso for too long. She reached out and squeezed his bicep. He laughed. She turned around and walked to the bathroom for a towel. When she tossed it to him, she plugged in her Christmas lights and turned off her overhead light.

Now, partially hidden in shadow, she sat on the bed and watched him try to dry himself in the golden glow. He, like so many men before him, was just bad at drying himself. She stood up and took the towel from him and ordered him to turn around so she could dry his back. She lingered, and leaned in towards his shoulder blade and put her nose up against his skin and breathed in.

"You smell like the storm."

"Should I shower?"

"No."

He was still holding his shirt in one hand so she took it from him and handed him back the towel. She went downstairs and put the shirt in the dryer, and then called upstairs to him.

"What about your jeans, are they soaked too?"

There was no way she could have said that to his face, and she put her left hand up to her mouth to contain what was probably going to be a long laugh.

"Uhhh. Yeah."

She paused, and took a breath to contain herself.

"Throw them down."

His wet jeans hit the stair landing with a splat about a third of a second after she finished speaking. They were soaked through. She put them in the dryer and paced back and forth for a minute. She was ready.

"What about your underwear?"

There was a pause from upstairs. A long pause. Laura suddenly realized why.

"Are you going commando?"

"Umm. Yeeees?"

Laura nodded and started the dryer. Trey was naked in her room. She walked as slowly as possible up the stairs, because if she sped up, she would have broken into a run. When she got into her room, Trey had the towel wrapped around himself and looked nervous as hell.

"Ehhh, do you have anything?"

Laura's wicked mind made her blush. She reached in her bottom drawer and pulled out a pair of faded pink sweatpants.

"They are the biggest ones I have," she lied, tossing them to him and then stepping out of the room to give him a little privacy.

"Do you," she spoke around the doorjamb that separated them, "need something for your, you know, chest."

"I'm okay if you are. You can come back in."

She laughed when she saw him. The sweatpants were snug on him, much tighter than anything he would normally wear, they only reached midway in his calves, and they sat low on his hips and hid practically nothing. She could make out the outline of his thigh muscles, and everything else. Sometimes she forgot how big he was, but in those tiny sweatpants, it was evident.

"Lay down, I'll do you first," Laura said, referring to their practice of sharing back rubs. Maybe.

Trey complied, laying on his stomach and exposing his swollen back. Laura turned on her CD player and played *Shepherd Moons*, and at that moment realized she was still wearing her skirt from the school day. She thought about changing, but it was a fleeting thought. She mounted him, sitting on the top of his pink sweatpants, and slowly slid her hands up and down his naked back, gently tracing his muscles, her fingertips feeling the memory of moisture on his skin.

The wind howled outside, and suddenly changed direction, pelting the window with sheet after sheet of rain. Thunder rumbled in the distance at a steady pace, like an oncoming train. Trey turned his head to look at the window, but said nothing. He closed his eyes as she slid her fingers up his neck and into his wet hair, giving a gentle massage to his head.

He knew why he was there. She knew why he was there. But they were both too nervous to take the next step.

Suddenly a brilliant light flashed and an immediate crack sounded. They were too close to call that sound thunder, it was the sound of lightning before the echo. They both squealed and clenched. Laura collapsed onto Trey, clinging to his back. The lights and music had stopped, but it took them a moment to realize the power was out.

"Holy shit," Laura said as she peeled herself off Trey's back. She exhaled and her heartbeat started to relax a little. She had lost track of where she had left off. She slid her hands down to his lower back, and slid herself back onto his thighs, having to feel her way in the inky black. Even with all the light gone, she could still make out his pink sweatpants.

"Can we talk?" Trey asked from the darkness.

A lightning bolt flashed and revealed his turned face had a look of concern. Laura knew she had no choice.

"Do we have to?"

Trey swallowed a laugh as he turned around. Laura laid beside him, like they so often had done before falling asleep together. He habitually lifted his head and she slid her right arm between the pillow and his neck. Her left hand she placed on his naked chest, her middle finger tracing a small figure eight around his heart.

"Something is different," he said, as multiple lightning strikes hit a couple miles away, the thunder shaking the house through his pause. "And that scares me."

Laura tried to look at Trey's eyes, but it was so dark, and he was looking up at the ceiling.

"I don't like not being able to see you," she said softly, her lips only eight inches from his ear.

"I'm being serious," he reassured her.

"So am I."

He forgot to breathe, and then took a huge, dramatic breath. But he didn't say anything after the breath. Laura sniffed a laugh.

"I thought that sigh was going to be followed by some big revelation," she admitted.

"I think I just forgot to breathe."

"Okay," she craned her neck to try to see his eyes. "I don't think that's possible."

"I got a lot on my mind."

"Yeah but," she thought about pushing it but figured it wasn't worth it. The mood had changed. She thought it wasn't going to happen. She let out her own small sigh. "Never mind."

"Laura, I'm in love with you."

Laura smiled and felt warm inside. She sat up, then threw her left leg over his body and straddled him sitting on his stomach. He could feel her naked thighs on his hips, he could see her silhouette outlined by the thin grey light of the storm, the last moments of an unseen distant sun that was about to set.

"What are you doing?" he asked as she positioned herself on top of him.

"I hate not seeing your eyes, especially when you say something like that," she said, putting her hand on his shoulders and leaning down close to him.

"This feels weird," he admitted. "It feels like you are holding me down."

"Okay," she said, sliding her hands down his arms and grabbing his hands and then pulling his arms above his head. She entwined her fingers in his and held his hands down as she leaned her head close to his face and whispered to him.

"Is this better?"

"It's far worse."

She didn't move.

"Say what you want to say."

Trey was about to tell Laura about Katherine. He really wanted to. But he had a feeling, if he did, it might not be well received. And he was not exactly in control of the situation at the moment.

"I don't know if I want to now," he said, only half-joking.

Laura smiled and let go of his hands and sat back. She let one hand rest on his stomach, tracing the muscles with her middle finger and her thumb.

"Okay. Now tell me how much you love me," she teased.

Trey cleared his throat.

"I'm scared I'm going to make a mistake," Trey admitted.

Laura smiled. "What kind of mistake?"

Trey shrugged and looked at her eyes. She was so beautiful.

"It's been a strange day."

Laura leaned down until her face was just above Trey's. He thought she was going to kiss him, and he closed his eyes to accept the kiss. But she stopped a few inches away from his lips. She smiled, stretching this moment into an eternity. They were both so scared to leap, but at least Laura was having fun with the terror of the unknown.

She rolled her head, brushing her nose against his jaw.

"Do you think," she whispered, "this is a mistake?"

She slowly skimmed her nose up across his cheek until her nose touched his, and their lips were almost touching. She circled his nose once with her own, and then slid down his other cheek and along his other jaw. He could feel the wet of her breath on his neck.

"What about this?" she whispered into his neck, her lips scraping against his stubble.

She moved her head up to look at his eyes for one moment, and in a flash of lightning she saw his eyes were still closed. She bent down and with her cheek she brushed along his eyebrow, her lips barely touching his closed eyelid. She silently moved to the other eye.

"And what about this?" her lips asked his eyelid.

He inhaled, afraid or unable to speak. She glided her nose down to circle his, once clockwise, and then once counter clockwise, and when she stopped, her lips were a millimeter from his own. Lightning threw shadows on their closed eyelids. When she spoke, their lips touched.

"Is this a mistake?" she whispered one last time, her breath mingling with his. He slid his hands along her knees and onto her hips, and they kissed.

The storm that raged outside went unheard and unnoticed.

27

Mistakes

Trey was blessed with many gifts, but timing wasn't one of them.

The pink sweatpants were crumpled in the middle of the floor. Laura's skirt was strewn over her CD player, her underwear and bra were both missing. The lovers were completely spent, sweaty and cuddling naked in each other's arms. They kept laughing at nothing.

They said all the nice and silly things people say at that moment. Laura's fingers were teasing Trey's hair. She asked if it was worth the wait. He told her she was beautiful. He kept running his middle finger back and forth across her left hip. They were so comfortable that they both felt they could say anything to one another.

But then Trey tested that theory.

"I guess this proves you're not a lesbian."

Remember the sound his wet jeans made when they splatted on the landing? The last line was the flirting equivalent of that sound. Trey managed to ruin the mood so fast that Laura pulled her hand from his hair and propped herself up on her elbow.

"What the fuck?"

Then he made it worse.

"I'm sorry, it was stupid. It was just something Katherine said."

"Uh huh," Laura backed away from Trey. It was pitch dark now, as the electric was still out. She could barely make out his form. "When did Katherine say this?"

"Uh. It was at lunch."

Laura was silent for a moment. She was now sitting up and crossed her arms in front of her breasts.

"But you weren't at lunch."

Trey still hadn't realized he screwed up. In his defense, he couldn't see her face well in the darkness, and he had just had sex, and... well, he was kinda dumb.

"We were in her car."

"Okay," Laura nodded, backing all the way against the wall. The wall was cold on her back, but other than the initial flinch she didn't care. The cold was somehow comforting. "What were you doing in her car?"

Trey heard the change in her voice and could feel her pulling away. He propped himself up on his elbow.

"Okay, so this might sound worse than it is."

"Uh huh."

"She wanted to apologize to me."

"For what?"

"Um. It's kind of a long story."

"I got time."

"Okay," Trey sat up. "She wanted to apologize to me because she thought it was wrong of her to make me choose between you and her."

Laura waited. Trey wasn't going to add any more details without being forced to.

"That's it?" Laura asked, almost rhetorically. "That's pretty mature of her. Did she like, want something from you? Like why a month later, you know?"

"Eeahh," Trey sorta sighed.

"Yes?"

"Um," Trey said, pausing like a discerning child at the side of the pool, not ready to jump yet. "Um."

"Jesus, just spit it out!"

"She heard you were a lesbian, and she felt bad that she made me choose between her and my lesbian friend. And then she kissed me."

Splash.

Laura stood up, completely naked, and walked out of the room. She went downstairs to the kitchen. Trey thought he heard her crying. He looked frantically for the sweatpants but couldn't find them, and then stumbled naked down the dark stairs, almost slipping twice. Laura was getting water in the kitchen. She was laughing so hard that it sounded like crying.

Trey stood at the doorway of the kitchen. He could barely make out her figure by the sink.

"Are you alright?" he asked.

"No," Laura laughed. "Not even a little bit."

Trey tried to move towards her but stubbed his toe on one of the island stools. Laura smiled at his pain, taking joy in a karmic universe. After some cursing he finally got close to her and reached out to hold her.

"Don't you fucking touch me."

"What did I do?"

Circuits misfired in Laura's brain.

"Are you joking me?" Laura was smiling, but furious. "Why is every man a fucking cheater?"

"What are you talking about?" Trey said, his voice getting hoarse.

"You kissed Katherine this afternoon and we had sex tonight. Was there anyone else in between?"

"No!" he stumbled over what he was trying to say. "I don't, that's not how... I didn't kiss her, she kissed me."

"You let her."

"I was trapped in a car and she was all, Laura's a lesbian, and I was just, I don't know, dumbfounded, and then she kissed me when I wasn't paying attention."

He was struggling to talk with a mixture of emotion and exhaustion. Laura saw him struggle. Until that moment she hadn't known it was possible to love and hate someone at the same time. She simultaneously pitied him and wanted to kick him in the balls. Instead Laura handed him the half-full water glass and watched him drink.

"My father cheated on my mother and I basically lost my family because of it. The first man I ever had sex with cheated on me the very next week. And now you cheated on me today."

"I didn't cheat on you! First of all, you and I hadn't even kissed, and secondly I didn't kiss her, she kissed me, I just... I was just so shocked when she told me you are a lesbian."

"I'M NOT A LESBIAN!" she screamed.

Trey froze. Her scream echoed and drifted away into silence until only darkness remained. He thought Laura might have been holding her breath. Trey took a sip of water.

"Well I know that now."

Trey was smiling. At that moment he thought he was much funnier than Laura did.

"So I had to fuck you to prove I wasn't a lesbian?"

"I'm just joking."

"This is a joke to you?"

"Stop it, Laura. Just calm down."

"So now I'm being hysterical? Wow!"

"Will you let me explain?"

"This ought to be good," Laura folded her arms in front of her, covering her breasts.

"Laura, I knew you weren't a lesbian as soon as I thought about it for a second. Because I know everything about you, and I would have already known if you were a lesbian."

"Ha. You know nothing about me."

"You're right. Fine. Whatever. I don't know anything about you." Trey shook his head incredulously.

"Except, you know... I do know you love dogs, but since your mom is allergic you can't have one. But every time you even see a dog you get sad and cry a little because you want one so badly."

"I don't cry."

"Yes you do. You cry. Actual tears. Every time."

"You cry."

"I know you love cats too and you cuddle with them when you catch one, even though *you're* allergic to them and you will sneeze for like an hour afterwards."

Laure smiled and rolled her eyes. "Please, everyone knows these things about me."

"No one knows these things about you except for me! I know everything about you. I know you love silver jewelry, mismatched socks, and flannel pajamas and don't like gold jewelry, crew cuts, and thong underwear."

"It's like choosing to have a wedgie, I don't understand the draw," Laura said, taking back the water and sipping.

"I know you love how high heels look on you but you hate wearing them."

"I'm legit concerned I'm going to break a leg."

"I know that you know that I know that you wear the orange sweater because I said I liked it once. And every time you wear it I know you are wearing it for me."

Laura smiled and put her left hand over her nose and mouth.

"I didn't know you knew that," she whispered.

"I know you hate ketchup but like a ketchup/mustard blend for pigs in a blanket. And you put mustard on weird things, things that shouldn't have mustard on them."

"I'm not accepting dietary criticism from the likes of you," she said, as she put the glass on the counter and crossed her arms again.

"I know Meg Ryan is your favorite actress and *Joe Versus the Volcano* is your favorite movie, even though it's weird. Your second favorite movie is *When Harry Met Sally...* And you love every movie she's in."

"She's a national treasure."

Trey smiled and stepped towards Laura and opened his arms. She slowly let down her hands and hugged him.

"I know you love books that make you cry. I know you want to love old movies but black and white films make you fall asleep."

She put her head on his chest and slid her hand slowly up and down his back.

"I know you care more about the lyrics of a song than the music, but some of your favorite music is in languages you don't speak with lyrics you can't understand."

"I can understand them, I just have no idea what words they are saying."

"I know you are suspicious of stand-up comedy."

"Hmm. Who isn't?"

"I know you yawn like a lion, but sneeze like a cartoon character. I know how you hiccup, how you breathe when you are tired. I know how you smell after you shower at school, and how you smell after you shower at home. Because at school you use Outrageous shampoo and at home you steal your mom's Salon Selectives."

Laura looked up at him with wide eyes.

"I don't even think she knows that."

"I know how your skin feels different on your shoulders than on your lower back. I know the sound of your voice when you're fighting to stay awake."

She kissed his chest. His hand slowly slid up her back to her neck.

"I know you love when I touch the back of your neck, and that the tops of your ears are ticklish. And I know if I trace the infinity symbol repeatedly on your shoulder blades that you will become so relaxed that you will fall asleep in my arms."

She put her right hand on his face and kissed him deeply. When their lips finally separated she touched her forehead to his ever so gently.

"But other than that," she whispered. "You don't really know much about me."

"Well," he smiled and whispered back. "I'm excited to find out more."

She smiled and kissed his ear while sliding her hand down his chest and stomach until she held him in her hand.

"Oh, look, you really are excited."

Trey reached down and picked her up and carried her up the stairs. She screamed, laughing and terrified. Somehow he didn't drop her until he set her down on the bed. But he was breathing hard and exhausted from the exertion. He collapsed next to her.

"Hey," she said, smacking him on the shoulder. "Get up and please me."

He laughed and complied to the best of his ability. They made love again, but less rushed this time. Then they tried showering together, but it was a challenge in the dark, and the hot water didn't last long enough. While there's nothing sexy about a cold shower, it was invigorating. After the shower they went downstairs, Trey wearing his pink sweatpants and Laura only in boxers, and they ate ice cream right from the container, sharing a spoon and a blanket when the ice cream made them cold. They made love again in the living room, and fell asleep, naked, on the couch.

It was a little before two AM when Dolores entered the Byrne household. The power was still out in Ocean Pines, so she had brought a Life Lite, a little plastic green disposable flashlight. She had been worried when she returned from the bar and Trey wasn't home. When she found Trey's car in the Byrne driveway, and her knock went unanswered, she chose not to wait outside in the rain. She didn't slam the front door to alert the inhabitants of her presence. For years afterwards she maintained that she called out from the doorway, but Trey never believed her, and Laura chose not to have an opinion of it. Either way, the fact remains, Trey and Laura only woke up when the flashlight was shining in their eyes. Dolores, who was shocked but smiling, said nothing as the teenagers scrambled to their feet, gathering a blanket and pillow to cover themselves while launching a volley of a thousand curses aimed squarely at themselves. Like the first lovers in the presence of God, Trey and Laura had never been more embarrassed in their lives, and in fact, never would be again. Trey took his wet jeans and shirt from the dryer and wore the pink sweatpants home.

***

The morning after, Laura and Trey met at English's for breakfast. They didn't plan it, it was just one of those beautiful moments of happenstance. Though they were both starving and exhausted, so breakfast and coffee was logical.

Laura had arrived first and was already on her second cup of coffee when Trey entered the dining room. She lit up as soon as she saw him, and unconsciously stood up. He laughed and tried to walk slowly towards her, so that he didn't break into a run. They embraced, right there in English's, and kissed, and laughed. It was awkward and lovely.

"I'm scared to ask," Laura said.

"She woke up right as I was leaving. She said I should give my esposa flowers today."

"Oh my God."

"Yeah, you know this is going to go on for a while," Trey said, referring to his mother teasing him. But it made Laura think of something else. Them. Their relationship. Suddenly she was out of the moment and wondering what this all meant.

Trey ordered and the waitress brought more coffee. He was looking at Laura. Her mind was racing, thinking about college, thinking about marriage, and a house, and children. She wasn't ready for any of that. Did she even want that? Trey kept looking at her with his big satisfied grin. Finally he spoke, as Laura was taking a sip of coffee.

"Do you think Candace knows yet?"

Laura snorted a laugh. She picked up a napkin to clean up where she spilled. She didn't say anything though. Trey could feel her silence, but had no idea she was thinking about their future in years.

"Maybe," Laura said thoughtfully. "Maybe we shouldn't tell anyone."

Trey shrugged.

"You're embarrassed by me?"

"No, it's just... I don't know. I need a minute."

Trey nodded. He was surprised. Laura should have made a joke then and she didn't.

"You are saying you need space?"

Laura sighed.

"No? I don't know. Not space. Can we talk about it tonight?"

Trey nodded.

"Mom works every night until one thirty or so. We have my house to ourselves, just come over whenever, we'll talk."

But they didn't talk about it that night. Throughout the day both her doubts and the thoughts of the future got pushed out of her mind by schoolwork and lacrosse. By the time she got to Trey's house she was hungry. For food, for sex, for music... for anything but talking. They listened to French jazz and traded tropical kisses. They ate pickles and cold pizza and made love like wild animals. She gave him a hickey right above his left nipple.

"Mine!" she stated after he yelped in pain. She sat back and admired his new temporary tattoo marking her conquest.

The third night was much the same. And the fourth, the fifth, the sixth, and the seventh. They were giggly and unfocused. They had their worst lacrosse games of the season but neither cared. They were having the best sex of their lives.

They didn't actually date, because they never left the house. They didn't cook. They didn't go anywhere other than school, lacrosse, and Trey's house. During the day they reveled in their clandestine love, at night they lived as nude creatures of lust. They alternated between fucking and making love and they finally knew the difference. They explored each other. The rest of the world disappeared. It was a week of secret thoughtless joy.

The eighth night they showered together until the hot water ran out. They listened to Pink Floyd and ate lunchmeat straight from the packages, the light from the refrigerator illuminated their skin. Their love seemed so natural and complete. But that was the night Trey couldn't hold back. Laura was on top of him, riding him, controlling their tempo. Her fingers were intertwined with his, and she held them above his head. He tried to stop, tried to pull out, tried to tell her that he was close but she was lost in a moment of ecstasy.

Up until that moment they had been using the "pull out" method that was so popular and unsuccessful with Catholics. The next day Trey bought condoms. Laura looked at the calendar and realized she was already three days late.

28

Lost Woman Song

Laura's period was always an unwanted surprise until she started dating Alex. For a few reasons she decided at that time to keep a little better track of it, and she eventually worked out that she got her period every thirty or thirty-one days. It had now been thirty-four days.

In her darker moments she was convinced that she was being punished by God for enjoying sex out of wedlock. It was a fleeting and yet recurring anxiety. When she took a breath and rationalized, she was smart enough to know what was far more likely than a cosmic or divine retribution for a few moments of joy—was that sex between a man and a woman had always been a part of a cause and effect equation that led to more men and women.

She didn't want to say anything to Trey yet, but she didn't want to hide it from him either. In truth, she had no idea if she was really pregnant. She wasn't ready to know.

But Trey and Laura had become too close too fast. So when at school the next day she tried to explain she needed a moment he pushed a little too hard.

"I can't come over tonight," she said.

"It's okay," he nodded. Then he leaned in close and whispered in her ear. "I bought condoms."

She felt a pang in her stomach. She shook her head at him. She whispered back, "It's a little late for that."

His eyes got wide and he took a step backwards. He tripped over someone's bookbag and fell over, in the process knocking down one of his lacrosse teammates and causing a huge scene. Laura walked away and went to hide in the bathroom.

After lacrosse Laura went straight home. Her mom was out with Bubby. Laura stared at her homework which had been neglected for the better part of a week. She had barely begun when Trey knocked on the door. She didn't bother answering. He walked in anyway.

"Laura?" he called from inside the door.

"I'm not home!" she called back.

He walked over and stood there looking at her. She sighed and looked up from her textbook. He had a strange expression, one that she hadn't seen before.

"What do you want?" she asked.

He got down on one knee.

"Laura Byrne..."

Laura started laughing.

"No. No. Stop it. Trey!"

He stayed on one knee.

"I'm serious," he said. "I love you."

"Okay, well, I don't even know if I am pregnant!"

"I don't care. I want to marry you anyway. I love you."

Laura stood up and walked over to Trey. She cupped his face in her hands and leaned down to kiss him. She was smiling, and her eyes were wet.

"Please get up," she said. "And go home. If you stay here I won't be able to control myself."

Trey smirked and sat down.

"I'm serious, leave now," Laura said. Trey complied, but as he left she pinched his butt which led to a lengthy make out session by the door. But he finally left Laura alone with her homework and thoughts.

Laura turned off the lights in the house and put on Ani DiFranco's album. She climbed into bed and thought about the future.

She knew she wouldn't marry Trey. Not now. She knew they weren't ready for that. But certainly they weren't ready for a baby either. If she had a baby now her life as she knew it would completely change. She thought about what the people in her life would think. She assumed Dolores would offer to raise the child as her own. She knew Jessica, Candace, her father, and his boyfriend Todd would all suggest she get an abortion, and be more than willing to drive her to the clinic. It was her mom that was the mystery.

Even if she didn't always go to church, Joyce at heart was a pretty solid Catholic. So much so that she even looked into getting an annulment after her husband cheated on her. While Joyce had many regrets, having Laura was not one of them. She dropped out of college to have Laura, though she was already married by then. She finished her last year of college only after Laura started kindergarten, and she still managed to build a strong and lucrative career. Of course, the situation was very different, as Laura was only in high school, and very not married. Still, Laura didn't know which way her mother would lean, but she knew she was too afraid to ask her.

Laura didn't want to get an abortion. She didn't even know what that really meant, or what the process entailed. She was afraid that if she had an abortion now that meant she would never be able to have children. Ever. She loved children. Whenever she thought about her future, Trey was her husband and they had one boy who looked like young Trey, and two girls who looked like young Lauras. That future was so distant it was almost another lifetime away. They hadn't even lived yet.

She never considered that if she had a baby she could give the child up for adoption, because she knew Dolores would never allow it. Or Dolores would adopt the baby. Laura wasn't okay with that either. Treating this child like her friend's little sister or little brother? That was no solution.

Laura was angry. Not at Dolores, not at Trey, not at society or nature, not even at herself. She was just angry. She was angry that her life was about to be turned upside down and she had no control over what would happen.

The whole house was dark and silent other than Ani and her guitar. "Lost Woman Song" came up. Laura knew every word of this song about a girl crossing a picket line to get an abortion. But for the first time, she felt the words.

Laura sat up in her bed and held a pillow in her hand. Laura rocked slowly back and forth and sang:

I'm just another woman lost
you are like fish in the water who don't know that they are wet
but as far as I can tell, the world isn't perfect yet

Tears fell onto the pillow. She didn't bother wiping her cheeks. The wet reminded her that she was alive. She so badly wanted someone to come through the door to tell her that everything was going to be okay. She wanted her mother. But the house was dark.

***

The next four days were torture for Laura. She knew she was going to have to take a pregnancy test or go to the doctor, but there was no way to do either of those things without someone finding out. She hadn't told anyone. She thought about calling Todd, but she felt bad about breaking the promise she made to him to always use protection. She thought about telling Jessica or Candace, and she almost did a few times. But then it would be real, and she wasn't ready for it to be real.

She kept Trey away from her at this time, but he still followed her and watched her like a sad puppy. All weekend she avoided him. She spent the entire weekend working on a term paper, which was a necessary distraction.

That Monday was a cold, rainy April day. Laura was eating lunch by herself in her car when suddenly she felt a sharp pain behind her left eye. She stood up and walked towards the school, and then suddenly felt nauseous. She thought about throwing up outside, but she knew someone would see. She made a beeline for the bathroom, and pushed the stall door open and stared at the toilet. Suddenly, it felt as if she was being stabbed in the side by something that was somehow both dull and sharp at the same time. For a second she couldn't breathe. And then another cramp hit her so violently her knees buckled.

Candace pushed the door to the bathroom open.

"Hey, are you okay?"

Laura was in the stall. As another cramp hit her she made a noise that sounded a little like a constipated ghost trying to poop.

"Oh my god, are you dying?" Candace said, half joking.

Laura had never been more happy to get her period.

Soon she was laying on the cot in Mrs. Pruitt's sick room. The lights were out and Mrs. Pruitt was holding a warm washcloth to her head.

"You know dear, when I was your age, I used to get the worst cramps. I actually passed out twice."

The medication had yet to kick in and another spasm caused her whole body to convulse.

"But it gets better dear, I promise it does. You'll grow out of it."

She left the washcloth on Laura's head and stood up and went to the door.

"Try not to worry dear. Stress always makes everything worse."

She shut the door and eventually Laura slept.

29

My Little Brown Book

When she walked out of the room, she saw Tyrone sitting in the chair. He was holding a bloody towel to his nose.

"Tyrone? What happened?"

"I don't know," Tyrone said, smiling and lying. It was clear he didn't want to incriminate himself.

"He picked a fight with two senior boys," Mrs. Pruitt said without looking up from some paperwork.

"Why?" Laura asked.

Tyrone shrugged. Mrs. Pruitt looked up.

"Laura, that's none of your business. Go to class."

An hour later Laura was getting changed for a lacrosse game when Candace came into the locker room. She opened up her locker, which was right next to Laura's.

"Sooooo," she said in a way that let Laura know she had some gossip. "Ty just got suspended. Three days."

"Why?"

"He beat up Jamie Thompson and Reid Derrickson."

"He's a sophomore and he gets in trouble for beating up two seniors? Oh, those poor guys. The teasing is gonna be relentless."

"Yeah, well..." Candace leaned closer to her. "You wouldn't be saying that if you knew what they said."

"What did they say?"

"Apparently they were calling you a dyke. That's why he hit them."

Laura's jaw dropped. She wasn't able to close her mouth because of the surprise, but she still laughed a little.

"If they only knew," she muttered to herself. "What I've been through this week."

"What?" Candace couldn't hear her over the din of the locker room.

Laura slammed her locker shut.

"I like Tyrone," she said.

"I like him too," Candace grinned.

"I think I should get him something. Do you think they make 'sorry you got suspended for defending my honor' presents? That would be a good greeting card. What does he like?"

Candace gave her a knowing look. It was a look that they both understood. A look that said, he's a teenage boy, he likes sex.

"Yeah," Laura smiled. "I'm not getting him that."

"You better not!" Candace laughed as she slammed her locker closed.

That afternoon Laura had her best lacrosse game of the season. A remarkable feat considering what she was dealing with. More remarkable was that by the end of the game she had broken the school record for points in a single game, points in a season, and she was only a dozen points away from breaking the career points record at her school. And she had no idea about any of it. She just relished the distraction which the game provided.

Joyce was in the stands, and took her to dinner afterwards. They went to Cactus Café so Laura could get her favorite shrimp fajitas.

"You know," Joyce said before their food arrived. "All the junior moms are talking about college visits. I think we need to get serious about this. It's time you start thinking about your future."

Laura started laughing and couldn't stop. It was the funniest thing she had ever heard her mom say.

"What?" Joyce was looking around, thinking she had missed something. She had no idea the word "future" could carry so much weight.

Laura kept laughing so much that she cried a little. This was an honest laugh. A laugh of relief. A laugh of hope returning to someone who had once lost it.

As soon as they got home Laura collapsed in bed and slept for eleven hours. Trey called, but she didn't answer. He went to see her, but Joyce told him that she was asleep.

He still had no idea that Laura wasn't pregnant.

***

The next day Laura went to Trey's house. It had only been fourteen days since they had first kissed, and she had felt like they had lived a few lifetimes in those two weeks. He was getting out of the shower when she arrived, and he was only wearing a towel.

He stood in the hallway looking at her, his skin still shiny and wet, his muscles as defined as they had ever been. He nodded to her, as if to say, *do you want to come into my bedroom*, but she shook her head and walked into the kitchen, sitting in the chair she had once scrubbed clean of his father's blood. The memory caused her to stand up and change seats.

"I'm not pregnant."

"That's good," he nodded calmly. He showed no signs of being relieved. "Laura, just so you know, I still want to marry you."

"Okay well, that's dumb."

"How is that dumb?" he said with a raised voice. "I know I'm not as smart as you, but there are things I know, and one of them is that I love you."

"And I love you."

"So we should get married."

"We are in high school."

"Not now, but when we graduate. Laura, I can't imagine my life without you."

Laura shook her head. She took a deep breath. She looked at the table and thought of the garlic soup and the green grapes. The Buckingham house never smelled like cooking anymore. She missed that.

"Trey, the problem is... I can't imagine my life without you either. But we haven't lived yet."

"What the fuck does that even mean? We're living, aren't we?"

Laura was shaking her head still. "It's too much, too fast. This week, I just felt like... I felt like my life was over before it even really began."

"I'm sorry. I'll wear a condom."

Laura laughed. "It's not that."

"What then?" he was pleading.

She paused and took a deep breath. "I don't know."

"Wait," he suddenly realized what Laura had come over to say. "No. Don't. I don't understand. Why?"

"I don't understand either."

"Laura, don't do this."

"We have to break up."

Trey froze. Tears dropped from his eyes. He didn't wipe them, and he didn't look away from her. His face was stone.

"I'm so sorry," she started. She felt her words choke in her throat. She looked away from him. "I never wanted to hurt you."

Trey sniffed.

"You can't."

"Trey, don't..."

"No, I mean... you don't understand."

"What?"

"Laura, you saved me. You know that right? That night, under my window, I was dying."

"You weren't dying..."

"I was. I was going to die, and I know it. I was in the darkest place I had ever been, and you came in there with me. And you... you held me," Trey choked on the last words. "You can't leave me alone. You can't."

"I love you so much," Laura said, her eyes filling with tears. "But we can't be together like that. Not now."

"Can we at least go back to being best friends?"

Laura smiled at the word *best*. It was somehow so innocent.

"You still want to be friends with me?" she said, wiping tears away. "After I did this to you?"

Trey took a deep breath.

"Laura, I can't imagine my life without you in it. If there's any way I can have you, I'll take it."

She nodded. He breathed, finally catching his breath. They sat in silence for a few minutes, neither knowing what they should do.

"Are you hungry?" Trey finally asked.

Laura shook her head. "It's so quiet in here."

Trey stood up and turned on the Marantz. The Duke Ellington and John Coltrane album was in, and "My Little Brown Book" played. It was a slow, sexy jazz number that they both knew well. A week prior they had made love to this song on the couch.

Laura smiled and bowed her head, afraid to look at Trey. He walked over to her and held out his hand.

"Dance with me?" he asked, his eyes still damp.

Laura stood up and slid her forearms onto his back, and leaned into him. They fit together so well. She nestled her head into his shoulder. They swayed together in the kitchen, in perfect comfort and sorrow.

30

Ladies Who Breakfast

Laura kissed Trey as the song ended.

"I'm sorry," she said right away and backed up away from him.

"It's okay," he reassured her. "I liked it."

"I know, but... it's not fair to you."

He rolled his eyes at her.

"Okay. What do you want to do? Do you want a backrub?"

"No," Laura shook her head. "I mean, yes, but I think that's a bad idea."

"You can leave your clothes on."

Laura stepped towards Trey, stopped, and then stepped away.

"Yeah, I need to go."

"Why?"

"Because if I stay I'll want to kiss you again, and that will lead to other things."

"So what should we do? Like how are we going to be friends if we can't be around each other?"

Trey immediately regretted saying that. But Laura smiled.

"I'm going home. Call me."

That night they spoke on the phone until they both fell asleep. The jokes had changed, they were more sexual. And the pauses were longer, as it took more time to think through what some words might lead to. But it seemed, for a moment, they had made a successful transition from lovers to friends.

That Thursday they went to see the movie *The Cutting Edge*. Technically, this would have been their first date, even though they were no longer "dating." Trey picked up Laura in his car. He paid for the tickets and popcorn. They held hands through the entire film and afterwards parked at The Point and kissed each other. Trey's lips tasted like popcorn. They reverted into the feral beasts they had been, but because Trey didn't bring any condoms, they settled for mutual tropical kisses. Laura apologized afterwards, and said they had made a mistake. Trey joked that she was being hard on herself and that she did a very good job. She punched him in the arm. He kissed her again, and she told him to stop. He said it was okay, it was just a friendly kiss. She kissed him. They sat on the hood of his car and looked at the moon and talked about how the only good love songs are sad and if Laura should go to Chicago again for the summer. They kissed again, and then agreed that it would be the last time.

That same Thursday, in the morning at school, Candace had told Laura that it was Katherine who was spreading the rumor about Laura being a lesbian. That got Laura thinking.

Since Easter was late that year there was no school on that Friday. Laura put a note on Katherine's car late Thursday afternoon asking her to meet at English's for breakfast the next day. Katherine was confused and suspicious, but curious enough to show up.

Early morning of Good Friday was cool and foggy, though the sun was doing its best to break through the clouds.

Laura got there first and was stirring the sugar into her cream and coffee when Katherine walked in. Katherine nodded, and confidently took her seat across the table, her perfect posture in contrast to Laura leaning on her elbows over her coffee.

"Good morning," Katherine said coldly as she sat. The waitress was right there and Katherine ordered pancakes and sausage, Laura ordered a scrapple, egg, and cheese sandwich on white toast with mustard. Katherine looked surprised at the order.

"What?" Laura asked.

"You should at least get that on a biscuit."

The waitress stood there unimpressed by the unfolding power dynamic. Laura nodded.

"Yeah, I should. May I get that on a biscuit please?"

Katherine nodded.

The waitress poured Katherine coffee and Laura slid her the creamer. Katherine held up her hand.

"I drink it black."

"Why?"

Katherine shrugged.

"Preference I guess. I find it hard to taste the coffee with all the cream and sugar in it."

Laura raised her eyebrows, not sure if that was meant as a slight.

"What about cappuccinos?"

Katherine lifted the coffee cup with two hands and blew the steam gently away from the lip before taking a tiny sip. She looked at the coffee before she drank.

"I've read about them, but I've never had one."

Laura raised an eyebrow and slowly nodded. At that point, it felt like it was a tie.

"So... I think we need to talk about a few things."

"Okay," Katherine said, putting her coffee cup down and giving Laura her full attention.

Laura looked around to make sure no one was near them or could hear them. Then she spoke in a hushed tone, a little more than a low whisper.

"First off, I am not a lesbian."

Katherine's upper lip curled ever so slightly into a subtle smile.

"I know."

Laura looked confused. Katherine gave her a moment to process.

"I saw the way Trey looked at you at lunch last Friday. I know that look. Love, concern, and fear all wrapped into one. He thought you were pregnant, right?"

Laura was dumbfounded.

"Same thing happened to me last year."

She picked up her cup and blew again, and took another tiny sip, then put her cup down. Laura was trying to figure out if she meant what Laura thought she meant.

"So," Katherine continued. "Did you bleed?"

Laura leaned back, shocked at Katherine's forthrightness. She nodded. Katherine smiled.

"Thank God, right!" she said, laughing honestly, and for a moment cracking her refined demeanor.

Laura nodded. Katherine looked Laura right in the eyes.

"God, there is nothing worse than that stress." She paused for a second and collected her emotions. "But then again... You deserved it. I mean, you basically stole my boyfriend, right? Isn't that karma?"

Laura shook her head.

"That's not... no, I didn't try..." Laura felt like anything she would say here would sound stupid.

"Okay, well, I don't feel bad for kissing him because at the time I thought you were... you know. And even if you aren't, well, he was my boyfriend first."

"That's not..."

"Let me ask," Katherine said with building agitation. "Would you be okay with me calling Trey every night when he gets back from your dates, and falling asleep on the phone with him?"

Laura looked at her expressionless.

"You don't need to worry because I'm not pathetic enough..."

"Okay," Laura calmly cut her off.

"Okay what?"

"Okay, you can call him every night and fall asleep on the phone."

Katherine's eyes narrowed. She hadn't expected this.

"What?"

"You can call him. You can fall asleep together on the phone. He doesn't owe me anything."

Katherine first shook her head then nodded while thinking both of what she heard and what she wanted to say.

"Did you," Katherine started. "I guess I mean, did he ever cheat on me with you, or with anyone?"

Laura smiled and shook her head.

"Why is that funny?"

"Oh, I was just thinking, Trey has enough on his hands with the two of us, I can't imagine another girl being thrown into the mix."

Katherine didn't smile.

"Yeah. You know that's maybe not as funny as you think it is."

"Maybe," Laura said. "I guess it depends on how well you know Trey."

Katherine frowned. At that moment the waitress brought their food. Katherine looked the waitress in the eyes, smiled, and thanked her. The waitress kindly touched Katherine on the shoulder. Laura asked for more coffee. After the waitress walked away Katherine looked at her food, but didn't move. She was measuring her next few moments. It was Laura who broke the silence.

"I have known Trey pretty much my whole life. We're best friends."

"Yeah, he mentioned that a few hundred times."

"It's more than that though. Dolores is like a mother to me. I mean, for most of our lives we've been like brother and sister."

"Gross."

Laura laughed.

"Yeah, granted, okay, but I can't imagine him not in my life, no matter what happens. He's a part of me."

"That's sweet," Katherine said sarcastically. "You are in love. I'm so happy for you."

"No, not like that."

Katherine shook her head and picked up her knife. She used it to spread butter on her pancakes and cut a few bite sized pieces.

"So you aren't in love?"

Laura shrugged.

"I don't know."

"But you guys are dating?"

"Not anymore," Laura remembered how Trey tasted of popcorn only hours before.

"Why not?" Katherine asked while she carefully placed her knife on her plate.

"I'm not sure."

"Okay," Katherine took a small bite and chewed while looking at Laura waiting in vain for her to expand on her thoughts. "So you will be together again?"

"I don't know."

Katherine put her fork down.

"So why are we here?"

Laura sheepishly looked at her food.

"I guess... for me to tell you I'm not a lesbian?"

Katherine shook her head at the absurdity of it all.

"You're paying for breakfast," Katherine said, picking up her fork and taking another bite.

Laura took a bite of her sandwich.

"You know," Laura said after swallowing. "You are right, it is better with a biscuit."

Katherine took a sip of her coffee and offered a sad smile. No one spoke for a moment while they ate.

"I loved him, you know," Katherine said out of the blue. "I think I still love him."

"I'm sorry," Laura said sincerely.

"You know you will have to marry him, right? Because there's no one out there who will be willing to share him with you. You can't call him up and talk to him until you fall asleep when he has a wife. You have to marry him, or you have to leave him and never speak to him again."

Katherine was sad but composed.

"It won't be fair to your husband, and it won't be fair to his wife. You're too close."

Laura stared at her coffee cup. Katherine's words weighed heavy on her heart.

"You realize this, right?" Katherine pressed.

Laura swallowed hard. She hadn't.

"You are going to hold his heart, and he's going to hold yours. And that's the best part of anyone. Yes, sure, you guys are good looking now. But the body breaks down, ages, gets wrinkles, gets fat. All of his beauty, all of your beauty, it's inside. And that's the part of him that you are claiming."

She tucked a lock of hair behind her ear and closed her eyes. She didn't cry, but she was sad.

"There's lots of handsome boys," she said with her eyes closed. "But Trey's got a good heart. That's what I fell in love with."

She looked up at Laura.

"Maybe," she continued. "It's because of you. Maybe he has such a good heart because he's had you in his life. I was so jealous every time he talked about you. I realize now you were the one good thing he clung to, through all those bad years. You were the thing that made him okay. That gave him hope. That showed him love. And that really sucks. Because maybe the one thing that makes him so great is precisely the same reason I can't have him. You."

Laura looked at Katherine and became sad. She hadn't expected anything like this when she asked Katherine to breakfast. Now, the waters had grown deeper and far more muddy.

"Would you want to be friends with Trey?" Laura asked.

Katherine looked at Laura, confused at first by the question. Then she realized Laura had trapped her.

"I guess, if I love his heart, I would have to say yes. Right?"

Laura couldn't hold back a slight grin.

"I like you," Katherine said to her. "You're clever."

Her eyes were smiling as she took another bite of pancakes.

31

Here a Star and There a Star, Some Lose Their Way

After breakfast Katherine went for a ride. She brought with her a canteen of water and her Emily Dickinson book. She rode through the last of the fog in a yet unplanted soybean field, and into the dappled sunshine of the woods, terminating at the secret stream. She let Dulcinea relax while she found a comfortable lean against the maple, flipping through the poetry, letting the occasional phrase trip upon her mind, but finding nothing in which to feast.

Katherine felt hollow. Uncomfortable in her own skin. She shifted her seat, again and again trying to make things right, but the roots were uncooperative. It was as if Dulcinea could sense her frustration. She wandered over to Katherine and nuzzled her, asking for some petting. Katherine stood up and obliged, scratching and hugging her best friend. She left the canteen and book under the tree, got on Dulcinea and rode.

They raced through the woods, jumping fallen trees and even another small stream. They broke into a gallop in the field, and Katherine let out a guttural scream she didn't know she had in her. She hadn't ridden Dulcinea like this before, not in an unknown place, not with such wild abandon. She laughed and screamed at the same time. For the first time Katherine let go.

When she arrived back at her house, Laura's car was parked in the driveway. Her mother met her at the door.

"Your friends are here," she said, with a forced smile.

"Friends?"

"Trey and Laura," she explained as if it was a regular thing. "They are having tea in the kitchen."

Katherine went through the dining room to the kitchen and didn't bother to hide her surprise. Laura smiled warmly. Trey was putting more sugar in his cup, and didn't look up right away.

"Sorry," Laura explained. "We didn't know when you were coming home, but your mom said it was okay to wait. She gave us cookies."

"Okaaaay?" Katherine said but meant *why are you here?*

"We wanted to know if you wanted to come over to play," Laura said, intentionally trying to sound like a kid. "We're going to play board games at Trey's house, Candace is going to come over, but you know, Monopoly is more fun with a fourth person. I thought you might want to join us. I can drive you home afterwards if you want."

As poised as Katherine normally was, her mouth hung open a little in stunned silence. But then, it was as if a switch inside of her flipped. She closed her mouth and looked back and forth from Laura to Trey. He had a dumb grin on his face, as if he was trying to hide something.

"Whatever. Sure, I guess," Katherine said, still not convinced she was going to go. "I need to shower, shall I just meet you there?"

Laura shrugged.

"We can wait," she said, picking up another cookie and raising her eyebrows with a smile to Katherine as she bit into it.

Twenty minutes later they were in the car, backing out of the driveway. Laura was driving, Katherine rode shotgun, and Trey was in the back, sitting in the middle of the seats. Laura waved goodbye to Katherine's mom, who was watching them with a slight air of suspicion from the front porch.

“We’re not going to play board games,” Laura said with a devious grin.

32

The Space Between

Katherine nodded nonchalantly and looked back at Trey, who had a more serious look than Laura.

"So, am I being kidnapped?"

"Kinda," Laura said, watching the road. "I really liked our breakfast this morning."

"Okaaaay. So your natural inclination is to then kidnap me?"

Laura grinned as she turned onto route 113 heading north.

"I went home and thought about it. It's pretty complicated, because we all have, like, these feelings, that are, I don't know... complicated."

"Uh huh," Katherine said suspiciously. Trey was now leaning on the back of their seats so he could be in the conversation.

"So I thought, you know, we have some options, but all of them end up kinda bad with someone being hurt, you know, and like fighting and like..."

"Wait, just stop," Katherine said.

"What?"

"You're not... proposing..." Katherine spoke carefully. "That we all..."

Laura laughed.

"No. God no."

"Let's not be too hasty," Trey said almost jokingly. Almost.

Laura looked at Katherine and slowly shook her head dismissively.

"You are really convinced I'm a lesbian, aren't you? Maybe you're, like, projecting something..."

"Well then what are you talking about?" Katherine said, cutting her off.

"I'm talking about all of us just being friends."

"Personally, I don't get it," Trey said.

"Exactly," Laura stuck her tongue out at him in the rear view mirror. "You don't get *it*."

"But why did we need to kidnap her?"

"Trey, you know we're not really kidnapping her, right?"

"Uh, no, I didn't," he said with heavy sarcasm. "But like, why the whole thing."

"I don't know. It like wouldn't work over the phone. Everything else would be too formal or weird."

"It's still really, really weird," Katherine said.

"Yup," Trey agreed.

"Look, here's our options. We can date and break up and never talk to each other and everyone can be sad and alone, or, we can choose to *not* date, not break up, and we can just be sad together. And I don't want to be sad alone, and I figured, Katherine doesn't want to be sad alone."

"And what about me?" Trey's voice was still a little higher than usual. He probably still hoped there was a chance for a threesome at the end of this conversation.

"You?" Laura looked in the rearview mirror to check that Trey was still smiling. "You get to hang out with two hot girls. I don't know dude, I think that will raise your stock in the eyes of others."

Katherine was silent. She didn't like the idea of Trey dating others. But she didn't like the idea of not being around Trey. Laura was kind of strange, but she had to give her credit, it took guts to even suggest something like this. And she only had a month left of school anyway, might as well make it interesting.

"So we're not playing Monopoly?"

Laura shook her head.

"Then where are we going?"

"We're going to the boardwalk!" Laura almost shouted.

Katherine rolled her eyes and groaned. "My dad says the boardwalk is where kids go if they want to get arrested."

Trey laughed.

"Nah, you can get arrested anywhere."

***

Like all great seaside resort towns, Ocean City had a boardwalk full of souvenir shops, restaurants, rides, arcades, and other amusements. Ocean City's boardwalk is located at the extreme southern point of the peninsula, the area directly north of the inlet where the ocean met the bay. Locals refer to the whole southern end of the boardwalk and the parking area there as *The Inlet*.

The boardwalk was over two miles long, but teenagers usually hung out around The Inlet, keeping close to the arcades and rides. Most businesses were closed for the winter, but this was Easter weekend, and a late Easter weekend at that, and the afternoon was sunny and warm. The arcades were open, the rides were operating, candy shops and pizza places had knocked the dust off and were stretching their arms after a long winter's nap.

The threesome went right to Thrasher's French Fries, a boardwalk institution. There are certain foods that can only be truly appreciated in a particular place. Like an apple, plucked off an orchard tree on a cool autumn afternoon, or a grape still wet with dew as the sun rises over a vineyard morning. These boardwalk fries can only be enjoyed properly when the wind is in from the sea, providing the final seasoning to the deep fried potato grown half a continent away.

Katherine was out of her comfort zone. She had never spent any time as a teenager at the boardwalk, and never been there at all without her parents. Sure, she went there as a kid, maybe once a summer when relatives from out of town were visiting, her father watchful and grumbling, her mother wide-eyed at the sea of humanity that had mostly given up caring what others thought. The most extreme and creative of the hoi polloi seemed to be drawn to this space with hunger and intensity. It was a carnival, a circus. The boardwalk was the space between the clean bright beach and the dirty dank bars, and the culmination of the two forces led to a fashion rarely considered acceptable anywhere else. It was where the most offensive t-shirts were both sold and worn, and where one went to show off tattoos and piercings long before they became an act of conformity.

Katherine took it all in. The sights and smells of the sea air, fried food, and humanity was electrifying. They strolled until they found a vacant bench. She sat cross-legged, her back leaning against Trey's shoulder as he sat facing ocean and she faced south down the boardwalk.

Laura held the fries and stood close enough to both of them so they could help themselves. She told a story about the time when they were kids and Trey decided to steal the barge, basically a large raft, that was being used to do repairs on the Ocean Pines boat ramp. They took it all the way out into the St. Martin's River, but once they got into the channel his stick couldn't touch the bottom anymore, and they were certain that they would end up drifting out to sea.

"He started crying."

"I didn't cry!"

"Yes you did."

"I was just worried for you."

"How did you guys get rescued?"

"A waterman noticed Trey crying and towed us in."

"So I basically saved your life."

Katherine and Laura were laughing. Laura touched Katherine's arm. It was a warm touch, and Katherine felt good. For a moment she thought about the boat ramp, how he took her there first night after they kissed, how it was also the first place she saw him naked.

They joked about other things. Stories new and old. Mostly they made fun of Trey. It was necessary, like the wise old women of the village insulting the meat. Without any guide or example they had to figure out how to balance the fact Trey had been inside both of them.

They pushed the limits of their new relationships. Each of them had to let go of a little bit of themselves in order to make this okay.

"Laura likes to have sex to T'Pau," Trey said apropos of nothing.

"I do not. Don't listen to him, it's an inside joke."

"Eew," Katherine offered.

They cackled like the gulls hunting for unattended Thrasher's. They laughed, even if they weren't sure what they were even laughing about, because it felt good. They were brilliant and exceptional teenagers that for once got to be dumb kids. They were friends. It was a good Friday.

***

The next day they went bowling in the afternoon. Candace and Tyrone joined them and Katherine bowled for the first time in her life.

At one point Candace cornered Laura at the snack bar.

"So, are Katherine and Trey back together?"

"No," Laura smiled.

"Huh. Are... are you and Trey together? Cause it kinda seems like you guys are."

"No," Laura said and laughed a little.

Candace paused obviously thinking about something. She looked concerned.

"Okay," she started slowly. "Don't take this the wrong way, but, are you and Katherine together?"

Laura sighed.

"How am I supposed to take that?"

"Okay, well, I'm sorry but how are you guys all hanging out and close and everything? Cause like, didn't Trey break up with her because of you? And now everything is like... cool?"

"Yeah, it's like, we're just going to be mature about it."

Candace stared at her. She had no expression as her mind raced. Then she grabbed Laura's arm and pulled her close. She spoke in a whisper, their noses only about three inches away from one another.

"Are the three of you, like... like... like uh, ménage a trois-ing? You have to tell me if you are, you have to, I'm serious!"

"Oh my god!" Laura laughed but with frustration. "You need to chill, seriously. Wow."

Laura started to walk away. Candace was following her.

"Um, that wasn't a denial..."

Later that night Katherine, Trey, and Laura went to The Point. Katherine walked to the bayside and looked out at Ocean City. Trey sat on the hood of his car, laying back against the windshield and looking up at the night sky. Laura was in the car looking through Trey's tapes for something she wanted to listen to, but not finding anything that she felt was right for the moment. Too many songs reminded her of making love with Trey. She felt that music was both sacred to her and unfair to Katherine. So she gave up and joined the others outside.

"You know Candace thinks we're all... you know... together," Laura said nonchalantly as she emerged from Trey's car.

"Ugh," Katherine shook her head.

"I still think it's a good idea," Trey offered.

"It's a terrible idea," Laura said.

"How do you know unless we try?" Trey really was trying his best.

Katherine walked over to where Laura was leaning against the car and she leaned next to her. She was smiling. They looked out at the lights of Ocean City together.

"Can I ask you something personal?" Katherine asked Laura.

"Sure."

"Do you think you ever could?"

"WHAT?"

"No, not with me and Trey, I just mean... ever. Do you think you could ever have sex with two people at the same time?"

Laura laughed. She looked back at Trey. He looked like he could be drooling.

"I mean, sure. Two guys at once, I could do that."

"Awwww!" Trey said. They all laughed.

Then they were all quiet, as their minds all went different directions.

"What's your father like?" Katherine asked Laura.

"He's nice," Laura said with a shrug. "He's smart, but, like only around smart people, if that makes sense. What's weird is that, I swear I remember him being so affectionate to my mom when I was little. But she hates him."

"What's your mom like?"

"She's smart too. She's a mom, you know. Not like Dolores."

"What's that supposed to mean?" Trey asked.

"Like, I don't know how to say it. Like I can tell Dolores anything, I think, but I can't really tell my mom anything, you know, cause she's still my mom. I mean, I tell Dolores things I wouldn't even tell the priest."

"What the hell does that mean?" Katherine asked.

"Like at confession."

"Oh," Katherine thought about it. "That's like a Catholic thing, right? I keep forgetting you guys are both Catholic."

"I'm barely Catholic," Trey said. "My dad never went to church, so I used to go with my mom and she had me take my first communion without him even knowing. But I didn't get confirmed or anything."

"Why did you stop?" Katherine asked.

Trey sighed.

"When I was a kid, I used to think that my dad hit me because of something that I had done wrong. Like, if I cussed, even if he wasn't around, he would hit me later, or the next day or something. Because I deserved it for doing wrong, like... like it was my fault. And, at church I was told that if I took communion then my sins would be forgiven. I was just a dumb kid, but I thought that if my sins were forgiven then my dad wouldn't hit me anymore."

Trey stopped talking and sighed. Everyone stayed quiet. Katherine's eyes were damp. Laura's left leg was shaking with anger.

"So that afternoon I went right up to him and told him that I had taken communion. I don't know, I thought I had some power over him or something. That was the first time he ever hit me with a belt. I was eight years old, and this grown man hit me as hard as he could... and he even felt like he had to use a weapon. I just... I couldn't figure out what I had done wrong."

"I'm so sorry," Katherine said, holding her hand in front of her mouth and trying to hold back her tears.

"I fucking hate your father," Laura growled through gritted teeth.

"Me too," Trey said stoically. "Me too."

***

A few days later the threesome was hanging out at Trey's house eating pizza and listening to music. Trey suggested they play strip poker. Laura told him to give it a rest, but Katherine didn't answer. Laura wondered if Katherine was considering it.

At some point Laura realized her back was sore and she was uncomfortable. She grabbed a throw pillow from the couch and laid down on the floor.

"Trey," she said. "Gimme a back rub."

He complied. Katherine was noticeably uncomfortable.

"Um, should I leave?"

Laura turned her head to look at her.

"No, my back just hurts from practice today. Trey's pretty good at it. Has he ever given you a backrub?"

Katherine shook her head.

"He'll give you one when he's done with me."

"Hey, what do I get?" Trey asked, sliding his hands under Laura's sweatshirt.

"Our appreciation and love?"

"How about one game of strip poker?"

"How about I give you a massage after you give me and Katherine one?"

"How about you both give me a massage at the same time?"

Laura exhaled as Trey pushed into her shoulder blades.

"I'm fine with that," she said.

Katherine had remained quiet. Laura had her eyes closed, but when she opened them she saw Katherine looked nervous.

"You okay?" she asked Katherine.

Katherine thought about the question.

"I don't know. We haven't touched each other since we broke up."

"Except for that time you kissed him."

Trey snorted a laugh. Katherine shook her head.

They traded backrubs and endured Trey's repeated suggestions of getting naked. Katherine had never had a massage before and never given one either. She felt vulnerable and nervous.

"You got a lot of tension," Trey noted. "Laura, feel this knot."

Katherine flinched. Laura didn't move.

"Nice try Trey," Laura said, smiling.

"No, I'm serious, it's like a huge knot. I'm just... whatever. Seriously, are you under a lot of stress or something?"

"Yeah," Katherine confirmed.

"Like what?" Laura wondered. "You're already accepted to college, you're going to be prom queen and valedictorian, and you're like filthy rich."

"I don't even know if I'm going to prom."

Laura laughed. "I think the world might actually stop spinning if you didn't."

"My parents would freak out if I didn't." She closed her eyes as Trey pushed into her ribs. "Ow!"

"That's so weird," Laura said, getting up for a slice of room temperature pizza. "My parents wouldn't even notice if I didn't go to homecoming or prom."

"My parents have plans for me. They're pretty involved. My dad thinks I'm going to get into politics."

"That's random. What does your dad do?" Laura asked.

"It's hard to explain," Katherine said. "Basically he just... owns things."

"Must be nice. So who are you going to prom with?"

Katherine shook her head.

"I don't know."

"Trey," Laura said. "Why don't you take her?"

They both turned and looked at her.

Laura wasn't entirely sure what she was trying to prove, or to whom she was trying to prove it. She felt her heart race with fear and excitement. This was one of those moments she balanced her heart against her head.

No one said anything. It was a long silence as each tried to read the others. Finally Katherine broke.

"You would be okay with that?" she asked Laura. "If Trey and I went together just as friends."

"Of course," Laura said, feeling her heart pound against her chest. "Why wouldn't I be?"

33

The Driveway

The morning after Prom, Katherine knocked on Laura's door with tears in her eyes. It was a warm early-May morning, the sun was shining, and fragrant hyacinths were blooming in Joyce's garden. Laura answered the door and invited her in but Katherine shook her head.

"I'm so sorry," she started. "It was all my fault."

Laura's heart sank. She knew something terrible had happened, and she knew it had happened to Trey.

"What happened? Is Trey okay?"

Katherine nodded. She was crying now and she put her hand over her mouth. She shook her head.

"I fucked up."

"Okay," Laura nodded. "Okay. What happened?"

"I kissed him," Katherine said quickly. Then she held her lips together tightly looking at Laura. It was clear she was afraid.

Laura felt like she might throw up. She had known this was a possibility but she told herself that Trey was free to make his own decisions. But still, she felt ill. She did her best to smile and shrug.

"We did more than that," Katherine continued. "I'm so sorry. I'm such a monster."

Then Laura did something that surprised even herself. She walked up to Katherine and hugged her.

"It's okay," she said as Katherine sobbed in her arms. "Seriously, it's okay. You're not the first person to regret having sex with Trey Buckingham."

Katherine choke-laughed through the sobs.

"How... are... you being... so cool... about this?"

"Honestly," Laura said. "I don't know."

Katherine eventually calmed down and went with Laura to English's for breakfast. Laura drove since Katherine hadn't slept yet and was seeing double. She explained to Laura how they had had a few drinks and one thing led to another, and then Laura asked her to stop giving her the details.

"Laura, I'm a terrible person," Katherine said, tearing up again in English's. "I... I only agreed to hang out with you guys in the first place because I just... *sigh* I love Trey so much and I just wanted to be around him. But you have been so nice to me and... I feel like I just stabbed you in the back. I'm so sorry."

She started crying again in English's. The same waitress, who at this point knew more about the drama in Laura's life than Jessica, walked up and offered more coffee. She looked at Katherine with a concerned air.

"Boy trouble," Laura whispered to her.

The waitress nodded knowingly and touched Katherine's shoulder gently before walking away.

"Here's the thing," Laura leaned towards Katherine and spoke quietly. "I love Trey, and I know he loves me. But I don't know if that's enough. Do you know what I mean?"

Katherine looked at her. She had stopped weeping, but her eyes were still wet. She shook her head.

"When I thought I was pregnant I thought my life was over. I mean...fuck, I don't want to live here forever. I don't want to live anywhere forever. I want to explore, I want to travel, I want to find new things and new people and not just... I'm not ready to put down roots."

“Like marriage?” Katherine said, confused.

“Yeah.”

“Neither am I.”

Laura sighed.

“I know, but. I feel like if I stayed with Trey he would convince me not to go. So I guess, I’m okay with you being with him, if you are okay with him being my best friend. Does that make sense?”

Katherine stared at her.

“Do you hate me?”

Laura shook her head.

“No, not in the least. I’m kinda impressed with you, coming to talk to me like you did.” Laura sighed. “You know, I actually thought this might happen, but I never thought you would be as upset about it as you are. Honestly, I didn’t think you cared this much about me.”

“I don’t have a lot of girlfriends,” she said to Laura. “I know this sounds crazy, but you might be my best friend.”

“That does sound crazy,” Laura said, smiling.

***

Laura dropped Katherine off at her home and told her she would come get her after she had some sleep so she could retrieve her car. Katherine was so tired she wasn’t even making sense when she said goodbye to Laura, although she did kiss Laura on the cheek and tell her that she loved her.

When Laura returned home Trey was waiting for her. He had tears in his eyes.

“No,” Laura said as she got out of her car.

“Laura, I’m so sorry.”

“I know, I already did this.”

Trey was confused. He hadn’t known Katherine had come over to Laura’s after he fell asleep.

“You fucked Katherine, I know.”

Trey sighed.

"I never wanted to hurt you," he said. Laura thought he sounded like an actor from one of the old black and white movies that she could never stay awake through.

"Come on," Laura said, leading Trey by the hand into her house. "Katherine said you had to give me a back rub as penance."

"What's happening?" Trey was thoroughly confused.

"Just shut up and give me a back rub," Laura said, peeling off her shirt. "And that's all you're going to do. Seriously."

Trey looked around thinking it was a trap.

"I'm so confused," he said.

"We all are," Laura mumbled, lying on the bed and closing her eyes.

***

Somehow, against all logic or sense, the three remained close. Katherine and Trey dated. Laura still got her backrubs from Trey, sometimes in front of Katherine, and Laura still fell asleep with Trey on the phone, though no longer in his arms.

That May, the three of them spent every night together. Laura and Katherine ate together at Buck's Tavern while Trey worked. Katherine went alone to Laura's lacrosse game to cheer her on. Trey and Laura drove all the way up to Montgomery County to watch Katherine compete in a horse jumping event.

They shared music, food, and conversation. At some point in the evening Trey and Katherine would break off to have sex. It was awkward but Laura teased them about it, and somehow that made it okay.

Rumors swirled around them. There was the rumor which claimed Laura was a lesbian, but there was another rumor that she was secretly having sex with Trey. Those rumors were old. Everyone knew boys and girls couldn't be friends, especially boys and girls that touched each other as much as Trey and Laura did. Now suddenly Katherine was part of the equation. She was Prom Queen, class president, valedictorian, rich, beloved... so naturally people couldn't wait to assume something licentious about her. It's easy to believe great people have flaws, and in this case the *flaw* was Laura. Adding Katherine into the mix of the two rumors about Laura neatly unified them in the most salacious way.

Eventually the rumor that Katherine was dating a boy and girl at the same time got all the way back to Katherine's parents. Even before they heard the rumor, they had already been concerned. Katherine's father had heard from more than one of his good-ole-boy friends that they saw Katherine hanging out at Buck's Tavern. Her mother didn't like how often Katherine came home smelling of the beach, even on school nights. Neither of them liked that she was dropped off right at, or a few minutes after, curfew every single night, usually by her boyfriend and another girl, or sometimes just the girl. Finally they knew why.

Everything came to a head early in the evening of the spring athletic banquet. Trey and Laura were both due to be honored as the most valuable players on their respective teams, and both were supposed to find out that they had broken the single season and career records for points. Katherine was going to the banquet to be with her lover and her friend, to support them, to cheer them for their accomplishments. She was wearing a turquoise summer dress with white flowers that she had picked out on a shopping excursion with Laura the weekend before.

Trey and Laura were just about to pull into the Bounds' long driveway, when Katherine's parents called her into her father's library.

"Sit down," her father commanded. He was sitting in his leather chair, a wall of books behind him. His wife stood by his left side, and placed her right hand on his shoulder. He sighed heavily.

Katherine sat and stayed quiet.

"This is not easy for us to say."

Concern flooded into Katherine. Her quick mind flashed a dozen possibilities, everything from her parents divorcing, her grandparents dying, or one of her parents being horribly sick.

"Well..." he clearly didn't want to continue. His wife squeezed his shoulder to give him courage. "It is come to our attention... well, that is to say, we have heard... uhhh."

"Katherine," her mother's tone was ice cold. "There is a rumor going around that you, Trey, and that girl Laura are in an unnatural relationship."

Katherine's mouth hung open for a second. And then relief washed over her, and she laughed.

"Ha! Trey wishes!"

Honestly, it didn't sound like something Katherine would ever say. It sounded like something Laura would say. But Katherine had been spending all her time with Laura, and her friend's sense of humor had rubbed off on her. It did not, however, translate well to her parents.

Her mother gasped. "What does that even mean?"

Her father turned red with rage, likely due to envisioning a teenage boy trying to convince his daughter to have a threesome. He stood up and pointed at Katherine.

"I knew this was all Trey Buckingham's fault. His father is a violent criminal and drug addict, and the apple never falls far from the tree. Are you doing drugs? Tell me! Are you?"

Katherine stood up as well and leaned over her father's desk.

"I don't do drugs and neither does Trey! And he's not violent. He's not like his father!"

"He's not violent?" her mother said. "He got kicked off the basketball team for punching the referee!"

"He didn't punch a referee!"

"He nearly killed his father!" her mother continued.

"WHAT?"

"This is what happens," her father said as he walked in front of the door to his library to prevent her from leaving, "when you spend your life in bars, letting your children grow up feral, like animals."

"Oh my God, dad, what are you even talking about?'

Katherine's mother stepped towards Katherine and pointed her finger right in Katherine's face.

"Don't you dare take the Lord's name in vain. Not now! Not now!"

"He's going to hit you," Katherine's father continued. "You know that's what happens with people like him. They hit their wives, and their children."

"Why?" Katherine walked through her mother's pointing finger to yell at her father. "Because he's Catholic?"

"What? He's Catholic?" Katherine's father was shocked.

"He is never!" Katherine's mother's eyes were wide with shock. "He's a BUCKINGHAM!"

"His mother is Catholic," Katherine turned to face her mom. "Who is a wonderful person by the way, and who Trey was DEFENDING when he *nearly* killed his father!"

"He's going to hit you because that's what he knows." Katherine's father said, trying to calm his voice down. "That's how he was raised. I didn't know he was a Catholic, and that just makes all of this worse."

"What does that even mean?" Katherine held up her hands towards her father. She felt the stress of feeling trapped.

"You aren't going to marry him, and that's that. For myriad reasons. The most important being that you are going to do great things and Trey Buckingham is not. He's not worthy of you. He's not good enough to be the wife of a US Senator."

"Wife?!?"

"Husband," Katherine's father was confused. "I misspoke. You know what I meant!"

Katherine pushed past her father and went out the front door.

"Fuck you and fuck the US Senate! I love him!" she screamed, slamming the door behind her. Trey, in his khaki pants, blue jacket, and yellow and blue tie, with Laura in her black and white floral cami dress, stood in the Bounds' driveway, having just gotten out of the car.

Laura and Trey froze trying to understand the scene. The door burst open and Katherine's parents came through almost at the same time. Trey's eyes fixed on Mr. Bounds. His leg started shaking and his fists were clenched.

Katherine's mom grabbed her arm.

"Calm down! Calm down!" she screamed at her daughter.

Katherine pulled her arm away from her mother. Standing in the driveway it was obvious how much taller Katherine was than her mother. She looked down and growled.

"Don't touch me."

Mr. Bounds then bellowed, "GET BACK INSIDE NOW!" which prompted the neighbors to call the police. The Bounds' home was on a four acre lot, as was the neighbor's home. That's how loud her father had yelled.

"You are being ridiculous!" Katherine yelled at both of her parents at the same time. "You act like my life is your life. It's not your life. I'm not a puppet for you to play with! I'm so sick of you trying to control everything I do. Let me fucking live my life! Aren't you proud of me? Haven't I done everything right?"

"Because of us," Mr. Bounds said.

"BECAUSE OF ME!" Katherine screamed. "I did these things, not you! I studied. I trained. I worked. I did these things! I did them! Not you! Not you. Not you."

"Of course," her father said quietly. "That's not what I meant."

"I don't care what you say, I know what you mean. Say whatever you want because I'm through listening to you. I hate you!"

Katherine turned to leave. She started to cry. She had never said that to her father before. He stepped towards her and grabbed her wrist.

"Katherine wait," he said.

"GET OFF ME!"

He didn't let go. In a flash, Laura was standing between father and daughter, pointing her finger right into Mr. Bounds face.

"She said let her go!" Laura yelled.

Mr. Bounds released Katherine's wrist and stumbled backwards, in complete shock. He was so focused on Katherine that up until that point he hadn't even seen the other kids in the driveway. Mrs. Bounds then got in between her husband and Laura and started yelling at Laura.

"Don't you dare yell at my husband!"

"I wouldn't need to yell at him if he wasn't such an asshole," Laura said, with anger, but calmer than the rest of the group. "She told him to get off her."

"It's none of your business!" Mrs. Bounds yelled getting closer to Laura. It looked for a moment like she might actually hit Laura. Her husband, recognizing the direness of the situation, grabbed his wife's arms to restrain her.

Trey, who had turned red with rage suddenly unfroze and taking a cue from Mr. Bounds, grabbed Laura to hold her back as well. Katherine was saying something to her father, but it was drowned out by Laura who was yelling at Mrs. Bounds.

"It is my business, she's my friend!"

"My daughter will never be friends with a DYKE LIKE YOU!" Mrs. Bounds screamed.

That was the moment Sheriff Bubby Davis stepped out of his cruiser and saw his girlfriend's daughter fighting with one of the most powerful men in Worcester County. To say he put on kid gloves at that moment would be an understatement.

He quickly stepped between Laura and Mrs. Bounds and separated the parties into two groups. With extraordinary patience he went back and forth mediating an eventual settlement. At one point, Katherine said she was moving out, and Laura kicked gasoline on the fire when she said Katherine could come live with her. Katherine's mother replied "over my dead body!" which was the last solidly dramatic line of the evening.

To Bubby's credit, he was good with teenagers, especially teenagers he liked, or at least, teenagers who he had reason to want their parents to like him. For whatever reason, his perseverance paid off and he was certain that the situation was completely diffused before he drove out of that driveway. It took hours. Laura and Trey missed their banquet, and the rumors only got worse from there.

Katherine agreed not to move out, on the condition that her parents agreed to stop telling her that she should break up with Trey. The three friends drove off together, and went to The Point. There, with the ever-present background of the twinkling Ocean City lights in the bay, they sat on the hood of Trey's car, looked at the stars, and shared some tears, hugs, and music.

34

Little Earthquakes

Jessica narrowed her eyes as Laura recounted the driveway fight, occasionally adding a "she didn't really say that" or "what an asshole" but otherwise just listening, smiling, and nodding. She thought it was funny that it was her fault that everyone suspected that Laura was a lesbian. Except for Dolores, of course, who had solid proof to the contrary.

"Your junior year was pretty fucking crazy."

Jessica was lounging in her bean bag chair doing her best to not spill her martini while shifting to try to get comfortable.

"This chair is not conducive to drinking martinis."

It was a little after two PM on a Tuesday in June, the only week Jessica was going to be home for the summer. She was taking a film class at Film and Video Arts in New York City that started the following Monday. In the spring semester she had become more interested in directing than acting and wanted film to be her focus moving forward, so she scrapped her plans to move back to the beach for the summer. Laura, while disappointed, was not surprised. Jessica didn't belong in Ocean City anymore.

Jessica took them to the kitchen so she could make herself another martini.

“So what I don’t understand is,” Jessica said as she poured the gin into the silver cocktail shaker. “Why were you okay with Katherine and Trey fucking? Like, did you like... did you like watch, or...”

“Ew! No!”

Jessica shrugged.

“Well then, why were you okay with it?”

“I think I got scared.”

“Of what?”

“You know, Trey once told me he couldn’t wait to get out of Ocean Pines and move to the city.”

“Yeah, like everyone.”

“Yeah... except he meant Ocean City.”

“Oh.”

“I mean, Trey and I tried being friends, and the first night we would have made love if he had a condom. It just, it didn’t work. But like, when we added Katherine, it kinda worked.”

“That’s diabolical."

“I didn’t plan it. Or maybe I did. I don’t know. I like Trey... no, I love Trey. I do. But if we’re so perfect for each other then why didn’t he wait for me? I think it’s weird that he’s just suddenly okay having sex with Katherine every night.”

“I don’t know,” Jessica shrugged.

“What?”

“I mean, you broke up with Trey. And... I don’t know, he’s a boy. They’re dogs.”

“I love dogs.”

“Ha. Puppy love,” Jessica smiled at her own joke. “And now you are going to work with him every day this summer...”

“Katherine is working at Buck’s too.”

“Holy shitballs, this town is so incestuous. You gotta get out of here. You got to come up and visit me in New York.”

“I’d love to.”

"I'm moving out of student housing and into my own apartment. My roommate's been a real bitch."

Laura just raised her eyebrow and said nothing.

"Alright, come on upstairs, we're gonna listen to Tori Amos, so no talking."

Jessica made Laura listen to the full Tori Amos album *Little Earthquakes*. She played it loud, as was proper.

Little Earthquakes was something new. A sultry female singer, a big dramatic piano, and heavy religious imagery drew Laura in immediately. The first song title was *Crucify* and had the line *I've been looking for a savior beneath these dirty sheets*. That was when Laura knew this album belonged to her. She closed her eyes and heard every word. Every song was about her, and Trey, and Katherine, and Alex, and Dolores, and even Joyce. During *Silent all These Years* she cried after Tori sang *I got the antichrist in the kitchen yelling at me again*. She saw Trey and Dolores in her mind in a way she never had before. She imagined the violence that she had never actually seen. And then she remembered the blood on the leg of the chair.

During *Precious Things* she laughed and opened her eyes when she clearly heard the lyrics *so you can make me come that doesn't make you Jesus.* She looked over at Jessica who was watching her and sporting a wide, triumphant grin.

In many ways it was a perfect record, until the second to last song. *Me and a Gun* described a rape so viscerally that Laura felt sick. It was as if something was suddenly pushing down on her chest. She took the dull pressure to mean anger, and stood up to leave. She couldn't even listen to the final song.

Laura needed air. She went out into the blazing afternoon sun, Jessica following, watching her with concern and still holding her martini. There used to be a black cherry tree on the south side of Jessica's yard, and on summer afternoons it would throw a hint of dappled shade on the west side of the dock, so Laura sat there, in the shade on the dock. Jessica joined her. Both girls faced west, their bare feet dangling over the side, tickling the tepid water of the bay. Laura looked around. Jessica's home was on a canal, but near the mouth so depending on which way you looked you could see either other homes, docks, moored boats, and people; or salt marshes, birds, sky, and the bay. Laura had chosen to turn her back on the world of man. Her eyes were full and glistening.

"Why do all the singers I love write so much about sex and violence?"

Jessica sipped her martini while composing her answer.

"Cause you don't really like bubblegum pop shit. You like singers who tell stories. And stories have conflict. Violence is the easiest conflict. But also, you like female singers who are personal and honest. And that's just the reality of too many women, that with sex comes violence."

No tears fell from Laura's eyes. She was terrifyingly still as she waited for wisdom from the world. No words were said for quite a while by these two teenagers sitting on the dock, watching the sunny afternoon wane. There was a cooling breeze gathering persistence, and the distant waves in the center of the bay bred tiny whitecaps. Occasional gusts created rustling of the cherry tree leaves, and caused more sun to hit their skin. Otherwise, it was oddly quiet there and then, facing away from the city, in a hot afternoon when even the animals seemed to be hiding from the sun and man.

Laura could hear the smallest hint of a rasp in Jessica's breathing. She started timing her breath, to join her friend. Jessica took shorter and more rapid breaths than Laura would, perhaps due to gin, cigarettes, or a year spent in New York City. At first, Laura found it hard to breath that quickly and shallowly, but soon the timing matched and both girls found more ease. Jessica didn't even consciously realize what Laura was doing.

"I think about Dolores sometimes," Laura said, watching the sun's reflection dance on the bay. "When she was our age. You know, like, she had no idea of the violence she was going to experience. She believed in romance, and like, happily ever after, you know?"

"Did she tell you that?"

"No, I mean, I just assumed."

Jessica looked at Laura.

"Why?"

Laura shrugged still looking at the bay, even though she could feel that Jessica faced her. She wanted to keep looking at the water.

"You think that because that's what you believe, right?" Jessica continued. "That you can get a happily ever after. Like that's the point of all of this, right?"

Laura met Jessica's eyes.

"Not the point, exactly. But yeah, I mean, that's got to be part of it, right?"

Jessica smiled and looked past Laura at the canal. A boat puttered slowly past, heading to the open water, and Jessica paused, staying silent as both girls returned the boat passengers' waves. As it got to the channel it sped away.

"I don't think it's a part of it," Jessica said.

Laura thought about her father and Todd.

"You know, you don't have to be married to have a happily ever after."

Jessica rolled her eyes, but didn't respond. Laura waited until she was sure she wouldn't.

"Can I ask you a question?" Laura said with a little more verve and a little less sadness.

"Another one?"

"Ha," Laura said sarcastically, pausing before she continued. "Are you, like, seeing anyone?"

Jessica fingered the rim of her empty martini glass and shrugged.

"Not really. There was a senior I was kinda hanging out with for a minute. But she turned out to be a LUG."

Laura shook her head implying she didn't know what Jessica meant.

"A LUG. Lesbian Until Graduation. Apparently it's pretty common. She's dating some dude now, an installation artist in Soho."

"Wait, what?" Laura was incredulous. "That's a thing?"

"Installation artists? Yeah, everyone's doing that now. I think it's kinda bull shit... like it's just arranging other people's art, but whatever."

"No, like someone can just decide to be straight after being a lesbian? You can't do that, can you?"

"Oh come on," Jessica teased. "You tell me you haven't thought about trying that out with Katherine?"

"No!"

"Not even a little."

"Only in Trey's fantasies," Laura said as a matter of routine.

Jessica smiled.

"He probably has a secret lair where he's trying to plot how to make that happen. With maps and spreadsheets and whatnot."

"Uhhh, I think you are giving Trey way more credit than he deserves."

They giggled.

"So, I'm still confused. Do you think my dad could have just chosen to not be gay if he wanted?"

"Oh..." Jessica didn't think the conversation was going there. She hissed with an inhale while thinking through her answer.

"Eh, probably not? I think people will someday figure out that sexuality is more fluid than we realize. Like maybe it's more of a spectrum, and maybe, not for nothing, for some people it might change in their lifetime? I don't know, I guess don't think we need to be so locked in to just one thing. Are you sure you've never been attracted to women, like at all?"

"I mean, I can recognize when a woman is beautiful, and I can admire her for it, but I don't want to like, lick her or anything."

Jessica laughed uncontrollably for a few seconds.

"So graphic," Jessica said, wiping a tear away from her eye.

"Well, you know what I mean," Laura said smiling as she looked out to the bay.

"You think you will get married someday?" Jessica wondered.

"To Trey?"

"To anyone."

Laura shrugged.

"Someday, I guess, yeah. I mean, it's what people do, right?"

"What do you think the point is, to getting married?" Jessica asked.

"What do you mean?"

"Well, I took an anthropology class this year and they said that the reason marriage existed in the first place was for meat security. So the wife could ensure that she would get meat."

"Why would the husband do it? To get vegetables?"

"No, to ensure his offspring was his. He trades meat for certainty that his line will continue. But, now that doesn't seem so important, the whole meat security thing, right? My mom used to always tell me that when she was growing up the only thing she thought women could be was a homemaker, nurse, teacher, or secretary. For her, there weren't other options. But now, we can be whatever we want. And we can buy all the meat we need from a store. So, why do it? Why get married?"

"Sex anytime you want?"

Jessica frowned.

"Yeah, but if that's true, doesn't it also mean you have to have sex whenever your spouse wants to as well? Which means, having sex when you don't want to? That sounds... wrong."

Laura smiled.

"I don't know. I kinda like sex."

Jessica looked away, out to the growing waves of the bay.

"You and everyone else I know," she said ruefully.

Laura was surprised.

"Are you okay?" she asked.

"I don't know. I think there might be something wrong with me."

"You mean like, sick?"

"Maybe," Jessica said with a sad smile. "Like in the brain."

"What do you mean?"

Jessica shrugged.

"I don't know. I just don't like sex. Maybe not always, but, pretty much always. I feel like I am doing it just because I have to do it in order to be with other people, or even just to exist in this world, but I don't ever like it."

"Even lesbian sex."

Jessica laughed hard again.

"The way you said that," she said, still laughing.

"What? I don't know your terms. Lugs and bitches and whatever else you city folks talk like."

"Don't act provincial," Jessica said, wiping a tear from her eye. "It's beneath you."

Laura looked back at the water.

"You know, my mom never said she was only allowed to be a teacher, or nurse, or whatever. I'm pretty sure she wanted to be a lawyer when she was growing up."

"Yeah, but your mom is younger than mine. When was she born?"

"1954."

"Oh yeah, that's almost a whole different generation than my mom. My mom was born in '41. A lot can change in thirteen years."

"That seems so long ago."

"It's interesting," Jessica kicked at the water with her toe. "The difference a decade, or even a couple of years can make for someone. Born at one time, you can come of age during a war, a few years after and you miss it. Look at the turn of last century. If you were born in 1895 you were like six times more likely to die of the Spanish flu than if you were born in 1910. Plus a guy born in 1910 would be too young to fight in World War I, and probably old enough to miss World War II. Or even, just look at our moms. Roe V Wade was 1973. You could have been aborted if your mom wanted. Two years earlier, I couldn't. Not legally, at least. It's kinda crazy when you think about how much our lives are dictated by the pure chance of the society into which we are born."

"But we're still in control of our lives," Laura was facing Jessica. But then she thought about when she believed she was pregnant, and how out of control her life felt then.

"Are we?" Jessica asked sincerely. "I don't know. I don't know if anyone really knows. I think the world kinda lays out a path for us, like a mountain road. And the lucky ones, like me, and I guess, maybe you too, we have some pretty solid guard rails on that road. But we gotta stay on that road, cause that's all there is. We go over the guardrail, it's death."

"And what's at the end of the road?"

Jessica smiled.

"Well, yeah, death's there too. It's probably not a perfect analogy, but there's something there."

Laura looked back out to the bay.

"Fuck that."

Jessica stood up and went inside to get another drink. She asked Laura if she wanted anything, but Laura just shook her head and kept looking at the distant growing waves and their tiny white breaks.

"Fuck that," Laura said again as Jessica closed the sliding glass door.

35

Irish Summer

That summer Laura worked at Buck's bouncing between the kitchen line and front of house, where she worked as a hostess or waitress. Other than the week Trey went to the Top 205 lacrosse camp he worked as a barback at Buck's. Katherine worked as a waitress, and Candace even worked as a hostess three nights a week.

Most of Laura's summer days were spent with Katherine. They had found Dolores' collection of romance paperbacks and took them to the beach, sharing the more graphic descriptions of sex with one another. Once a week Laura went with Katherine to the stables and they rode together.

That summer firmly established Dolores as a motherly force in the restaurant world of Ocean City. Part of this was because she was an early adopter of using the J-1 visa kids for her workforce. J-1's are temporary work visas for international students, and that year, most of the J-1 kids were from Ireland. Since Dolores knew what it was like to be a young twenty something in a foreign county, she took these kids under her motherly wing; mostly by imploring them to drink less, giving them aloe for their horrific sunburns, and tricking them into eating the occasional vegetable.

Dolores made a daily shift meal for the staff, which came to be called the family meal. She strove to make it as healthy as she could, and encouraged all of her employees to come to Buck's to eat together every single day, even if they weren't scheduled to work. What was likely intended as concern for the gastrological health of the employees she thought of as her children had an interesting side effect. Bringing workers to Buck's on their day off created a real family atmosphere and made it far easier to get a shift covered when needed. Since Dolores worked every day in the summer she always made the family meal everyday herself.

Laura worked Tuesdays and Thursdays cooking on the line, and on those days she always came in early as a prep cook, which meant she could help Dolores with the family meal. Those were her favorite days. It was a little bit like old times, cooking together in a kitchen, just the two of them. The lighting was different, the kitchen was bigger, the meals were bigger, but something sacred remained.

Between work and going to the beach and stables with Katherine, Laura rarely saw her mother. This annoyed Joyce, even if she was spending almost every night with Bubby anyway. Bubby, who was getting pretty serious about marriage at this point, figured out a work around. Once a week they would do a date night at Buck's, so Joyce could see her daughter. Even if they only had a few moments together, proof of life was enough for most parents in the 1990s.

Laura was having an easy, carefree summer. She liked the Irish students, found their accents charming, and loved how they never let an opportunity to make a quip pass them by. The one she gravitated to the most was a twenty-one-year-old medical student from Dublin named Conor. He was smart, handsome, thin, and sarcastic; the latter being her favorite quality. He was a waiter, and when she was a hostess she flirted relentlessly with him, and he matched game for game.

"Oh for fucks sake. Are all American's fucking thick or just the ones you seat in my section?"

"What you got today?" she said not even looking up from the menus she was wiping down.

"The gobshite at table twenty just told me I speak English really good. Where the fuck do I start with that? Does she not know we speak English in Ireland? And it's speak English really *well*, not good, you fucking Muppet."

"Honestly, I have no idea what she's talking about. I can barely understand you half the time."

"Oh bollox, and what about the other half of the time?"

Laura looked up.

"Oh, that's when I'm not listening."

He was always a good sport, and didn't stop flirting even when his fellow countrywomen teased him about American jails being no joke.

The Irish kids she met that summer were all a few years older than her, and they were smart university students who were well-read and well-traveled. But they treated her as an equal, not as a kid, other than the jokes about her being too young for Conor.

Laura rarely drank because she didn't want to drink and drive and she usually didn't have a ride home otherwise. Somehow this led to her being a designated driver for her Irish coworkers, driving six to eight drunk students from bar to bar, seeking live music and good craic.

So even though she was often sober, she spent those warm nights in the outdoor bars of Ocean City. Sitting at a beach bar she was surrounded by drunk and affectionate friends, with her toes in the sand, listening to live music, and feeling the soft cool ocean breeze.

***

On the last day of July, Katherine and Laura were lying on blankets in the sun, each reading a romance paperback they had taken from Dolores' collection. Both of the book covers had a shirtless man kissing a woman in a dress that seemed to be falling off. But on Katherine's book the man was also riding a horse.

"You know," Katherine said three-quarters of the way through her paperback. "I don't think there's going to be a horse in this story."

"If it's anything like this one," Laura held up her half-read book. "I hope there's not. I mean, this is just straight up porn."

Katherine put her book down. She looked up at the surf. A boy was chasing a girl, splashing water on her. The girl was screaming with laughter.

"Have you," Katherine started and then sighed. "Have you seen Trey at all this summer?"

Laura put down her book and sat up.

"Uh, yeah, like every night at work."

"I mean, outside of work."

Laura shook her head. She hadn't realized it, but she hadn't seen Trey once outside of work all summer long.

"We haven't gone out on a date since he came back from camp," Katherine said. "And last time we were... you know, together..."

"Yes, I know," Laura said, pointing to her book as reference.

"It was a week ago. During the day, at his house. Honestly, things are not the same as they were... before."

"Before what?"

"Before you. Trey is different."

"Like the sex isn't as good?" Laura said half-sarcastically.

"It's not that," Katherine continued. "I don't know how to make sense of this, but it's as if there's a piece of him that's missing. Remember what we talked about at English's a million years ago, how you'll always have his heart?"

"But I don't," Laura looked at the waves. "I literally never see him."

"Yeah," Katherine said. "I don't think that matters. I think you still have it. Maybe more than ever."

"So this whole thing, all this craziness we've been through, it was just a fling?"

Katherine reached out and held Laura's hand. She could tell she was annoyed, she could hear it in Laura's voice.

"Not for me. I swear to you. It wasn't for me."

Laura repeatedly assured Katherine that she was okay but she was lying. Laura wasn't sure exactly why she was upset, but she felt like she had been slighted somehow. She found excuses to not go to the stables or beach with Katherine for the next three days. The fourth day, she decided she was being a baby and she went to the beach with Katherine. They laughed about their books, but both girls had realized something between them had changed.

That night Laura drove Fionnuala, Aiofe, and Meabh to the Angler Bar and Grill, a bar right on the docks not far from the Inlet. Conor was there, drinking a beer from a plastic cup, dangling his feet towards the water, and looking out at the marina. Laura wandered up, and sat beside him, silently pondering the boats and the ripples that rocked them. He smiled but kept his eyes fixed towards the water. She asked him what he was thinking about.

"You," he lied.

"Fook off," she said in her best Irish accent.

He toasted her.

"Nice one. Yer getting it."

Laura lovingly bumped his shoulder with her own.

"You better watch yourself," Conor grinned. "Yer man over there is gonna get jealous."

Laura looked and saw Trey was at the bar.

"You're not very smart, are you?" Laura smiled.

"Not really, no. I mean, I'm a bit of an eejit in Ireland, but I'm a fucking genius in America."

Laura ignored the slagging.

"Trey is with Katherine."

Conor leaned away from Laura and squinted his left eye trying to focus on her.

"I thought you were smarter than that."

"What?"

"Yer man is not with Katherine now, is he?"

Conor nodded to Trey, who was talking to Fionnuala. Laura looked back at Conor and he raised his eyebrows. Conor whispered to Laura.

"He keeps looking over at us. I have a feeling I'm about to get my ass kicked."

Laura leaned back and rolled her eyes again. Conor rolled his eyes, mocking her.

"He wouldn't kick your ass. We haven't done anything."

"Ya better make fucking sure he knows that. He's a big dude."

"And why haven't we done anything, again?" Laura asked, changing the tone slightly.

Conor smiled at her, realizing he was more drunk than he had thought. He considered trying to wink, but had forgotten how to do it without looking strange.

"Lots of reasons. Too many. Oh, don't listen to me, I'm hammered. But yer man there, he misses you. Won't be long now."

"You're drunk."

"Doesn't make me wrong. Speaking of wrong, you know what I heard today? Only eight percent of Americans have their passport. Fucking eight, like two less than ten. Boggles the mind."

"How many people in Ireland have passports?"

"I don't know. Fucking all of them?"

Laura looked away at the water thinking for a second.

"Well, it's just a tiny little country."

"Fuck off." Conor took a deliberate breath to steady his mind. "The Irish, we read and we travel. That's what we do. And that's why everyone likes us."

Laura raised her eyebrow.

"Are you sure it isn't your modesty?"

"That too of course. But look, it's true, I might have a pint now and again. But that's the point, what good is a pint if you can't tell a story while drinking it? And how are you going to have a story if you don't read or travel?"

Laura was charmed. She leaned in and kissed him. She put her right hand on his cheek to steady his face, and they were both leaning dangerously close to the water. He tasted of beer and cigarettes. Her lips were parted, his were not. He didn't pull back, not right away, but he didn't kiss her back either.

The kiss lingered longer than it should have. It was a drunk bar kiss initiated by perhaps the only sober person there. No one but Fionnuala saw Trey throw his beer down in disgust.

Conor was trying to say something, perhaps apologize, perhaps make a joke, but neither option came out fast enough. Trey grabbed Conor's shirt with his left hand and pulled him up.

"She's only seventeen!" he growled.

"No fucking shit..." Conor tried to explain that he didn't do anything, but the wrong words came out first.

Trey punched Conor in the left cheek with his right hand. The same hand that once knocked his father unconscious, and the same arm that once broke the referee's nose. Conor dropped to a knee, then spun around and wildly swung at Trey, missing his head by a few inches.

Laura jumped to her feet and grabbed Trey's arm.

"TREY, WHAT THE FUCK?" she yelled as six others rushed in to separate the two. The bartender kicked all of them out, probably because one of them had said very loudly that someone was seventeen. Even in Ocean City, that wasn't the kind of thing you wanted to broadcast in a bar.

Trey stormed off and left. Laura turned to Conor as they were escorted out.

"I'm so sorry," she said, her arm around his shoulder. "We'll get you some ice."

"Nah, I'm grand."

"You warned me, I'm so sorry."

"Hey, I'm fucking serious. I'm grand. I got pissed, I got kissed, and I got a puck in the gob. It's all I need for good night. Come on, let's go find another pint. Ah, no, you know what, it feels like a good night for rum!"

The following day Conor showed up for the family meal as if nothing had happened. He wasn't even scheduled to work that day, but he wasn't one to miss a free meal. As soon as he showed up, Trey walked right up to him and handed him an envelope with hand written apology. Before Conor even read it he shook Trey's hand and said something that sounded like *eh, you are alright, I'll get ya next time.*

When Laura had a moment alone with Conor, she again tried to apologize for kissing him, but he waved it off. He pulled the letter out of his back pocket and waved it at her.

"I'm gonna frame it. Written proof of my first American donnybrook," he said, winking at her. "Come outside."

She followed him out the side door and they walked to the deck that overlooked the marsh. Ducks immediately swam towards them.

"These ducks are like pets," he said laughing. "They see people and they come running. Look, Laura Byrne, yer a sweet lass, ya really are. What I wouldn't give for you to be a couple years older, or me to be a couple years younger."

He laughed to himself. She softly shook her head.

"In a couple of years it won't matter," she said.

"You bet," he sighed. "So in a couple of years, you come visit Ireland. I'll show you the craic."

Laura laughed.

"You still don't get how bad that sounds to an American, do you?"

"No, and God willing I never will."

"You know, I don't have a passport."

"Fucking hell. Are you serious?"

Laura nodded. He looked out at the marsh and the swarming ducks.

"America," he said, almost as a question.

***

Three days later Katherine broke up with Trey. Neither of them told Laura. It was Candace who broke the news to her when they were working together at the hostess stand.

"You seriously didn't know?"

Laura shook her head.

"I thought you and Katherine were like best friends. Or you and Trey were best friends. Or you know, something like that."

Laura looked at Candace trying to decide if she meant anything more than her words were saying. She decided that she did.

"It's been a complicated year," Laura said.

"I bet."

Laura took a deep breath.

"I know I don't say this enough, but you are really important to me."

"Because I tell you all the gossip," Candace wasn't smiling.

"Because I know you have my back, and I will always have yours."

"Damn right. Even if you are in a messy love triangle."

They looked at each other for a moment, then burst into giggles as two middle aged men walked up to the hostess stand looking for a table.

***

The next morning Laura went to the stables to ride with Katherine. It was going to be their last ride before Katherine left for school. Katherine rode Dulcinea and Laura rode an old, gentle horse named Buttercup.

For the first time they went deep into the woods, Katherine leading Laura to the small clearing with the stream and the maple tree. The summer had turned the clearing into a glen of wildflowers in bloom, full of black-eyed Susan, scarlet beebalm, blue cornflower, and purplestem aster. When the girls dismounted, Buttercup and Dulcinea feasted on the flowers while the girls put their hands in the steam which had lost its clarity. They stretched, picked flowers, and explored the edge of the woods.

Laura found a book on the ground. Forgotten to the elements it had grown to have three times the width it once had, and was covered in leaves and organic growth. Laura wiped off the rot and saw it was Katherine's Emily Dickinson book, opened to the poem *Hope is the Thing with Feathers*.

"Oh," Katherine said when Laura held it up for her to see. "I wondered where I lost this."

Katherine held the book and looked at it.

"I left it here the day you showed up in my kitchen. I guess I haven't been back since."

"It seems kinda symbolic, no?"

Katherine looked around and smiled. She tossed the book gently back to the forest floor.

"I used to come to be alone, when I felt lonely."

"That doesn't make any sense."

"It does when you have four brothers."

Laura bent at the knees to pick some more wildflowers.

"The last few months," Katherine said while looking at the maple tree she once lounged under. She admired how it now had a crown full of leaves. "I felt like I became someone else. Maybe this is just what happens, before college."

"Are you nervous?"

Katherine shook her head.

"It's not that. All week I've been getting so emotional. Like I'm doing everything for the last time."

"Maybe you are."

"Yeah, maybe... Laura, look, we need to talk," Katherine said. She took a deep breath. "Trey didn't take the breakup well."

Laura kept picking flowers.

"Oh yeah?" she said not looking up.

"We were in his house, in his bedroom. I didn't plan on breaking up with him, but he was so distant, and then he got in a fight with Conor."

"That was my fault."

"Laura, no. It wasn't."

Laura stood up and looked at Katherine. They were both silent for a few seconds. Katherine let out a big sigh.

"When I broke it off, he kinda pushed me out of his room."

"He pushed you?"

She nodded.

"Not to the ground or anything, but he was really angry. He said I had ruined everything. I'm pretty sure he meant that I had ruined everything between him and you. Then he slammed the bedroom door so heard he broke it. It came right off the hinges. Then he kicked it like three times. Honestly, I kinda just ran out of there."

"Fuck."

"He showed up to work like nothing had happened, but he's not talking to me. I think I really fucked things up."

Laura shook her head.

"Trey made his choices."

"Yeah, but I didn't make it easier."

Laura shrugged.

"I had a good summer. And I'm glad we're friends."

Katherine looked at Laura with a pained smile.

"Honestly," Katherine said. "The best thing about me dating Trey was getting to know you."

Surrounded by wildflowers, they hugged. Laura handed Katherine the bouquet she had picked.

"I can't wait to someday tell Trey you said that," Laura said with a smile. But Katherine didn't smile.

"Please wait until I'm in Providence before you do."

36

Autumn of Longing

Preseason soccer and field hockey started two weeks before the school year. Dolores decided that Trey and Laura had worked too hard over the summer, so she cut their hours down to only weekends once sports began. The third day of preseason thunderstorms canceled both practices. Laura suggested Trey come over to her house so they could talk. She said she would make dinner, but then Joyce called and said she would be out for the evening. Laura changed her mind about cooking, and they ended up eating leftovers and talking about nothing for a while in the kitchen.

Finally Laura asked Trey if they could really talk.

"I thought we were talking?"

"Katherine said you pushed her."

"That's bull shit."

Laura looked at him but didn't say anything. They both knew Katherine was not someone to make up lies.

"Okay," Trey explained. "She broke up with me and then tried to kiss me, so I pushed her away from me."

"And you ripped your door off your hinges."

"Well I was fucking mad."

"Obviously."

"Laura, what the hell. I feel like I've been a fucking plaything for you and Katherine to pass back and forth and no one gives a shit about me."

"I never heard you complain about fucking Katherine."

"You're not listening! Laura, you broke up with me! I swear to God, I don't know what to tell you. I've broken up with one person in my life, and it was Katherine, so I could be with you. And not even as a girlfriend, just to be with you as a friend! I don't know what the fuck you want from me!"

Laura was quiet. Trey's voice quivered, and it sounded like he was on the verge of tears.

"Look, I just wanted to be with you, and it was your idea to hang out with Katherine, not mine. And then she started fucking me, and yeah, okay, I liked that... but like, you and her just hung out every day without me, and I never saw you... and you flirted with Conor, and like, everyone else at the restaurant except me... and it just really hurt, you know? It was like, when I came back from camp it was like you didn't want to talk to me."

"I didn't know," Laura said, trying to remember the order of events from the summer. "It didn't seem like that to me."

"Laura, I swear to God I never wanted any of this to happen. I just wanted you. Anyway I could have you. I need you."

Laura kissed him. She kissed him hard, up against the cabinets, and he kissed her back, grabbing her back and pulling her into him. As they spun around he even knocked over a water glass that didn't break, but spilled water all over the counter and floor. They stopped to survey the damage. Trey picked up the dishtowel and wiped it up.

"I'm sorry," he said.

Laura had no idea what she was doing. Suddenly she wanted Trey so badly. She took off her t-shirt and was standing in the kitchen in her sports bra while Trey was on his knees mopping up the water.

"Alright," she said smiling. "Come upstairs and you can give me a backrub."

She walked towards her room, peeling off her sports bra and shorts on the way. She turned on some music and laid in bed completely naked. Trey stood at the door, frozen.

"Come give me a backrub."

"Is that all you want?"

"Yeah, why do you ask?" Laura said, nonchalantly. She turned her head to face him and she had a wicked smile.

Trey undressed in a flash.

"Hey, what are you doing?" Laura said giggling. She missed seeing Trey naked, and she missed playing with him more. "Why are you getting naked to give me a massage?"

She turned her body to face him and met his kiss as he crawled into bed with her. When she wrapped her legs around him, she had never felt so comfortable.

But it was too soon after Katherine had broken up with Trey. They both knew it.

They talked for hours afterwards, occasionally kissing each other. Eventually they decided that the only way to ensure that they would always remain friends was to stop kissing. Neither of them liked the idea, and both of them broke the "no kiss" rule a couple times that evening, but when they finally parted they had agreed to go back to just being friends. It was a strange start to another strange year for Laura.

The beginning of senior year is challenging for anyone, but it's especially hard on those people who have no idea where they want to go to school, or what they want to do with their lives. The ranks of those lucky few who, from an early age, have been drawn to a profession, did not include Laura.

Two weeks into the school year she was eating dinner at home with her mom when the phone rang. Laura answered as her mom gave her a look of *tell Trey or Candace we're eating dinner*, but the person on the other end identified herself as Coach Bridget Maddox, assistant lacrosse coach at the University of Notre Dame.

"Oh, hi?" Laura was not sure what she should say.

"Did Coach Hartman tell you we would be giving you a call?"

"She did not."

"Oh, well, I went to school with Coach Hartman, back in the stone age, and she called me up and couldn't stop saying nice things about you. Said you are the fastest player she's ever coached, and she said you're even tougher than me, which...," she laughed awkwardly. "Well, we'll see."

Laura was surprised. Coach Hartman was a perpetually grumpy coach. In fact, the only time she ever said anything really nice about Laura was at the spring athletic banquet, which Laura missed because she was busy threatening Katherine's dad in his driveway.

"That's nice of her."

"Yeah, so, you weren't on our radar at all. You don't go to any camps or anything, huh?"

"Um... no?"

Coach Maddox laughed again.

"Okay, so do you want to come out and do a workout for us?"

"I guess. I have to check with my mom."

Coach Maddox paused. Laura waited.

"Can I ask, is anyone else recruiting you?"

Laura shook her head.

"I don't think anyone is recruiting me."

"Well," Coach Maddox said matter-of-factly with a smile in her voice. "We are."

"Oh. Thanks. What do I need to do?"

"Okay, I'll send you a letter. Don't sign with any other school before you see me. How soon can you get out here?"

"You are in Indiana, right? My dad lives in Chicago, it's pretty close, right?"

Joyce put down her fork and looked on with concern.

"Yeah, depends on where he lives, but it's like two hours give or take. Your parents are divorced, huh?"

"Yeah, for a while now."

"Yeah, mine too," she let that thought settle for a moment. "So when can you come out?"

"I mean, I guess after field hockey season."

"Right. Coach Hartman told me you just broke the career assists record last week. Congrats."

"Oh, thanks. I didn't realize."

Coach Maddox laughed through a sigh. "Call me, okay? Promise?"

"I promise."

Laura hung up the cordless phone, and placed it back on the charging jack.

"Who was that?" her mom asked.

"Um. The lacrosse coach at Notre Dame. They want me to come do a workout for them."

Joyce's eye got wide. Joyce was a Catholic girl from the Midwest. To her, Notre Dame was Harvard and the Vatican all rolled up into one. She shot out of her chair and gave Laura a mama-bear hug.

"My baby is going to Notre Dame!"

"Mom!" Laura said, rolling her smiling eyes.

***

Three weeks later, on the first Friday of October, with Coach Hartman's blessing to miss a practice, Laura flew to O'Hare Airport, where she was met by her father. He drove her directly to Notre Dame, where they found Coach Maddox waiting for her.

She was introduced to three of the sophomore players, and they helped her through a few drills. They seemed so much older than her, even though they were all the same age as Jessica. But they seemed bigger somehow, and harder. Not only their bodies, but the space around their bodies too. Laura couldn't explain it, but it felt like they were more than the sum of their parts.

Laura ran some timed sprints. At one point she looked over at her father, who had the biggest smile on his face. She realized he had never seen her play a sport, and he had no idea how fast she was.

Afterwards Coach Maddox showed Laura and her dad into her office. It was a tiny, windowless room, not much larger than a closet. It was full of files and loose papers, and had a small combo TV/VCR surrounded by dozens of VHS tapes.

"Coach Hartman didn't lie, you're fast," Coach Maddox said as she cleared some file folders off two of the three chairs in her office. She motioned for them to sit down. "What's it like playing for her?"

"She's nice," Laura shrugged.

"Really?"

"No," Laura said, blushing a little. "I don't think she likes me."

Coach Maddox laughed and pulled out a file. It had a Xerox of Laura's school picture paperclipped on the outside.

"That's funny. This is what Coach Hartman sent us. 'Fast, smart, tough. The only girl I ever coached I would be afraid to play against.' So..." Coach Maddox shut the file and looked up at Laura. "I think you are wrong."

Laura blushed more. She didn't know what to say.

"So here's the thing, we need a big commitment from you. But I promise you this, if you come here and play, it will change your life. You're fast, and that's great, that can't be taught. But we're going to make you much better. And I don't even mean as a player, I mean as a person. Because that's what we're about."

She stood up and extended her hand.

"Grades, SATs, everything looks good. You'll have to send in a formal application, but, I'll be honest, we want you here."

Laura stood up and shook her hand. She looked at her father who was beaming.

"I've arranged for the two of you to go on a campus tour. And if you have any questions, just call me. Okay?"

The private campus tour was given by a beautiful blond senior boy named Michael who was on the fencing team, majoring in pre-med, and involved in theater. He was from northern California and was funny and charming. The air was crisp and the sun hung low in the clear sky. The campus was green, golden, and red. It was the week before midterms, the day before the Stanford game, and a nervous energy was palpable. Thousands of RVs from forty-nine states had rolled in to surround the stadium. The tailgates had begun, even though the game was still a day away.

Michael focused on showing them the things that made Notre Dame special: the Hesburgh Library with the thirteen story-tall "Touchdown Jesus" mosaic, the neo-gothic Basilica of the Sacred Heart, the administration building with its legendary golden dome, and Laura's favorite – the Grotto of Our Lady of Lourdes. The grotto was a small, man-made, stone cave with ivy growing around the outside. Inside were hundreds of candles, each lit for a prayer.

"This is a pretty popular spot for students," Michael explained as they arrived at the grotto only moments after the sun had set. "Especially during finals week."

"Why?" Laura's father asked.

"Sometimes it's easier to pray than study," Michael said, opening the iron gate to let them in. His voice turned into a whisper while in the sacred space. "It actually caught fire once in 1985, the night before the Michigan game. We lost the game though, so, I guess it doesn't always work."

Laura didn't think places like Notre Dame existed in America. It was old, beautiful, glowing, and warm.

That night she went back to Chicago with her father. Todd had pizza waiting for them. Laura was exhausted from the incredibly long day, flight, seven hours of driving, college workout, tour, and excitement of a new adventure. She took two bites of pizza and fell asleep.

That Saturday morning she went with her dad to the coffee shop she once worked at. It felt smaller than she remembered. None of her former coworkers still worked there.

Her father had tried to get tickets to the Notre Dame/Stanford game but it had been sold out for the better part of a year, so Todd prepared a little watch party for them. He had all the necessary snacks: potato chips, French onion dip, pigs in a blanket, and nachos. Laura's dad wasn't a big football guy, in fact he didn't even fully understand the rules, but Todd explained it to them.

Todd, who grew up in Queens, New York, was a closeted lifelong New York Jets fan. In fact, when he was a child his father took him to a game at the old Polo

Grounds, back when the Jets were still called the Titans. Laura had no idea of this secret part of Todd's life, as he didn't fit the stereotypical football fan of that era. Laura, for her part, had never watched a football game on TV before, and had never watched any sport played beyond the high school level at all.

She was half a continent away from her home, and it seemed like she might have had a preview of her future. As she watched the students cheering on the television she realized that she could be one of those people in less than a year's time.

The three of them went to dinner. Laura ate steak and French fries. Laura asked Todd about his parents. He told her about how his father kicked him out when he found out Todd was gay. He told a funny story or two about life in Greenwich Village as a teen in the seventies. He talked about Stonewall, which happened before he lived there, but how the spirit was still palpable. Laura told them about Jessica and how people thought that Laura was a lesbian. Her father was concerned, but Todd relished every word of the story.

After dinner her father went to bed, but Laura and Todd stayed awake talking until two AM. She told him all about Trey and what happened with Katherine.

"Oh my God, she is such a bitch, but is it wrong that I kind of love her? Do you have a picture?"

Laura shook her head.

"Don't worry. Niki Taylor. I've got her right here," he said pointing to his head and then smiling wickedly as he sipped his wine.

"She's not a bitch," Laura said after some thought.

"Well, in this case it's kinda half a compliment."

Laura rolled her eyes.

"And you and Trey? You really think you are done? Seriously?"

"Yes. It's over. For real this time."

Todd laughed.

"Oh honey. It's a long year," he said prophetically.

***

Three days later, in his bedroom, Trey stood in front of Laura, naked other than the towel wrapped around his waist. It was a windy day outside, with low, fast moving grey clouds promising—but as of yet not delivering—rain. Laura chose to shower at school but Trey had played a game at Pocomoke that afternoon, and drove straight home afterwards. Laura correctly suspected that he waited until he saw her car pull up before he got into the shower, so she had gone into his bedroom and refused to leave or even look away so he could get dressed. It was a silly battle of wills which meant nothing.

She wanted to mess with him, because they were friends, and because he kept trying to get naked in front of her. But she also wanted to call his bluff because she loved him and liked seeing him naked.

"How are you planning on drying your hair without taking off your towel?"

Trey pursed his lips and looked at her, sitting on the bed with her sinister smile of victory. He walked towards her and bent his head down, rubbing his hair against her shirt.

"Stop it," she said, laughing and trying to push him away. It was like pushing away a boulder, he was so thick.

"Stop it. Stop it!" She was getting frustrated. She punched him hard in the shoulder.

He sat back.

"Sorry, okay, chill. What's up your butt?"

She shook her head softly, not saying what she wanted to say. She thought about Katherine, and suddenly she wanted to leave. But as she was about to stand up, he spoke.

"So, wanna go to Homecoming with me? Or are you going to do the whole, make people think you are a lesbian thing again?"

He was grinning, thinking he was funny, or cute. He saw right away that she didn't agree with his assessment.

"I was just joking," he tried.

"Yeah," she looked him right in the eyes. "The whole thing is a joke, right?"

"What? No, I really want to go to Homecoming with you. Shit, Laura, come on. I love you."

"You have to stop saying that."

"Why? It's the truth."

"Can you put some fucking clothes on?"

He stood up, took off his towel, and tossed it at her. She caught it, called him a dickweed, and whipped it back at him, snapping it on his ass. His face turned purple with a combination of rage and embarrassment.

"Laura, what the fuck is your problem?"

Laura sat still, honestly pondering the rhetorical question for about seven seconds.

"You," she said, standing up and walking out.

37

Homecoming Again

Trey reached out his hand to stop her, pleading with her not to leave. Even though he was naked he followed her down the hall and to the door, but at this point she was running, and she was faster than he was. He ran back to his room and quickly pulled on a pair of jeans, grabbed a white t-shirt, and ran out the door, but she was already in her car by the time he got outside, and she was down the street before he could make it to the end of the driveway.

Laura went home. Before she even walked through the door she could smell that her mom had been cooking. It was chicken cordon bleu, her "special occasion" dinner. Bubby was there, sitting at the dining room table in his uniform with a napkin tucked under his lantern jaw. From the state of their plates, they had just started eating. Red wine was in both of their glasses. Her mom lit up as soon as she walked into the dining room, and she stood up right away and quickly moved to give Laura a huge hug.

"Oh sweetheart, I'm so glad you are here. Sit with us and eat, please," Joyce went to the cupboard and pulled down a plate. She picked up the serving spoon with her right hand, and held Laura's plate with her left hand. That's when Laura saw it. The single round cut diamond flashed in the light. Laura turned her head to look at her mom. Joyce was doing everything she could to be busy, and Laura realized her mom was nervous.

"Can I have some wine?" Laura said, looking down at her plate.

"Um..." Joyce looked at Bubby who just shrugged a *why not* kinda shrug.

Joyce took down a wine glass and with her left hand poured the tiniest amount of wine in Laura's glass. Laura lifted Joyce's hand further, in the process brushing the diamond.

"Come on," she said as she pushed her mother's hand up. "Is that rock so heavy you can't lift your arm?"

Joyce put the bottle down and rolled her eyes to look at Bubby. She sighed.

"Are you going to change your last name?" Laura said without a hint of a smile, picking up her glass and shooting looks back and forth between Bubby and Joyce. "Do I have to change my name? Wait, do I have to call you dad now? Do you prefer daddy?"

Laura was being a little wicked, but Bubby laughed at her teasing, and that softened her mood. Laura put her wine glass down and smiled at him. He did make her mom happy. She knew she shouldn't take out her anger at Trey on these two. She turned and looked at her mom. Joyce's face was red with embarrassment.

"Come on mom, let me see it properly."

Joyce held out her hand and Laura inspected it.

"Damn, that's a big one," she took her time inspecting it. Then she picked up her glass and looked back and forth at the two of them again. "Congrats, really. When's the wedding?"

Joyce laughed and hugged Laura again, who didn't get out of her chair, so it was awkward.

"Mom, you're going to spill my wine."

"Just what a mother of a teenage girl loves to hear," Joyce wiped away a tear as she sat back down. "Why do you always tease me?"

"Because I love you."

At that moment there was a loud knocking at the door. Bubby instinctively stood up, feeling the energy of the knock being one of heightened emotion. Laura closed her eyes, knowing it was Trey, and knowing she didn't want to deal with him then. From the dining room table Joyce looked through the sidelight and saw Trey standing at the door.

"Oh it's Trey. Let me see if he wants to eat," she said waving him in.

Trey walked into the dining room flushed and sweaty. He apologized to Joyce and said hello to Bubby. Laura finally looked at him inquisitively.

"I couldn't find my car keys, so I ran over."

"Have some water sweetheart," Joyce said, pouring him a glass. He smiled and nodded and took a sip, still standing, and never taking his eyes off Laura. Laura stood up and went over to her coat, pulling his keys out of the pocket and tossing them to him.

"Whoops," she said as sarcastically as possible.

Trey nodded and walked over to her.

"Can we go talk?" He whispered to her.

"I'm going to eat my dinner."

"Trey," Joyce said breezily. "Let me fix you a plate."

Trey sat down and they all took a couple bites in silence. Finally Bubby remembered something.

"Trey, did ya'll play Pocomoke today? How'd you do?"

"We won. One, nothing."

"Trey scored," Laura said, not looking up from her food.

"Alright," Bubby nodded in approval. Joyce smiled and offered a *well done* accolade.

"Eat your food, son," Bubby prodded. The "son" hung in the air, echoing in all their minds, except for Bubby's. He didn't even realize he had said it.

Trey took a few tentative bites. Laura cleaned her plate, chugged her wine, and reached for the bottle for a refill. Joyce stopped her.

"Don't you have homework?"

"Phss," Laura said dismissively. Joyce moved the bottle away from her. Laura stood up and picked up her plate.

"May I be excused," she called over her shoulder as she walked into the kitchen. She hadn't asked that of her mother in many years. Joyce rolled her eyes and looked at Trey.

"I'm sorry Trey, I think she's in one of her moods."

"He knows what he did!" Laura called from the kitchen as she put her plate in the dishwasher.

Trey shook his head and sighed, his eyes going back and forth from Bubby to Joyce.

I really don't, he mouthed. Bubby laughed and nodded.

"Just apologize," he whispered. Joyce shot him a disapproving look. Bubby put up his hands and whispered *I'm sorry*. Joyce picked up her wine and took a sip. Bubby raised his eyebrows at Trey and shrugged, as if to say, *you see what I mean?*

Trey asked to be excused which made Joyce laugh. He picked up his plate, but at that moment Laura walked through the dining room and headed outside. Bubby told Trey to leave his plate and go, and he complied, running after her and catching up to her in the driveway.

"Don't get in your car, come on."

"Why not?"

"Because you're angry, and because you just slugged a glass of wine, and because I want to talk to you."

Laura kept her hand on her car door but didn't open it. She looked at the trees which were bending in the wind. It was getting colder, and it felt like it was about to rain.

"Let's go inside and talk," Trey pleaded.

Laura shook her head. She didn't want to take Trey into her room. Nowhere else inside would be private. They could go for a walk, but it was cold and windy. He was shivering. She would have given him a sweatshirt, but nothing she had would fit.

She walked over to the garage door and pulled it up. She unfolded a chair and put it right in the middle of the garage, then motioned to him to sit down, while she paced just outside the garage door. He sat and waited for her to gather her thoughts, or pace out her frustration.

Laura's mind raced. She didn't want Trey to take her for granted, which she felt like he was. And yet, she didn't want to be Trey's girlfriend. But she wanted to be naked with him, and kiss him. And for him to be her best friend. Yes, she wanted Trey in her life, but she didn't want to *need* Trey in her life. She felt burdened by his love, and yet hurt when he took her for granted.

Unfortunately, pacing was only making it worse.

Trey was the one that broke the silence. He had tried to be patient but he could feel her frustration building and he thought it was better for her to release it.

"Is this about Katherine?"

Laura shook her head and nodded at the same time.

"You pushed me away. You keep pushing me away. What was I supposed to do?"

Laura threw up her hands defensively.

"You can do whatever you want."

"You didn't want me. That's what you told me. Did you want me to wait forever for you? Because I would of, and I will, if that's how you want to play it."

"It's not a game," Laura growled.

"Are you sure? Because, right now, it feels a lot like a game."

Laura sighed and softly shook her head. She kept pacing in the driveway. Trey stayed seated in the chair, but leaned forward, interlocking his fingers and resting his elbows on his knees, while looking down at the cracked concrete floor.

"What do you want me to do?" he pleaded.

"Just acknowledge my feelings."

"I'm doing that. That's why I ran over here, that's why I want to talk to you. I am acknowledging your feelings. What else can I do?"

"Nothing."

"Well," he said thoughtfully, "I'm doing that too."

She let a sly laugh escape her countenance against her will. He looked up, sat back in the chair and smiled triumphantly. Huge raindrops started falling, one violently hitting Laura's cheek. She grimaced.

"Laura, it's starting to rain, come in here," Trey stood up and offered Laura his seat.

"Jesus Christ just let me be," Laura held up a hand towards Trey.

She shook her head and looked up at the huge, dancing trees. They were taking the brunt of the storm, as they always did. The rain changed into smaller and more frequent drops.

Trey looked around the garage and found a massive beach umbrella. He opened it with a giant *whoosh* sound, and stood next to Laura holding it over her. She stepped away.

"I don't want that."

"Come on, you're getting soaked."

"Why do you feel the need to try to fix everything?"

Trey shrugged.

"I guess,' he started thoughtfully, "if I see a problem I want to fix it. That's just who I am."

"But what if you can't fix it?"

"Then I don't want to see it."

Laura shook her head and walked a few more steps away from him and his enormous umbrella. He closed it and went back in the garage, watching her pace again.

"That's not healthy you know," she said, not looking at him.

"Standing in the rain? I know."

"No. Not wanting to see something you can't fix. It's not healthy."

Trey thought about it.

"It's healthier than wanting to do something that's impossible, knowing that no matter what you are going to fail."

"Is it?" Laura wondered.

"You can't change the past."

Laura smiled.

"That's not what I'm thinking about," she said as she closed her eyes and turned her face up to meet the rain. The now tiny drops were cold, and fell more viciously against her eyelids and lips, where they felt like tiny pin pricks.

"Are you trying to get sick?" Trey broke her trance.

"No," she said, still looking up with her eyes closed, the occasional drop falling into her mouth. "You know this rain was once an ocean. Or a tiny brook, or a mud puddle. It might have given life, or taken it away. Or both. And now, it's trying to find its way back to the ocean."

She took a deep breath. Trey was just watching her.

"What the fuck are you talking about?"

"I love the rain."

"And I love you," he said from the dry garage.

Laura heard him, but it was as if he was speaking to someone else. His words didn't penetrate her. It was the storm that cleansed her, bathed her, and made her new.

Trey stood in the garage watching her with concerned eyes. Laura was soaked. The rain clung to every molecule of her clothes, and coated every inch of her skin. She opened her eyes and smiled. She walked very slowly into the garage and lifted her arms for a hug. Trey fell into her. She held him tight for a few seconds, and then broke the embrace, still holding him by the shoulders. She put her head into his chest and rubbed her wet hair against his shoulder.

"Now we're even," she said sadly.

38

Halloween in Greenwich Village

Laura and Trey did go to the Homecoming Dance together. Trey was Homecoming King, Candace was Homecoming Queen, and Laura watched as two of her best friends danced to *Holding Back the Years* by Simply Red. Trey and Laura kissed in Laura's driveway, but after a minute she stopped it and walked inside without saying anything.

Things got uncomfortable. Field hockey and soccer season ended. Trey got suspended from school for two days because he got into a fight with the basketball coach's son. According to Trey, Tyrone started the fight, but somehow didn't get into trouble. Trey quit the basketball team. Laura decided not to play basketball. She claimed it was to focus on lacrosse, but she was lying.

Trey worked five days a week as Buck's became the place to go in the off season in Ocean City. Dolores had gotten creative with her menu and moved away from the "nothing but fried cheese" of the past. Her big innovation was a tapas sampler platter, long before anyone outside of the big cities in the United States knew what tapas was. It was all the rage in Ocean City that autumn.

Laura's father surprised her with tickets to the Notre Dame/Navy football game, which was played that year in the Meadowlands on the afternoon of Saturday, October 31st. Unfortunately because of work he couldn't make it himself, but Todd volunteered to meet her in NYC and be her chaperone.

Jessica was living in a Hell's Kitchen apartment just off of Ninth Avenue, so a plan was hatched that both Todd and Laura would stay with her, and they would all go to the Greenwich Village Halloween Parade after the game.

For those who have never been to both a Notre Dame/Navy football game and the Greenwich Village Halloween Parade, it would be hard to imagine the stark dichotomy of these two worlds. Of the 58,769 who attended the football game, and the roughly 1.5 million who attended the parade, there couldn't have been more than two dozen folks who went to both.

The clean-cut, pure, macho, healthy, sunny, antagonistic, testosterone-filled rage of the football game was contrasted by the dirty, sexual, welcoming, kind, queer, frightening, shadow-infused parade. Both gatherings were joyous. Both were beautiful. Both made sense to Laura.

After the parade they wandered the streets of the Village, eventually crossing over to the east side and going to Veselka Diner for perogies, borscht, latkes, and breakfast. They all drank coffee and Ukrainian beer.

Veselka was a twenty-four hour Ukrainian soul food restaurant at the corner of Second Avenue and East 9th Street, which was already an East Village institution by the time Laura set foot in the door. Its tight tables were crowded at all hours of the day and night, though the sobriety of the clientele changed when the natural light gave way to the artificial. On this particular night, the tables were populated with everything from clowns, cats, cheerleaders, and centurions, and admittedly just a few more vampires than usual.

The conversation drifted. They discussed the game, the parade, the city, the various apartments Todd once called home, Jessica's fall semester classes, and Homecoming. Eventually Laura shared the news about Joyce being engaged.

"Your father will be very pleased to hear that," Todd said earnestly. "He likes that kind of thing."

"What kind of thing?" Jessica asked.

"Monogamy," Todd said with a slight air of exhaustion. "Besides, there's little your father wants more than to be sure Joyce is happy."

Laura laughed.

"Don't laugh, I'm serious. He loved your mother. He still does."

"Sure. But why did he cheat on her?"

"Oh, sweetie, it's not that simple. He loved your mother, but he didn't love himself. Not enough to admit who he was."

"Isn't that a little hypocritical, Mr. Byrne liking monogamy," Jessica mused. "No offense implied, of course."

"Baby cakes, first, you can't offend me, believe me. And second, neither of you will ever know what it is like to be living a lie. Believe me, things were way different sixteen years ago. It was a lot harder for a gay man to admit he was gay."

"Okay pumpkin," Jessica put her forefinger up, "I mean I know a little bit. Like, hello, I'm a lesbian."

It was just at that moment that the four top next to them with three over six foot tall drag queens and one guy dressed as the Terminator were standing up to leave. One of the drag queens put a hand on Laura's shoulder and leaned down.

"I so don't want to leave, I'm loving this, and girl, I'm here for your hair. But I got a joke. What does a lesbian bring to a second date?"

Todd and Jessica rolled their eyes. Laura shrugged.

"A moving truck. What does a gay man bring to a second date?"

"I don't know," Laura said, politely smiling.

"What's a second date?" the drag queen said, snapping after the punchline and laughing and waving as she walked away.

"That joke was old when I was in high school," Todd smiled.

"Is that true though?" Laura innocently asked.

"I mean," Jessica tried to sound like an authority. "It's a stereotype. It's not like every lesbian is like that, or every gay man is like that. But there is truth to it."

"It's just a joke," Todd said. "People are people. Different strokes for different folks. I will say, some gay men go a little nuts when they first come out of the closet. But men being dogs is nothing new, gay or straight."

"Did my dad?"

Todd was drinking coffee and almost snorted it from the sudden laughter.

"Uh. No. Quite the opposite. Your dad has been with three people his whole life. Your mom, yours truly, and the guy he cheated on your mom with. You know, his name is Randy. I shit you not. Randy! He came to visit once..." Todd lowered his voice to a loud whisper. "I don't care for him."

"I never met him."

"No, you wouldn't have. Your father was so embarrassed by the whole thing. And I think Randy was just a means to an end for him."

"It's weird to think about my father's love life."

"Yeah why is that?" Jessica asked honestly. "I'm not judging. I do the same, I don't think of my parents as real people, just as constants."

"Until they are suddenly not," Laura said.

"Sweetie," Todd looked so sincerely at her. "Your father never would have left you if he could have avoided it. It's the biggest regret of his life."

Todd put his hand on Laura's hand, and patted it.

"You know, it's one of the reasons why I fell in love with your father. He was broken-hearted. Not for your mom, and obviously not for Randy, but for you. He was broken-hearted because he lost you. I thought that was just so sexy. I wanted to be with someone who could love that fiercely. I'm not built that way, but I'm drawn to those that are. And if monogamy is his condition for me to be with him, then I accept it. It seems like a small price to pay for a love like his. Well, maybe not small, but acceptable."

The waitress was refilling coffee and Jessica ordered another beer. A group of four costumed twentysomethings sat next to them. A Freddy Kruger, a Marty McFly, a Beetlejuice, and a "Like a Prayer" Madonna.

"I certainly never imagined I would live in Chicago. I mean, hell, I would have slapped myself silly if I went to 18 year old me and showed me what 36 was going to look like. Thank god I still have my looks though, right?" he said the last sentence to Laura touching her arm and laughing.

"But how do you know? Like how did you know that my dad was the one?"

"Oh sweetie, no one knows. Not really."

"Is it a big sacrifice for you, to live in Chicago?" Laura asked.

Todd laughed.

"Honestly… no, not as much as I make it out to be. Chicago is great, it's got art, culture, theater, shopping, a good community. The gays there are real salt of the earth, they iron their flannels if you know what I mean."

Laura had no idea what he meant, but smiled and nodded.

"It's just not as good as New York, obviously. But it's not like I moved to rural Iowa to be with him."

"Would you, if he asked?"

Todd was silent as he thought.

"I don't know. I want to say I would, but I would probably be lying. I would be miserable there. I wouldn't be living my life, I would be living someone else's. And I didn't come out of the closet to live someone else's life. It wouldn't matter, because your father loves me too much to ask something like that of me."

"He adores you?"

"Worships, dearie. Worships. That's why I work so hard to keep this figure," he said as he took a huge bite of his hazelnut praline torte.

Jessica and Todd shared jokes and quips that Laura didn't hear as she was lost in thoughts of Trey and the unknowable future.

39

The Final Year

It was the day after Thanksgiving, when Laura and Trey were chatting in the kitchen of Buck's. Laura had just finished her first shift working on the line since the summer and was still in her dirty apron. She had made coffee and was sitting on the chest freezer, sipping it. Trey was standing close enough to smell the sweet and bitter on her breath. They were alone, the bright lights reflecting off the silver and white, hiding nothing. He made her laugh. It was a dumb joke, but an honest laugh. She touched his arm, and didn't let go.

He looked down at her hand and smiled. She tugged, ever so gently to pull him close. He closed his eyes and she kissed him. He tasted the coffee, while she tasted the sweet alcoholic remnants of the rum and coke he snuck when his mother wasn't looking. It was a good kiss. A rare kiss. Unlike most of their previous times together, it was in a well-lit place that was full of people only minutes before, it was private and somehow public, and unexpected. It was gentle, soft, unrushed, long, and necessary.

They stopped when they heard a crash coming from the dining room. Someone had dropped a tray full of clean silverware. They smiled at one another, sheepishly.

"That was nice," Laura said, still holding Trey's arm. She slipped her hand down to hold his hand, then she pulled it up to her mouth and kissed it. Then they hugged for a long time, holding each other as if they had been apart for many years.

There was no agenda, no outside world, just a gentle kiss and a simple embrace.

In some ways, this moment was the beginning of their first real relationship. After this kiss, on almost every night in December they would fall asleep in one another's arms. They were lovers and best friends. And they told no one.

Now that both of them had turned eighteen, neither mother seemed to think they needed to enforce a curfew. Not that it mattered, Joyce was usually at Bubby's, and Dolores was often at Buck's. Laura and Trey always had a quiet home to share their nights. They rented every classic film from the video store. Laura taught Trey how to cook garlic soup. They made each other mixtapes.

This was the time when they learned to make love without haste. To linger and explore. They made their own time. To them the outside world all but disappeared.

***

A week before Christmas, Katherine called Laura. They had briefly spoken on the phone a few times, but it wasn't a regular thing as long-distance calls were expensive. Trey was in her room. He was sitting on the floor against her bed, flipping through mixtapes looking for the right music for that night. The only light in her room was from Jessica's Christmas lights.

Laura noticed right away that Katherine sounded upset.

"What's wrong?"

"Oh," Katherine sighed. "I'm just being stupid. I'm not able to come home for Christmas."

"What? Why?"

Trey took interest in Laura, as he probably could hear Katherine's voice coming through the receiver. He put down the tapes and got on his knees. Laura was wearing sweatpants, and Trey grabbed them by the cuff and slowly pulled them towards him.

"My dad is taking the family to Paris. I'm leaving right from school. Then when we come back we go straight to the ski trip. I was really hoping to see you, and catch up."

Laura grimaced at Trey and swung her hand at him. But he had pulled her sweatpants off and revealed red lace panties. He kissed her knee and the inside of her thigh.

"Um... uh... Yeah, I can't feel sorry for you. Paris and skiing?"

"Yeah," Katherine laughed a little. "I know I'm being ridiculous. I just wanted to see you. I miss you."

Trey kept kissing up her leg, higher and higher.

"I miss you too," Laura said between breaths.

Trey used both hands to pull her panties off. Laura closed her eyes and stopped protesting. Trey kissed her thigh, and her stomach, and then her other thigh. She arched her back.

There was a long pause on the phone while neither girl said anything.

"Are you and Trey together?"

"Yes," Laura said. She wasn't sure if Katherine was asking if he was currently in the room or if he was now her lover, but both were true. It was the first time she admitted it to anyone. At that point even Jessica and Candace didn't know they were dating.

"Okay," Katherine said. "I'm... I'm glad."

Trey took off his pants and Laura shook her head. He slipped a condom on. Laura mouthed *NO!* and Trey froze. But then she pulled her sweatshirt up and circled her nipple with her finger.

"Thanks," she said after far too long of a pause.

Trey smiled and went back to tropically kissing her, making it impossible for her to breathe normally.

Katherine started talking about a psychology class that she thought Laura would find interesting. Laura tried to pay attention but Trey had gotten very good at finding the right spots. Laura gave up and closed her eyes, and put her left hand on Trey's head, guiding his tongue. Katherine stopped talking. Laura's breathing got more shallow and she dropped the phone.

"Oh my god," Katherine whispered when she realized what was happening. She strained to hear all she could.

The bed creaked as Laura swirled her hips. Trey adjusted his spot and pulled Laura down towards him. Laura suddenly remembered she had been on the phone and grabbed the receiver.

"I'm sorry," she said in between breaths. "I dropped the phone."

"Uh huh. So what are you doing right now?" Katherine said, a smile in her voice.

"Nothing," Laura said, pushing Trey's mouth away from her. He smiled and slid his body between her legs until his face was next to hers and he started kissing her neck. He was right against her, and very slowly pushed inside her.

"So," Katherine said with a slight giggle. "What do you want to talk about now?"

"Um," Laura's mind was empty. "What... ever."

"You know I can hear him breathing, right?"

Trey pushed deep inside. Laura let out a gasp.

"Oh my god," Katherine said laughing. "I heard that!"

"I should go," Laura said, feeling wonderful and terrible at the same time.

"No... no. Just tell him to hurry up, this call's expensive." Katherine said wickedly.

"I should go," Laura said again.

"No," Katherine said. "I kinda like this."

Laura let go of the phone, but the receiver stayed by her mouth. Katherine heard every breath. It didn't take long for Trey to finish. Laura's breathing returned to normal, and she picked up the phone, but no one said anything. Trey had a big grin on his face, and Laura punched him in the chest.

"So," Katherine said. "That was hot."

"We'll never talk about this again," Laura said while still trying to catch her breath.

"Oh yes we will," Katherine laughed.

"So... I guess, have fun in Paris?"

"I'm gonna think about you the whole time," Katherine said.

"Oh, I don't know what that means anymore," Laura whined.

"Good!" Katherine laughed. For another minute or two they said their good-byes.

***

In the first week of February Laura found out she got into The University of Notre Dame. Trey, who had been heavily recruited by many schools, got a scholarship offer to play lacrosse at the University of Maryland, College Park. Trey and Laura congratulated each other but for the next week or so avoided talking about what would happen when they went to schools that were 600 miles apart.

On Valentine's Day, Trey took Laura to dinner at a French restaurant in Seaford, Delaware called Bon Appetit. It was romantic for a few reasons: because it was French, because it was different, and because it took an hour to get there. It had snowed just a little the day before, and while the roads were clear, the endless fields of Delmarva reflected the white moonlight, and lent a hint of magic to the drive.

Trey was uncharacteristically nervous, which made Laura remark he was acting weird. He gave her a red rose and a red box of chocolate that was shaped like a heart. On the drive there they had listened to *Black Eyed Man* by the Cowboy Junkies, but on the way home they listened to a mix Trey had made which included many of the songs from the mix Laura once shared with him in her bedroom. He even included "Careless Whisper."

Instead of returning to either of their homes, he drove to The Point, and got out of the car, walking around to Laura's side and opening the door. It was cold, and the wind swirled, gathering a further chill from pockets of icy plants that surrounded the parking area. Laura didn't understand what was happening, but got out of the car, and together they walked to the water's edge.

Trey knelt down and pulled a small square box out of his pocket.

"Laura, I think you know..."

"What the fuck?"

"What?"

"What is this?" she waved her right hand back and forth between the box and Trey.

"I love you more than I ever thought possible. And I want to spend the rest of my life with you. No matter what happens, no matter that we're going to be apart for four years, no matter what you want to do, I'll wait for you to come home. Will you marry me?"

Laura screwed up her face and looked at Trey with pity.

"No."

"No?"

"God no."

"Why not?"

"Um, are you serious? Jesus Christ dude, we haven't even lived yet."

"Don't you love me?"

"Of course I love you. What does that have to do with getting married?"

"What?" Trey stood up now. "I think that has a big part of what to do with getting married."

"I know, like... that's not what I mean. You know what I mean?"

"I don't know what you mean."

Laura put her hand on Trey's arm.

"Trey, I love you. And okay, maybe, somehow, we might end up together, but I don't think so."

"What the fuck?" Trey pulled away.

"Well, are you going to live in a city?"

"Yes!"

"What city?"

"The city," Trey said motioning to Ocean City.

"That's not a fucking city!" Laura yelled.

"But it's our city!" Trey pleaded.

"It's not. It's not mine."

Trey sighed and looked away from her.

"No, wait. Look, Trey... I don't even know if I ever want to be married. I don't know. I feel like that's what people do because everyone else does. Maybe people just get married because they are afraid to face the world alone."

"No, they get married because they love each other."

"Okay, sure. That's why your parents got married, and that's why my parents got married, and look what happened. I mean, Jesus fucking Christ, do you know of a good marriage that exists?"

"But we don't have to be like everyone else."

"EXACTLY! That's what I'm saying."

"But I mean, we can get married and not be like everyone else."

"Okay, but why can't we not get married and not be like everyone else."

"I don't understand."

Laura sighed. "Will you move to New York with me?"

"Why do you want to live in New York? Because of Jessica?"

"No, because it's exciting and... and... different."

"I can't leave," Trey shook his head. "My whole life is here."

"It doesn't have to be."

"I don't understand why I'm not enough for you."

Laura looked to the ground, softly shaking her head. She knew there was nothing she could say to fix this. "Can I give you a hug?"

"I don't want a hug."

She looked up and met his eyes. "But I do."

Trey capitulated. Laura held him close and put her head on his shoulder. He was radiating heat. She kissed his neck softly.

"I love you. Here. And now." she said. "Shouldn't that be enough?"

He didn't respond other than to take a deep exaggerated breath.

"I think I'm always going to love you," she said as she brushed his cheek with her hand and kissed him on the lips. "No matter where I go, no matter what I do. I'm always going to love you."

A single tear fell from Trey's eye. Laura wiped it away with her thumb. He breathed heavily.

"Can I see the ring?" she whispered.

They broke the embrace and he rubbed his eye with the back of his hand holding the box. He held his hand out to her and offered her the closed box, but she didn't take it. He shrugged, shook his head a little, and then opened it for her. It was a small single diamond set in a silver ring, and it caught the moonlight just so. She smiled.

"Oh... oh Trey..." Laura put her hand to her mouth. "Jesus, that's really pretty."

"You can have it," he handed her the box.

"I can't," Laura shook her head.

"Just wear it on a different finger."

"I can't. I'll know what it means to you."

He pulled it out of the box. He held her hand and slid it on her ring finger. It was a little loose.

"All it means is that I love you. You know that's true."

"I can't."

"Stop saying that. Say you won't, but don't say you can't."

Laura sighed.

"Look," Trey said. "It's a gift. We both know what it means to me. You can choose what it means to you."

Laura took it off her ring finger and slid it on her middle finger. Then she flipped off Trey.

"What do you think?"

"Come here," he said, smiling. "I want to see it closer."

When they kissed, she could still taste the salt of his tears.

40

The Final Season

Monday morning Candace was waiting for Laura in her parking space. As soon as Laura parked, Candace got into the passenger seat.

"So... how was Bon Appetite?"

Laura smiled and shrugged. Candace was the only one at school that knew that Trey and Laura were dating.

"How was the Snow Hill Inn?" Laura countered.

Candace held up her left hand and showed Laura a gold ring with five diamond chips.

"What?" Laura said. "You are not getting married. He's only a junior! Cradle robber!"

"I told him he needs to wait until I graduate college. But he's the one. I'm sure."

"How do you know?"

Candace shrugged.

"I don't know. I just do."

Laura gave her a hug and offered various congratulations. Then they sat still for a minute. Laura reached into her blouse and pulled out a long necklace. Hanging from it was the ring.

"What does this mean?" Candace asked, inspecting it.

"I don't know."

They looked out at the lacrosse field and sat in silence until they had to leave.

***

A few weeks later lacrosse season started. The third game in, while playing on a muddy field in Easton, Trey tore his ACL, MCL, and PCL in his right knee. Trey's athletic career was over. University of Maryland rescinded their scholarship offer, though Trey still had the option to attend the school if he liked. He declined.

Laura was unstoppable that season, and set a career points record that was so high it took almost three decades to break. Trey never went to any of her games, never watched her once. He said it was because he couldn't drive, but Laura didn't believe it. She thought it was too difficult to watch a sport he knew he could no longer play.

Trey was driven home from school by Chandler Dare, a senior theater kid whose family had moved to Ocean Pines the year before. Trey had been given pills to help with pain and swelling. When they ran out, Chandler got him weed. Trey started smoking every day after school. He was often asleep when Laura came to see him after her practice or games.

Trey was still on crutches during Prom. Trey was Prom King, Candace was Queen. He didn't want to dance, and said he couldn't, so Tyrone filled in for him. Laura sat with Trey for most of the night, they swayed to the occasional slow song together. Laura danced a couple of times with Candace, but otherwise spent prom sitting in a chair.

The day before graduation, Laura went to the beach with Candace and Tyrone. Candace was going to Temple University in Philadelphia, which Tyrone informed them was only 151 miles away. He already knew the route.

Laura left the beach and drove to Trey's house. He was on the couch, and had crumbs on his shirt. He had fallen asleep while listening to Pink Floyd.

"Jesus Christ, what are you doing?"

Trey opened his eyes, but they were just slits. He was off crutches now, but still kept a brace on his knee.

"My knee hurts."

"You should have come to the beach with us."

"I can't."

Laura leaned down to kiss him. He smelled like weed.

"You're not fucking paralyzed. You hurt your knee. Get over it. This shit is exhausting."

"Come on, gimme some sugar baby," Trey said, trying to be cute.

"You gotta get your ass off that couch if you ever want any sugar again," Laura said. She shook her head as he closed his eyes again. She turned around and walked out the door.

The following day Dolores hosted a graduation party at Buck's for Trey's classmates and their parents. It was a joyous occasion full of laughter, hugs, and tears. At one point in the middle of the party, Dolores took Laura out to the dock. As soon as they walked onto the deck the ducks came rushing over. Laura remembered Conor.

Dolores handed Laura an envelope full of cash, and a heartfelt card. Laura gave her a hug.

"Mija, I am so very proud of you, you know that right?"

"Of course."

"I feel like it has been so long since we have just been able to sit and talk, like we used to. I miss those days."

Laura thought about what Dolores meant by that. She couldn't possibly miss the days when her husband terrorized her. Laura wondered if everything was always going to be a compromise.

"Mija, there is nothing in this world that would make me happier than you marrying Trey and living here forever, raising little grandbabies for me to spoil."

Laura froze.

"Maybe someday you will come back," she continued. "It's a long life."

She paused now as they looked out onto the marsh and bay. In the distance, untamed mallards were flying low, and an egret was stalking the shallows.

"But now, you need to run away."

Laura looked at Dolores. "What do you mean?"

"I love Trey, but he's turning into a real shit. He's not ready to be a man. Don't think... look, I know he had a hard life, and maybe some of that was my fault."

"No it wasn't."

"Okay but maybe a little. But listen, he needs to take the next step. He has to do it on his own. He smokes this pot just like so many others that just get stuck out here in this fucking marsh."

She exhaled shortly out her nose, as if she was trying to cleanse the smell of the marsh from her body. Laura couldn't remember if she had ever heard Dolores swear before. She wondered if that was the result of working 18 months in a restaurant.

"He's a dark cloud," Dolores said to the marsh.

Laura just looked out at the bay. The sun was settling in the horizon. Laura wondered if Trey reminded Dolores of her husband, but she didn't want to ask.

"Maybe someday you will come back," Dolores continued. "Or maybe you won't. But either way, you will always be my daughter."

The women embraced while Trey smoked a joint by the dumpsters with the fry cook and dishwasher.

41

Grunge

Even though they saw each other almost every day, Trey and Laura grew apart. Trey worked six nights a week as a barback. Laura worked two nights on the line, and three in the front of the house. New Irish J-1 workers invaded the restaurant bringing their wonder, passion, and energy. Laura met so many new short-term friends, just like when she was a kid in Ocean Pines. She took up running, and every day she ran at least three miles before going to the beach. She was glowing.

Trey faded. He didn't consciously avoid the sun, but with the habitual weed and working late he rarely fell asleep before sunrise. He was pale and thicker than he used to be. He just barely kept the worst of his depression at bay with a heavy dose of Pearl Jam, Soundgarden, Nirvana, and cannabis. He never exercised, he just worked and slept.

They stopped having sex. There was never a conscious decision to do it, it just happened because of their lifestyle. Laura didn't want to hang out with the bar staff until two am every night, so she just went home and went to sleep. She tried to wake Trey up once in a while to get breakfast, but he was exhausted. He had lost the spark.

There's always a few days in early August when a strange weather pattern settles in over Ocean City, and the days are grey and the nights are cold. This year it happened on August 1st, which just happened to be the day Laura decided she couldn't take it anymore. She went to the Buckingham home around ten AM, just after her run. Dolores had already left for work, so she let herself in and went to Trey's bed.

He was sleeping alone, as he always did those days. She woke him up by shaking him.

"Stop it!" he finally said, with his eyes still closed.

"No," said Laura. "Not until you wake up and go to breakfast with me."

"I just went to sleep!"

"I don't care. Let's go to English's. Come on, it's a perfect day. It's cold, it's grey, I'll let you listen to Pearl Jam."

Trey opened one eye and looked at the bay window, the same window they had hid beneath so long ago.

"I don't care."

"Yeah, no shit. That's all you do now is not care."

"Whatever. Just break up with me here, you know you want to."

He closed his eye again, perhaps so he didn't need to look at Laura. She looked around his room. It was littered with dirty clothes and it smelled like he hadn't changed the sheets all summer. She saw a large envelope on the floor face down, and she knew what it was. Their prom pictures, which he still hadn't given to her. She shook her head.

That's when she noticed two fist sized dents in the wall. Right next to each other, right by the door. Her mind flashed to an image of Katherine. She thought about how the spirit of Trey's father still haunted that house, and the blood she once scrubbed off the kitchen chair. She stopped looking around and stood perfectly still, watching him. That's the moment she realized that while she loved him, she really hated him.

"You are turning into your father."

Trey's eyes shot open, and his face reddened. He sat up and grabbed the first thing he saw, which was a little lamp that sat on a bedside table.

"Don't you ever fucking say that to me again!" he growled and flung the lamp against the wall between them, shattering the lamp.

"We're done," Laura said coldly before running out the door and all the way to her car. She had no idea if he tried to follow her, she was always faster than he was, but he could no longer run anyway.

She drove straight to Buck's and told Dolores she needed to quit. Dolores didn't ask why. Dolores gave her a big hug, and promised her she would always be her mother, whenever she needed one.

Three days later Laura left a note on Trey's car. It read:

Dear Trey,
I'm sorry it had to end this way. I really do love you, but we don't work anymore.
If you ever hurt Dolores, I'll fucking kill you.
Laura

Trey cried when he read it, and tore it to shreds.

42

Our Mother

Laura packed her bags and kissed her mother goodbye two weeks earlier than scheduled. She was done with Ocean Pines, and wanted to waste no more time there. She called her father, who was elated to welcome her for two weeks before school started.

Having a mini vacation in Chicago with Todd sounded like the perfect plan.

"My dear," Todd sermonized in a professorial tone. "There are two proven cures for a broken heart. Spa days and shopping. Thankfully your father's credit card is available, and I'm gonna go ahead and clear my schedule. You can't heal on your own dear, you can't heal on your own."

But after three days of shopping, manicures, and mud baths Todd was concerned. He had never seen Laura like this before. She may have been forcing smiles and trying her best, but it was as if someone had stolen her joy.

It was a hot afternoon and they were carrying two shopping bags each. Todd took her to a small café for a frappe. They sat by the window and watched people walking by.

"I thought you were sad, but I think I was wrong. You're not sad, are you?" Todd asked.

Laura shrugged. She honestly didn't know what she was.

"Sweetheart, I think you are angry."

Laura nodded. That felt right.

"Do you want to talk about why?"

Laura shook her head. She wasn't sure she even knew why she was angry. Todd waited, took a sip of his frappe and looked out the window. He was a good listener, because he was never in a hurry to hear anything.

"I don't know why," Laura finally said.

"It's okay not to know," Todd said with a smile. "But it's not a good way to start a new adventure."

Laura shrugged again. Todd took another sip and looked out at the people walking by.

"Someone stole your spark. When that happens, you can't wait for them to give it back. You have to go find it again."

"What if it's gone forever?"

Todd laughed.

"God I miss being young," he said wistfully. Laura looked at him. He looked her right in the eyes.

"Impossible."

When Laura checked into her dorm she found out her roommate wasn't coming and she would have a room to herself. She was looking forward to having a roommate for the first time in her life, and this just added to her anger. Two hours later she was in the Joyce Center listening to The Vice President of Student Affairs give a welcome speech. The woman got up and said, "you do not change Notre Dame, Notre Dame changes you." The words bounced around Laura's head, and she heard nothing else. A minute later, long before the speech was over, Laura stood up and walked out of the auditorium. She was ready to quit the school at that moment. She was ready to quit everything. She had an unfamiliar energy, telling her to run and never look back. She walked back towards her dorm prepared to repack the bags she had just emptied.

"Did you forget something?"

Laura turned to see Coach Maddox coming out of LaFortune Student Center. Laura just shook her head.

"Aren't you supposed to be at orientation?" Coach Maddox asked with a questioning head tilt.

"I made a mistake."

"Oh," Coach Maddox nodded. "I got it. Come on inside, I'll buy you a soda."

They went into the student center, which was almost abandoned, since the upperclassmen weren't at school yet and the freshmen were all at orientation. Coach Maddox walked up to the bored cashier and pulled out her wallet.

"What do you want?" she asked Laura.

"Coffee."

Coach Maddox smiled, nodded, and ordered.

"Yeah, you're the coffee girl."

"What?"

"Every other kid I have ever seen has shown up to tryouts with Gatorade or water, you came with a gas station coffee."

Laura just shrugged.

"So," Coach Maddox continued. "Are you homesick?"

"No."

"Okay. So then, what's going on?"

"I just... I just feel like I'm not in control of my life."

"Hmm."

"What?"

"Well," Coach Maddox was looking right in Laura's eyes, as if there was a secret she was trying to uncover. "This is something I usually hear from juniors, not freshmen."

"I was hoping to have a roommate, but she didn't show up."

"Oh, that sucks, I'm sorry. But we might be able to fix that."

Laura sighed.

"The lady giving the speech, she said Notre Dame changes me, but I don't change Notre Dame."

"Okay."

"It upset me."

Coach Maddox smiled.

"Why?"

"It made me feel like my existence doesn't matter. If I wasn't here, things would go on just as they would, the same way. Like I'm nothing."

"I don't think that's what she meant."

"I don't see any other way to take it."

"Is that all?"

Laura shrugged and sighed. Coach Maddox waited.

"I broke up with my boyfriend. I know everyone who goes to college breaks up with their boyfriend, but... I don't know."

"Just because it happens to everyone doesn't mean it hurts any less when it happens to you."

"Everything is shit."

"Grab your coffee, I want to show you something."

They walked out of LaFortune and towards a small courtyard in front of O'Shaughnessy Hall. Coach Maddox pointed to a stone well and bronze sculpture of a woman drawing water and Christ leaning on the well and speaking to the woman.

"This is the story of the Samaritan woman at the well. Do you know the story?"

Laura shook her head.

"Jesus meets this Samaritan woman at a well and she gives him water and he gives her eternal life. It's an important story because Jews and Samaritans didn't really get along. But that's not what I like about it." Coach Maddox pointed to two other statues of men flanking the courtyard. One was looking towards the well, and the other was looking away. "This is what I love about this sculpture, these two other statues."

Laura looked at where she was pointing.

"So that's the Apostle John," Coach Maddox pointed at the one looking at the well. "See, he has a pen and a book, and he's recording what he is seeing. And the other one is Luke. Since Luke is looking away, this explains why the story of the Samaritan woman isn't in the gospel of Luke, but it is in the gospel of John."

"Okay... I'm not really sure of your point."

"It's just chance. Sometimes the ball bounces your way, sometimes it doesn't. You can't control everything in your life, you'll go nuts if you try that."

Laura looked silently at the woman and Jesus.

"Laura, I'm not saying this because I want you to play lacrosse, but you can't just quit. You got to give it a chance. The ball isn't bouncing your way right now, but things change. Give it a shot. I'm almost positive things will get better..."

Coach Maddox kept talking. Laura nodded but didn't remember anything else the coach said. She just kept looking at the woman at the well.

Laura stuck it out. Two weeks into the semester Laura's friend Anne got permission to move into Laura's room. Laura enjoyed having a roommate. They went to football games. They went to parties. They stayed up late talking.

Anne was from Sacramento, California. Laura knew of Sacramento only because in Ocean City at the entrance to Route 50 there was a sign that read "Sacramento, CA 3073 miles." Anne grew up just a few miles from the sister sign advertising Ocean City. Laura thought there was something magical about them finding one another in the middle of the country.

She found some of her classes fascinating, especially an art history class and a theology class that taught her about the Gnostic Gospels. She got a job at Lula's, a small coffee house just off campus. She went on a few dates, but the boys were either cheating on their girlfriends from home, or trying to find a wife. She wanted no part of either of those scenarios.

Lacrosse ended for Laura on the second day of fall ball when she tore her Achilles tendon. She needed surgery, and was still in a cast for her first semester finals.

She chose to spend Christmas with her grandparents in Iowa. It snowed. She sat by the fire, read novels, and slept.

Her second semester at Notre Dame was hard. It was cold and the snow was heavy. She missed playing sports. She missed the ocean. She missed being touched and being loved.

Early in the semester she had one of those long, philosophical talks that you have in college with a couple of her neighbors. Abortion came up and Laura said nonchalantly that she was pro-choice. One of the other girls asked her to leave the room. None of them ever talked to Laura again.

The following week the Vice President of Student Affairs banned the Gay and Lesbian Alliance from meeting on campus. This became a big controversy. Laura joined the banned organization. Anne joined out of solidarity for Laura.

An unknown person wrote *Leviticus 18:22* with a permanent marker on their door. The next week someone wrote *Baby Killer* just below it. While she was showering in the shared bathroom someone called Laura an apostate. The curtain was closed and she couldn't even tell who it was. After the shower she had to look up the word.

Laura's heart had hardened.

After final exams that spring Laura quit Notre Dame. She was in the wrong place, and knew it. She spent a week in Chicago, sold her car, bought a train ticket to New York, and moved in with Jessica.

In the end, the VP of Student Affairs was right. She didn't change Notre Dame, but Notre Dame certainly changed her.

43

The Long Autumn

Manhattan was dirty and smelled of urine and cigarettes. It seemed like everyone smoked cigarettes everywhere, as this was long before the indoor smoking ban or the legalization of cannabis.

Laura tried an occasional cigarette but it wasn't for her. The one time she actually succeeded in inhaling she thought her lungs were going to explode, so she never did that again.

Jessica lived in a high ceilinged railroad apartment in Hell's Kitchen, and slept in the back room past the kitchen. It was a small room, with only enough space for her double bed and a dresser. In the living room there was enough space for a futon and Jessica's stereo and growing CD collection, a coffee table and a broken recliner that no longer reclined, except when you least expected it.

Laura had her own "room" in Jessica's apartment, though her room was actually a converted coat closet. It had a sloped ceiling because it was underneath the hallway stairs. She could hear every footstep of every person going up or down, but she got used to it, and eventually would only wake if someone was actually running down the stairs. It had nothing in it but a mattress, which was too big for the closet so the sides were curled against the walls.

It didn't matter. She had a cheap place to sleep and felt like she was in the middle of the world. She got a job working as a waitress at a luncheonette on the

Upper West Side called E.J.'s, which was known for their crunchy French toast, delicious milkshakes, and terrible coffee. It paid the bills and then some.

It was a hot summer when she moved to the city, and through most of that season she went everywhere wide-eyed and observant, just waiting for the promised violence to happen. But Laura was fortunate. While the city was dangerous that summer, through a combination of vigilance and luck she avoided the ferity that had given the city such an ugly reputation.

By the time autumn relieved Manhattan of its maddening heat, Laura relaxed. Most days, unless it was raining hard, she would walk from her apartment on Ninth Avenue and 52nd Street to E.J.'s on Amsterdam Avenue and 81st Street. Every morning she made a habit of changing her route just a little, exploring a new street, putting it in her personal map and making it a part of her world. Most afternoons she walked east to Central Park, meandering through that most remarkable creation in the most remarkable city which she now called home. There is no pretension in falling in love with a place and time, when that place is Central Park, and that time is autumn.

One important aspect of New York that may have been overlooked by those that didn't spend enough time there, was the humble coffee cart. There were countless coffee carts that appeared sometime in the final moments of the night, and would usually disappear around midday. Every cart offered coffee and pastries of some kind, and the "fancy" ones would even make a sausage, egg, and cheese sandwich.

In 1994 they were everywhere in Manhattan, including on the north end of 52nd Street, right across Ninth Avenue from Laura's apartment. Each morning she stood in line, but before she even had a chance to say good morning, Gaspar had her coffee ready.

Gaspar had no idea what Laura's name was, but he knew she drank a small coffee, light and sweet. He always chatted just a little, usually about the weather. He was young, handsome, and a little tired looking most of the time, except for autumn, when everyone is inspired in New York.

The city was so massive and crowded with strangers, that these moments of familiarity mattered. Even days when Laura didn't go to work, she would go down to get her coffee and say good morning to Gaspar, and let him give his weather report.

The fall of 1994 was long and gentle. It was one of those exceptionally great seasons. Warm days with forgiving breezes, cool nights, and the occasional soft rains to cleanse the city and start all over again. On those grey rainy days Laura would sit by the fire escape in her kitchen, with the window wide open, drinking her cart coffee and listening to *Kind of Blue* by Miles Davis as the music melded perfectly into the sound of the city in the rain.

She bought a Walkman and added music to her wanderings. Pairing music with a city day is an art akin to picking the right wine for a meal, and Laura was well on her way to becoming a sommelier of sound. She would raid Jessica's ever expanding CD collection pushing her past the modern singer songwriters and dipping her toes into the pool of blues, jazz, and classical music. And she spent long afternoons at the Tower Records listening stations and digging through their "World Music" collection.

It was just after dark on a Tuesday the week before Thanksgiving when Jessica discovered that a small box arrived in the mail, addressed to her, and possessing a familiar return address. Jessica grinned and ran up the stairs. Laura had just lit three candles and a stick of incense which she had purchased from a street vendor that afternoon, and she was unpacking the pad Thai and spring rolls that were delivered moments before Jessica went to check the mail. When Jessica pushed the door open, she held up her hand displaying the box proudly and raising her eyebrows.

"Hmmm," Jessica said grinning as Laura recognized Trey's handwriting. "It appears Trey sent *me* something."

She ripped it open and a cassette tape slipped out with a small note.

Jessica,

You have always been so kind to share music with me over the years, I wanted to return the favor.

Sincerely,

Trey Buckingham

"Well that's formal," Jessica remarked while looking at the tape. The track listings were handwritten on the paper covering. "Ha... ha ha... ha ha ha ha ha... Wow..."

"What?" Laura asked, trying not to show too much interest. Trey hadn't attempted to contact her once since she had left Maryland for Notre Dame fourteen months before. Jessica kept smiling the further down the track listings she read, with the occasional chortle escaping like punctuation after each of the final few artists' names.

"Bitch, I am a pawn in your love game," Jessica shook her head enjoying the whole experience. "This tape is so for you. It starts with *I Will Always* by The Cranberries, I mean, that's a good one but, shit, that ain't for me... I don't know *Glycerine* by Bush, I've never heard of them, but *Ice Cream* by Sarah McLachlan? Trey wanted to send me that? *Fade Into You* by Mazzy Star? Okay. Fucking *Raining in Baltimore* by Counting Crows, come on. Dude, these are 'I love you Laura and I'm nothing without you' songs, not 'hey buddy Jessica, here's some cool music.'"

She struggled to read the writing on one of the songs.

"Alright, I don't know *Seduced* by Mary Coughlan, but if that one is for me, I might need to watch myself around Trey."

Jessica forced a faux exasperated laugh. Laura was still not getting it.

"Aw, you don't get it? This is his way of sending you a love note."

She handed Laura the tape.

"Put it in," Jessica prodded her. "Let's hear how much he still loves you. Plus I wanna hear that song *Seduced*."

These are the first words Laura has heard from Trey in over a year. She didn't know The Cranberries, and with the Irish accent she missed the first couple of lines. It just made her listen harder. Then she clearly heard:

Be whatever you want to be
Go wherever you need to go

Laura sighed through a torrent of memories. For a decade, Trey was there. Almost every day, through every struggle, pain, joy, and discovery, he was there by her side. They were together from the first, those autumn days riding bikes together, cooking in his home, when her father left, and when his father was taken away. They were both there when they innocently collapsed in exhaustion, dreaming in each other's arms. They... the concept of *they* was once more than the sum of its parts, *they* were more than two things put together, and *they* were more than just a single thing. They were everything to each other.

And again the lyrics were clear:

I will always go beside you

Laura took a bite of the pad Thai. She didn't feel like eating. She sat back on the futon and closed her eyes and remembered Trey.

44

Quitting

That autumn and winter Jessica was busy with school and work, and Laura used her free time to explore her city. When it got cold she bundled up and kept exploring. Through Jessica and work she met a handful of friends, all actors, writers, poets, dancers, musicians, or filmmakers currently working as waiters, baristas, strippers, temps, or bartenders. She went to all her friends' plays, showcases, gigs, and screenings. She was in her honeymoon period with New York, and went to every museum, even all the way up to the Cloisters.

Laura thought about Trey more than she admitted, and she often walked through the city listening to his mixtape. It wasn't a perfect mix, it was a little all over the place with Bush, Live, Candlebox, The Offspring, Counting Crows, Radiohead, Screaming Trees, and STP which all had a certain vibe. She felt like those were "Trey" songs, like where he was now, alone and without her, pining, and kinda sad. She didn't like that version of Trey. Then there was Sarah McLachlan, The Cranberries, Mazzy Star, and Mary Coughlan which were all songs she imagined were Trey and Laura together, holding each other again. Those were the songs that made her smile.

Then there were three wildcard songs.

First, *Hallelujah* by Jeff Buckley. She hadn't heard it before, not even the John Cale cover or the Leonard Cohen original. It was the kind of song that made her fall in love with Trey all over again. That first sigh...

Second, *Brokedown Palace* by the Grateful Dead. There was a time when Trey was really into the Grateful Dead. He was never a Deadhead per se, but he knew most of their studio albums. And let's be honest, everyone who grew up around Ocean City knows the American Beauty album by heart, so that was a nice addition to the mixtape. It made her homesick. The Grateful Dead and Ocean City, peas and carrots.

Third, *Southern Cross* by Crosby, Stills, and Nash. When Trey and Laura were growing up, the music that was considered Classic Rock was only about ten to fifteen years old. In fact, the year Laura and Trey met was the same year Crosby, Stills, and Nash released *Southern Cross*. It's one of those songs that got loads of radio play on classic rock stations, which was really the only non-classical radio alternative to top 40 pop music in the 1980s. Everyone knew that song, it was part of the background of their lives.

Classic Rock has a built-in nostalgia that's part of its hook. The familiarity mixed with the message of the lyrics affected Laura. Even in those still twentieth century years, that song was a sepia sunset memory of halcyon days gone by.

And that's part of moving to the city. No one moves to the city as a blank slate, everyone comes from somewhere, and brings their energy, their experience, and especially their language. One of Laura's languages was music, and *Southern Cross* would always be as much a part of her as Hell's Kitchen or anywhere else she lived.

The tape worked. For the first time in fourteen months, Laura thought she might have made a mistake letting Trey go.

***

Her mom repeatedly asked her to come home for Christmas, but Laura said she had to work. So in early December Joyce came up to the city and for two nights stayed at the Algonquin Hotel. She did the mom thing perfectly, taking both

Laura and Jessica out to dinner and even to see *Les Misérables* on Broadway. When you're a broke kid living in the city, the only way you get to see Broadway shows is when someone from out of town visits and takes you.

After the show they were sitting in the Blue Bar of the Algonquin, blissfully ignorant of the rich literary history of that space. Joyce, like many of her generation, appreciated a good hotel lounge over a noisy bar, especially when there was something important to say. Laura sipped her house merlot while leaning back against a soft cushion and pondering the tragedy that was Fantine.

"So..." her mom trailed off while she took her own sip of wine and looked back and forth between Jessica and Laura. She heaved a big sigh and let it slip. "We need to talk."

Laura snapped back to reality and steeled herself for the incoming bad news. Jessica leaned in, happy to have a distraction from schoolwork and her impending senior project. Joyce frowned, not sure where to begin.

"Spit it out mom."

"I have taken a job in Baltimore that starts in January."

"Woah, congrats Mrs. Byrne, that's awesome," Jessica clinked her martini glass against Joyce's wineglass.

"Yeah mom," Laura said, more pensively than positively. "Congrats. Is Bubby moving with you?"

Joyce shook her head.

"I'm sorry to say we broke up."

Laura looked at her mom and gently nodded. All she could think about was Bubby and Trey sitting at dinner together, the table otherwise empty.

"I'm sorry mom. Are you okay?"

Her mother shrugged.

"I think so. He is a good man, but he's just not right for me. He wants a family, and... I don't want to be a mom."

"Ouch," Laura smiled.

"Oh hush, you know what I mean. I'm forty-three years old, and I've been a daughter, a student, a mother, and that's it. I want to live my life, does that make sense?"

"Mrs. Byrne, I totally get it. You don't need to explain yourself to me, that's for sure." Jessica ate her last olive and nodded to the waitress for another martini.

"Yeah, mom, of course. It makes total sense."

Joyce nodded sadly.

"This means I need to sell the house. Which means you need to come get your stuff."

Laura thought about her childhood room. It seemed fuzzy to her. Other than a few photographs stuck into the dresser mirror she couldn't remember any details.

"I don't need any of that stuff, you can throw it out."

Joyce was visibly upset.

"What about your trophies, you worked so hard for those?"

"Oh please."

"What about your letters, or your photos, or your clothes?"

Laura closed her eyes. She could only see a few photographs. Trey was in all of them.

"It's just stuff. I have everything I need."

Joyce sighed in frustration. But Laura shook her head.

"It's just stuff."

***

Three days after Christmas, on a frigid gray day, Laura was almost finished her shift when her manager Milo told her that he seated table 25. She gave him a, but-I'm-almost-finished-my-shift look, to which he responded that the customers asked for her specifically.

When she popped around the corner of the booth she was surprised to see Tyrone looking at her and grinning.

"What the hell?"

Candace, who had been hiding her face behind a menu, squealed, jumped up, and gave her a big hug.

"Oh my God, guys, what are you doing here?"

"Why didn't you come home for Christmas!" Candace demanded more than asked. "I miss you."

"I miss you too. Are you guys ready to order?"

Candace looked at her like, *what the hell?*

"Look, I'm almost done my shift so if you order I can punch out and then hang out with you, but I gotta put the order in before I punch out."

"I haven't even looked," Candace said, shaking her head, still confused.

"I'll take a burger," Tyrone didn't need to look. Candace gave him an exasperated look.

"Candace get the Chicken Ruben, you'll love it. You guys want milkshakes? They're a pain in the ass but I'll do it for you."

"Just coffee," Candace said with a forced smile.

Laura grabbed three coffees and sat with them for a couple of minutes before the food arrived. Candace explained that they were in the city to see the show *Stomp*, Tyrone had gotten her tickets for Christmas. They were staying in New Jersey with a friend of his from college, as he was now a Freshman at Rutgers. She said they still had a few hours before they were meeting Tyrone's friends for dinner.

After lunch Laura suggested they walk over to Central Park. It had snowed overnight, and while the streets were wet and noisy, the park would be blanketed and peaceful. Candace shrugged acceptance and asked Laura if she wanted to finish her coffee. Laura laughed.

"Our coffee is terrible. Let's get a cart coffee."

Most coffee carts were gone by the early afternoon, but Laura knew a place by the Museum of Natural History that stayed until 3:30, and they were able to get there as he was starting to pack up.

Coffees in hand, they walked into the park at 77th street and south to Strawberry Fields. It was dusted with a thin sheet of snow, as was the Sheep Meadow, and all the places off the paths. They walked around the lake to Bethesda Fountain, and then up the hill to Bow Bridge. The entire walk Candace filled in Laura on gossip from home, but she never brought up Trey once.

When they got to Bow Bridge, Candace stopped talking and sipped her coffee. She was chilly, but charmed by the view. She realized Laura hadn't spoken more than a couple of words since they left the restaurant. She looked at her. She had forgotten how pretty Laura was, even with food stains on her shirt and a smudge of chocolate ice cream on her chin. Candace took off her mitten, licked her thumb, and wiped away the smudge.

"Moooooom," Laura joked.

"You're really pretty," Candace said in an almost listless way.

"Not for New York," Laura laughed.

Tyrone walked over to the other side of the bridge and leaned against the railing, looking out towards the east side of the lake. Obviously giving them privacy.

"So is this it?" Candace asked.

"Oh come on, it's a beautiful day. Look at this view."

"No, I mean, you. What are you doing with your life? You know you have to go back to school, right?"

Laura grimaced and shrugged.

"Why?"

"Um, so you can get a job and do something with your life. Unless you are planning on marrying rich or something. But even then you should probably go to school."

"I don't think I'm ever going to get married."

"Okay," Candace waved her hands to say, *What's next?* "So then? Are you, like, gonna be a waitress your whole life?"

"I don't know."

"Look, I know Trey fucked you up pretty bad..."

"Trey didn't fuck me up."

Candace looked at her and tilted her head to the left while half rolling her eyes. "Okay, really? Because you haven't been home since you broke up with Trey."

"That's not true," Laura said, leaning against the bridge and looking out onto the water. Ducks were swimming in the unfrozen lake.

"When? When were you home?"

"What I mean is, Ocean Pines is not my home anymore. Maryland is not my home."

"Oh, so now you are a New Yorker? That's it, you're from New York now? Your home is, what, Jessica's apartment?"

Laura smiled imagining what Candace would think if she saw Laura's closet that passed for a bedroom.

"Not exactly. I don't think I really have a home, not the same way I did. It's hard to explain."

"Okay, well, like this is all well and good, but what about in five years, or ten years? What are you going to do then? You're too smart to waste your life."

"I'm not wasting my life. I'm exploring."

Candace shook her head.

"Psh. Okay, well, like, can't you explore once you get your degree? I mean come on, this is how the world works."

"Moooooom."

"I'm being serious Laura. You're going to wake up one day and regret your choices."

"Okay. But everyone has regrets. I want my regrets to be on me. Can't I do that? Can't I make my own way? Not do what I have to do because I've been told that it's the time to do it, because some 'world' works a certain way."

"Okay, well in the meantime the world is going to leave you behind."

"I never asked for it to wait. I don't care, I really don't. I don't. I mean, whatever that means, fuck that."

"My God, Laura, listen to yourself. You're so lost," Candace shook her head softly and sadly.

"I don't think I'm lost."

There was a long pause. Finally Candace spoke.

"Well, if you say you are not lost, fine. But it sure sounds like you are looking for something. And I don't think you know what that something is."

"Exactly," Laura said, relieved. "You're right, I don't. That's it. I guess, I want to find what I'm not supposed to find."

"Cool," said Tyrone to the east side of the bridge, who apparently was listening the whole time. Laura smiled. Candace shot him a disapproving look.

It was getting dark. As they walked south it began to snow again.

45

Old Friends

A week of heavy rain prompted Laura to start taking the subway to work. So she got in the habit of taking the C train from 50th street up to the Museum of Natural History and walking from there. She still took the long way home.

This is when Laura started carrying a book with her wherever she went. One necessary technique of self-preservation in the subway is to not make eye contact with any of the violently insane subway people. Which meant one had to either have a newspaper or a book.

One early evening she was reading a novel on the N train heading south to Union Square to see a co-worker's actors showcase, when she heard a familiar voice.

"Will you look at this, an American who can read. Now I've seen everything."

She looked up to see Conor's broad smile. He was dressed in a dark suit and holding the grab bar. After an initial shock she stood up and gave him a hug. At that moment the train braked suddenly and she slammed into him, and they nearly fell over.

"Was it good for you too?" he joked, taking a seat next to her.

"What are you doing here?"

"Funeral," he said smiling.

"I'm so sorry."

Conor shook his head.

"Sorry, that wasn't funny. Actually I'm here for a wedding. My best mate up and decided to become an American. I guess he was tired of being clever and charming, maybe he thought he would try being rich for a while."

Laura was having a hard time following.

"What about you? College?"

"Nah."

"Fucking hell. Really?"

Laura shrugged. For some reason Conor's response made her embarrassed. He noticed.

"Oh fuck, is one of your boyfriends here? I should keep an eye peeled, eh? Is it that guy?"

He pointed to a man sitting across from them that couldn't have been less than seventy years old, dressed in a suit and holding a cane. Laura sighed. The old man winked and shook his cane at Conor.

"She kissed me, I swear," Conor said to the old man and held up his hands defensively. Laura laughed.

"Where's the wedding?"

"Tribeca. Where are you off to?"

"Union Square. This is my stop," Laura stood up.

"I'll walk with you."

"Aren't you going to be late for the wedding?"

"I'm not the one getting married," he shrugged as they walked out of the subway car. "Though I do have the rings. Sean's gonna be fucking furious."

They walked through Union Square, heading east and south. Laura was working her way towards St. Mark's Street.

"So, Miss Laura Byrne, what are you up to these days?"

"Just waiting tables. Living in New York."

"Quite the upgrade from waiting tables in Ocean City. Maybe someday you'll make it to Dublin. You know, the big time."

Laura nodded sarcastically. She told him about Candace coming to visit and her lecture.

"Oh for fucks sake. I like Candace enough and all, but what business is it of hers how you live your life?"

"She's my friend. I think she's just concerned about me."

"Ah yeah, sure, a friend's eye is a good mirror and all. But come on, you look good. You're reading fucking Russian literature for fun," he gestured to her book. "Don't worry about Candace. No one knows what the fuck they're doing."

Laura stopped walking and looked Conor right in the eyes.

"I'm scared I'm wasting my life."

He smiled.

"Course you are. Everyone is."

He took a breath and waited to see if she wanted to say anything more. She didn't.

"There's a fella I was at school with, he was a couple years ahead of me, I saw him around the way the other night and tells me he's a Buddhist. Like apropos of fucking nothing, 'Hey Conor, alright? I'm a Buddhist now.' Just like that. And I don't fucking know what that means, so I ask him if he's still allowed to drink, and he says he is, so I say, 'Great, buy me a pint and tell me all about it.' And he does."

They started walking again as Laura felt this story had legs.

"So he says to me, 'Conor, I worked in a bank, and I was gonna kill myself. I was at the end of the line, you know?' I didn't, but I nodded along, cause, you know, he paid for the pint. And then he says to me, 'I just wanted things. Clothes and shoes and whatnot, you know?'"

"Honestly," Laura interrupted, "In this country clothes and shoes are considered necessities."

"Nice one," Conor smiled. "No what he meant was like nice shit, you know designer stuff. Armani, Gucci, something Italian."

"Okay."

"Anyway... he says, 'Whenever I got something, I was so fucking proud, like I had accomplished something. And each new thing was like a new award I gave myself. But then one day I was walking home right by Seapoint, and there were all these schoolkids screaming. One of their pals had tried to go swimming and was drowning.'" Conor paused here and touched Laura's arm. "Now this fella was a top notch athlete in school, football, hurling, rugby, he was the tops. But he says to me, he says, 'Conor, I froze up like a statue. I stood there looking at this drowning child and I was thinking about my fucking Italian shoes.'"

Conor raised his eyebrow and nodded, pausing again for dramatic effect. Laura's eyes were wide.

"Did he save the kid?"

"That's what I asked! And he said, 'Conor, I wouldn't be standing here today if I didn't save that child.' But you know, he thought about his shoes. He paused in that moment that could have meant life or death, you know? And that stuck with him. That thought fucked him up."

"What happened to the shoes?" Laura said, smiling.

Conor's face reddened.

"That's precisely what I asked! Fucking hell. Ruined, by the way. But that's not the end of it, cause he saves this kid and then he goes right to the pub and gets polluted. That night he makes up his mind he's gonna quit, you know, because he blames the job on the shoes or something. But what he doesn't know is, that kid he rescued is the grandson of his boss's boss's boss at the bank. The big cheese. Head honcho. Grand Pooh-bah. So he tries to quit and instead they give him a promotion and gobs more money so he can buy all the shoes he'll ever want."

"Holy shit."

"My exact response again! Maybe I said 'fucking hell,' but same sentiment."

"Wait," Laura was trying to connect the dots. "How does this make him a Buddhist?"

"I'm getting to it. So he says to his boss that he doesn't care about the money, he's quitting for real. But the bankers think he's just burned out, so they offer him to take a three month holiday and then decide if he wants the job after that. So he agrees, buys a backpack and goes east."

"To India?"

"To Amsterdam. And he goes to his hostel and orders the most expensive spliff they have."

"What's a hostel?"

"A hostel. Like a regular youth hostel."

"I don't know what that is," Laura said flatly.

"Fucking hell, a youth hostel. Like a hotel for young people. Anyway..."

"There's hotels for young people?" Laura was surprised by this.

"Are you fucking with me now?"

"No."

"They are like hotels but they have bunk beds and six or ten people to a room. That's how young people travel. For fucks sake, how do you not know about them?"

Laura shrugged.

"Fucking America. Anyway, he's in this hostel and gets the best grass they have."

"Hostels sell weed?"

"Only in Amsterdam. Let me just get through this, I got a wedding to get to. Anyway he smokes this grass and he gets super paranoid. Like he thinks everyone in the coffee house is like KGB agents or something."

"I thought you said it was a hostel."

"It was both, just... Right, so he up and bolts, because of the KGB. Now keep in mind, he's had a few pints, and he's knackered from the plane and now he's high as a kite. He walks the streets and he's going through the red light district and he's all turned about. He's by a canal, because, Amsterdam, and all of a sudden the heavens opened and it's pissing rain. Now everyone's running for cover, someone bumps him, he slips, hits his head, and goes right in the drink."

Laura narrowed her eyes trying to tell if Conor was serious.

"What did you used to call this? Blarney?"

"No blarney, I swear on the holy Mother. He wakes up two days later in the hospital, head all wrapped up, bad concussion. And he has no idea who he is, right? Total amnesia."

"Okay," Laura rolled her eyes. Conor smiled, clearly enjoying that she wasn't believing the story.

"Listen, at this point he doesn't even know his name. He says the last thing he remembered is swimming at a beach... *as a child*. So they ship him off to a psych ward and soon as he gets there, bam, his memory comes back, like a lightning bolt. He remembers his name, his flat number, his job, the Italian shoes, the drowning lad, the name of his hostel, even the grass and the KGB agents. Right, it all comes back. But he doesn't say anything to anyone. Instead, he sits there for hours with a bandage on his head, just watching all the other lunatics."

"Wait, aren't you a doctor? Is 'lunatics' a medical term?"

"I'm dumbing it down for you, cause, you know, you're not in university."

Laura punched him in the arm. Conor grabbed his arm.

"Fucking hell, every time I'm around you I get my ass kicked. Anyway, he starts to think maybe he should stay there, work some stuff out. Honestly, it probably wasn't a bad idea, cause he was like, at the end of his rope. But then the psychiatrist comes in. They brought in this young Egyptian doctor specifically to talk to him because she speaks English. Apparently she's a real knockout. And he just melts, you know, he lays it all on her, the whole thing. And she's like, you're not a looney, so you gotta go."

"Thanks for translating."

"Your welcome. But then she says she's a Buddhist and she gives him the name of her temple and says he should go to a meeting there and learn about meditation. Now, at this point I said to him that Egyptians are Muslim not Buddhist and he says Irish are Catholics and not Buddhist and yet here we are. So I shut my gob."

"You being quiet might be the most unbelievable part of this story yet."

"Yer one to talk. Anyway, he went to the temple. And he said to me, 'Conor, I learned more about myself in one hour in that temple, than I did in 24 years of church.' And I said, 'it's that good, huh?' And he said, 'no, it was just the right thing for me at the right time. It was what I needed to hear.'

"So I said to him, 'Did you quit your job?" And he said, "Why? It wasn't my job that was my problem. It was my mindset.' He said, 'With everything I wanted that I didn't need, I was throwing another piece of my life away. But I didn't know any better. But now I do.' So he's a Buddhist."

"That was the most random story ever," Laura said with smiling eyes.

"What? You said you felt like you were throwing your life away. Just like yer man, the Buddhist."

"Seriously that was so long ago I don't even remember feeling that way now," Laura said with a laugh.

They were at the corner of St. Mark's and Third Avenue. A street of head shops, tattoo parlors, and t-shirt shops. Basically the boardwalk of New York City. Conor asked for Laura's novel and wrote his address in Ireland on the inside cover and handed it back to her.

"I gotta fly. I truly love conversing with you, Laura Byrne. If you ever come to Ireland, you have a place to stay."

He turned and hailed a cab right away. As he opened the door he turned back.

"I misspoke. *When* you come to Ireland you have a place to stay. As long as you like."

Moments later the cab disappeared into the yellow and red sea of the East Village twilight.

46

Death

Spring in New York kinda sucks. It's cold, it's humid, it's hot, it's windy, there's no breeze, it rains and snows at the same time, and then it's a million degrees and then it's cold again, all in about an hour.

Jessica had a mini nervous breakdown that April, and was hospitalized for a few days. She was very dehydrated, but Laura also knew she hadn't been sleeping, she was drinking and smoking far too much, and was pretty stressed in general. Not to mention, April weather in New York is enough to drive anyone insane.

Even so, Jessica still managed to finish her Senior Project and graduate on time. Laura went to her graduation and sat with Jessica's parents and her oldest sister, who apparently lived in Connecticut and worked in the city, and yet she and Laura had never met before that day.

As spring turned into summer Laura got in the habit of bringing her bathing suit with her on sunny days so that after work she could go to Central Park and sunbathe while reading. It wasn't the same as going to the beach, but there was something about the park in the summer that made New York feel even more like her home. It was a hot summer, but every summer seemed hotter on the island of Manhattan than it did 200 miles south on the peninsula of Ocean City.

After graduation Jessica got an internship at a small boutique commercial production house, and worked on independent films on the side. The internship turned into a full time job, and she was able to quit the bar she waitressed at.

For the first time since she had moved to New York, Jessica and Laura's schedules lined up pretty well and they started to spend more time together. Their many talks, sometimes at bars, sometimes at their apartment, often went deep into the night.

It was a cool, rainy August night when Jessica came home from work with a magnum of cheap Chilean red wine. She ordered Chinese food, Moo Shu Pork with extra pancakes and Singapore Mei Fun, claiming that those were the best dishes to pair with her "fine wine" selection.

Laura noticed that Jessica was a little drunk already, and she explained that she had gone to a work happy hour. The owner of the company had bought her a martini and two shots of Jameson before he slid his hand up her thigh.

"Eww." Laura's skin crawled. "Isn't he old?"

"Yeah. Like super old. Like pushing fifty. What's even worse is he whispered to me 'My wife is out of town' in like a really raspy voice. Like anything about that is sexy."

"I'm sorry."

"Yeah, whatever, I'm sure he'll be all weird on Monday."

"Did you tell him you're a lesbian?"

"Oh, he already knows. I honestly don't know if that makes it better or worse."

Laura was at the stereo and was flipping through CDs looking for Ani DiFranco's *Not a Pretty Girl* album, which had come out about a month prior. Soon as Jessica heard the first notes she smiled. She popped the cork and poured generously. They sipped their wine letting Ani do most of the talking.

The food came and Laura unpacked it while Jessica gestured with her wine as she complained that there were never enough pancakes. They ate and agreed that *32 Flavors* was the best song on the album. Jessica leaned against the back of the futon and sighed heavily, thinking about Monday morning already. She finished her wine and held her glass out for Laura to refill.

"You seem," Laura treaded delicately as she poured, "frustrated all the time lately. Maybe your job isn't right for you?"

"Of course it's not right for me. But I have to do it."

"Why?"

"Cause that's how it works."

Laura had taken a huge chopstick full of Singapore Mei Fun, with three rogue, yellow, angel hair noodles clinging to her chin. Jessica laughed and handed her a paper towel, which in their apartment always stood in for napkins.

"Fair enough," Laura said after swallowing. "But I know you. It doesn't matter if you work at this job or not, you are going to make it someday. You're driven." Laura was a little drunk too, but she meant what she was saying.

Jessica sighed.

"You don't know that."

"Yes I do."

"I mean, you can't know that. I have been thinking about this lately. Everything that you are certain of as fact is likely to someday change. You can't trust it. All you can trust is the moment."

"You mean you can only believe what you see?"

Jessica scrunched up her nose and closed one eye as she thought about the question.

"Emmm... not really. Sight is bullshit. Of the five universally accepted senses, sight is most likely to deceive us. I don't think we see half of what we think we see, and we don't see half of what is there. Well, taste is kinda weak, too."

"Because you smoke too much."

"True. But even if I didn't, it constantly changes. Hormones, mood, illness, lighting, all those things can affect taste. Maybe scent and touch are real. Scent can store memories forever. Touch confirms something is, like, actually in the room with us."

"Are you purposely forgetting hearing? Come on... music?"

"Sound and truth? I don't know. There's no truth at all in what people say, right? Half the time we don't even know what people are saying, we just assume we know what they are going to say. No one listens. Most conversations are just pastimes anyway. Like games... like this one. And, you know, if you think about it, we learn to ignore the sounds that are most familiar. It's fucking awful. Our hearing ignores that which is closest to us. And yes, the best of sound, is undoubtedly, music. But you can't find truth in music. Truth means nothing to music. It withers, dies, or maybe worse, becomes forgotten. The right music makes truth unimportant."

Laura laughed. "Did you smoke weed tonight?"

"A little bit," Jessica said smiling.

"Wait a second," Laura remembered. "I thought you didn't believe in the soul."

"Of course I don't," Jessica shrugged and sipped her wine, inspecting it. "That's just made up bullshit by the church to get money from poor people. But that doesn't matter to the right notes. The right notes transcend the bullshit."

Laura was confused.

"I don't understand."

Jessica sighed. She took a deep breath and held it, then released it slowly.

"Fuck it... I... *sigh* Fuck. I don't think I'm a lesbian."

Laura's eyes got big.

"WHAT?!?"

"Yeah. I mean, I don't like guys, but I don't think I like girls either. I don't know, I just don't want, you know, sex. I like this," Jessica gestured with her hand back and forth from her to Laura. "I like talking and friendship and being with you, but I don't want to *be* with you."

"You don't want to lick me."

"I don't want to lick anyone! I wish we could just have this forever, but, I know, we can't cause... you know... you like dudes."

"Barely."

"I mean, don't get me wrong," Jessica put her wine glass down and picked up the Moo Shu. "I'd suck a dick to get a few more pancakes with my Moo Shu, but, you know, I wouldn't like it. Means to an end and all."

"So would you marry someone for pancake security?"

"Fuck off," Jessica used a chopstick as an extended middle finger to flip Laura off.

Laura laughed.

"We're sisters," Laura reminded her. "Remember that. You're always going to have me."

Jessica grinned with a mouth full of cabbage and egg.

At that moment the phone rang. Jessica picked it up and said "hello" with her mouth still full. She listened for a second, swallowed, and lost her smile.

"Okay," she said to the receiver while looking at Laura. She handed the phone to her friend.

"It's Joyce," she said seriously. Laura held the phone to her ear.

"Laura, we need to talk."

Laura sighed and waited.

"It's Trey's father. He had a heart attack in prison."

"Oh."

"Laura, he's dead."

"Good," Laura said unconsciously. Joyce paused. Laura didn't say anything else.

"The funeral is Monday morning at St. Mary's Star of the Sea. I thought you would want to know."

Laura held the phone away from her ear and closed her eyes. For a moment it looked like she was going to hang up.

"Laura? Are you there?"

"Mom, can I borrow your car?"

"Yes dear, of course. Come home."

Sunday night she was on a train to Baltimore, feeling far more lost than she had ever been.

***

It was still dark Monday morning when she left Baltimore in her mother's car. She wanted to leave early in case there was bad traffic, as going to the beach in the summertime could be challenging. Her mother offered to go with her, but Laura asked to go alone.

Laura didn't know what to expect. She wanted to be there for Dolores and Trey, even though she hadn't spoken to either of them in years. Somehow the three of them had all been brought together by this man who she didn't really know. She needed to see it through, even if she didn't know what that meant.

She had brought seven tapes, two made by Jessica, four by her, and the mix Trey sent Jessica. She tried an Ani, Tori, Indigo Girls heavy tape, but the mood wasn't right, and so she changed it out as she passed over the Severn River. She put in the mix that she once shared with Trey, a tape she hadn't listened to in a long time. *Something I Can Never Have* took on a whole new meaning as she inched closer to her childhood home. But after the Nine Inch Nails she put Trey's tape in. She felt she owed him at least that much.

The sun rose as Laura got to the Bay Bridge. Ducks were flying low and the Chesapeake Bay was calm, almost like a dark mirror reflecting the first rays of the sun. There were no boats on the water yet, and just a single tanker that seemed far closer to the rising sun than it did the bridge. There were no clouds in the sky, not even on the horizon. She was sure she had never seen a sky so barren of clouds before.

Even though it was summer, it was so early on a Monday morning that there were almost no cars on the road until she got to Easton. Even then, traffic was light. She stopped for a coffee at a gas station outside of Easton, and it was some of the worst coffee she had ever had. It tasted chalky and old. She drank it anyway.

She got to Berlin hours before the funeral, so she stopped at English's for breakfast. She sat in her favorite booth, and the waitress recognized her, asked her where she had been, and said nothing more about it. She got the scrapple, egg, and cheese on a biscuit with mustard and drank three cups of coffee, even though she was wide awake.

"Only person I've ever seen eat that with mustard," The waitress said as she dropped off the check. "Hard to forget something like that. Don't be a stranger, sweetie."

They smiled at each other and Laura drove to Ocean Pines.

She drove past her old home, and there were three cars in the driveway that she didn't recognize. She wanted to knock on the door, but instead she drove away wishing she hadn't gone down her street.

She drove toward the Buckingham home, but chickened out at the end of the block and did a U-turn. She wasn't ready. She drove into Ocean City, and walked into the church, sitting all the way in the back corner.

She was so early that neither Trey nor Dolores were there yet. In fact, she was the first person in the church other than the priest, who was someone she had never met before. Laura never understood why Catholic priests were constantly moved around from parish to parish, but at that moment she was glad to not be recognized.

She was nervous. At least a few times she considered leaving and driving back to Baltimore. However, the thought of Dolores one day finding out she was there and didn't stay even long enough to say hello made her sick to her stomach, so she stayed. A few mourners walked in and took seats near the front, but no one that Laura had ever seen before.

She almost didn't recognize Trey when he walked in. His hair had grown long, and he looked thin, especially in his face. Laura was pretty sure his suit was the same one he wore to Homecoming senior year, and it still fit, if not a little loosely. But even if he was thin, he was healthy looking, his skin was dark, as if he had spent the whole summer at the beach.

Laura stood up and froze, not sure what she should do. An old man had come up to Trey and was talking to him. Laura didn't know if she should look at him or not, but just as she thought about looking away he looked up and saw her and gasped. He held his left hand to his face, his forefinger between his eyes, and made a sound like he had the wind knocked out of him. Laura walked up to him, ready to apologize and leave, when Dolores walked through the door.

"Mija," she said as she enveloped Laura with a huge bear hug.

"I'm sorry," Laura said. "I'm so sorry. I'm just so sorry."

"Mija, oh, you don't have to be sorry for anything," Dolores looked at her but wouldn't let her go. "I've missed you so much."

"I've missed you too," Laura said honestly, tearing up while she hugged Dolores again.

The hug ended only when another mourner tapped Dolores on the shoulder to offer her condolence. Laura and Trey drifted to one another. Laura put out her hands for a hug and Trey capitulated. They held each other gently, and for a long time. It was their first real hug in public since the lunchroom in high school.

"I'm sorry," she said.

"No," he said calmly. "There's nothing to be sorry about."

"I mean about your dad."

"Yeah," Trey said. "Exactly."

Laura looked at him trying to read his face, but he was hiding his emotions well.

"You're sitting back here?"

Laura nodded.

"Do you want to sit up front with us?"

Laura shook her head. Trey shrugged.

"Well, can I sit in the back with you?"

Laura swallowed hard.

"Sure."

They had just sat down when Dolores walked over to them.

"Children, come up and sit next to me, please."

Laura smiled. Trey looked at Laura and shook his head in faux and performative disbelief.

The service flew by. Dolores and Trey both cried. Laura put her arm around Trey. At the Sign of Peace they hugged, and Laura thought Trey might never let her go.

There were about thirty people in attendance, only one of whom Laura recognized. Katherine's father, Mr. Bounds, came late and left early. Laura later learned he was there at the request of Katherine, who was taking summer classes in Spain and couldn't get home. The other mourners were family or high school friends of Trey's father. Trey didn't speak and wasn't a pallbearer. He drove his mother to the graveside. Laura drove separately. At the grave there were only twelve people, the pall bearers and two of their spouses, the priest, Trey, Dolores, and Laura.

After the quick graveside service everyone left except for Trey, Dolores, and Laura. It was noon, and the sun was blazing. There was still not a cloud in the sky. Laura was squinting because of the sun's reflection from the cars. Trey took off his sunglasses and handed them to her. She tilted her head and smiled, but took them and put them on.

"Do I look too cool now?" she whispered to him.

Trey smiled. Dolores wept loudly. Trey and Laura walked to her and held her as she cried. They were tears of sorrow, longing, anger, pain, and hatred. Trey and Laura cried too. They couldn't help being that close to so much pain without joining in.

"It's over mom. It's over," Trey kept saying until her tears relented.

She smiled a sad smile and put her head on his shoulder, knowing full well it would never be over.

They all went back to Buck's for a reception that the staff had prepared. There was far too much food as less than a dozen people showed up. Dolores wasn't up for a real conversation. Laura talked about New York and Dolores listened, smiled, and patted her on the thigh occasionally.

Dolores was broken, and Laura hated seeing her this way. Dolores knew it and excused herself to go do work, which really meant to go cry some more in the office.

Trey walked over to Laura's table and sat next to her.

"I'm sorry," Laura said again. "Today must be hard for you."

"It's hard for me to see my mom in pain. But don't get me wrong. I'm great."

"Still though..."

"No. Seriously. My dad is dead and you are here. It's like a dream come true."

Laura looked down and sighed.

"Do you think," he asked cautiously, "that you could drive me home. There's something I want to show you."

Laura raised an eyebrow and he smiled.

"Seriously, it will only take a couple of minutes."

Laura nodded and they walked out to their cars. Trey got his sunglasses out of his car and grabbed a box of mini chocolate donuts which had partially melted in the sun. He popped one in his mouth and offered the box to Laura. She took one, popping it in her mouth and laughing as she chewed. Then they got into her mom's car and headed back to Ocean Pines.

"I like your hair," Laura said in the car. Trey smiled and shrugged.

"Thanks?"

"I really do. You look good. Healthy. Mini chocolate donuts aside."

"Breakfast of champions."

"I'm serious though. It's good to see you looking like this."

He looked at her to confirm she was being serious. He was confident she was.

"I surf every day now. Well, almost every day."

"And you stopped smoking pot?"

Trey laughed.

"Oh, Hell no. I mean, probably more than back in the day. No, definitely more. You know there's really not a lot to do in this town but surf and smoke pot, right?"

Laura sighed and concentrated on the road.

"I'm going to school at Salisbury. I'm a semester behind, but, you know, that's not much of a surprise. I heard you are living with Jessica, how is she doing? Did she like the tape I sent her?"

She raised an eyebrow.

"That tape was for her?"

"What?" he said with a crooked grin. He flipped on the stereo. The Counting Crows' "Raining in Baltimore" played. He looked at her.

"My tape?"

Laura shrugged.

When they got to Trey's house, out of habit, Laura parked in the drainage ditch across the street. He looked at her.

"You can pull in the driveway," he said.

"I don't think I can," Laura said as she turned off the car.

As they walked towards the house they saw a group of six kids riding bikes around the cul-de-sac, playing some game that grownups wouldn't understand. Trey waved to them, and one of the kids waved back.

"I suddenly feel old," Laura said.

"Just wait," Trey smiled as he opened the door.

They walked into the Buckingham home. Laura paused at the doorway.

"It seems bigger than I remember. Isn't it supposed to seem smaller?"

"I think you have gotten used to those New York City apartments," he smiled and held out his hand to direct her to his room. Laura tentatively stepped inside.

"Um, why are we here?" she asked as she walked down the hallway.

"You'll see."

"Or," she stopped and faced him. "You could just tell me."

He sighed. "I've got some stuff of yours. You might want it."

He opened the door to his room, which was as messy as it ever was in high school. He picked two Baja hoodies off the floor from in front of the closet and tossed them on top of some folded clothes on his dresser.

"Are those clean?"

"Like fifty-fifty."

Laura shook her head.

"That's not how clean works."

"Relax," he said, opening his closet. Inside was a large wooden chest. Laura had never seen it before. He dragged it out of the closet and into the middle of his room. He opened it.

Inside were letters, trophies, photos, and clothes. All of it was Laura's.

"What the hell?"

Trey backed up to the door.

"Well, your mom said you didn't want it anymore, and she was going to throw it out, and I asked if I could have it, and..." he saw her face was a mixture of confusion and surprise. "Please don't be mad."

"I'm not mad, I'm confused."

"Do you want a drink?"

Laura shook her head.

"You want some weed? I'm going to go smoke some weed."

Laura shook her head again.

"Alright, well, take as long as you want. I'll be honest, I looked at the photos, but I didn't read the letters or anything."

Laura pulled out her old Iowa Hawkeyes hoodie and held it up.

"Oh, yeah, you loved that. And that orange sweater is in there too. You always loved that sweater."

"*You* always loved that sweater," Laura was still looking at the chest.

Trey nodded in agreement. Wordlessly he walked out back to go smoke pot. A minute later he walked back in.

Laura was still holding the sweatshirt and looking at photos. Everything she had thought she had lost. Everything she had chosen to let go.

"That was fast," she said without looking up.

"Eh... the kids were out there, I didn't want to."

She sighed.

"Can we talk?" she asked.

"Always."

Laura put the sweatshirt down and closed the lid of the chest.

Laura walked into the kitchen and Trey followed her. She paced back and forth gathering her thoughts. Trey pulled two glasses down and filled them with water, handing one to Laura. She took a sip and put it on the table. She sighed again.

"I don't want those things anymore."

"Okay."

"So why are you keeping them?"

"In case you change your mind."

Laura shook her head.

"No. I won't. I needed to get rid of them in order to become the person I need to be. The person I want to be."

Trey shrugged.

"But that is who you are."

"No," Laura was getting angrier. "It's not. That's not who I am anymore."

"Yeah, it fucking is," Trey was calm as he sat in a kitchen table chair. "That chest in my room is you."

"That's kinda sick, Trey."

"What? No it's not. Look, no matter what you think, everything in that chest is you. And those kids playing in the cul-de-sac, that's you, and that's me too."

Laura sat down across the table from him.

"Trey, you have to let me go."

He smiled and slowly sipped his water.

"You're crazy," he swallowed a laugh. "I haven't called you, written you, or tracked you down, even though it would have been easy to do any of those things. I've done nothing but let you live your life. You came back here."

"Which was a mistake."

"Why?"

"It just was."

Trey nodded.

"Okay, well, before you go, let me just say something, okay?"

Laura sighed a little too dramatically.

"Sure."

"No matter where you go, and no matter how long you are gone for, I'll be here waiting for you."

"Trey, don't wait for me, I'm not coming back."

"And that's fine. I hope you have a good life. But if you do come back, I'll be waiting here for you."

"You're not going to get married and have kids?"

"I don't know, maybe. But I'll leave them all for you."

"You're sick."

Trey laughed.

"I'm only kinda joking. I mean, I know you'll meet someone better than me, but there's no way I'm ever going to meet anyone better than you. It's not going to happen."

"Trey, stop it. Seriously, you need help."

"No shit."

"I don't want you to keep my stuff and I don't want you to wait for me, and I don't want you to think about me."

"Why not, why can't I do that if I want to?"

"Because I love you, too, you stupid shit!" Laura raised her voice. "I want you to be happy and content and fulfilled and not pining for a fucking box of memories literally hidden in your closet. The symbolism here, it's... Jesus fucking Christ man!"

"Too on the nose?"

"Yeah!" Laura said with a cracked smile.

"If you love me so much, stay the night."

Laura laughed hard and honestly. She laughed so hard that tears came to her eyes and she needed a minute to catch her breath. Trey smiled and waited until she was done.

"I'm serious. Come on, I'm not trying anything here. One last night. No sex," Trey explained. "Just stay here and sleep with me, like the old days."

"Ha! Dude... Dude. Dude. No way."

"Why not?"

"Stay the night in your room with your creepy murderbox? No thanks."

"What are you talking about?"

"Dude, you're a little obsessed."

Trey shook his head.

"I'm really not. I work, I surf, I smoke weed, and I sleep with a bunch of Irish girls in the summer. I'm not smelling your sweatshirt every night before I go to bed, I'm not asking the Irish girls to wear your orange sweater before I do them from behind or anything."

Laura sighed.

"Wow! That was so specific. You did that, didn't you?"

"No!"

"But you thought of that really fast."

"I just thought of it right now," he said laughing. "I swear."

There was a three second pause when no one said anything. But Trey couldn't help himself.

"I wish I thought of it before."

Laura stood up.

"I'm out."

"I'm joking."

Laura sat back down. She sighed again. Her head was spinning a little. She had drank far too much coffee that day, and hadn't slept much the night before.

"Honestly," she said after taking another sip of water. "I am really tired."

"Please stay the night. Or just sleep a little. Don't get back on the road like this."

"I'm like seeing double," Laura exaggerated.

"Just rest. You need it."

"No fooling around though, right?"

"No monkey business."

"Seriously."

"No hanky panky."

Laura frowned.

"See, I feel like you're flirting here."

"This isn't flirting. I can show you flirting."

"Don't make me regret this."

Trey smiled and picked up the phone and handed it to her.

"Call your mom so she doesn't worry."

Laura was embarrassed.

"I don't know her new number."

Trey stood up and walked into his room.

"I got it," he said over his shoulder. "She gave it to me when I made my murderbox."

He walked back into the kitchen and handed her his address book. She looked at the number, trying to decide what to do.

"Please stay," Trey said with a calm voice.

47

Afterlife

It was the end of her shift in mid-September when Milo caught Laura at the computer about to clock out.

"I sat table 25. Just a single. After that you can go."

"Dude, you're killing me."

"Come on, you got your side-work anyway."

"I'm done my side-work," she called back as she turned the corner.

As she turned the corner she froze in her tracks. There she was, a tiny little thing, shaved head, nose ring, Dr. Martens, ripped jeans, writing furiously in a little black notebook, what looked like... yes, it was song lyrics. Laura was sure that Ani DiFranco was sitting at table 25 and now she had to do her best to play it cool.

"Hey, how's it going?" she said way too loud, startling most of the restaurant. "Sorry. Can I get you a drink?"

"Coffee," she said without looking up. She was scribbling away in her notebook and not even looking at the menu. Laura almost ran for the coffee and was back in a flash.

"Here you go. Are you ready to order?"

She looked up from her notebook and smiled at Laura.

"Sure, can I get a veggie egg white omelet with a salad instead of home fries?"

"Totally, yeah, absolutely."

"Cool," she smiled and went back to the notebook.

Laura went to put the order in. As per usual, Milo was there furiously typing away on the other computer. He didn't even look up.

"Laura, I didn't know you had your side-work done, Tanja can take table 25, you can punch out if you want."

"No!" Laura said forcefully. "No, no, no. I'm good. I'm gonna get her some water."

Laura dropped off the water and smiled. Then she felt like she was acting weird and she backed away quickly.

Laura was used to famous people coming into EJ's. That week Laura had waited on Billie Jean King and Howard Stern, and she didn't even acknowledge their celebrity. You get used to famous people while waiting tables in New York. But to her, Ani DiFranco was not a famous person, she was a divinity. Hence why Laura was acting so... awkward.

When the bell dinged to alert the food was up, Laura flew across the dining room and snatched it out of the runner's hand in order to drop it off herself.

"Can I get you anything else," she said a little too eagerly.

"Sure. Can I get some more of that world's worst coffee?"

Laura laughed too enthusiastically and she grabbed the pot from the warmer.

"Like water dressed in brown, right?"

That's when she saw it. A spark of recognition mixed with a very subtle, appreciative nod. Laura quoted her own lyrics back to her, so she knew Laura was a fan. They had connected. She was in. *Ani nodded to me*, she thought. As she watched her hero take a bite of food, she realized she was creepily staring. *Oh my God, Ani caught me* staring, she thought erroneously. So with nothing else to do, she walked over and asked her if the food was okay.

"Yeah, yeah, it's fine." She said, but as she looked at Laura her eyes narrowed a bit. "Hey, are you okay?"

"Not really."

"Yeah, you seem a little jumpy."

"Can I sit."

She shrugged.

"Sure."

"Okay, so here's the deal. Oh, this is going to be a long story."

She chuckled and looked around to see if this was a practical joke. "Can you give me the short version?"

"I don't think so," Laura said smiling.

They both laughed a little, the difference being Laura didn't laugh out of fear.

"Okay, well, how about you can talk until I finish eating. You think you can finish it by then?"

"Alright, I'll try. See the thing is, I'm in love, but I don't want to be."

She put her fork down.

"Oh, well... that's new." She picked up her pen and made a note. "Alright, fuck it, give me the long version."

"So there's this boy. When we were eight... wait, do you know Ocean Pines, Maryland?"

"No. Hold on a second, so I know what I'm getting myself into here. What are you?"

"What do you mean?"

"Like are you an actor, or musician, or writer, or what? Like why are you here?"

"Oh, I'm nothing."

"What do you mean you're nothing?"

"I'm just a waitress."

She picked up her fork and took a small bite thinking.

"Anyway..." Laura went to continue but she stopped when her new friend shook her head.

"No, hold on. I'm still processing what you just told me. I don't think I've ever met a server in New York that's not trying to be something else. Like you don't want to do anything creative?"

"I mean, I'd love to, but I don't have any talent for it. I can't sing, I can't play music, I think I'm a good dancer, but no one else does."

They laughed.

"You could write."

"I can't."

"You're illiterate?"

"No, I mean, I can't do it. I can't make the words say what I want them to say, they just all come out wrong."

Her friend nodded.

"Well it takes practice. Anyone can write," she said before taking another bite of food. Laura looked down at the plate. She was a quarter of the way through the omelet, and though she had only taken one bite of salad so far, Laura felt like she was running out of time.

"I know me, and I know that's not for me. Anyway..."

"Yup, back to Maryland."

"Right, so there's this place called Ocean Pines in Maryland. And it's like this huge community but no one lived there except for me and this boy named Trey. It was just us growing up."

"Like Mayberry?"

"No, not at all. It's really full of trees, and there's no streetlights. It's more like Hansel and Gretel. Except we weren't brother and sister, but we kinda were, which makes this all kinda fucked up."

"Okay?"

"It's bigger now, but we were the first kids there. And we grew up, together, I guess sort of like in our own womb in this dark and lonely place."

"Woah. Hold on. You said you're not a writer?"

"No."

"So you are never going to use that nurtured in a womb of darkness thing?"

Laura shook her head.

"You okay with me taking it?" She said pulling out her notebook and pen and writing it down. She raised her eyebrow waiting for a response.

"Of course." Laura was beaming, but trying to stay cool.

"Anyway, go ahead."

"It was just that... from the beginning we were thrust together because there was literally no other choice. He was the only boy and I was the only girl, and that's just how it was. And our last names are even really close, so like when we were seated alphabetically in class we'd be seated next to each other. I mean, our pictures were next to each other in the yearbook for fucks-sake. It's like, no matter what, we were going to be together."

"And did you get together?"

"Yeah... yeah."

"Was the sex bad?"

"No, well, yeah, I mean, originally, yeah, like really bad. Well not bad, but... like... problematic. And there was another girl involved."

"Hello," she interrupted. "Now we're talking. Was the girl with you or him or... both?"

"Just with him. Well, she and I were best friends for a minute, well, not best friends but... But it's not about that, we're getting off track. Like I'm going to compare everyone I meet to him and how are they supposed to compare to this guy that I grew up with and have known my entire life?"

"So this is just about a boy?"

"No, it's about me. Look, there's this big huge world out there and I want to explore it. I'm not an artist, I can't create something from nothing, I just don't have that in me. But I love everything about art. I know who I am, I am curious. And when I can't explore, I start to feel like boxed in, then the world gets harder. I get angry.

"And I know everyone will look at me and think that what I'm doing is selfish, and honestly I don't think they are wrong. But what the fuck? I haven't chosen anything in my life. Just one thing after another happens to me and I don't want that life, I don't want to be something that happens to someone else either. I want my own regrets you know, I don't want to blame the world, I want to blame myself.

"So like I hadn't seen him in two years, but I went to his dad's funeral and then we slept together that night."

"Woah, back to the action," she said as her eyebrows jumped up.

"Well, we didn't have sex. Okay well, we did have sex, but not until the morning, so that didn't count. We just slept together and held each other and it was really nice."

"Stop, wait. I'm curious, why doesn't morning sex count?"

"Oh, you know, you're sleepy and... well... you know how sometimes you are not entirely awake, but also not asleep. Like a waking dream?"

"Uh huh."

"Yeah, well. I don't know, it just happened."

"Stop. Did he have sex with you while you were sleeping?" she asked, suddenly very concerned.

Laura laughed. "Oh, no, I, uh... I woke him up."

Her friend nodded approval and took another bite of her omelet. "No notes, carry on."

"Anyway, it's not about that, right? He says he'll love me forever no matter what I do, and he says he'll wait forever for me and all that nonsense, but I asked him flat out can he just be my friend and nothing else. Can we just be friends forever, and go love other people and marry other people if we want and just be friends and he said no. Which is kinda bull shit if you ask me."

"I see you keep looking down at your ring. Did he give that to you?"

Laura looked at her diamond ring on her middle finger. She had only started wearing it again after the funeral.

"Yeah. Years ago."

"Why do you wear it?"

Laura sighed, looking at the ring.

"Because I love him."

"So what's the problem?"

"Because I don't want to be a wife and a mother and just live in the same place until I die. And he does want that, and honestly he belongs there. He fits there. He wants to live there. He found his place."

"But it's not yours?"

"I don't think I have a place. I mean, I have spent a lot of time thinking about this and I really don't think there's anywhere that I belong, not really."

"Where have you been?"

Laura shrugged. "Maryland, Indiana, here."

"That's it?"

Laura nodded.

"Babe, come on. There's a big world out there. You probably belong somewhere, but maybe you gotta go find it."

"And I turn my back on love?"

Her friend smiled. "Aw shit. You gotta love yourself first, otherwise it's all just a waste of time."

She took a final bite of the omelet. Laura sped up.

"I feel like the whole world is changing. Art, music, films, everything, it's all just, I don't know... like technology is driving us and we're just going along for the ride, you know? Everyone I know is doing what they are supposed to be doing, and they all seem certain that there's only one way. I don't think it's fear or ignorance that drives them, I think it's the crushing weight of fate that locks us in these predetermined paths. And all the artists, and all the poets, they're all screaming the same thing, right? They are saying break free. Take the untraveled path. Free your mind. But even though those artists' work are taught in the best schools, those same schools themselves tell you to get in line. I know, I was at that school, you know? Like we're told to read these books but not to act on the knowledge in those books, and it makes me think that this whole earth is just a wheel in a cage. And I know that's a cliché but that's the thing, right? Everything's been said before, everything's been done before and now we're just going through the motions.

"But what if there's another way? What if it's possible to live in-between the paths. I know this sounds crazy, I do, and I know I'm kinda rambling and I know that I'm young and sorta cute and healthy and strong and all those things that make life easy for now. Everyone says I'm going to wake up one day and regret every decision I am making. Maybe they are right. Maybe I'll end up homeless or insane, or dead in someone's murderbox."

"Stop!" She put up her hand. "What the hell is a murderbox?"

"It's a thing Trey has, it's just pictures and sweatshirts and stuff, it doesn't matter."

"It sounds like it matters."

"Okay but, even if it ends badly, it ends badly because I chose it. And it felt right to choose it. So if something is wrong with me then, in the future, that must mean something is wrong with me now, which is possible I guess. But it's also possible that something is just wrong with the world, even though in the end, it's the same result. And I get that this is just mental masturbation here but it matters because this is a fucking life, right? This is my life. So if something is going to be wrong in my life, let it be my fault."

Laura took off her ring and slid it to her friend.

"I want you to have this."

"Fuck no," she said pushing it back to Laura. "Shit, first off, that's how curses start. I don't fuck with the universe like you do."

They both laughed.

"Look babe, everything is a compromise. You just gotta find the right compromise for you. Otherwise you are gonna end up ranting on a street corner somewhere. Or, I guess, in someone's murderbox, whatever the fuck that is."

She took her last sip of coffee.

"I'm so sorry, but honestly I gotta go. I wish I could help, but I think that maybe you know what you want to do, already, right?"

Laura nodded. Her new friend smiled.

"Can I get my check?"

Laura shook her head.

"No," she put her ring back on. "I got it, this one is on me."

They both stood up and shared an awkward hug.

"You're a pretty cool waitress."

"Yeah," Laura smiled, a little embarrassed. "And you're just pretty cool."

When Laura walked back to the computers Tanja was putting in an order for the four top at table 13. She smiled at Laura.

"Who was your friend at twenty-five? You guys were having a pretty serious conversation, huh?"

"Uh, that was Ani DiFranco."

Tanja laughed.

"Uh, no. That wasn't Ani DiFranco."

Laura looked at her new friend walking past the large plate windows.

"Right there, that's Ani DiFranco," Laura said emphatically.

Tanja shook her head.

"No, I'm telling you I've met Ani DiFranco like three times. That's not her. I mean, she kinda looks like Ani looked three years ago. She's probably a fan of Ani DiFranco."

Tanja walked away. Laura looked out the window and smiled. Milo came up and began tapping away at the computer.

"You ready to check out?" He asked.

Laura nodded, looked Milo in the eyes, and quit.

***

Jessica went with Laura to the airport. Visitors could go all the way to the gate and wait with the ticketed passengers, and that's exactly what Jessica did. It was one of those sunny days in October, when the blue sky was made a deeper blue by the contrast of the occasional white pillowy clouds ambling listlessly along. Jessica wanted a cigarette, so they went to the bar and Jessica bought Laura a gin and tonic, which was the drink she said her father claimed was the healthiest when flying.

"Something to do with quinine," she said gesturing in the air with the hand holding her cigarette.

Laura smiled and looked at her friend, her best friend, knowing that she would remember this moment for the rest of her life. Jessica saw her look.

"Bitch, you're going to miss me so much," she took a sip of her martini. "But not as much as I'm going to miss you."

The Bruce Hornsby song "Mandolin Rain" was playing in the airport bar. Laura listened and closed her eyes for a moment. Jessica was watching her.

"What are you thinking about?" Jessica asked.

"This song reminds me of this time with Trey. When we were hiding from the rain, under his window. It feels like a lifetime ago."

"Yeah, well, you and Trey have a lot of songs." Jessica ordered another martini even though hers was still half full. "He won't wait forever, you know."

"I don't want him waiting now."

"You don't love him anymore?"

Laura looked right into Jessica's eyes.

"I think I've always loved Trey Buckingham. And I always will."

Jessica looked away and focused on her drink. She stabbed the last olive and ate it.

"Maybe that's all love is," she said with her mouth full. "Something to give music meaning."

"That's all love is?"

"Maybe that's all life is," Jessica finished her first martini in one big gulp when the other appeared.

Laura sighed and took a sip of her drink. She was nervous. Jessica took a long drag, then French inhaled, which had become her thing lately, and then exhaled up above their heads.

"Luxembourg," Jessica shook her head. "Such a bizarre choice."

"It was the cheapest ticket."

"I know," Jessica sighed. "Still though."

"I probably won't stay there long."

"So, like I can't even write to you?"

Laura shrugged.

"I mean, at some point I'll need to work. So I'll write you when I get a job somewhere, and then I'll let you know where I'm going."

"You can go to Ireland and live with your handsome doctor."

Laura shook her head. "Maybe someday, but not yet."

"You want your stupid Buddhist moment first."

"I don't think you should call it that."

"Seriously though, when are you going to come back?"

Laura shrugged. Jessica shook her head.

"I don't know what you think you are proving with all of this, but you can't just turn your back on your whole life and think you stand on your own feet. I mean, come on, no man is an island."

Laura smiled.

"Well it's lucky then that I'm no man."

"Hmm." Jessica frowned. "You can run anywhere you want, but you're always going to be that girl from Ocean Pines. And I'm always going to come visit and remind you."

"I hope you do."

"I'm going to send you a tin of Old Bay every time I get your new address."

Laura laughed. The airport loudspeakers announced her flight was boarding. They stood up and walked to the gate.

"I don't care how far you go, or how long you are gone," Jessica's voice quavered as she tried and failed to hold back tears. "If you ever need me you just tell me and I'll be there, okay?"

"Okay," Laura said while she fumbled for her ticket.

They hugged and Jessica wiped away some tears. Laura handed her ticket to the flight attendant and walked through the gate.

"Laura Byrne!" Jessica called after her, getting Laura to turn around in the jetway and look back. Jessica was smiling a sad, knowing smile. It was as if, in this one instant she could see through time, all the possible pasts and the probable future. She caught her breath and held it, for one brief and eternal moment. "You're always going to be my sister!"

Laura's hand shot to her face, covering her mouth, hiding her sad smile, and somehow holding the tears in her eyes. With her other hand she managed a half-wave; and unable to speak, she turned away and walked through the tunnel, soon to be flying through the bluest sky she had ever seen, away from the sun, and into the dark, unfamiliar night.

Acknowledgements

This story is fiction, technically, but built on many microtruths. For everyone involved in those moments, at The Point, under the window, at the boat ramp, on the subway, at the Grotto... or just those who shared a cup of coffee with me, thank you.

I have always heard it said that whenever you write a book there are too many people to thank, and now that I'm putting together the acknowledgements I can confirm that is true. So many people helped me, from Coach Tom Wescott telling me I should talk to Hannah Purnell about equestrian events (and Megan Wallace giving me Hannah's number), to Josh Nordstrom letting me steal a great line from his life, it's just too many to remember. I'm sorry if I have missed anyone.

That said, thank you to Aaron Rosenberg and Brandi Bowles for their advice and sharing a little of their expertise. And Hannah Purnell for all things equestrian. Nancy Howard answered a few questions about when things happened in Ocean City in order to help me keep my timelines straight.

I would never have kept going if it wasn't for Ryder Myrick, who read the first iteration of the first chapter and somehow convinced me it could be a novel. His insight into literature, his advice about the characters, and his encouragement pushed me to see this through. Thank you.

I probably would have given up again if it wasn't for Andrea Yablunosky who might very well be the biggest fan of this book. I think she has already read it four times. In fact, she has already outlined the plot for the "second season."

Huge thanks to first readers Sharyn O'Hare, Josh Nordstrom, Kathryn Barrett-Gaines, Linda Schneider, Amanda Pollack, Marie McFarland, Jennifer Moskowitz, Ava Rupert, Jackie Davis, Clint McIntyre, Caitlin Brown, Sara Hoffman, Gunnar Reynolds, Stephanie Nasteff-Pilato, Meg Sudlik, Erika Meister, Igor Tymiński, Meabh Ni Bhroin, and Richard Walshe. I needed those notes! Special shout out to Mom, Josh, Linda, Sara, and Marie for making it all the way to the end!

Thanks to Mark Weinstein, Lauren Downey, and Jaime Coyne at Kevin Anderson and Associates, for their professionalism, honesty, and thoroughness. I especially owe an immense debt of gratitude to my editor Jaime Coyne who helped me understand how to bring these characters to life, while assisting me in the gruesome murder of my darlings. Jaime, more than anyone else, made this novel readable. I think (hope) she might have even taught me how to write a novel. KAA was worth every penny.

Special thanks to the beta readers Caroline O'Hare, Brad Beebe, Valerie Murphy, Megan Wallace, Megan Leslie, and Sharon Curtiss. All of you gave me great notes and really helped shape the book. Sharon Curtiss even proofread an early version!

Speaking of proofreading, Megan Leslie managed to proofread and edit the entire book in like 48 hours. It was incredible. I promise you every remaining mistake is mine and not hers though. Thank you Megan, it's such a better book than it would have been without your help.

One of my absolute favorite moments from this whole process was talking to beta readers Keena and Lily Gumbinner about the novel. Since one of the things the book is about is mothers and daughters and the change that happens between generations, it was so special to have those conversations. Especially since the mother, in this case, introduced me to some of this music in the book. Thank you both so much for reading and giving me notes!

Thanks to my brother Tom, who still hasn't read the novel, but has long encouraged me to write a book, especially while I'm trying to run a DnD game.

And finally, the three most important women in my life helped shaped this book more than they realize. Thank you Mom for teaching me how to cook, and for always reading. Thank you Caroline for introducing me to the music of Ani DiFranco, designing the cover, and understanding that this is something I needed to do. And finally, thank you to Olive for saving my life, for giving me the idea of the haunted house, and for introducing me to the music of Taylor Swift. I am so proud of the reader and writer you are becoming. I love you all.

About the Author

Dan O'Hare is a Realtor, lacrosse coach, filmmaker, environmentalist, and author. Originally from Ocean Pines, Maryland (in fact, supposedly the first person born there), he has also lived in Indiana, Colorado, New York City, Ireland... and for a short time, in a cargo van, down by the river. He now lives with his wife and daughter in Salisbury, MD.

www.ingramcontent.com/pod-product-compliance
Lightning Source LLC
LaVergne TN
LVHW100509110826
845146LV00002B/568

* 9 7 9 8 9 9 9 4 4 2 5 0 5 *